Casserole Diplomacy and Other Stories

An On Spec 25th Anniversary Retrospective

Casserole Diplomacy and Other Stories

An On Spec 25th Anniversary Retrospective

As Selected By:
Diane L Walton, Barry Hammond, Ann
Marston, Barb Galler-Smith, Jena Snyder,
Susan MacGregor, Robin S. Carson

Tyche Books Ltd.

Casserole Diplomacy and Other Stories:
An On Spec Retrospective Anthology

As Selected by:
Diane L. Walton
Barry Hammond
Ann Marston
Barb Galler-Smith
Jena Snyder
Susan MacGregor
Robin S. Carson

Published by Tyche Books Ltd.
www.TycheBooks.com

Copyright © 2014 Copper Pig Writers' Society
First Tyche Books Ltd Edition 2014

Print ISBN: 978-1-928025-05-4
Ebook ISBN: 978-1-928025-06-1

Cover Art by Herman Lau
Cover Layout by Lucia Starkey
Interior Layout by Bart R. Leib

All rights reserved. No part of this book may be reproduced or transmitted in any form or by any means, electronic or mechanical, including photocopying, recording or by any information storage & retrieval system, without written permission from the copyright holder, except for the inclusion of brief quotations in a review.

The publisher does not have any control over and does not assume any responsibility for author or third party websites or their content.

This is a work of fiction. All of the characters, organizations and events portrayed in this story are either the product of the author's imagination or are used fictitiously.

Any resemblance to persons living or dead would be really cool, but is purely coincidental.

Contents

Foreword	Marianne O. Nielsen	i
Foreword	Diane L. Walton	iii
Happy Eating on Ugrath 3	Jason Kapalka	1
Star-seeing Night	Alice Major	11
The Reality War	Robert Boyczuk	19
Casserole Diplomacy	Fiona Heath	37
Jubilee	Steven Mills	51
No Such Thing as an Ex-Con	Holly Phillips	67
Closing Time	Matthew Johnson	85
Foster Child	Catherine MacLeod	101
More Than Salt	E.L. Chen	113
Where Magic Lives	S.A. Bolich	131
The Black Man	A.M. Arruin.	145
Pizza Night	Laurie Channer	155
Boys' Night Out	Rob Hunter	169
Mourning Sickness	Robert Weston	185
Sticky Wonder Tales	Hugh Spencer	197
Emily's Shadow	Al Onia	211
The Resident Guest	Sandra Glaze	225
Come From Aways	Tony Pi	237
Still	Greg Wilson	255
The Asheville Road	Corey Brown	279
Buddhist Jet Lag	Christian McPherson	295
A Taste of Time	Scott Overton	297
Penultimate	F.J. Bergmann	307
Pilgrim at the Edge of the World	Sarah Frost	309
Afterword	Diane L. Walton	321

The following people deserve our sincere thanks for years of service (listed in alphabetical order):

The On Spec Editorial Collective, past and present:

Robin S. Carson
Barb Galler-Smith
Catherine Girczyc
Barry Hammond
Susan MacGregor
Ann Marston
Steve Mohn
Derryl Murphy
Marianne O. Nielsen (past General Editor)
Holly Phillips
Robert Runté
Hazel Sangster (past Managing Editor)
Phyllis Schuell
Jena Snyder (past General Editor and Production Editor)
Diane L. Walton (current Managing Editor)
Peter Watts

Guest Editors:

Hazel Sangster — Theme: Youth Writing and Art -Vol. 2, No. 3 (#5) Winter 1990
Spider Robinson — Theme: Humour — Vol. 3, No. 3 (#8) Winter 1991
Lorna Toolis and Michael Skeet — Vol. 4, No. 2 (#10) Fall 1992
David Nickle and Karl Schroeder — Vol. 5, No. 3 (#14) Fall 1993
Leslie Gadallah — Theme: Hard Science Fiction — Vol. 6, No. 1 (#16) Spring 1994
Barry Hammond — Theme: Horror & Dark Fantasy — Vol. 7, No. 1 (#20) Spring 1995
Barry Hammond — Theme: Cross-Genre — Vol. 8 No. 1 (#24) Spring 1996
Robert J. Sawyer — On Writing column
Robert Runté and Peter Watts — Theme: Canadian Geographic — Vol. 9 No. 1 (#28) Spring 1997
Gerald L. Truscott — Theme: Music — Vol. 10 No. 1 (#32) Spring 1998
Lyle Weis — Theme: Earth, Air, Wind & Fire — Vol. 11 No. 1 (#36) Spring 1999
Marianne O. Nielsen — Theme: Future Crime — Vol. 12 No. 1 (#40) Spring 2000

Editorial Advisory Board:

Douglas Barbour
J. Brian Clarke
Candas Jane Dorsey
Leslie Gadallah
Pauline Gedge
Monica Hughes
Alice Major
Robert Runté
Karl Schroeder
Phyllis Schuell
Brad Thompson
Gerry Truscott
Lyle Weis

Art Directors:

James Beveridge
Lynne Taylor Fahnestalk
Tim Hammell
Derryl Murphy
Jane Starr
Diane L. Walton

Production Editors:

Lynette Bondarchuk
Cat McDonald
Jena Snyder

Support Staff, Summer Students, Web Gurus, Proofreaders and Volunteers (in alphabetical order):

Stacey-Lynn Antonation
Colin Bamsey
Matt Bamsey
Sara Bamsey
Alan Barclay
Lynette Bondarchuk
Gareth Boyce
Beverly Byron
Scott Cairns
Isaac Calon
Katerina Carastathis
Mark Chan
Elaine Chen
Karen Desgagné
Steve Fahnestalk
Karen Grant
PJ Groenveldt
Chris Hammond-Thrasher
Josie Hammond-Thrasher
Cath Jackel
Chris Jackel
Brent Jans
Janice Jessop
Jen Laface
Cara Koropchuk
Roberta Laurie
Danica LeBlanc
Rick LeBlanc
Colin Lynch
Kathy MacRae
Ashlin McCartney
Andrea Merriman
Shellon Miller
Tobey Morris
Dave Panchyk
Laurie Penner
Heather Price-Ferguson
Paul Rodgers
Brandon Schatz
Larry Scott
Kelly Shepherd
Jane Spalding
Claire Stirling
Melody Szabo
Donna Weis
Michelle Wilson

Cheerleaders (just because):

Jane Bisbee

Michael Penny

FOREWORD
MARIANNE O. NIELSEN
FIRST GENERAL EDITOR OF *On Spec*
(1989-1992)

In 1988 and for many years before that, the members of the Edmonton-based Copper Pig Writers' Society bemoaned the lack of English Canadian speculative fiction magazines—not only as venues for their wonderful stories but as places to find English Canadian writers and writing. The French Canadian magazines had created their own niche and were doing well. We, on the other hand, looking for English markets, were tired of rejection letters from American magazines that stated "too weird," "too off the wall," and most depressing, "too depressing."

One day, we were sitting in my living room lamenting the usual rejection letters, when we looked around the circle and realized we had all the talent we needed to establish our own magazine—writing and editing skills, organizational skills, business smarts, contacts in writers' organizations, networks of editors and writers, government agency contacts, typesetting and layout skills, and a bunch more. I left the room to go to the bathroom and came back to find myself elected "General Editor and Sharkbait."

The first years were interesting—and not necessarily in a good way. Finding funding was tricky, our pockets got emptied regularly until eventually the Alberta and then Canadian governments gave us enough to cover materials. We were all volunteers though, but saw giving our time to be a worthy endeavour—not only were we working to introduce Canada and hopefully, some of the rest of the world to the amazing talent among Canadian spec fic writers, we were working with new writers, often giving them the chance to redraft a story if we saw potential in it. The first Cory Doctorow book I saw on the stands in the US made me glow with pride because I knew *On Spec* had published his first story.

Since we knew some amazing spec fic artists, we decided we had to publish artwork to complement the stories. THAT upped the cost, but it was worth it to see these talented people move on to book covers and WorldCon art shows, and even working for big name special effects companies.

In 1992 I had to resign from *On Spec*. I decided to go back to university and get a Ph.D. and found out the hard way that when you start footnoting your short stories, it's time to stop writing fiction. Many academic articles and books later, I still regret that decision, but I am thrilled every time my copy of *On Spec* arrives in the mail, full of new writers and new artists to enjoy. And the stories are still delightfully weird and off the wall, but not as depressing any more, it seems.

I hope you enjoy this collection of stories from the past 25 years of *On Spec* as much as the editors did when they got to read them for the first time. Every brown manila envelope was full of possibilities...and here are some of the best that flew, crept and bounded out of those envelopes.

FOREWORD
DIANE L. WALTON
CURRENT MANAGING EDITOR

We were pretty naive when we decided to start *On Spec*, weren't we? But back then, there didn't seem to be any impediments we couldn't deal with, and the potential rewards of fame and fortune and glamour would be . . .

[REWIND]

On Spec is and has always been a labour of love for everyone closely involved. Nobody got rich; nobody got famous, other than perhaps being biggish frogs in a small lily pond, and as for glamour—hardly! It's a lot of work to make this little journal happen four times a year. But we still love hearing from readers and writers and artists, making new friends and reuniting with old ones. We love the thrill of finding a story in the slush that has the spark of creativity to make an editor sit up and take notice. We love the moment when we tell a writer we want to buy their work, especially if it is their first time in print. We love the moment when we say to a new visitor to our dealer table at a convention, "So, have you heard of *On Spec*?"

Labour of love, indeed! It's been a great ride so far, with so many people to thank for their time and effort.

The stories in this book were selected by the current editorial team, with great help from Jena Snyder, who was there from the start. We picked stories that resonated with each of us—personal favourite stories that each continue to stand on their own, regardless of the year they first saw print. Some of the earliest stories didn't make the cut, because they had already appeared in our *First Five Years* anthology (Edge Science Fiction and Fantasy Publishing), and you can read them there. This book will show you what we've been doing with our time since then. And we want to thank Tyche Books for this opportunity.

While we were making our choices, it was just like visiting with old friends. If this is your introduction to *On Spec*, we have some friends we'd love for you to meet.

Happy Eating on Ugrath 3: A Model for Study
Jason Kapalka

START REPORT
04/06/99 HardCopy File for Reference
ScriptTrans 02/08/97-04/23/98 Sys53/SecC
TRANS frm HAPPYFOOD INCORPORATED/ Administrative Division
RECEV stn HappyFood Franchise #2232575/Ugrath 3

Dear Mr. Nogren:
    Congratulations on your safe planetfall on Ugrath 3, and the problem-free setup of HappyFood Franchise #2232575! We suggest you immediately begin thawing the Food Processing Clerks in your freezer—FPCs require a few days of orientation and training before they are competent to work the HappyFood Franchise equipment.
    As you know, Ugrath 3 is a small world which has been out of direct contact with the Core for some forty years now. Nonetheless it is a prestigious assignment for a HappyFood

Franchise manager! The colonists there have been living on a limited diet of local foodstuffs for some time now, and in general, have large credit accounts due to the lack of consumer outposts. The time is ripe for Ugrath 3 to have a HappyFood Franchise established.

Remember Yucatan 5!

Eighty years ago it was a small colony like Ugrath 3, but thanks to assertive marketing, HappyFood Inc. now has over 300,000 franchises there while the competition has been unable to gain a significant foothold.

While training your Food Processing Clerks, we suggest you have them use HappyFood Inc.'s new slogan as often as possible, especially at the conclusion of a transaction. Studies have shown that repetition of this variety will embed the desired associations in subjects within a short time.

"Healthy, hearty, happy eating to you!"
EndTrans

TRANS frm HAPPYFOOD INCORPORATED/ Administrative Division
RECEV stn HappyFood Franchise #2232575/Ugrath 3

Dear Mr. Nogren:

We are happy to see from your account files that your HappyFood franchise is off to a good start. But by no means can you rest on your laurels just yet! Action must be taken to consolidate the gains made during this initial period.

Your present markup rate of 240% is acceptable, but in the light of the Ugrath 3 colonists' high disposable income, and the lack of competition at present, we feel it would be wise to increase this to 300% over a two-month period.

One other suggestion is in order. You do not mention having trained your Food Processing Clerks for suggestive merchandising. If you have not yet done so, proceed to with all dispatch!

The procedure is simple, and well within the FPCs' capabilities. For example: if a customer buys the Jumbo Bacon Barbecue HappyBurger (Simulated), have the FPC ask if they would like the Cheesy Potato Skins (Simulated) with it, while nodding their head slightly up and down. Studies show that even the suggestion of a nod increases the customer's chances of saying yes to such a question. Do not be afraid to aggressively use suggestive merchandising! Choice is a burden to most customers, and they will be pleased to have your staff suggest food item selections.

Healthy, hearty, happy eating to you!
EndTrans

TRANS frm HAPPYFOOD INCORPORATED/ Administrative Division
RECEV stn HappyFood Franchise #2232575/Ugrath 3

Dear Mr. Nogren:

Recent invoices from your HappyFood franchise indicate a period of slowed growth. Going over your daily reports, we believe we have pinpointed the problem.

There seems to be a misunderstanding on your part of the Truth in Food Marketing codes. While food unit archives and daypart reports must, indeed, list a particular meal's full title, it is unnecessary to print it on your menu, or have your Food Processing Clerks pronounce it during transactions. Specifically, we see your menu lists items like the "Happy Lobster Pack (Simulated)" and "Milk Substitute Reconstitute HappyShake." It is not necessary to include the terms "Simulated" or "Milk Substitute Reconstitute" in the names of these items. In fact, we strongly suggest you discontinue the use of such terms, as we believe they are responsible for the dip in your day profit reports.

In other developments at HappyFood Inc., some recent outbreaks of scombroid on developing planets have been traced to contaminated morlen, a mainstay of the Happy Seafood menu. Consequently, HappyFood Inc. has decided to discontinue the use of the Happy Morlen food product, item number 343-86ux in your catalog. From this time onward, food item 343-86ux must be referred to in all cases as Happy Fish.

Healthy, hearty, happy eating to you!
EndTrans

Jason Kapalka

TRANS frm HAPPYFOOD INCORPORATED/ Administrative Division
RECEV stn HappyFood Franchise #2232575/Ugrath 3

Dear Mr. Nogren:

    We are happy to see that you have complied with our advice regarding the daypart menu terminology. Perhaps not coincidentally, your accounts indicate that the Ugrath 3 Franchise is now growing rapidly in popularity with the colonists. At this rate, your franchise will be one of the most profitable and prestigious establishments in HappyFood Inc.'s galaxy-wide chain.

    On a more sombre note: we are sorry to hear about the demise of two of your Food Processing Clerks in a microwave accident. Still, remember the clone tanks in your Franchise can generate replacements within a few weeks. We have sent a copy of HappyFood Inc.'s FPC training Videodisc #4354 along with this month's shipment of food materials. This enjoyable vid uses advanced subliminal imagery to teach your FPCs to deal with death or maiming due to cuts, slashes, laser burns, or radiation spills in a cheerful manner that will not interfere with their regular duties. If you watch this vid yourself, remember to wear the enclosed protective glasses to prevent any unintentional b-mod spillover.

    You also mention some requests by the Ugrath 3 colonists for information on the nutritive makeup of HappyFood products. By all means, give them a copy of HappyFood Inc.'s Infobook #3490, detailing the healthy, natural wholesome materials HappyFood products are made of and/or inspired by. Regarding Unigel, the principal taste component of some meals: do not give your customers erroneous information regarding this substance! Remember: HappyFood Inc. won the 2095 court case in which Unigel was alleged to possess certain deleterious and addictive properties.

    Healthy, hearty, happy eating to you and your customers!

EndTrans

TRANS frm HAPPYFOOD INCORPORATED/ Administrative Division

RECEV stn HappyFood Franchise #2232575/Ugrath 3

Dear Mr. Nogren:
    We are concerned with your latest report which indicates you have introduced new menu items to the morning daypart menu, incorporating local foodstuffs. You should be well aware of HappyFood Inc.'s policy on new menu items: it is necessary first to submit Form XVI (Request For New Food Item Approval), listing the proposed item's name, portion, yield, unit servings, advance instructions, ingredients, procedure, and storage information, so that the Research & Development Division can examine and test it. While it is often profitable to incorporate local foods into your menu, HappyFood Inc. uses a standardized recipe system for a good reason. Travellers from different planets are always assured of receiving a familiar meal at a HappyFood Franchise, with no need to risk the possible hazards and unpleasantries of local foods which may be somewhat exotic to the traveller. Hence, please submit any menu items like this "Bacon and Eggs" you suggest to head office for verification first in the future.
    In addition, we see that you are offering the Happy Chicken (Simulated) with Reconstituted Potatoes and Happy Salad (Simulated) as a combination dish; all very good, but you offer it at a discount of over 12%! The Happy Chicken food item is not currently listed on your afternoon daypart menu; thus, no audit trail exists for it, and the customer perceives value because there are no other menu combinations to compare it with. *Therefore*, there is no reason to discount. You are only training the customer to "buy cheap." To repeat, there is *no* value in deep discounting.
    We feel certain you will correct these small problems and go on to make HappyFood Franchise #232575 a profitable link in the chain of HappyFood Franchises stretching across the galaxy. In fact, we insist you implement the aforementioned measures immediately.
    Healthy, hearty, happy eating to you!
        EndTrans

Jason Kapalka

TRANS frm HAPPYFOOD INCORPORATED/ Administrative Division
RECEV stn HappyFood Franchise #2232575/Ugrath 3

Dear Mr. Nogren:

We here at the Internal Monitoring Branch of HappyFood Inc. are sorry to say that the reports sent to us by head office concerning your HappyFood Franchise on Ugrath 3 are quite disappointing. As you are aware, you were chosen for this prestigious post on the basis of your past performance with the HappyFood chain of food processing establishments; however, the most recent information received from your Franchise is forcing us to consider disciplinary action.

You have received repeated warnings to desist in various non-standard procedures: excessive discounting, unauthorized food item introductions, and unnecessary food composition documentation. Despite your assurances of compliance, all our data indicate you are continuing in these non-standard practices. In addition we have reason to believe the suggestive merchandising training of your Food Processing Clerks has been substandard. But even more disturbing than these problems is the recent rumour of "redecorations" supposedly undertaken in your HappyFood Franchise. We must order you, in no uncertain terms, to stop any such modifications and return the Franchise to its regulated appearance.

HappyFood Franchises on the various colonized planets are to remain as similar as possible in all regards; this is merely an extension of the policy of standardized recipes. A HappyFood customer should be able to enter an establishment light-years away from his or her home and feel comfortable, as if he or she is returning to a familiar place, not entering some bizarre, foreign, possibly dangerous eatery; to this end the Food Processing Clerk clones have standardized facial features as well. The lighting and furnishings of the standard HappyFood Franchise have been carefully researched and designed for optimum effect, producing an impression of comfort from a distance, which gradually fades upon continued exposure or actual contact with the flexiplastic chairs. In this fashion, both the demands of "initial appeal" and "quick turnaround" are satisfied, as customers are encouraged to enter the establishment but discouraged in the act of loitering.

Cease with these "ambient lighting" and "padded seat" experiments; remove any tables and furnishings of plant fibre and replace them with the standard flexiplastic. If you have stopped broadcasting the HappyTunes music product over your interior speakers, resume immediately. As with the other components of the HappyFood Franchise, HappyTunes are integral to maintaining a standardized and profitable environment.

We hope that these disciplinary problems can be quickly forgotten, and that your HappyFood Franchise will go on to be satisfactory in all regards. Still, we must emphasize that noncompliance will result in the termination of your position as Manager of HappyFood Franchise #2232575.

Healthy, hearty, happy eating to you and your customers!

EndTrans

TRANS frm HAPPYFOOD INCORPORATED/ Administrative Division
RECEV stn HappyFood Franchise #2232575/Ugrath 3

Dear Mr. Nogren:

Your behaviour has exceeded all the prescribed bounds of HappyFood Inc. professionalism. As of this date, you are relieved of your post as Manager of HappyFood Franchise #2232575. Close the establishment immediately and return to head office for disciplinary action. Another Manager will be sent to Ugrath 3 shortly to try to undo the damage you've caused.

It is a blemish on HappyFood Inc.'s reputation that you have been allowed to continue in your course for as long as you have. Recently we discovered that many of your food invoices have been falsified, and that you have discontinued the use of many standard food items, particularly the Happy Fish product and those consisting of or using additives of Unigel, in favour of food items harvested and eaten locally. This alone would be bad enough to warrant your removal, but various other indiscretions have been uncovered. Hidden monitors in the Franchise have indicated that many customers linger in your establishment for up to three hours, a completely unacceptable figure; you have allowed your Food Processing Clerks an unheard-of degree of autonomy, to the point that few, if any, still wear their regulation flexi-uniforms; some, apparently, have been allowed to cultivate cranial hair growth of nonstandard appearance. That your profit analyses still show favourably has yet to be explained—the suspicion is that these too have been falsified.

Perhaps you are aware of how disruptive your activities are, and how devastating to HappyFoods Inc. it would be if such practices became standard: soon each Franchise would be different, and local entrepreneurs would begin to successfully compete with us, drastically slashing profits.

In light of all this, your farwave transmitter has been disabled by a remote signal, a contingency built into the equipment for just such rare occasions as this. Do not bother trying to call for friends or colleagues to take you off-planet. Your automated shuttle will not respond to your course orders, but will take you directly to head office for your disciplinary treatment.

There will be no further warnings. Return immediately on pain of extreme disciplinary action.

EndTrans

TRANS frm HAPPYFOOD INCORPORATED/ Administrative Division
RECEV stn HappyFood Franchise #2232575/Ugrath 3

Nogren:

You were warned.

A division of Internal Monitoring Armed Response troubleshooters are on their way to Ugrath 3 as you receive this. They have been told to expect a traitor to HappyFood Inc. and all that HappyFood stands for, and will react accordingly. I'm sure you're familiar with the stories told of the Armed Response teams. Perhaps you thought these teams were fictional. They are not.

After you have been removed, the HappyFood Franchise on Ugrath 3 will be shut down for several years to allow the damage you've done to repair itself. We only hope you found your pathetic little rebellion to be worth all this.

Peaceful surrender to the Armed Response team may possibly result in your survival, in which case extremely severe disciplinary treatments will be administered on your return to head office. Frankly, we here at head office are hoping you do not give up quietly; all of us will enjoy watching the combat vid records afterwards.

Healthy, hearty, happy eating to you . . .
EndTrans

TRANS frm HappyFood Franchise #2232575/ Commander Divot Armed Response Trouble-shooters Unit
RECEV stn HAPPYFOOD INCORPORATED / Administration Division

Commander Divot reporting:

As ordered, I brought Unit 5B down on Ugrath 3, with full armament distributed to trouble-shooter personnel. We approached HappyFood Franchise #2232575 with caution, as per your instructions. However, upon entering the establishment, we were unable to locate any activity of the treasonous nature you specify in your last message. In fact, HappyFood Franchise #2232575 is undoubtedly the finest Franchise either myself or my men have had the pleasure to dine in.

Obviously, some sort of bureaucratic or computer error is involved here. Possibly it involves the farwave transmitter of the Franchise manager, one Mr. Nogren; the device has malfunctioned in some way. Perhaps he was merely unable to get his reports through to head office due to this mechanical problem. The techs on my team were able to fix the transmitter, however, so, you should be getting a report from him any time now.

The quality of the Franchise's service and food here is amazing! Last night we dined on a seven-course meal, featuring native Ugrathian Kik-fish (similar though superior to Happy Lobster), and various wonderful vegetable dishes that showcased the fine berries and fruits of Ugrath 3. Mr. Nogren informs me that the principles behind his renovation of the Franchise here are applicable in any Franchise in the galaxy, and we assisted him in sending full documentation and video reports of his establishment to the galactic net, where it can be accessed by Franchise owners everywhere. Of course, this was only a short time ago, but already the response from other Franchises has been phenomenal!

My team has persuaded me that it would be best to remain here on Ugrath 3 until the mistake in our original mission orders has been clarified. Hopefully you will be able to locate the error and determine the actual location of this treasonous Franchise you warned us about so thoroughly. In the meantime, I suspect my men are anxious to sample more of the Franchise #2232575's remarkable cuisine.

Indeed, I admit I too am tempted by Mr. Nogren's description of tonight's meal: Raga-fish stew with boiled jubes (much like Happy Leeks, though I feel that jubes have a more piquant, enticing flavour) and side dishes of various sweetmeats. I am certain that once word of Mr. Nogren's innovations spreads, we will be able to enjoy meals of this quality on every planet in the galaxy. Surely a promotion is in order for Mr. Nogren!

We await your response eagerly.

Healthy, hearty, and happy eating to you!

EndTrans
EndReport

Originally published in Spring 1994 Vol 6 No 1 #16

Jason Kapalka was born and raised in Edmonton, Alberta. He is the cofounder of PopCap Games, the video game developer responsible for *Bejeweled*, *Plants vs Zombies*, *Peggle* and other popular titles.

STAR-SEEING NIGHT
ALICE MAJOR

*If the stars came out only once in a thousand years
what a wondrous sight we could think them.*
— *Emerson*

Star-seeing night.　　This may be a star-seeing night.
Radios ricochet,　　repeat from balconies.
Electrostatic tingle　　of tongues.

Faces turn to the closed clouds,　　the sun-occluders,
the world-sheath warm　　from the lungs of a weary planet
that struggles　　to secure its shaken balance
through cloud, now a constant.　　Moisture claimed by sky
and held hostage.　　Whole cities
sunk in deepening ocean.　　Sun no more
than a pale suspect.
　　　　　　Sometimes a slow swirl
opens in the thick air,　　a heavy-lidded eye.
Once the year before in　　Buenos Aires. Once
a decade back, over　　the drowned streets of London.
Whole generations have　　emerged and died
with no glimpse　　of galaxies.

Alice Major

But now the eye   may open. Here.
People remind each other   of the ritual,
practiced every year—   preparing for stars,
dowsing lights   to dim a vast
metropolis.   Its meaning almost lost,
but now renewed   and relevant.

Stars. We may see   the stars tonight.

Sky sucks daylight   down its grey throat.
Dusk creeps in the alleys.   Radios confirm the clouds
will part by midnight.   People form processions,
reverent as novices,   make their way to rooftops,
whisper together   as the wind tugs vestments.
Fall silent   as the sirens start to wail
demanding darkness.   The city dims.
A rising wind tears   rifts in ragged clouds.
A still, still-small eye   opens. First star.

Nikki

Nikki, six years old, bundled
in her brother's coat, blinks away
sleep's slow sedative.

> *Will we see the moon? she asks*
> *Maybe, if the clouds break soon enough*
> *they tell her. Aren't you a lucky girl*
> *to see the stars?*

But moon and stars to her are mere
abstractions. She knows about them
as she knows elephants and sailing ships,
has seen stars in photographs taken
high above the clouds' narcotic quilt
—jewels thrown savagely on black cloth
by some magnificent thief.
Still, she expects the stars will wear
five neat points, imagines the moon

with a fat nose, like the symbols
used even to this day on nursery walls.

Vega

She knows the stars. Their patterned stories
trace her longings on the silent air
behind her eyelids. She craves their glories—
bound Andromeda. The great square
of Pegasus. *(Wingbeats. Rescue.)* The chair
of Cassiopeia. Their names on her tongue
are crystal—light made sound, a thoroughfare
of bells. Arcturus. Aldebaran.
And Vega of the Lyre—herself as heroine.

"Vega knows the stars." Her husband claims
a share in her excitement, vicarious
and teasing. "No, don't say that." Pained
by his intrusion, she blushes, shrugs
away his arm. He is no Perseus,
although she loves him. Her longings are
mute but stubborn, gleaming, nebulous.
A perfect marriage made of stars
beckons to her, sidereal, singular.

Diana

"Here, Mrs. D. I'll turn the bed.
They say you'll see the moon
from this direction." *Poor old
thing. She's just not
coming back from that last
treatment. It's gone too far.*

   pain
    dull apron
   on abdomen
      pain

Alice Major

>   remembered pain
>   like thick weight
>   of monthly blood
>   blood waiting
>   to be born
>
>   remember moon
>   seen when?
>   sixty years. We
>   lived somewhere
>   else else
>   where?
>
>   half full moon
>   D-shape
>   I remember
>   pregnant
>   wait I was
>   pregnant. Elsie?
>   moon a big belly too
>   pressed against
>   sky.
>   Elsie born
>   that night
>   remember
>   pain

The cataract   clears. The iris opens.
A city stares into the black   sky bowl.

One point   on the western rim of cloud
turns to supple   silver fabric—peau-de-soie
then lace, then filaments   that trail long fingers
of desire after   the escaping moon.

Diana

Look Mrs. D . . . A full moon.

Star-seeing Night

*I doubt she even hears us. Such
a pity—it's just too late
for her to take this in. Hope
I don't go like that.*

    aching
    moon arc complete
    as a crone's
    wheel complete
    as a life flow
    of silver flower
    light
        bud, bloom
    splendid fruit

    birth only
    a beginning else
    where
        now the ache
    of utter
    contrast silver
    against dark
    arc spun end
    to end
        end over
    end splendour
    all the way
    round.

Vega

Vega knew the stars—her secret dower
of pattern. But not these stars, incessant
rain of light, a pathless, brilliant flour
sifted on the night. Pattern irrelevant,
garbled, a wilderness of radiant
white noise. "So, where's your star?" Husband tries
to take her arm. "Where's Vega?" Exuberant
he gazes up at star drifts. Tears fill her eyes.

Alice Major

"I told you—I don't know." Her face shuts out the skies.

Nikki

*Nikki, wake up.
See the stars.*

Nikki struggles through muffling
layered sleep. Her world of muted days
and cloud-reflected city glow at night
has
   vanished. Overhead
the stars hang near,
intense and lapidary, as though
the gem-encrusted fabric of the sky
drooped with their weight.

Wondering, she lifts her hand. Sudden
hunger makes her fingers curl,
coveting glory, coveting their fire.
Stars suddenly as real
as the fizz of soda pop, as close
as sparklers on her birthday cake.

*Will they be here tomorrow?
No, just tonight.
Aren't you a lucky girl
to see the stars
at least this once.*

But luck drains out of Nikki's eyes,
like starlight through her small
plump fingers.

*They won't be here
tomorrow?*

The loss assaults her. Some birthright
snatched away before she knew

the heritage was hers. She is angry.
Her voice beats wings
above the reverent murmur of the crowd.

No! No!
I want them again
tomorrow.

The stars sing back to her,
their voices incandescent.

Pale faces flower   in the pricking flame
of starlight.   The watchers seek
to memorize   unearthly messages
ciphered by far-off suns   and sent
across millennia.

Some among   the multitude begin
to drowse   and screen the dark
hollows of their mouths,   heavy eyes
able to absorb   only so much glory,
cups that fill   too quickly.

But most cradle wonder   like a quiet infant
all night in their arms,   yearn upwards
to the moon's bridge,   to the stars' black lake,
to the wide-set floodgates   of the firmament
until the clouds come.

Originally published in On Spec Fall 1994 Vol 6 No 3 #18

Alice Major has published nine highly praised poetry collections and a book of essays, "Intersecting Sets: A Poet Looks at Science." She served as the first poet laureate for Edmonton.

THE REALITY WAR
ROBERT BOYCZUK

Magic! Bertwold thought, grinding his teeth and staring at the castle wedged neatly—and quite impossibly—in the heart of the pass. *Nothing good ever comes of magic!* Beside him, Lumpkin, his crew chief, mined his nose abstractedly, evincing no interest whatsoever in the castle.

The two men stood at the juncture where the road turned from gravel to dirt. All work had ceased; picks, shovels and wheelbarrows lay in the long grass next to the idle road crew. Behind them the paving machine huffed in a quiet rhythm, its bellows rising and falling, as if it were a beast drifting off to sleep. The digging and grading machines had already been shut off and lay like giant, inanimate limbs on the road. Bertwold had fashioned them thus—in the shapes of human arms and legs—to assuage the King's distrust of machines. But now their very forms irritated Bertwold, reminding him of all the hoops he had already had to jump through to win the Royal contract.

And now this.

Clasping his hands behind his back, Bertwold stared miserably at the castle.

Its outer walls were fashioned of basalt, rising seamlessly from the ground to a height of nearly ten rods. Each corner boasted a square tower surmounted by an enormous ivory statue. Curiously, all four of the carvings appeared to be of imperfect figures, each lacking one or more limbs. The statue on the nearest corner was missing a head and sporting two truncated stumps where there should have been arms. Within the castle itself, visible above the crenellations of the walls, were apical towers of coloured emerald and ruby glass; and between them, the tops of ovate domes that shone with the lustre of gold and sparkled with the cool radiance of silver. Thin, attenuated threads, the colour of flax, (walkways, Bertwold reckoned, though they were empty) wound round and connected the buildings in an intricate pattern that was both complex and beautiful to behold—and, he thought with a slight degree of irritation in his engineer's mind—altogether impossible.

"How long has it been there?" he asked at last.

"We're not sure, boss," Lumpkin said. "It was there when we came out this morning to start work."

"Have you sent anyone to . . ." Bertwold hesitated, not sure exactly what might be appropriate in this case. ". . . to, ah, ring the bell?"

"Well, no sir. I tried to order a man to do it, but they're scared of its magic, you see . . ."

Turning to Lumpkin, Bertwold tapped him on the chest with his forefinger. "Then you go and find out who lives in that *thing*, and what they're doing there. You, personally. Don't send a labourer." Lumpkin opened his mouth, as if to say something, but Bertwold cut him off. "Or I'll find someone else who's hungry for a promotion." Lumpkin clamped his mouth shut. "In the meantime, I'll get the men back to work. We're still at least half a league from the castle, and there's plenty of road yet to lay. As far as I know, there's nothing in the contract that prevents your men from working in the presence of the supernatural."

Lumpkin, now a shade paler, nodded and swallowed hard. Spinning on his heel, he stumbled away, the gravel crunching under his boot soles.

Bertwold sighed. He had not counted on this when he had won the king's commission to build the greatest road the land had ever seen. He looked at the castle, imagining the pass as it had been yesterday, and the day before, and every day before for as long as men remembered: a wide, inviting V of sky that gave

onto the tablelands beyond.
Why would anyone want to drop a castle there?

Lady Miranda peered through the arrow slit. *Ants*, she thought, watching as a clutch of figures emerged from a tent and scattered, busy with their unfathomable, pointless tasks. *Insects.*

She looked at her right hand, then at her left, and pursed her lips. Between the two there weren't enough fingers remaining to end this quickly. Perhaps if she asked Poopsie . . .

No, she thought, *he'd never agree.* He was still off somewhere, sulking. It had been as much as she could do to convince him to move the castle from that horrid swamp to where they were now, even though he'd undershot their destination by over a hundred leagues. If she had been the one with the talent for moving, it would have been done right; but her talent was transubstantiation, of little use in such endeavours. She knew he should have offered his entire leg and not just the shin, for the gods were capricious and not entirely to be trusted. But that was Poopsie, always trying to cut corners, to save a finger here, a toe there, and ending up paying a much higher price for it in the long run. She'd wanted to warn him, but had, with difficulty, held her tongue. Now he'd have to go an entire arm or the other leg to unstick them if they ever wanted to leave this absurd spot.

And they must.

The mortals would never leave them alone until both she and Poopsie had been whittled down to their trunks. Humans *were* ants, swarming over their betters and bearing them down by dint of sheer numbers. Crush a hundred and a thousand would return. Their thickheadedness was simply incomprehensible.

Like the one who had disturbed her sleep yesterday morning. Lumphead, he had called himself. Lumphead, indeed! A thoroughly nasty bug of a man. Imagine the nerve, asking *her* to move the castle! *Never!* She had shouted, outraged at the impudence of the request, though it was the very thing for which she wished. How dare he! Her anger rekindled for an instant as she remembered his effrontery—and how she had reacted instinctively without thinking. Then she smiled, recalling the startled look on Lumphead's face as she had reached out and touched his nose, and broccoli had sprouted in its place.

It had been worth her little toe.

Bertwold tried hard not to stare at Lumpkin's nose.

Instead he watched his three sappers wrap burlap around the explosives before carefully packing them on small, two-wheeled carts. Another coiled varying lengths of fuse around his shoulder.

"Ready, sir."

Bertwold nodded at the fusilier who had addressed him. "Then let's get on with it."

"Yes, sir!"

The men lifted the handles to their carts and began jogging along the dirt path towards the castle, the wheels raising small clouds of dust. *Ha!* Bertwold thought as he watched his men draw closer to the base of the wall. *Let them magic their way out of this!*

Lady Miranda's beauty was legendary. At least in her presence.

Studying herself in the mirror, she daubed an exact amount of rouge beneath her eye patch. She frowned, then turned her head so that her face was in profile, her patch blending in with the dramatic shadows and angles of her sculpted features. She had changed into a slinky black velvet number that matched the colour of the patch. *Yes*, she decided, *perhaps I can use it to good effect*. The patch certainly added to her air of mystery, making her flawless skin appear even more striking. Picking up a silver-handled brush, she began stroking raven hair that fell to the small of her back. She smiled. *Ya still got it, baby*, she thought. Then, with just a slight degree of irritation: *Lord knows I might need it soon*. She sighed. Certainly she'd been careful, very careful, to dole out her magic in small doses over the years, saving it for only the most pressing occasions. Her appearance had, after all, been her saving grace; it was how she'd attracted Poopsie—and his countless predecessors. She'd managed to remain relatively whole while her suitors had whittled themselves down to slivers of flesh to gain her favour. But Poopsie had reached the point where he was becoming more and more reluctant to do so. He, along with his ardour, was thinning out. That's what had landed them in this cursed mess in the first place.

The mirror chimed, snapping Miranda out of her reverie; its surface shimmered like a windblown lake, distorting her reflection. A moment later, a pasty-faced cherub wearing a headset appeared where her reflection had formerly been. "Ladyship," it intoned in a thin, reedy voice. "The bugs are restless." The cherub disappeared and was replaced by a scene outside the castle. Several figures toiled along the road, dragging wooden carts behind them. The view narrowed, drawing in on the men. Visible, some rods behind, and exhorting the men on loudly, was that hideous lumpy fellow whose nose she'd transformed the previous day; and beside him stood another man, a head taller, and broad of shoulder. A breeze flicked his locks of golden hair restlessly in the wind. Miranda ordered her mirror cherub to zoom in.

She sucked in a breath. He was a big fellow. A towering bear of man, arms locked defiantly across a barrel chest, a scowl twisting up his face. And a striking face it was. Eyes grey as sea mist, nose long and straight, cheeks prominent and sculpted like her own. And four, perfect, fully-formed limbs. Miranda's heart skipped a beat. *Why*, she wondered with no small amount of bitterness, *couldn't more immortals look like that?*

"Milady, the ants draw nigh . . ."

A V creased Miranda's brow; she shifted her attention back to the figures dragging the carts. *Explosives*, she suddenly realized with distaste.

She expelled a sharp breath and cursed loudly. They would be at the gates in a few minutes. It was too late to find Poopsie.

Gathering up her skirts, she dashed out of her sitting room and down the stairs, taking them two at a time, emerging in the courtyard. She ran over to the front gate and knelt in the dirt, her velvet gown forgotten. Placing her palm flat on the ground, she concentrated on the two remaining fingers of her left hand and began chanting under her breath. Almost immediately her fingers stretched, then liquefied, soaking into the earth and transmuting the hard-packed, washed-out dirt to a lumpy beige mass centred around her palm. It glistened in the sunlight. The transmutation grew, milk-white circles forming in pockets on its surface. It continued to spread, now moving away from Miranda, following the path under the gate and out towards the men trotting up the road.

Bertwold watched the sapper slip and fall. The man tried to rise, but the more he struggled, the further he sank into the ground. He managed to drag himself up slightly on the protruding edge of his cart, but his efforts only mired the cart deeper. He wiped his face with the back of his arm and spat something from his mouth. "*Oatmeal!*" he screamed.

"What did he say?" asked Bertwold.

"Ootmal," said Lumpkin, his voice altered since his nose had been turned to broccoli. "The rood's been tooned to ootmal."

"Oh," Bertwold said. "I see."

Two of the men—along with the cart—had already slipped beneath the surface. Another had managed to half-swim, half-crawl to safety at the side of the road where the ground was firmer.

Bertwold stared at the castle and ground his teeth.

A moment later there was a muffled roar. The oatmeal road exploded upwards like a fountain; it showered down in thick droplets splattering all those who had gathered to watch, a large lump narrowing missing Bertwold and plopping wetly atop Lumpkin's skull.

Miranda reached the ramparts just in time to see the ensuing explosion. She laughed aloud as the oatmeal rained down on her enemies. *Chew on that, silly mortals!* she thought. *Vulgar food for vulgar pests.* That big one didn't seem to be quite so haughty now that he was wearing a suit of oatmeal.

Miranda felt exhilarated, alive. And something else, too. A strange, yet not wholly unpleasant tingling. Perhaps, this was just what she needed. Nothing like a bit of excitement to shake the dust from your bones.

She clambered onto the thick edge of the crenel so she would be visible to those below. Then she waved, looking directly at the big man, laughing and knowing her laugh would be carried clearly on the tongue of the wind to those annoyingly perfect ears...

There was no denying she was beautiful.

Bertwold stared through his brass telescope at the infuriating woman. She sat on the parapet, brushing her hair as if nothing were amiss, acknowledging his presence by blowing him an occasional raspberry. *Cheeky impertinence*! he thought. He was angry at her—and angry at himself for finding that damned eye patch so fascinating!

"Weel?"

"Well what?" Bertwold answered irritably. He stepped back from the telescope and made a mental note that, at a more discreet moment, he would suggest a thorough steaming might help Lumpkin in the preservation of his wilting nose.

"Whoot shud I teel the mun?"

Bertwold turned. Some of the crew were playing cards, others stood in small groups, talking in low voices. Bertwold stared at a digging machine, its oak bucket cupped in the shape of a human hand, resting uselessly on the side of the road.

"Assemble the men," he said. "I have an idea."

Bertwold stood behind the machine, pleased that its design and construction had proceeded so smoothly. It had taken only a day, remarkably, really, when he thought about it. Perhaps his men shared the same agitation to get on with things that dogged him; or maybe they were just anxious to complete the road and return to their families. Whatever the case, the guilds had worked cooperatively for once, and would have posted their first injury-free day had it not been for the knifing.

Bertwold walked the length of his new machine, checking the work. Inside the frame from the levelling machine, they had placed the arm from the digging machine, hinged on a massive, metal pin. Bertwold nodded at the end of his inspection, deciding it would make a passable catapult.

He surveyed the castle wall with his telescope, settling on a spot midway between the towers.

The men stood ready.

Bertwold barked an order and three bare-chested men bent to the task of turning a large windlass that drew the catapult's arm lower. A ratchet snicked in time to the men's grunts. When the arm would go no lower, a second crew wrestled a round, black bomb into the cupped palm at the end of the arm. Lumpkin, who Bertwold had placed in charge of the catapult, jotted a few quick calculations on a pad he held in his hand, and directed the men to angle the cart ever so slightly. A moment later, he turned to Bertwold and said, "Weady, Sur!"

Bertwold nodded.

"Fur!" Lumpkin shouted at a burly man holding a mallet.

The man raised his eyebrows in a quizzical look.

"Fur! I said!"

"Beg your pardon?"

"Fire," Bertwold said quietly.

"Oh," the man said, then turned and knocked the ratchet stay free with his mallet.

The arm flashed upwards, and the cart jerked sharply, its wheels momentarily lifting off the ground. Bertwold watched the bomb arc towards the castle.

It struck near the top of the wall and exploded, a thunderous sound rushing back to them a second after the flash. A section, just above the point at which the missile struck, slowly tumbled backwards and out of sight, leaving a small, but noticeable gap, like a missing front tooth.

The men cheered and Bertwold turned to look at Lumpkin. Though it was hard to tell, he thought he could detect a smile of satisfaction beneath the green mass of broccoli.

"Aieee!" shrieked Miranda, dancing backwards when the wall tumbled down, narrowly missing her and burying Poopsie, who had been seated in the rose garden. "Aieee!" she said again. Then, recovering her composure, she stamped her feet in indignation. *How dare they?* she thought. *The insolent insects!* "That's it!" she said to the rubble heap that had been Poopsie. "Now I'm really mad!"

"Now, now Miranda, better not to get yourself worked up," Poopsie's voice was barely audible from beneath the debris.

"They're only doing what mortals usually do. Let's think about this thing rationally..."

"No!" Miranda shouted as a large section of the fallen wall began to stir, loose dirt and stones trickling off its edges. "I will not let this go unpunished!" The chunk of wall floated upwards, then hovered. Another piece began to shift.

"Please, Miranda, before you go throwing away perfectly good body parts on a pointless gesture." Poopsie's voice was clearer now, and Miranda recognized the wheedling tone. She knew it was his own precious body parts he was really worrying about. "After all, we're the ones who landed in the middle of their pass. It's not as if they came here just to raze the castle." A geyser of dirt and stones shot from the hole and fell to the ground, forcing Miranda to hop back two more steps.

"Are you taking their side?"

Poopsie clambered from the pit as best he could on his one good leg, covered in dirt but otherwise unhurt. "No, dearheart. I'm just saying you have to see it from their point of view." The stone slabs suspended in the air dropped back into the hole with a *whump*.

"Humph," she said. She eyed him closely, wondering what part of himself he had sacrificed to escape the rubble. He shook his head like a wet dog, and dirt sprayed out in all directions; it was then she saw his left ear was missing.

"Just give me a moment to gather my thoughts, and I'll move the castle like you wanted," he said.

There was another thunderous explosion, and part of the castle wall to Miranda's left cascaded downwards, shattering the glass roof of the aviary. A flock of brightly-coloured birds, including her favourite gryphon, took wing, rising over the wall and scattering on the wind.

"I've decided that I like it here," Miranda said. "I think we should stay."

"Stay? No, don't be silly." Poopsie bent down and placed his hand on the ground at Miranda's feet. "Brace yourself," he said.

But before he could do anything, Miranda seized his hair and, in an instant—and at the cost of her big toe—transmutated him to a parrot with a tiny wooden leg.

"Awk!" Poopsie squawked, flapping his wings and hopping about on his one good leg.

"There!" said Miranda petulantly. "Now you shan't be able to work your magic until I release you!"

Another explosion rocked the castle, and Miranda stepped up to the wall, placing her palm on it.

"Awk! Miranda, wait!" Poopsie screeched, but it was already too late, for her long raven locks were melting away as she worked her magic, running down her cheeks and neck like trails of blackened butter, leaving streaks that shone darkly in the sun.

Bertwold watched as a fourth projectile misfired, shattering uselessly against the wall and dropping to the ground in a curl of smoke. Already there were two large gaps near the summit of the wall, and an irregular tear where the third bomb had hit beneath the tower. He did a quick count of the remaining ammunition—fourteen missiles—and decided that it would be sufficient to finish the job. He ordered the men to concentrate their fire to the right of the largest breach.

"Fur!" Lumpkin shouted.

The bomb tore up and away, dwindling to a small dot. It struck—but much to Bertwold's consternation, it neither fell nor detonated. Instead it stretched the dark surface of the wall as if it were made of rubber. A moment later, the wall snapped back in their direction and the black dot began to grow rapidly.

Oh, oh, Bertwold thought.

Lumpkin bolted down the road, leaving a trail of florets in his wake. Bertwold overtook him just before the bomb struck.

He was pitched, head over heels, into a deep ditch they'd been using as a latrine. A series of rapid explosions followed. The ground shook beneath him. Dirt rained down, then smoking bits of debris, sizzling as they extinguished in the fetid water. A moment later a dark cloud boiled around him, choking him and making his eyes water. He struggled to his feet.

"Sur?"

Bertwold blinked back tears.

"Butwuld?"

The smoke dissipated, and Bertwold could make out the blurry face of Lumpkin, who stood on the bank above him. Lumpkin's clothes were singed and torn, and the tip of his

The Reality War

broccoli was blackened, but otherwise he seemed unhurt.

"The catapult?" Bertwold asked, grabbing Lumpkin's shirt and bunching the material in his fist. Then, before Lumpkin could answer, Bertwold pulled himself up the shallow embankment, throwing his foreman off balance, so that, with a yelp, Lumpkin tumbled into the latrine.

Bertwold staggered up the slope of the bank. Before him, where the catapult and stockpile of ammunition had been, there was an enormous, smoking crater.

"Got them!" Miranda lifted the hem of her gown and did a little jig. "Maybe now he'll understand who he's dealing with!"

Poopsie shook his head ruefully, ruffling his feathers, scratching behind his left ear with his tiny wooden leg. "I wouldn't count on it," he squawked, and flapped onto Miranda's shoulder. "Please, Randy, just change me back and I'll get us out of here. Let's leave before something serious happens . . ."

Miranda shooed him away with a wave of her hand. She crossed her arms, and her expression hardened. "No. He started it. Now let him finish it—if he can!"

"What are they doing?" Lady Miranda wondered aloud. For the last five days the annoying humans had left them in relative peace. Poopsie chewed quietly on a cracker, but refrained from commenting.

Miranda leaned forward between the merlons of the parapet, about to drum her fingers in consternation when she remembered her digits were all gone. It only added to her pique.

"Awk, Randy," Poopsie squawked in her ear, "they're not worth the effort. Awk, awk! Let them be."

Miranda winced; every time Poopsie talked he was sounding more like a parrot. And it was getting harder and harder to coax him from the trees.

"Awk! Change me back and let's be on our way. Awk!"

"No," she said. "Not until this is finished." She gave him another cracker.

What were the bugs up to?

She stared down the valley at the mortals' camp and shook

her head in bemusement. They'd dismantled all their limb-shaped construction vehicles. At first, Miranda thought they'd given in, and were simply packing up to leave; but instead of slinking away, they had erected an enormous pavilion and dragged the disassembled parts of the machines underneath its broad canvases. Miranda bit her lip so hard she drew blood. The pain surprised her, made her curse softly under her breath at the waste of a perfectly good blood wish. *It's their fault*, she thought, her anger slowly rising as she dabbed at her lip with a lace handkerchief. *And they shall pay.*

Bertwold admired his latest invention.

It had taken them the better part of a week to build the thing. In the process, they'd had to cannibalize every single construction machine. And they'd also exhausted their supplies. For the last two days his men had worked on empty stomachs and Bertwold had spent almost as much time mollifying their growing discontent as he had spent overseeing the construction work. But it had been worth it, he thought. This was the best machine he had ever built.

"Fire up the boilers," he said to Lumpkin.

At Bertwold's words, Lumpkin jumped. He looked drawn, and more than a little nervous; this Bertwold could understand, having seen the other men eyeing Lumpkin's nose hungrily. Bertwold's own stomach rumbled. For a moment his vision misted over, and he could only see the yellow of a rich cheese sauce running over green of broccoli and his mouth began to water...

He shook his head to clear it.

Focus, he admonished himself. *You'll need all your wits to operate the machine.*

"Awk!" Poopsie flapped his wings, screeching as he circled the room in agitated motion. "Awk!"

"What is it?" Miranda sat before her mirror; she had spent the morning in the cellar, rooting through old trunks, trying on wigs.

"Follow me! Follow me!" Poopsie shrieked. Then he darted

beneath the door jamb and flew out of sight.

Miranda leapt to her feet and sped after him, out onto the parapet where he perched, his little wooden leg tapping an agitated tattoo on the crenel.

"Look!" he squawked, pointing a wing.

Miranda turned. Her jaw fell open.

The roof of the humans' pavilion had been rolled back, revealing a huge machine fabricated in the form of a man. It was sitting up, as if it had just woken. Steam curled slowly from vents in its neck. As Miranda watched, there was a piercing whistle, and the machine rumbled to its feet, towering over the camp, its face now level with hers. With a grinding noise it teetered, steadied itself, took one lurching step, then another, walking in an exaggerated gait, moving cautiously along the edge of the oatmeal swamp, heading towards the castle.

Poopsie hopped on her shoulder. "Quick!" Poopsie screamed in her ear. "Change me back! Change me back! I'll get us out of here! Awk!"

Miranda raised her arm to bat him away, then stopped abruptly. "Okay," she said. She plucked him from her shoulder with her good arm—the one with two remaining fingers—and he yelped, a strangled sound that Miranda felt vibrate through his windpipe. She closed her eyes and concentrated; her arm began to dissolve, to fuse with Poopsie.

He grew.

Already larger than Miranda, he continued to grow with each passing second as her arm disintegrated. By the time she was up to her elbow, he was a forty foot high parrot, his wooden leg the size of a small tree. When she finally withdrew, only a small flap of flesh left where her arm used to be, Poopsie's head extended past the castle's highest tower.

"Now," Miranda shouted, pointing to the man-machine. "Get him!"

Poopsie blinked, once, twice, and cocked his head. His eyes were dull and remote, and Miranda could no longer detect any sign of human intelligence in them. "Poopsie?" she asked. "You there?"

Poopsie screeched, an ear-splitting reverberation that shook the castle down to its foundations. He launched himself from the parapet, his wings beating so hard that Miranda was nearly blown from the wall. He swooped past the machine, and dove towards the clutch of workers in the encampment. At the last second he banked and climbed into the sky, a tiny figure with a bright green nose struggling in his talons. In seconds he'd dwindled to a small dot on the horizon.

Oops, Miranda thought.

As if enraged, the man-machine leapt forward, its whistle shrieking in anger.

The parrot was monstrous, huge, large enough to knock even the machine over.

Bertwold watched it dive towards him and he froze, his hands on the levers, unable to move. It grew larger and larger until he could see nothing else, and he covered his eyes, waiting for the moment of impact that would topple him to his death. But nothing happened. Or at least nothing dire. The machine rocked gently as the parrot swooped past. When Bertwold lowered his arm the eyeholes showed only empty sky. He pulled a lever and the head swung round a full circle. But the bird was nowhere to be seen.

"Right," Bertwold said. "That's it for you." He reached for a lever.

The motors roared; steam vented in screeching whistles. The machine jerked forward, breaking into a mechanical trot. Then it lurched sickeningly. Although the engines continued to bellow, the machine had come to a standstill.

Bertwold grabbed another lever, pulling sharply on it; the machine roared even louder, and this time he could hear its metal joints squeal deafeningly under the stress. A rivet popped out of a plate above his head, and shot across the chamber, ricocheting off the opposite wall, and clattering noisily to the floor. Bertwold eased up on the lever, and the machine seemed to sigh; then it settled on an awkward angle, the landscape ahead of him tilted a few degrees. *What the . . . ?*

Bertwold unstrapped himself and took two quick steps to the right eyehole. Far below, the machine's feet had already disappeared, swallowed in the golden brown, lumpy earth.

Bertwold cursed aloud. In his anger, he'd forgotten about the rotting oatmeal!

He dashed back and worked furiously at the controls, but no matter what he did, no matter how hard he pushed or pulled the groaning levers, he couldn't free the machine's legs. His beautiful new machine continued to sink. As he sweated and cursed and sweated some more, the landscape rose, bit by infuriating bit, before him.

Bertwold stood beside his machine, just beyond the edge of the deadly oatmeal. Only the machine's head was visible, its chin nestled firmly in the brown morass. Bertwold felt like crying. Instead, he continued to brush oatmeal from his jerkin in as dignified a manner as he could muster. It left sad brown streaks wherever it touched.

Down the road, the encampment was deserted; his men had abandoned him. *One giant parrot and they fled like frightened children.* Bertwold shook his head. He had expected better of them, especially Lumpkin, always faithful Lumpkin. *Oh well,* he thought. *Wherever he's gone, he's probably better off now.*

"Halooo . . ." The voice startled Bertwold. It was a woman's voice, a mellifluous, lilting tone that made his blood quicken. It had issued from behind the castle gate. "Is anyone out there?"

Bertwold turned and cleared his throat. "Yes?"

"Um," the voice began. "I'm in a bit of a fix. I was wondering if you could, uh, possibly give me a hand."

Bertwold strode up to the gate. In its centre was a square peephole that was shut. "What sort of help?" When there was no answer, Bertwold said, "Why don't you open the gate?"

"I'm afraid I can't," the voice said. "You see, that's my problem."

"Then at least open the peephole so I can see who it is that I'm addressing."

"Oh well, if you insist!" The voice sounded annoyed, almost petulant. There was a rasping sound followed by a grunt. Then the small wooden square swung inward. Bertwold's heart faltered. Framed in the opening was the beautiful face he had watched through his telescope, although now a wig sat askew atop her head. Bertwold gaped; the woman blushed. Then she inclined her head in a fetching manner, hiding her eye patch in half-shadow. Bertwold sucked in a sharp breath.

"I'm afraid I can't open the door," she said in a forlorn voice that rent Bertwold's heart. "I'm trapped." She stepped back and he could see that she had only one arm, and that arm had no fingers. "I managed to pull the bolt on the peephole with my teeth, but the gate is barred." She gave him a melting look. "I'm afraid you'll have to find your own way in."

Bertwold's heart sang in his chest.

Fall was nearly played out and winter would soon be upon them; large flakes of snow drifted down and settled on the ground. The pass, paved road and all, would soon be closed until spring. Miranda stared at the castle, at *her* castle, and the causeway that had been cut through it like a tunnel, and felt a brief, almost imperceptible, flash of something that might have been anger.

But it passed quickly.

As if sensing her agitation, Bertwold reached out and put his arm around her shoulders. She turned and smiled at him.

It had been his idea to come back here, and she could see it troubled him no less than her. The way he had looked at his machine, or the head of it anyway, that poked above the ground in the midst of the inexplicable broccoli patch. It was, she thought, quite clever, still widely regarded as his best work, something of which he could rightly be proud.

"Ready?" she asked, and he nodded.

They walked back to their carriage. When she reached out to open the door, he closed his fingers over her wrist. "Problems?" he asked.

She drew her brow up in puzzlement.

"The cold," he tapped her arm. "I was worried about the temperature. How's it holding up?"

She flexed her arm, curling her fingers, all five of them, into a fist and released them. An almost inaudible whirring followed her movements. "Works perfectly," she said, reaching out and pulling his head to hers until their lips touched lightly. "Just like magic."

Originally published in On Spec Fall 1994 Vol 6 No 3 #18

Robert Boyczuk has published short stories in various magazines and anthologies. He also has three books out: a collection of his short work, *Horror Story* and *Other Horror Stories*, and two novels, *Nexus: Ascension* and *The Book of Thomas, Volume I, Heaven* (all by Chizine Publications). More fascinating details on Bob, and downloads of most of his published work, are available at **boyczuk.com**.

Casserole Diplomacy
Fiona Heath

Edna was doing the dishes when the aliens knocked on the back door. She was in the kitchen at the back of the house, facing the woods instead of the highway that cut through the isolated area she had lived in for most of her sixty years. A little television sat on the counter near the sink. Images whirled by on the screen but the volume was so low Edna's slightly deaf ears caught only the occasional car crash or gun shot. She preferred it that way, only keeping the TV on for company with Jonno gone and the kids so far away. The kitchen was clean and well kept.

The walls with their faded orange floral paper and fake wood cupboards were scrubbed and almost shiny. The captain's wheel clock hung on the wall beside the embroidered Lord's Prayer Edna had made for her thirtieth wedding anniversary. Cat and mouse ceramic salt and pepper shakers stood on the speckled Formica table beside a book of crossword puzzles. Yellow nylon curtains, closed against the night, hid the array of Florida seashells on the windowsill. The seashells were mementoes of Edna's only trip in an airplane. The sea in Newfoundland only gave up broken shells and driftwood. Edna liked the creamy pink of the southern conches and would often sit at the table absentmindedly stroking the shells as she did her puzzles.

She had been cooking all day and was just finishing cleaning up. Tomorrow was the Bonavista Ladies' Social and she had made her best dishes for the luncheon. Edna was renowned on the peninsula for her cooking. Years ago, her bakeapple pie won first prize three years in a row at the County Festival. That was when there were still bakeapples to be picked in handfuls off the roadside. These days she only ever collected enough for a few pies and a single freezer bag for winter.

Thinking the knock must be Sherri, her closest neighbour, who lived in an identical house across the highway, Edna yelled, "What are ye knocking fer—it's open as always, dearie." Her hands stayed busy in the sink of hot water and dishes. The aliens knocked again. Edna sighed in love and exasperation, pulling her yellow gloved hands out of the sink, and shook off some of the water. She stepped over to the door and opened it. "Sherri, love, what are ye think . . ."

Edna stopped talking as she saw three aliens crowded onto the back steps. The aliens stared back at her. Edna was so surprised not to see Sherri, not to see a familiar face on the back steps, that she was less surprised at how unfamiliar her visitors were. Strangers were only visible in the tourist months of July and August. Out of season strangers were fantastic enough that being from another planet was only an extra oddity. And it was obvious they were aliens, with smooth yellow faces—*kind of like my gloves* flitted quickly through Edna's mind—and awkward white rain slickers that didn't seem to fit properly. Edna could just make out muddy white jeans at the bottom of each slicker.

Edna knew about aliens. She had watched the *X-Files* once at her daughter Katie's in Halifax. Sometimes she read the *National Enquirer*, mostly for the Hollywood gossip, but she skimmed the alien abduction stories. Her heart began to beat a little faster. Perhaps they were here to take her away to the stars. No one would believe her story, that was for sure, a widowed woman living alone outside Maberly, Newfoundland. She was just the type they take. There was that farmer from Nebraska who had been experimented on and now could see rings of light around everything electric, but no one believed him. Edna clutched the doorframe. She looked closely at the aliens, struggling between fear and a quiet kind of thrill. She

Casserole Diplomacy

realized they were each holding a container. The containers looked strangely familiar—like grey metal Tupperware. The aliens gestured at her with the containers. Edna realized they had brought food. *Why, they've just come to visit.* Edna was surprised; she had never read anything in the *Enquirer* about aliens visiting before abducting people. She relaxed her grip on the doorframe. Even though they were yellow-coloured strangers, it was a dark and chilly night for April and they had come round to the back door like any sensible person.

Everyone in Maberly knew the front door was for strangers, tourists and government officials, all the come-from-aways who were trying to experience the authentic Newfoundland. The back door was for friends and neighbours, people who lived here and treated each other like human beings—not cardboard images. Since the aliens knocked at the back door, they probably knew someone from around here, or came from a place with back door folks too. Perhaps they were friends of her Stan down in St. John's. They lived crazy lives in that city, Edna knew, what with the university and the CBC there. The aliens might be odd-looking all right, with rubber glove skin and strange oval eyes, but they knew enough to be back door folks. Now that she was looking at the three of them closely, their expressions seemed hopeful rather than aggressive. They were just coming for a visit, like any neighbour might. With their hands full they couldn't abduct her too easily. Edna prided herself on her hospitality—the whole town knew Edna wouldn't turn a sick owl away from her door—and no one was going to say Edna Calhoun didn't know how to treat aliens well on a cold night like this. She smiled at them and stood back from the door to let them in.

The aliens crowded quickly into the warm kitchen. Edna realized she'd kept them standing there a few minutes while she thought. She pointed to the table. "Take off your slickers. There are hooks on the back of the door. Sit yourselves down now. I'll just put the kettle on for some tea." She peeled off her gloves and walked over to the old gas stove, taking the kettle and filling it under the tap in the rinse sink. "I was finishing the dishes from the day, but I'll just leave them for now."

Edna lit the stove, carefully as always, and put the kettle on the back burner. When she turned around, the biggest alien came towards her and thrust all three metal Tupperwares into her hands. She (at least Edna thought it was a she) had orange eyes, oval and gentle. "Well, thank you kindly," Edna said. "But I'll have no one saying Edna Calhoun can't feed her guests."

The aliens looked at her. Edna sighed. She was hoping to only give them tea with some cookies she had made a few days earlier, but the Tupperware tins were large and heavy. They would expect a meal. Edna put the Tupperware on the counter beside the stove and opened the fridge. She could give them the food she'd made for tomorrow. With Jonno gone, Edna no longer had a freezer filled with good food waiting to be eaten. No point when it was just her in the house. Edna only liked cooking for other people. All the pleasure was in seeing other people enjoy her creative labour. But company was company and Edna wasn't going to behave badly like other folks she could mention. Like Carol Anne Wheeler who had given the Simpsons tea and toast when they had dropped in, coming back for a visit after retiring into St. John's to live with their daughter. *Even with nothing in the house, you could whip up some muffins or Pillsbury cookies as quick as can be. Best thing too, when fresh out of the oven. Toast!* Edna snorted to herself. She'd have to get up early and cook something else for the luncheon but she'd make sure these aliens were well fed tonight. Good thing she'd been to town only yesterday and bought her week's groceries at the Valu-Mart.

Edna wondered if the aliens could eat regular food. They never came for dinner in the *National Enquirer*. Edna froze. What if she was the dinner? What if the Tupperware held the condiments? She glanced back at the aliens, who were sitting neatly around the table. They looked somehow oversized for the furniture, even though they weren't much bigger than Edna, and she was getting round these days. They were chittering quietly to one another, sounding like squirrels with deep voices.

It made Edna a little uncomfortable, not knowing what they were saying, but she couldn't believe they were a threat, even with yellow skin, too many teeth and not enough fingers. *Not knocking at the back door, not sitting at the kitchen table, calm as can be. They must have come a long way for this visit. Company is company, Mrs. Calhoun, and you just let them be themselves, and give them food and drink to warm their bellies.* You don't have to say much to come-from-aways, even alien ones. Who just want to pry into the life of regular people, as if the ticket for the ferry ride over gave them permission to be nosy like tourists in a zoo.

The shortest alien came over to Edna as she took dishes and containers out of the fridge. He had a little fringe of wispy, crinkly yellowish hair on his neck and the back of his head. He was a bit tubby and reminded her of George—one of Jonno's youngest fishing partners. George had loved her codcakes—when there was still cod to make them—he would stand beside her while she fried them up and sniff loudly and ecstatically. "Edna's codcakes. Boy-o boy-o. What's better for a hungry man than a plate full of these here codcakes? I could eat nothing but Edna's codcakes day in and day out and I'd be a happy man!" Edna would scowl and push him away with a threatening spatula. George would jump out of her way, blowing kisses. She would smile and end up laughing as she turned back to the sizzling pan. Edna missed George, gone when the cod was gone, to Cornerbrook, trying to find something to do now that his life on the sea was over. Edna couldn't help but like the alien George as he chattered excitedly beside her, gesturing at the food and the table.

"All right," Edna said. "You can set the table. The cloth lies in the bottom drawer." She pointed. George the alien followed her finger and opened the drawer, pulling out the top cloth and looking at her. Edna nodded. "Just spread that over the table." She pointed back to where the other aliens were sitting. George grimaced in what was probably a smile and took the faded but clean orange and white checked cloth back to the table. All three of them examined it quickly and then George smoothed it over the table. He had forgotten about the salt and pepper shakers and the puzzle book, but the big alien pulled them out, making a deeper noise that might have been laughter.

George came back and stood beside Edna, looking expectant. Edna smiled shyly back as she continued to take the covers off the dishes. "Well, I guess it'd be all right if you were to put the utensils out as well. They'd be there in the top drawer." She pointed again. George opened the drawer with interest and made the laughing noise. Edna watched as George scooped up a big pile of cutlery. She shook her head with amusement as George took the pile over to the table where the three of them broke out into excited chitterings. The stout one picked up two forks and touched them to his face, peering at it. "No, no, we only need one of each to eat with, and some serving spoons." She picked up a fork. "One for me." She pointed at herself. "One for each of you." The aliens smiled back at her and each one picked up a fork from the pile. "Right," said Edna, as she gathered up the rest of the forks. She put away the forks and then returned to the table and picked up a knife. Before she could say anything, the aliens dove into the mess of utensils and pulled out knives. The big female one who reminded her of Jonno's kindly old Auntie Simmons had taken a butter knife. "No, that's for the margarine—take one like this. Though I suppose we'll be needing it too." Edna offered a regular knife in exchange and laid the butter knife off to the side of the pile. George looked at the others and they all looked at Edna. Before she could say "Right," they all reached for a spoon, checking to see they all had the same size. Edna smiled and put the rest of the utensils back in the drawer.

Edna finished getting the dishes ready while the aliens chittered over the utensils. She knew they were also sneaking glances at her hands but that didn't worry her. Even with a touch of arthritis they were still shapely for her age, not like Sherri's poor hands gnarled like tree roots. The casserole was still slightly warm so she popped it in the oven for a quick reheat. Luckily she had made the cold salads and the dessert earlier in the day, so they were all ready to eat.

This time the third alien—the middle one—came over to help. He looked more alien, more jaundiced yellow instead of the sunny yellow of the other two. She wasn't sure, but she thought he might be older. The other two seemed to defer to him. He seemed more excitable, the kind of person who flew into tempers if not humoured properly. He was happy enough right now, and peered at her in a short-sighted kind of way, *as if he needs glasses*, Edna thought. She took a serving spoon from the jar beside the stove and stuck it into the potato salad, handing him the bowl. Glasses took it delightedly, sniffing with what must be his nose, a protrusion between orange eyes and grimacing mouth, but tilted so far up, Edna could stare right into the two air passages. She turned away, feeling like she was seeing something she shouldn't. Glasses took the bowl over to

Casserole Diplomacy

the table and came back for the green Jell-O salad and then the red. The lime wobbled with carrots, celery and green pepper. The red was sweeter with peaches and pears and mini marshmallows. Both were moulded into wreaths. Edna herself brought over the teapot and the mugs.

Edna Calhoun sat down at her kitchen table with the three aliens. Spread out on the orange and white checked cloth were the three salads, the cat and mouse shakers Katie had sent her ages ago, the teapot and mugs, utensils and a butter knife. Edna sighed. "Old age is making me forget me manners. I've forgotten half the meal." She went back to the cupboards and brought out the plates. She went into the pantry and brought out a jar of dill pickles and a loaf of bread. Edna used to make her own dill pickles, never as fine as Ruth's but with a respectable crunch, but she had let the garden go after the kids had left. The store-bought were tasty and cheap. *Not much point into going to all the trouble of pickling for two*, she had said to Jonno. No point at all just for herself. Finally she went and got the margarine out of the refrigerator.

Edna settled back into her vinyl chair. The aliens looked at her, smiling with all those teeth. Edna smiled back. "Well now. I don't hold with no prayers or anything, so let's all just help ourselves to this good food."

Edna pushed the potato salad towards George, who was sitting on her right. On her left, Auntie Simmons touched her forearm gently. Edna was surprised. Their skin didn't feel like the rubber yellow glove—more like peach fuzz. Edna looked at Auntie. Auntie turned to Glasses. Glasses, Auntie and George linked their hands and took Edna's. She liked the feel of their skin—soft and warm like a baby's. Together, the aliens chittered briefly in sing-song voices as they smiled at each other. Edna smiled too. They sat their quietly, enjoying the moment. To Edna, the room seemed to shrink and expand at the same time, After a couple more moments, they dropped hands and Glasses said awkwardly, speaking for the first time in a voice as textured as his hands, "Thank you."

Edna tried not to blush as she said, "You're welcome." Her voice came out funny. She felt like she did when Jonno smiled at her when they woke up beside one another in the morning. She stared at the tablecloth as she pushed the potato salad towards

George. "Help yourselves."

Everyone did. Edna opened the bag of Wonder Bread and offered it around. The aliens were very excited by the plastic bag, with its yellow, red and blue dots and stripes. They gestured for her to repeat its name. Edna said, "Wonder Bread. You get it at Valu-Mart, the grocery store." The aliens sat for a moment then broke out into the laughing noise. Edna smiled too, although she wasn't sure just what the joke was. Wonder Bread. How much English did they understand? "I guess it does sound kind of strange."

While the aliens were tasting the salads, Edna got up and took the casserole from the oven. It smelt as good as it always did. She should have served it at the same time as the salad, but "better late and hot than early and cold." That's what Jonno always said when she started to fret about food being ready to serve at the same time. He said it too, when he'd had a late time fishing and would try and sneak his big burly body into their bed so she wouldn't wake up and be angry. But she was always awake, wondering if the sea had gotten him, if this was the night, and her anger only covered her relief. Jonno knew that and would only say *better late and hot than early and cold* as he threw his arm around her so they could laugh together. She'd been lucky in the end, people said, with him dying neat and clean in the living room of a heart attack instead of out there on the cold sea with the fish to find his bones. But she'd have preferred it if the sea had taken him, the sea he loved, rather than sitting at home with the life gone from him. *He was dead before he died*, she thought bitterly. *The damn government took that when they took back his fishing license. No more cod. As if we hadn't been telling them high muck-a-mucks that for years, and they'd taken no more notice than a child notices a mosquito. Jonno's heart went out with the tide every time he got a cheque instead of a fishing quota, and it never came back, either.*

Edna shook herself. Thinking about Jonno like that with company here. She didn't know what got her thinking so sad. At least Jonno had gotten a good forty years on the sea, like his dad and his granddad. It was Stan who'd only gotten to taste it. Poor Stan, lost in the big city, hanging out with all those strange radio people. She brought the tuna melt casserole over to the table and sat back down. Auntie Simmons smiled kindly at her. George looked at the casserole and at Edna's face and leaped up with a chitter of glee to dash into the kitchen and take a serving spoon from the jar. He stuck it proudly into the casserole. Edna had to laugh. "Thank you, George, guess I was forgetting again. This is a tuna casserole. Won second prize at Bonavista Festival last year." Edna was very proud of the casserole. Edna had created it herself and hadn't told anyone her secret ingredients that made it the richest and tastiest around. She'd improved it since the fair, and this year she knew she'd take home the first.

Edna tried to explain Jell-O to the aliens. They hadn't asked in so many words, not having said anything in English since Glasses said "thank you," but simply kept looking at the Jell-O salads then at Edna until she felt she had to say something. Edna wasn't sure herself how to describe it. She was talking about hot water and many colours when the front doorbell rang. Edna was astonished. "Why, that hasn't rung since . . ." Her voice faltered. *Since the ambulance came to take away Jonno*, she thought. Auntie Simmons and George had funny expressions on their faces. George let out a squeaky chitter as they both turned to Glasses. Glasses made a gesture with one yellow hand and looked directly at Edna. Edna looked into his orange eyes, then at George and Auntie Simmons. She got up heavily from the table. "You just sit tight and keep on eating. Don't ye worry."

Edna had to pull hard to open the front door once she got it unlocked. She tugged it open a few inches and looked out to see two men in suits on the tiny front porch of her bungalow. The older one looked very formal, grey hair slicked smooth on his head, like he'd never been in a head wind his whole life. The younger man, skinny and tall, had very curly brown hair that didn't know which way to go. He looked excited.

The older man spoke in a clipped mainlander accent. "Sorry to trouble you, Mrs. Calhoun. We've reason to think there is a dangerous offender in the area . . ." He paused briefly. ". . . from St. John's. We're just doing a routine check. Have you seen or heard anything out of the ordinary today or tonight."

The young one broke in: "In the woods, have you heard any

noise or seen strange lights in the woods?" The older man shot him a mean look and Curly subsided.

Edna stared at them, thinking. Government folks. Suits. At her front door spouting about Danger. Danger. It was obvious they wanted the aliens. Would almost smile if she were to stand aside and motion towards her kitchen. Edna was not a brilliant woman, but she was shrewd. She could see how hungry Curly was for a taste of the aliens. On the verge of the highway, she could make out dark shapes of cars. She could see Sherri's front light on—they must have a couple of men over there too. The suits must want them bad. Wanted to take them away and act like they know best. The same way they knew best when they resettled all the folks from Kearley's Harbour, closing down a whole community just because they said so. They never stuck around long enough to see the results either. Her Aunty Gwen moved after her whole life on the water. Within the year in St. John's she'd gone blind and died. She may have been seventy-one but they were long livers in her family, nearing ninety most of them. Standing just behind her front door, looking at the contained arrogance of the men, Edna was suddenly furious, furious as she'd ever been. Furious in a way she had lost in the tidal wave of grief she'd felt looking at Jonno keeled onto the carpet, gone from her for good. Opening the door wider, Edna drew herself up as stern as her rounded body allowed, solid as a lighthouse. She glared at the men.

"Who d'ye think ye are? Disturbing me in my house with nary a warning? What's yer talk about lights and bad people? In this place? We'd be lucky if we get a drunk from Bonavista on the highway. What are ye thinking of? Disturbing an old woman with scary talk. Get away from me now. Get back to where ye came from."

Mr. Formal looked startled. "It's simply a public service . . ." Edna glared again. He shot Curly a rueful glance that implied "typical newfie" and pulled a business card smoothly from his coat pocket. "If you hear or see anything out of the ordinary, call right away, although I'm sure you're right. There is nothing to worry about." Edna took the card ungraciously.

"Nothing to worry about?" she snapped. "I've got plenty to worry about. No cod. No more summer berries. Storms one day and a drought the next. A pension that gets smaller every month. Everybody leaving like Maberly died and was left out in the sun, stinking. What's left in this place 'cepting worries and memories, boy? You leave us be with your big city talk of bad people. Everybody here knows where the rotten apples are." Edna thought she saw Curly's face turn red as she struggled to shut the door.

She stood for a moment behind the shut door, her heart pounding against her chest. Edna hadn't yelled at anyone since she was young. She felt ashamed of herself, screaming at strangers. Screaming at human strangers, to protect the alien ones in her kitchen. She took a deep breath. *What's there to feel bad about, Edna dear? It'll make a good story to tell the girls tomorrow, and however much they purse their lips, you know every woman there will wish she'd done the same. I won't tell them about the aliens, though. Don't think they'd understand that part.* She tried not to think about how she didn't understand her behaviour either. They were aliens in her kitchen after all, strange no matter what names she called them. She was probably betraying all of humanity by closing the door on the suits. She didn't care. Edna realized the tension she'd been feeling in herself all evening was now gone. She no longer believed the aliens would hurt her. She sighed, knowing they'd be leaving like all the come-from-aways, leaving her to live her days alone. Edna shook her head. *As if you'd be going anywhere but the cemetery*, she told herself. *I'd never leave this place. It's in me bones.*

Edna looked at the business card Mr. Formal had given her as she listened to a car start up and move away. It was plain white, with only a name and the Government of Canada symbol in the upper left hand corner. She left the card on the side table in the living room as she walked back towards the warmly lit kitchen.

The aliens looked as if they hadn't moved since she left. Frozen into positions around the table, it didn't even feel like they were in the room. Edna made her feet louder as she walked in and settled back into her chair. "Without Jonno to play his fiddle, guess the government has to provide the entertainment too. Don't ye worry. They were just looking for an escaped criminal." Edna looked at Glasses. "I told them there were none of those here in Maberly."

Glasses smiled gently as the three of them seemed to unfold a little and relax. Auntie Simmons reached over and stroked Edna's arm, leaving it warm. "Well, I think it's time for dessert." Edna went over to the fridge and brought out a pink and frothy angel food cake. "Now this is a Betty Crocker cake mix. I don't know who she is, exactly . . ."

After the meal was finished, plates scraped clean and mugs of tea polished off, Edna and the aliens sat contentedly back in the white vinyl chairs. The aliens had coaxed Edna into telling the ingredients for all the recipes as well as the best stores for value. They repeated the occasional word back to her in their funny deep squirrel voices. She showed them the packets of Jell-O and mini marshmallows and the cans of tuna in her pantry. The aliens chittered excitedly. She even broke down and told them the secret ingredients of her tuna casserole. French's prepared mustard, two egg yolks and pesto sauce that Kate sent up from the city. "Why not? I know you won't tell anyone in Bonavista."

The aliens left after helping her do the dishes. George and Auntie Simmons had washed and dried and put away under her direction while Glasses stood in her pantry and stared at the cans of tuna. As they all stood by the back door, George, Auntie Simmons and Glasses touched Edna's heart, her hands, their own mouth and their middle. Then they each bowed and said a halting thank you. "Thank you for welcoming. Enjoyed. Not forget. Thank you." George added, "Tuna. Very fine, very fine," and winked.

"You're welcome," Edna replied warmly. "You drop by my back door any time you're hungry." Edna looked at the aliens. "I guess you won't be back in Maberly any time soon."

They looked back at her with quiet eyes. Edna touched her heart, pressed her hands together and then leaned over into Auntie Simmons and touched her gently on the mouth and on her stomach. Auntie took her hand for a moment and her orange eyes held Edna's faded blue ones. The aliens went out the back door. Edna shut and locked the door behind them. She pushed aside the yellow curtain but couldn't see out into the dark.

Edna threw away the green and brown and grey food in the

metal Tupperware left by the aliens. Some was still steaming hot and some refrigerator cold, but it still smelled odd and you never knew. Better safe than sorry. She stacked the containers beside the sink for morning, thoughtfully caressing each smooth finish.

As she settled into bed, setting her alarm for 5:30 a.m. to cook for the Bonavista Ladies' Social, Edna thought over her evening. *I never thought aliens would be such back door folks. Just like everyday people. Jonno would have liked them. Glad those government folks are too stupid to know which door to use.* She wondered where the aliens had come from, even though she hadn't asked the whole night. It wasn't any good to ask come-from-aways too many questions. No point in getting involved with people always on their way to somewhere else. But now it would be kind of nice to know which star they were from so she could remember them on clear nights.

Edna took a long time to fall asleep. When she did sleep, she dreamed she and Glasses were dancing in the middle of the sky to Jonno's fiddle playing. George was juggling codcakes and Auntie Simmons was knitting a huge peach blanket that swirled around her ankles but didn't trip her up. She could hear Jonno's laugh.

The following month, the *Chiladans*, from a small planet in a minor solar system humans hadn't yet identified, landed in New York City. Their graceful craft was unnoticed by all the very expensive equipment maintained for just such an event, and suddenly appeared hovering over Times Square. The *Chiladans*, well-skilled in diplomacy, immediately declared their peaceful intent and invited the Secretary General of the United Nations and the leaders of the G-7 to dinner aboard the ship as a sign of their good will towards Earth. After a shared meal, the humans could inspect the ship for weapons. After an intense forty-eight hours of crisis conferences, the leaders of Earth agreed.

Each dignitary was flanked by two security guards as they made their way aboard the sleek grey ship. The aliens in the reception hall were a little surprised by the extra guests, and sent someone to check with the chef.

Glasses shrugged. Edna had taught them to make plenty. He

told the aide not to worry, and sent George for extra plates and utensils. The aliens ushered the leaders of Earth into a large and airy room filled with orange and red plants that appeared to be growing out of metal walls. The chairs and couches, in cool sandstone and clay colours, were low to the ground, and flanked by shelves filled with more brightly coloured and flowering plants. In the centre of the room, beside a large oval table, stood Glasses, the best *Chilad* chef of off-world cuisine, and Auntie Simmons, the dessert chef. Spread with a large orange and white gingham cloth, the table displayed a feast of potato salad, two kinds of Jell-O salad, pickles and white sliced bread. In the centre was a steaming vision of Edna's tuna casserole.

Originally published in On Spec Spring 1997 Vol 9 No 1 #28

Fiona Heath is now a Unitarian Universalist minister who she speaks, writes and teaches about the intersection between science and spirit. *Casserole Diplomacy* was her first published story. She lives in Waterloo, Ontario with her partner and son.

Jubilee

Steven Mills

I'm a Presbyterian Church minister, for what that's worth. Not a lot these days. Not since the noises in the church basement.

"Mice," Mr. Berkowitz said, and bought some traps. He laid them in the corners, and near the back of the fridge in the mint-green kitchen. Mrs. Miller stepped on one, broke two arthritic toes in the snap, and, popping nitro pills like Pez candies, had to be rushed to the hospital.

Mr. Berkowitz caught no mice, but the noises persisted. The Board of Managers agreed to have a work bee on the Saturday next, the twenty-fifth, to tear the paneling from the basement walls so they could expose those "wretched vermin" to the light of day. And smite them.

That Sunday worship sported a typically low July attendance, about sixty-five parishioners and a handful of visitors. Unfortunately, my sermon on the Water-to-Wine story in John 2 was a little flat: I could hear the crinkling of candy wrappers begin at the four-minute mark. Usually I can hold the sweet-tooths off for nine or ten minutes, but with this muggy July heat I just didn't have it in me.

Right after the Prayers of Thanksgiving and Intercession, toward the end of the service, I paused and stared as bubbles thick as dirty motor oil simmered on the Presbyterian blue carpet. I cleared my throat and announced the final hymn, "Rejoice, O People," number 299. In that moment the bubbles swirled together and a white lamb slurped up out of the floor. It shook its floppy ears, skipped down the aisle and sprang up onto the pew beside Mrs. Miller.

Mrs. Donnally fainted into the aisle. People rose from their seats. "It's a miracle!" Hands waved, palms to heaven. People stepped over Mrs. Donnally to get a better view. "Amen! Hallelujah!" Shouting drowned out the first chords of the hymn.

The lamb blinked again, then morphed into a woolly behemoth of mucilaginous slime, howling and towering over Mrs. Miller.

Someone in the choir said, "Holy shit!"

It reached down, clamped a shaggy limb onto Mrs. Miller's blue-tinted head, then lifted her right out of the pew, and shook her. Slime spattered the wall. The Board of Managers just had the sanctuary painted a delicate robin's egg blue the month before.

Parishioners scrambled to get away—tumbling over the backs of the pews, or scrabbling on all fours underneath the pews. Somebody snatched Mrs. Donnally from the path of the faithful rushing toward the doors.

The sour-smelling fingers held Mrs. Miller under both sides of her jaw and behind her recently-coiffed head while she hung there, kicking. Stubborn, she dug her hands into the slimy wool and tried to pull herself free.

Then the creature plopped Mrs. Miller onto her butt-worn pew and shrank back into a lamb. It leapt off the pew and darted up the aisle, melting into the carpet as it ran. Oily smutches rippled to the four corners of the sanctuary.

Mrs. Miller scraped mucilage out of her hair with her hands.

I thought I was dreaming. I just kept thinking, *Mrs. Miller—good choice!* Quite unbecoming of course, but she and I had had our battles, and had settled on a polite, seething truce for the past few years. But I dream about her often. Usually she does not fare well.

So I figured this was just another one of my tabloid-style dreams. Slime Lamb Attacks Church Elder in House of God. Nothing unusual.

But no, this actually happened.

The sanctuary was empty now, except for Mrs. Miller and me.

She raised her arm, like God in Michelangelo's *The Creation of Adam* on the ceiling of the Sistine chapel, although I don't think creating was what she had in mind. She pointed at me. I was barely protected by the pulpit.

"You!" she hissed. "This is your doing!"

I've come to realize over the years that there are parishioners in every congregation who view the minister as responsible for whatever ills befall the family of God—poor attendance, tight budgets, fallen angel food cakes ("It was a mix, it should not have fallen, would not have fallen if you hadn't let all that cold air in, Reverend."). Mrs. Miller was one such bane.

"Me?" I said.

"Yes, you. I've known all along. The handiwork of the devil."

"You don't even believe in the devil, Mrs. Miller. You told me so yourself."

She eased to her feet, back straighter than usual (a little bit of free slime-chiropractic work never hurt anyone, I thought), and stalked out of the sanctuary to meet the approaching wave of sirens.

I sat down in the chair behind the pulpit.

I've read that God exacts retribution: locusts, floods, plagues. And I admit, Mrs. Miller can indeed be trying. So maybe that's what this was, godly retribution.

Or maybe there *is* a devil. Ha. Maybe he's looking for recruits—little spindly blue-haired ones.

Well . . . maybe it *was* me. Maybe I *did* let my fear of her get the better of me. If I'd—

Now just hold on a minute. We're talking a lamb grew out of the church floor and turned into a slime creature. Yeah right, in my dreams.

I shrugged to myself. Yikes. What if it were true. I could have toasted Mrs. M. right then and there. (Opportunity knocks, and if you don't—)

"Excuse me." The RCMP officer was standing at the back of the sanctuary, hat in hand. "Can I talk to you?"

"Yeah, sure," I said.

He came forward, extracting a notebook and pen after

tucking his hat under his bulging arm. I notice biceps. Mine are kind of weenie. Too many years of books, not enough football. I regret that sometimes, the—

"Can you tell me what you saw, Father."

"Just call me Dave, Officer," I said. I told him about the lamb. He nodded, but he didn't take any notes.

I called Mrs. Miller on the phone the next day, even though it was my day off.

"I had to use beer," she said, "real beer to get that goo out of my hair. I actually had to go into the liquor store. My word, if anyone saw me. And stink, I'll probably smell like a barnyard for the rest of my days."

And through the phone line I could taste her indignant acrimony. There was a distinctly Mrs. M. taste to the energy, a bitter, aspirin-like flavour. I could tell as clearly as if I were reading her mind that she believed quite sincerely that I had *created* that lamb to attack her.

On Tuesday afternoons, I do my hospital visiting. One of my least favourite duties. That smell in hospitals—maybe it's the cleaner they use, or maybe there's anaesthetic floating around in the air. Bleah. Makes me nauseous. Even after twenty-nine years of ministry.

I found Lisa Michaels sitting up in bed, flipping through an issue of *Sports Illustrated*. The one with the bathing suits.

Lisa has been depressed ever since her breast cancer diagnosis. The surgeon removed a lump six months ago and gave her a clean bill, but then last week she found another lump. She and her surgeon began discussing the M word. And now here she was, contemplating surgery.

"Hey, Lisa," I said.

"Hi, Dave." She whipped the magazine across the room. It smacked against the wall and dropped into the garbage can. A perfect shot.

I went and got a chair, but before I could get my butt into it, Lisa said, "Dave, will you say a prayer for me? I know this is all supposed to be God's will, and such, but I just don't want to go through with this. Will you say a prayer? For healing?"

Jeepers. These are the put-your-money-where-your-mouth-is kind of prayers: let's see what this God of yours can actually *do*, choirboy.

Lisa is a very sincere Christian and a committed churchwoman. But it's been my experience that God doesn't seem to have a whole lot to do with cancer—neither giving it nor taking it away. Although a person's good faith does seem to help keep their immune system strong. It's not that I don't believe in miracles. I do. Honest. I've just never been party to one. God never seems to want to use me to pull them off.

"And do a laying on of hands," she added.

I smiled (although it felt more like a grimace), placed my hand on her shoulder and closed my eyes to hunt around for some appropriate words. I felt her fingers curl around mine and she slid my hand down onto the side of her breast, and squeezed. I pretended not to notice. But there was the lump, irregular and hard, about half the size of a golf ball.

Her terror wailed loud inside my head. I tasted dry wood ash—my mouth seemed filled with it and my body overflowed with a scorching mix of Lisa's fear and grief and ember-hot rage.

"Dear God," I said, stunned. And then the lump was in my hand, a slippery mass of hard tissue.

She gasped. I gasped. I jerked my hand away. The cancerous lump smacked on the floor and rolled under the next bed.

Lisa ripped open her gown, groping at her heavy breast.

She shrieked and leaped from the hospital bed. "It's gone!" she shouted. "It's gone!"

I dropped to my hands and knees and grappled for the lump. I needed the evidence. Lisa was pulling at my clergy shirt.

There. I had it.

She jerked me to my feet and threw her arms around me. She was laughing and crying. She thrust her breast at me. "Feel it."

I felt it. The lump was gone. Or rather, it was in my left hand. We just stared at it.

That Sunday, worship was a tad tense, but at least the sanctuary was packed. Lookie-loos, reporters, even the police were there. I was sweating, wishing I'd polished my sermon a little more—I'd pulled it together later than usual Saturday night. It had been a very weird week.

The service started off smoothly though. Call to Worship. Only the usual peculiar noises from the basement. Prayer of Adoration and Confession. No lambs slopping up out of the floor.

First hymn. And it was a bad one. Don't know what I was thinking when I picked it. Maggie, the organist, butchers it every time.

I could see little bumps of dark goo—as Mrs. Miller called it—bubbling around Maggie's Phentex-slippered feet.

The hymn finally ground into its Amen without an eruption of slime violence. The bubbles glooped back into the carpet, leaving only a thin, viscous film.

Jennifer Keeley (her maiden name), recently divorced from her husband Roger (speaking of slime) and raising three kids, rose to read from the Old Testament—Leviticus 25, the Jubilee section.

Roger had gone off to find himself last year after being fired from Sears, but all he found was a twenty-three-year-old "chickie-poo" with big red hair and even bigger boobs. That's how Jenny put it. I never much liked Roger. His little adventure seemed to tear the guts out of Jenny's self-confidence.

I slipped down into the front pew as I usually do for readings—a much better view, and it allows me to nip over my sermon notes without the congregation seeing.

Jenny cleared her throat and began to read. "And you shall hallow the fiftieth year, and proclaim liberty throughout the land to all its inhabitants; it shall be a jubilee for you when each of you shall—"

She faltered. I looked up. She was fiddling with the buttons on her blouse—or rather, clenching them.

Then I could feel it. The slippery tendril of energy coming from somewhere behind me in the pews. Suddenly I could taste it, a corn-syrup sweetness with an after-taste of fish. Made me think of portly Edgar McDonald for some reason, a quiet member of the Board of Managers whom everyone liked.

I was about to turn and confirm the source when I heard a soft pop, then a ping, and then Jenny's green skirt hit the floor around her high-heeled ankles. I don't know what Edgar hoped

Jubilee

she was or wasn't wearing under that skirt, but he wanted to know, wanted to know something fierce. I hope the pink cotton underwear and knee-high nylons were worth it.

Jenny's face streaked scarlet. I assumed embarrassment at first, but then I heard it inside my head, the soaring howl of her humiliation and rage. "Sweet Jesus," I muttered, as I watched the acrid power roar out from her, blasting every stitch of clothing off Edgar McDonald's pasty Scottish body.

There was a collective gasp, and then a silence so sudden and so deep that God should have been checking in on us.

Glenda, Edgar's wife, generally had that demure, eyes-downcast look. Not at this moment, though. In fact, she had the look of someone with a confirmed hunch. And if Jennifer Keeley didn't kill Edgar outright, I was certain Glenda would.

Mrs. Miller started in on her nitro pills—I could feel her eyes searing my head. The press went wild, flashes blinded me. Jenny yanked up her skirt and started down the aisle. I could feel her pooling her energy. I intervened—I had visions of her splattering poor Edgar into bloody little bits of middle-management flesh. It would take weeks to clean him off the newly-painted ceiling.

"Get the hell out of my way, Dave," Jenny growled at me.

"Jenny..."

"Y'know, Dave, it's high time I had a little chat with Roger," she said.

Roger? Yeah, Roger, her ex.

She tugged on her skirt. "There are a few things I've been meaning to say to him," she said, "but I just haven't been able to work up the nerve before now."

Indeed, Jenny suddenly seemed to have her old confidence back. I got the hell out of her way.

People started yelling. Someone threw a sports jacket over Edgar. The press and police surged forward.

There seemed to be no use continuing to worship, so I just raised my hands and hollered out the benediction. Maggie, the organist, leapt in with the chords of the choral Amen, but they were drowned out by all the shouting.

The air conditioner in the manse's living room was losing the battle. I was down to my underwear, T-shirt and bare feet. Not a pretty sight.

The spaghetti sauce was plop-plopping on simmer in the kitchen while I was waiting for the noodle water to boil. I like my big meal at lunch time.

I set my beer on the end table, grabbed the remote and turned on the TV. I hoisted my feet up onto the hassock. Monday is my day off. Mondays, beer, and TV are a tradition for me, a tradition that started with my first congregation, where the retiring minister, a wrinkly Edinburgh Scot, stayed on as a parishioner, having ministered there for nineteen years. He insisted that Monday was the cleric's Sabbath, and was to be spent with a good thick book and a bottle of good scotch whisky. To help him relax. I never could get the hang of the whisky.

And after the mayhem following yesterday's service, I certainly needed to relax.

I sipped my beer and flipped to the read-along cable news channel. Along the bottom of the screen I read, "—rain falling in Africa. Astronomers announced today that the Hubble Telescope has detected another fold in space. This second wrinkle is between the orbits of Uranus and Neptune. Last week, astronomers announced the discovery of the first fold. They assure—"

I turned off the TV and got out of my chair, beer in hand, and began to wander. Out the living room window I could see four 1967 Corvettes—each a different colour—parked in Joe Frederick's driveway. The kind he goes on and on about. The kind he never used to have.

Two houses up is Brigitte's place. She's a single mom on social assistance. The ceiling in her kitchen fell in last month and that slimy troglodyte-cum-landlord told her if she wanted it fixed she could bloody well go turn a few tricks and make the money herself.

Brigitte's finally lost it, I thought. She was outside, standing on a kitchen chair, picking leaves off the spindly maple tree the city had planted last year to "green up" the neighbourhood. I got my binos and took a closer look. Gadzooks. She was picking *money off the tree*. Fifty dollar bills, and stuffing them into a green garbage bag.

The phone rang. I set the binoculars on the TV and went into

Jubilee

the kitchen. The noodle water was boiling finally.

"Hello?"

"Reverend?"

Oh joy—Mrs. Miller. I gave up trying to get her to call me by first name years ago. And I sure as heck don't call her by hers. What is it anyway? Starts with an L, I think.

"Mrs. Miller. Well, what can I do for you?" (This is my polite way of helping parishioners get to the point when they phone.)

"Francis wants to talk to you."

Francis is Mrs. Miller's forty-five-year-old handicapped son. I could hear him in the background. "Hi Dafe. Hi Dafe. Hi Dafe. C'mon. C'mon. C'mon. Hi Dafe."

"Put Frank on the phone."

"No. He wants you to come here. He wants to say . . . He . . . Please, Reverend, come talk to him." Mrs. Miller has never actually *asked* me for anything before. She's always told me what to do, what she thought I should be doing that I wasn't, mostly ordering me around like a ten-year-old kid. Like she orders Frank around, actually.

"I'll be right over," I said, and hung up. I turned off the gas under the spaghetti sauce and the noodle water, then poured my beer down the sink. It'd be flat by the time I got back anyway. What good is beer without fizz?

I slipped on my Birkenstocks. Figured I'd just walk over. Mrs. Miller lives quite close to the manse. Too close.

Jeepers Murphy! I need to put on some shorts; I'm in my flipping underwear. I hate summer.

The midday heat was stifling.

I nipped across the street and scooted down a back alley, taking the shortcut to Mrs. M.'s big two-story house.

I noticed that the Berkowitzes had replaced the chain-link fence around their back yard with a heavy, high board fence, and painted it a lovely emerald-green colour. There was such a curious sweet-cinnamon energy swirling in their back yard, and suddenly I was able to look right through the new board fence as if it weren't even there. Just because I wanted to see what they might be up to.

Mr. and Mrs. Berkowitz were lying under their oak tree,

which was now much taller and fuller than it used to be, giving them sweet, cool shade in the midday heat. They were nude, lying on the afghan she'd crocheted last winter. There was a plate of Fig Newtons between them. They were talking and laughing and eating Fig Newtons, and all the while Mr. Berkowitz stroked Mrs. Berkowitz's breast with the backs of his curled fingers.

I always knew they really liked each other.

Frank was up in the mountain ash tree when I got there. Mrs. Miller was on the lawn, in front of her favourite perennial bed, demanding that he come down right this instant.

Frank is a worker, always cutting grass or raking leaves or shovelling snow around the neighbourhood. He has a regular paying clientele of church and non-church folks. I've always wondered how much of that money Frank got to keep—I figured the old bat was probably robbing him blind. I'm sure that this is my own hardness of heart. Mrs. M. just can't be that mean. And not that she needs the money either. Her dead husband left her and Frank very well cared for financially.

"Leave me alone! Leave me alone! Bossy, bossy, bossy! I want to leave, I want to. You're not the boss of me y'know, you're not. I'm grown up."

"Hey, Frank," I called out.

"Hi Dafe!" Frank gave me a big grin. "I'm gonna fly away, Dafe, live by myself. Just wanna say, 'Bye. I'm gonna fly!' Bye Dafe!"

"How'd he get up in the tree?" I whispered to Mrs. Miller.

"Don't talk 'bout me!" Frank hollered. "Not nice!"

"I'm sorry, Frank. You're right. It's not nice. I'm sorry. How'd you get up in the tree?"

"I fly!" he said. "I fly!" He began flapping his arms. "Bye Dafe! Bye Mom! Bye!"

"No!" Mrs. Miller pleaded. "No, Francis! Don't leave me!"

But he did. Flapping his arms and kicking a little with his big feet, he leapt from the tree and flew up over the two-story house. He looked jerky at first, like when he walks, but soon his arms flapped smoothly with the strength years of raking and shovelling had given him. And then he was gone.

Jubilee

Mrs. Miller started shaking all over. I'd seen her shake like that before when she was so mad at me she could hardly talk. But I was sure it wasn't rage that had control of her now.

She started to wail, tears erupting from her eyes. I cuddled my arm around her—she's actually quite tiny—and walked her up the stairs to the porch. Tea, I was thinking. I'll make her some tea. My own heart was breaking for her. For Mrs. Miller. Good heavens, I thought, what's the world coming to when I feel sorry for this little demon?

"I'll make us some tea," I said.

Tuesday morning I stopped in to visit Julia Castle, an elderly woman on our membership roll who never comes to church.

"David, how timely. I was thinking I might call you today and ask you to come by," Julia said. "I have something to get off my chest. Please come in." She stepped back, sweeping me inside with her hand. Her apartment was refreshing and cool.

I have spent many hours here with Julia over the past ten years. Although her heritage is staunch Scotch Presbyterian, she hasn't been to church since she was in her twenties. She professes atheism, but gives regularly to the congregation and reads systematic theology for fun. Julia is frightfully well-read (she thinks television is for idiots). In fact, I don't think the woman sleeps much anymore, but instead spends her long nights devouring books.

She made tea and brought out the Peek Freans, my favourite, and some home-made scones. Julia hasn't made scones for tea in years. Serving me with her Royal Albert Country Rose china, she chatted lightly about her various neighbours' feats and foibles.

Finally, she sat in her Queen Anne chair with Matthew Fox (named after the theologian), her golden Lhasa Apso, curled up in her lap like a cat. Matthew Fox looked quite comfy. Stroking him lightly, she sighed.

"I am afraid that I am finally losing my faculties," she said. "And since I have no other living relatives, as you know, I want to confirm with you your role as executor of my will."

I took a Peek Frean. Julia isn't one for histrionics.

"I don't really know how to explain," she said, "so I'll simply come out and say it. I have been having delightful intercourse with Matthew Fox all week." I have explained to Julia on several occasions that we rarely use the "I" word for anything but sex anymore. She doesn't seem to pay heed to my advice. On the other hand, Julia doesn't get out much, so it probably doesn't matter. "You see," she continued, "he . . . he has been participating. In fact he is becoming quite the interlocutor. I am discovering that he has a unique and poignant perspective. Quite refreshing, I might add."

I swallowed my Peek Frean.

"The first thing he said to me was 'No.' Just like a child. An important first word for anyone wishing to develop a critical mind, don't you think? 'No, what?' I asked him. We were about to have tea, just like this. 'No, thank you,' he said. 'That's very good,' I told him—it's always important to reward good manners—but that wasn't what I meant. I explained that I wanted to know why he said 'No.' 'I don't like Peek Freans,' he said, 'and we always have Peek Freans now. You used to make scones. I like those better.' So I made him some scones. He was quite beside himself with delight."

Matthew Fox looked up at her, a perfect Disney-dog gaze.

"It's not you, Julia," I said, thankful that I would no longer have to share the Peek Freans with the dog. "You're not losing your marbles. The universe has gone kind of wonky. Not really in a bad way, though." Slime grabbing Mrs. Miller by the head wasn't such a bad thing, was it?

I told her about Mrs. Miller and about Frank and Lisa and Brigitte. I left out the part about the Berkowitzes. "I'm not really sure what God has in mind," I said to her as a kind of conclusion.

Julia stroked the rim of her teacup with her index finger. "Honestly, David, it sounds to me as if God is quite out of the picture. God just doesn't have this rich a sense of humour; God has more of a knock-knock joke sense of humour."

I chewed. Atheists will use anything to get a leg up in the existence-of-God debate.

Julia fed Matthew Fox a piece of scone.

I stopped in at Mrs. Miller's on the way home from Julia's.

Jubilee

I'm not sure why. I just felt I needed to.

I had never heard Nathan shout before, but he was shouting now. "You asked me to come, and I agreed. But I've had enough. I'm leaving!"

Whoa. Wait a second. Nathan is dead, remember? You buried him, for Pete's sake. Three years ago.

"Please, Nathan. Please stay." Mrs. M. was actually begging.

She must have felt me come into the dining room because she turned to me, her eyes wide. "I just want to talk to him, if only for a while. It's been so long. Please, David, please make him stay."

David. Wow, she was desperate.

"Hey, Nathan. Uh, good to see you again. You're looking great." He looked younger than I remembered. In fact, he looked better dead than he had those last couple of years before his heart attack.

"Hi, Dave. You're looking pretty good yourself. You lost some weight?"

I blushed. "Yeah," I said. "I've been working out this summer." That was a bald-faced lie, but I pumped my arms up and down to show him anyway. I made a mental note to order some new short-sleeved clergy shirts—mine *were* getting snug around the biceps.

"Reverend!" Mrs. Miller stamped her foot.

"See?" Nathan said. "You always nose in, take over the conversation, work it around to something you want to talk about. And since I'm here anyway: that's not all. Remember how you were always accusing me of running around on you, rolling in the hay with some secretary from work? Well, I'd have been nuts to: you'd have skinned me alive. So just so you know, I never did, even though you never believed me. You're just a jealous, bitter-hearted woman. And you have been from the day Francis was born."

"That's not true. Tell him that's not true, Reverend."

I held up my hands, more to protect myself than to defer. I'm as afraid of her as Nathan was. But he's already dead and I'm not, and I don't want to be, so I just kept my mouth shut.

There was silence. A stalemate. But something had changed in Mrs. Miller. I could taste it, more like black pepper, less like aspirin. She looked at Nathan and spoke, her voice soft, quiet, like I've never heard it before. "Did you ever love me, Nathan?"

"Yes, Lil, I did. For a long time. Then, after Francis was born, things changed. Inside me, inside you; between us. And it was never the same after that." He sighed. "How is Francis?"

"He left home, Nathan. He flew away."

Nathan simply nodded, as if Frank's flying away was an ordinary thing. An expected thing.

"What's going on, Nathan?" I asked.

He looked at me and shrugged. "The universe is growing up, Dave. It's transmogrifying—I think that's what Calvin would call it."

"John Calvin, the Reformer?"

He snorted. "No, Calvin of *Calvin and Hobbes*!"

"Oh," I said. "*That* Calvin." Mrs. Miller used to complain that Nathan did all his reading on the toilet. (The things people tell you when you're a minister.)

Nathan shrugged again. "The universe is going through a gawky adolescent period right now. Bending, folding—melting down all the walls. Your lives will soon be more like my life, more like what life is like on this side.

"But until those barriers are gone completely, I'd rather stay over here on my side." He turned to Mrs. Miller. "It's been too long between us, Lil."

Something snapped inside my head. I heard it, like the crack of a timber under weight. I tasted wood ash again.

Mrs. Miller nodded slowly. "All right," she said. She took a moment to look at him, to really look at him. "Good-bye Nathan."

Nathan said nothing in response, but waved to me, then slowly dissolved into the air.

Mrs. M. tipped her head back and howled. Like one of the Hounds of Hell. The windows rattled. I slapped my hands over my ears. The house began to shake and white-hot flames roared around us. But there was no rage left in her, just sheer, unadulterated grief.

I reached out, pulled her tiny body against mine, and held her hard. I was no longer afraid. Of her, or anything else.

Her howling filled me, wound through my body, coursing electric. I tasted her bitter life. It melted in my mouth. The bitterness became turmeric, then lemon rind. I wanted to spit it out of my body, but it was part of me now. Had always been part of me.

After a long time the howling ebbed. Then slowly, the flames fell back, as this first wave of grief eased.

Then there was silence. And the gentleness that comes after the long, harsh storm.

So, the universe is transmogrifying, I thought. Growing up. The dead should know.

Might as well get used to it, I told myself.

And so, as I held Mrs. Miller, I rained iris blossoms on us, right there in her dining room, because I remembered that she said once how much she loved irises. They rained like purple snow, their rich sweetness surrounding us, filling the air we breathed.

Originally published in On Spec Summer 1999 Vol 11 No 2 #37

Steven Mills lives in Burnaby, BC, with the delight of his heart, Holly Phillips, in a tiny 17th floor apartment with a cat who is rather unsure of her own mind. His first short story sale was to *On Spec*! He has published over a dozen stories and one novel, *Burning Stones*.

No Such Thing as an Ex-Con
Holly Phillips

Was it irony that when Kev told her the company had won the bid for the new courthouse park, the only thing Emily felt was relief? Relief that Mr. Berl couldn't use the excuse of a slow spring to fire her. She knew damn well he'd only hired her, an ex-con, because she was Kev's friend.

(*No such thing as an ex-con*, Bernice had told her the morning of the parole hearing.)

Even when she was there, planting with the rest of the crew, Emily didn't give it much thought. The new courthouse was nothing like the old one, it sparked no memories. She dug holes and tried to remember what had been on that corner before. As a bike courier, she'd known every building in every block this side of the river. Still hard not to miss the riding, but at least she was fit again. No hope of getting her old job back, of course, a felon isn't bondable.

Felon. Convict. Accessory to murder.

Stomp the spade deep, heave out the heavy load of black wet dirt. The hole had to be big, they were putting in four-year-old elms here, American elms that could resist the blight.

"Emily Lake." The man's voice asserted rather than

questioned.

Emily looked up. "Detective Bailor." She shook off her gloves and cap, raked her short hair into spikes and jammed the cap back on.

"I heard you were out," he said. "What was it, three years?"

"And a half." With a kind of delayed shock, the hatred she'd once learned for that raspy smoker's voice welled up and burst in her chest like a bubble of mud.

He nodded once, looked her over. Looked over the worksite. Nodded again and left, crossing the plaza to climb the stairs to the courthouse doors. The rain started up again, dripping off the bill of her cap. She pulled on her wet gloves and went back to her shovel.

"So who was that?" Kev asked when they quit for lunch.

"Some guy," Emily said, shoulders hunched, face like stone.

No such thing as an ex-con.

Ugly, running into Bailor like that, but she couldn't blame him for the nightmares. Those were already waiting, same as they always were, filling her boarding house room like the fat stench of decay. Memory. What god laughed when he came up with that one?

The women, of course, mute ghosts haunting her in memory as they'd haunted her in fact. And the dreams of murder, the ache of terror when she'd been sure she was going nuts, the unbearable relief of the letter to the cops, that had not, in the end, been any kind of relief at all. All of that in Emily's mind as she showered off the mud and sweat, ate a sandwich and crawled into bed. She only knew she cried in her dreams by the pain in her throat in the morning, every morning.

Bailor came again, of course. She was checking the inventory of the plants just delivered by the nursery. Another rainy day, the sheets of paper on the clipboard were soaked and flimsy, hard to read. She was trying to decide if that was 10 junipers or 18 when that familiar rasp said, "They working you hard?"

It had to be a 10, because otherwise they were short by nine plants. "Yeah." Her pencil made a hole in the paper.

"Had any more dreams?"

God, she thought wearily, *what a shit*. But when she looked up, she saw no mockery in his small blue eyes. He looked uneasy behind the cop's moustache. All the same, she said, "Screw you, Bailor."

He snorted, "You used to have better manners."

"Yeah, well, prison's funny that way." She dropped her eyes to the clipboard, made a careful note.

"Actually," Bailor said, and stopped.

Rain pattered on the plaza bricks, on the inventory list, on the bill of her cap. She looked up.

Bailor stood, raincoat bunched up so he could shove his hands in his pockets, watching dirt spill from a tear in a root ball's burlap cover.

"Actually," he said again. Then, "Aww, to hell with it." He turned and stomped away, growling over his shoulder, "See you around, Lake."

At night, the dreams.

Bailor's smoker's voice, "Look at this." A woman's face, teeth bared above the ruin of her throat. "Look at this." The smell of stale smoke on his breath. The slashes across her breast. "Look." Photographs of death. "Look." Mementos of torture. "Look at this. Look at it, damn you!"

"I've already seen it!"

"Where?"

"Right there!" Pointing to the empty corner at his back. Empty in his eyes. Not hers.

"Don't give me that shit." Small blue eyes in the red slab of his face. "Don't you dare give me that shit."

"But it's true. I can't help it. You think I wouldn't rather be crazy? You think I wouldn't rather do anything than live with this? With . . . *them?*"

But dream-Bailor is gone and only the women are left. Amanda. Glennis. Cherie. Pam. They wear the wounds of their murders scrawled across the bodies no one but Emily can see. Pam stares with empty eye sockets. Glennis holds her own guts in her hands. Amanda's bloated and soft from the nights in the river. The nights she'd waited until Emily had written the letter to the cops telling them where to find her. Amanda, Glennis, Cherie, Pam, in death and rage, crowding close. Until she wakes.

When she showed up at the worksite, Kev took one look and said, "You look like shit. Nobody'll fire you if you take a day off."

To do what, watch the empty corners of her rented room? "I'm fine." The nursery's delivery truck was already there, *beep beeping* as it backed over the curb. Emily tossed her lunch bag into Kev's truck and headed over.

"Hey," he said.

"I'm fine," she told him, face hard as concrete.

No such thing as an ex-con. It was there in his face. "Sor-ry," he said. They unloaded the plants in silence.

The sun came out that afternoon and the work drew a small crowd of onlookers, people on their way to or from the courthouse. Every gray raincoat that stopped pulled Emily's head around, all afternoon, until a scowl was fixed on her face. But Bailor didn't show until quitting time.

"You need a lift home?" Kev asked her.

"No thanks," She crumpled up her lunch bag, her eyes evading his. "I'll take the bus."

"Suit yourself." He jerked open the driver's side of his truck, then said, "If you're in some kind of trouble, I hope you know you can ask me for help."

"Yeah." She stuffed the lunch bag in her jacket pocket. "Thanks."

"I put myself out on a limb, getting you this job."

"I know."

Kev shrugged, climbed into his truck. "See you Monday." He slammed the door, started the engine. Drove off, leaving muddy tire tracks across the plaza.

Emily turned and waited for Bailor to approach. He looked as tired as always, permanent stains around his eyes. He was still walking when she said, "What the hell do you want with me?"

"You need a ride?"

Her stomach churned, scalding her throat. "Yeah."

He turned, jerked his head for her to follow.

He drove a Ford sedan, newish but already dented in the driver's door. There were paper cups stained with old coffee on the passenger side. Emily stomped them flat with her boots. Bailor started up the car and backed out of his parking spot. *Reserved for police vehicles only.*

He said, "So how's it going, now you're outside? You're on parole, right?"

"Eighteen months to go."

"That's a pretty good job you got there. You're lucky. What'd you do before, bike messenger, right? How come you didn't go back to that?"

"You need to be bonded."

"Oh yeah? I didn't know that." He stopped at the lot exit. "So, where am I taking you?"

"Broadbent and Third."

"Okay." He pulled out, cutting off a tentative town car. "What I said the other day. When I asked if you'd had any dreams again. That was kind of the wrong thing to say."

"No shit."

"Thing is." His thick fingers tightened on the wheel. The first two on his right hand were stained yellow, but the car smelled mostly of old coffee and dog. There was a pale stripe across the ring finger on his left hand. He cleared his throat and swallowed. "Thing is, I didn't mean it that way. I mean," his hands so tight the bones showed at his knuckles, "I actually want to know."

Emily stared out the windscreen, squinting through the tension. "You sure the hell never did before."

"Yeah, well." He cleared his throat again. "How come you never copped a plea when we had your whole damn confession?"

"That wasn't a confession. That was . . . you know what that was."

"Yeah, right. Psychic bullshit. Even your dumb-ass public defender knew you were going down. Even if," he added, in a mutter, "Slobodski did say he never heard of you."

She leaned her head back against the seat. "I couldn't plead guilty to something I didn't do."

"Man," he said, still as if talking to himself. "I've never seen anything like it. The way you tore into the prosecutor, screaming about ghosts and dreams, the judge banging her gavel . . ."

Another nightmare, a different kind. Emily closed her eyes.

"What do you want, Bailor?"

They were crossing the bridge, she could tell by the way he rode the gas and brake. Rush hour traffic. She would have been home by now if she'd ridden her bike.

"You read the newspapers?" Bailor finally said.

"No."

More silence, as if he were chewing it over. "I got a case. Child abduction. Fifteen years a detective and this is the first one I've had. Couple of boys. First one seven weeks ago, the second one just last week. Both of them eight years old, both of them kidnapped right out of their beds. Good families, no divorces, no angry grandparents. Everything says stranger abduction, and with two kids gone now . . ."

Emily rolled her head to look at his face and recognized the hard look there. Desperation. She'd felt it from the inside.

"What do you want from me?" she said, but it wasn't really a question anymore. She just wanted to hear him say it. Her guts like a fist clenched under her ribs.

It didn't look like it was any easier for him, but he got it out: "I need your help."

"Again," she said. "You need my help again."

Bailor clenched his hands on the wheel, and his jaw on the words he still refused to say.

He dropped her off on the corner; she wouldn't tell him the number of the house. Not that he couldn't find out easily enough. He handed her a business card with his pager number scribbled on the back.

"Listen," he said as she climbed out of the car, "these kids . . . They don't have forever."

"I'll call you."

He leaned across the seat to see her face. "You know how many women Slobodski would have killed if we hadn't caught him? That's how many kids this freak could kill. You know what I'm saying?"

She propped her arms on the roof of the car. "Do you believe I never knew Slobodski, or those women, or saw any of the murders except in dreams? Do you believe in ghosts? Do you believe I told the truth?"

He straightened and put the car in gear. "What I believe," he said, "is that I will do any goddamn thing it takes to find those kids. Any goddamn thing at all."

She pushed off from the car. "Go to hell, Bailor." She slammed the door and he drove off, turned the corner without signalling, and was gone.

According to his card, Bailor'd made sergeant since her trial. Detective Sergeant Willis G. Bailor.

She wondered what the G stood for.

When the cops had arrived at her door, she actually cried with relief, though they'd mistaken it for fear. The ride to Headquarters had been almost a pleasure. The whole world brighter, the November sunshine rich as gold, as her relief that she was not insane. What she had dreamed was true. But then, sitting in the interview room, she realized the dead women were still with her, naked, expressionless. Dead. And then the questions. How did she know about the body in the river? How did she know the details of the crimes? Why did she tell no one sooner? And especially, repeated so often the words blurred into sound: Who was he, who was the killer?

And all she could say was, "I dreamed their murders. I see their ghosts. I don't know who he is." While the dead women watched from their corner.

And then being locked into that narrow cell, she and the four dead women, blind Pam, disemboweled Glennis, bloated Amanda, breastless Cherie. That night, that was the heart of all her nightmares, when she first knew that she had fallen so far into hell she might never climb out again.

I dream their murders. I see their ghosts. I don't know who he is.

She dreamed them still. The only thing that had changed was that now she had a face for him, the murderer, whose hair was cropped and clean and whose eyes were small and brown and so shallow they were almost blank. She saw him often in the news, waiting for her own trial, charged with accessory to murder after the fact—just the one count, for Amanda whose body she had told them how to find. Of course she was an accessory, however strenuously Slobodski, the killer, denied it. Because after all, how else could she have known?

She'd known she would be convicted. The plea they'd offered would have gotten her half the time—a generous one, the prosecutor said, because she had at least told them where to find Amanda. And although no one ever said as much, it had been finding Amanda that led Bailor to the witness who'd seen the van Slobodski'd driven. That was the big break in the case, and the deal was the only way they could bring themselves to thank her—the only way short of believing her. But how could she take that deal, say she had conspired to cover up the killer's crimes, when she knew better than any but his victims just exactly what those crimes were? She couldn't, not even when he was convicted, not even when he hanged himself in his cell, not even when the dead women had left her at last, satisfied by his death.

Because of course, they hadn't really left her at all.

She still dreamed them every night.

Imagine if they were children, how much worse those dreams might be.

She called Bailor's pager at dawn, sitting on the bottom stair by the pay phone. A cold draft seeped under the front door and across her bare feet. She pulled her hands up her sleeves as she waited for Bailor to call her back. It took him about a minute and a half.

"Bailor."

"Do you know what you're asking me to do?"

A breath. "Emily."

"Do you?"

"I'm asking you to help me find a couple of kids."

"You're asking me to climb back down into hell."

Silence.

"Bailor?"

"Yeah."

"I lived those women's murders. Do you realize that? Can you imagine what it's like?"

"I know exactly what that's like."

"Why, because you saw their bodies?"
"I talked to their families—"
"I felt his knife!" Silence. "You really don't give a shit what happens to me, do you?"
"Do you care what happens to those kids?"
She propped her head on her knees and whispered into the phone. "Tell me you believe me."
"Tell me you'll help."
She blinked wetness from her eyes and realized it was tears. "What do you want me to do?"

Bailor picked her up at eight, two jumbo coffees steaming on the dashboard. He looked her over critically as she got in the car, and said, "That's the best you could do?"

She did up her seat belt as he pulled away from the curb. "What did you expect, Dior?"

Dress up, he'd said. *Wear something professional.* The "best she could do" was a second-hand pair of wool pants and a black turtleneck.

"What's it matter what I look like anyway? You get me a job interview with your boss?"

He shot her a look over his coffee cup. "You need something of the kids', right? To do your thing? So I called the parents, told them I'm bringing over a criminal psychologist, a whaddyacallit, a victim profiler. They watch TV, they think every police department's like the FBI." He gave her another look. "Maybe they'll think you're a child genius. You look about sixteen."

Emily said nothing, drank her coffee. She could blame the caffeine for sweaty palms and a jumpy heart, but not for the gut-deep certainty that she was doing absolutely the wrong thing. She was no psychic. She'd just stumbled into a few months of hell, stumbled on through into prison, and now she'd stumbled out again and what was she doing, courting a return?

She swallowed the same mouthful of coffee twice and said, "This is nuts, Bailor, you know that, right?"

He emptied his cup and tossed it over his shoulder into the back seat. "You backing out on me, Lake?"

Yes. She couldn't say it. "No."

They were driving the road that wound uphill into the Glens.

Old-fashioned frame houses, trees lining the streets.

He said, "Don't say anything, okay? Just look intelligent and let me do the talking."

Yeah, right. Intelligent. She'd be lucky if she could manage sane. "Can I ask you something?"

He grunted.

"If this works . . . I mean it isn't going to, you know that. But if it does . . ."

"What?"

"You going to charge me with accessory again?"

The car came to a stop. Bailor set the brake and turned off the engine. Then he said, "Nobody's going to know about this, Lake. Got it? If you get anything I'll call it an anonymous tip."

She rolled her head on the headrest and looked at him. He was scowling out the windshield. He looked tired and angry, which was okay, but he didn't look scared. It wasn't fair. She wanted him to be scared, as scared as she was.

He undid his seatbelt, opened the door. "Okay?"

She put her half-full coffee cup on the floor. Undid her belt. Got out of the car.

"These are the Levesques," Bailor told her going up the front walk. "Their kid was the second one taken. An only son." That was all he had time to say before the front door opened. The Levesques must have been watching for them.

A tall thin man and his small plump wife. Emily found it impossible to meet their eyes, and she never did get a clear picture of their faces. Mr. Levesque's hand was as damp and cold as Emily's, his wife's voice jerky as she offered them tea. Bailor said something soothing, Emily hardly heard what. She felt like an imposter. Nothing new there, it was how she'd felt since she'd gotten out. But this was worse, because the Levesques, blinded by their hope, couldn't see her for what she was.

Bailor herded her up the stairs, leaving the kid's parents to wait below. The boy's bedroom was at the end of the hall, door sealed with a yellow strip of tape. Bailor pulled the tape to dangle down one jamb and opened the door.

Just a kid's room. A twin bed with a blue quilt, a kid-sized table under a window. Plastic soldiers and a poster of Ken Griffey Jr., a baseball glove propped proudly on the bedside table. There was also a nightlight there shaped like a baseball, milky plastic that would shed just enough light to keep the corners empty. *A good idea*, Emily thought. *I should get one of those.*

Bailor cleared his throat. "So, you, uh, getting anything?"

Emily jammed her hands in her pockets and scowled at him. "Yeah," she said. "You want a cigarette, don't you?"

He scowled back. "I'll wait outside," he said, and stepped into the hall. Just before he shut the door he said, "By the way, in case you're interested, the kid's name is Ben."

She stood for a minute, hands in her pockets, listening to the Saturday morning quiet. Someone down the block was mowing their lawn, probably for the first time that season. They should fertilize, after.

Emily shook her head, went and sat down on the bed. *You need something of the kids', right? To do your thing? Jesus, Bailor, how the hell would I know? I never "did" anything. They just came.* She shuddered, now, remembering. She picked up Ben's baseball glove and put it on. It fit her well; his dad must have got a size he could grow into. She worked at the leather of the webbing, softening it, while she looked around. There was a picture on the table by the window, a skinny black-haired boy wearing his baseball cap backwards, Griffey-style.

A floorboard squeaked, paused, squeaked again. Bailor was pacing, impatient, wanting a cigarette. *Some psychic*, Emily told herself. *What ex-smoker doesn't want a cigarette?* She pulled off the glove and propped it back in place. The lawn mower had stopped. She got up and went to the door.

She was wrong, he wasn't pacing, just rocking on his heels. "So?" he said.

She shrugged, hoping he wouldn't see her relief.

He swore under his breath and stomped off down the hall to the stairs. "I'll let you know as soon as we have anything," he said to the parents as they opened the door. They didn't say anything to Emily, but she could feel the weight of their eyes. That terrible hope. Something she'd discovered: the dead don't hope for anything.

The next stop was the other side of the Glens, the ritzier part with newer houses and a view of downtown. Bailor said, "We think he targets the classic middle-class suburban families." He made them sound like a sub-group of criminals. "The Karsovs are professionals, she's an architect, he's a vice-president of something." He glanced at Emily. "This kind of thing can tear a family apart."

"I know."

"Yeah, I guess you saw enough of that on the street."

She clenched her teeth, hating how much he knew about her: the foster homes, the runaway years. They had used that at her trial, proof she had to be dysfunctional, that she could know any number of murderers.

The Karsovs' house was a big stucco affair, set behind a three-car garage, and a lawn like a fairway. The doorbell bing-bonged, starting a blur of movement behind the oval of frosted glass.

"What's his name?" Emily asked.

"Andrew Dean," Bailor said. "Andy."

The door opened, revealing a woman with curly gray hair, too old to be the mother. She ushered them into the foyer at the same time another woman came down the curving stairs, talking even before she'd reached the bottom.

"My mother came down to sit with me, Greg had to go in to work, some things just won't get done without him, can I offer you some coffee? We made cinnamon rolls this morning, they're Andy's favourite." And she started to cry.

Her mother said, "I think the detectives probably just want to see the room, Glory."

"Of course," Mrs. Karsov said. She didn't seem to notice the tears. "I'll show you the way—"

"I know where it is, Mrs. Karsov," Bailor said gruffly. "We'll just take a look and get out of your hair."

The two women stood at the bottom of the stairs watching them climb.

Bailor pulled off the tape as before and opened the door.

A big room, a lot bigger than Ben's. A wall of plastic baskets full of toys, a futon with a Batman quilt tucked tidily under the pillows. The ceiling was painted as a blue sky with clouds. There was a picture in this room, too, a school photo that showed a round freckled face under ginger hair, a grin that threatened mischief.

Bailor lingered in the doorway. "We thought maybe the perp knows the families, or at least the kids, because of the names. Andy, Ben, like he was doing them in alphabetical order. And they're only sons. But we haven't found anything else they have in common, except they both slept with nightlights on. Maybe he's a nightlight salesman. You know how many places there are to buy nightlights in the city? Forty-eight that we know of so far." He sounded discouraged, his voice rasping in his throat. "Goddamn it, I hate this case."

Emily looked at him. "You got kids, Bailor?"

He glowered at the floor between her feet. "Jeff. He had leukemia. He was ten."

She stared at him a moment, then looked away out the window. "I'm sorry."

"Yeah." He cleared his throat. "Just do what you do," he said, and slammed the door shut.

The house was too new for the floorboards to squeak. She went over to the bed and sat. The room was empty. Nothing to say Andrew Dean wouldn't come through the door the next minute, kick off his shoes, and grab the half-constructed spaceship in the corner. Relief poured through her, and a tide of guilt. Too bad she couldn't help. Too bad for those poor little boys suffering god only knew what horrors, too bad for their parents, too bad for Bailor. But okay for Emily, who had enough nightmares already. And she'd tried, right? She'd done her best. What else could she do?

To put off facing Bailor, she lay down on the bed. The clouds on the ceiling were blurred around the edges; someone had done something clever with a sponge. They probably glowed in the glimmer of the nightlight, like real clouds did, just before the moon rose. *Nice*, Emily thought. When she'd scraped together the cash for a deposit on her own apartment, maybe she'd paint her bedroom ceiling like that. Something to gaze at when she woke up sick, cold and shaking.

She rolled over onto her side, and there he was. Andy's ghost with his half-made spaceship in the corner.

He had freckles all down his shoulders and arms, the contrast like a tan against the white of his narrow chest. His face was solemn, a little bewildered, as if he didn't quite know why he was there. His belly button stuck out like the navel on a navel orange. He bore no wounds, as the women had, and none of their anger. Maybe he was still so young he didn't know he should be angry.

And yet, meeting the dead boy's eyes, Emily caught a glimpse of the darkness behind them. The darkness, the filth, the pain and fear, the moment of his death—just a glimpse, but it tore open the scars where her heart used to be. She rolled off the bed and stood.

"All right," she said. "All right."

Bailor knew when he saw her face. "Jesus," he said.

"Come on," she said.

He didn't ask. Just took the stairs at a run. In the car he said, "Where?"

She looked around. Andy was behind them, standing in the street, waiting. "Back that way."

He pulled out from the curb with a yelp of tires, spun the car around with a jerk that spilled the coffee at Emily's feet. She barely noticed. "Go," she said.

He went.

Andy led them, showing her the turns to take, out of the city, across the river and into the farmland beyond. Fields of black furrows ready for planting, trees, farmhouses, tractor repair shops.

"What is it?" Bailor asked her. "What do you see?"

The naked boy always ahead of them, standing still.

She shook her head. "Just drive."

There were lakes out this way, too, most of them ponds that watered cattle and fields. But a few were left half-wild, surrounded by cottages and trees, rowboats on sagging docks. Andy led them down a road that skirted one of these, Pickcreek Lake, and to the mouth of a driveway.

"Here," Emily said.

Bailor drove past the driveway, parked just down the road.

He turned off the engine, pulled a cell phone out of his jacket pocket, looked at it, put it back.

"Stay put," he said as he opened the door. "I'll be right back."

"Wait a minute!" She climbed out too, slithering on the edge of the ditch. "Bailor—"

"Just wait here. I can't keep you out of this if you come around and mess up the crime scene."

"But..."

But what? He was already gone, jumping the ditch to disappear among the trees.

Emily slammed her door, the sound a shock in the rural silence. Andy stood with his back to her across the ditch. His shoulder blades sharp as incipient wings under the frail, freckled skin.

"Shit," Emily said.

Andy looked back at her, his death in his eyes. She jumped the ditch and followed him through the woods.

The house at the end of the driveway sat in a small gravel clearing, a tiny sagging house full of an inhabited silence, windows curtained and dark. No sign of Bailor. Andy disappeared.

Mouth dry with fear, Emily snuck through the trees, around the house toward the lake. She was a city person, the wet mat of leaves felt treacherous under her boots. Behind the house, the lake, a gray oval of water fringed by trees. A couple of wooden docks poked out into the water, but the houses they belonged to were hidden.

There was a dock here as well, a long crooked affair of weathered planks and old tires reaching across the marshy ground between the yard and the lake. Andy stood among straw-coloured reeds, looking at his feet that made no dents in the saturated ground. That's where he was, Emily realized, shivering with cold. She'd forgotten her jacket.

So she'd found Andy. Where was Ben?

Terrified of the house's blank windows she crept around the back of the garden shed, heart in her mouth. Still no sign of Bailor. Staring around her at the trees, the lake, she leaned against the shed. It was prefabricated out of corrugated metal, cold under her shoulder, its paint white and new. New. An old house with no garden and a brand new garden shed? Her heart lurched back into her chest and started to pound.

The shed had a door at either end. She had seen without really seeing that the doors facing the house were open, showing the line of rakes and shovels, the rideable mower in the center of the floor. A mower for a gravel yard.

Goddamn it, where was Bailor? Emily leaned against the door and almost fell when it slid quietly open on oiled tracks. The floor was rough cement. Pale light poured through the shed: tools, mower, garden chairs. No boy.

But he had to be here. Why else the shed full of useless tools? Emily walked over to the mower, careless of being seen, and then froze. Her foot coming down had made a hollow thump. She looked down. At first it just looked like the same concrete as the rest of the floor, but then she saw the grain, and realized it was plywood painted gray. She dropped to her knees and looked again. Hinges and, under the mower, a padlock through a hasp.

"Hey!"

The shout stopped her heart. She looked up to see the man standing at the back door of the house. He was in a sweatshirt and jeans, half his jaw white with shaving cream, a razor in his hand. He had pale hair in a crew cut, pale eyes that looked lashless and raw. Fear in his face that mounted into fury.

"Hey! Get away from there!" He started down the stairs. "That's private property!"

Emily threw herself at the mower. It started, sweet and quick, the rattle of its engine loud in the metal shed. She drove it forward onto the gravel, left it running as she scrambled off again. He was at the other door of the shed, still shouting, the neck of his shirt white with shaving cream.

"Get out of here!" he shouted. "Get out before I call the police!"

"I am the police."

Bailor, his footsteps covered by the noise of the mower. The blond man spun, whole body braced with shock.

Bailor's problem. Emily snatched a rake off the wall, jammed the end of the handle through the padlock hasp and heaved. Muscles honed over weeks of digging strained until they burned. The hasp didn't budge. She wedged the rake handle further through the hasp and heaved again, using her legs and back as well as her arms. There was shouting behind her, a scuffle half drowned by the mower's faltering engine. The rake handle digging into her collarbone, blood pounding in her temples, sweat stinging in her eyes.

A high shout, "No!" The crack of breaking wood.

The hasp came loose.

She threw the rake aside, hauled up the trap door. Blackness down below, a reek of sewer and mud. Bailor was at her side, panting.

"No ladder," she said.

"Here." There was one in the corner, aluminum, new. He dropped it into the pit.

The mower stuttered and died. Silence.

"Ben?" Emily kneeled at the edge of the hole. "Ben?"

And from below, a tiny voice. "No."

Bailor was already on the ladder, climbing down.

A skinny little kid, black with filth and bruises. Eyes clenched shut against the light of day. It was Ben. He'd denied his presence there, not his name. That one *No* was all he'd say. But he was alive.

Emily pulled off her shirt and wiped him clean while he crouched, shivering, on the floor of the shed. She shivered too, in her undershirt. Bailor handed her his jacket. For the first time she saw his gun, black and snub in its holster on his belt. She wrapped Ben in the jacket and then wrapped her arms around him too, looking over his head toward the house. In the space between shed and steps lay the blond man. He was on his back, arms flung wide, legs twisted. The front of his sweatshirt was dark with blood.

The crack that she'd thought was the plywood breaking.

He wasn't dead. As she stared, his hand weakly moved toward the hole in his chest. Ben shivered steadily in her arms.

"Jesus, Bailor," she said.

He looked down at her. "Yeah," he said. "The paperwork's gonna be hell."

They carried the boy to Bailor's car and laid him curled in the back seat, then stood together on the side of the road, waiting for his backup and the ambulance to arrive. Emily shivering in her white undershirt.

"What did you touch?" Bailor asked her.

It took her a minute to understand. "The shed door, in back. The mower steering. The padlock. The rake."

He nodded, looking wearier than ever. "I'll go back, wipe your prints. Keep you out of this, like I said. You can hitch a ride into town."

She looked at him. "Bailor . . ."

He looked off down the road. "He was carrying a straight razor. Did you see it? I didn't think anybody used those anymore." He shrugged. "I'll get shit for not calling backup, but nothing worse. Believe me, with this guy, nothing worse."

Emily nodded, wiping her dirty hands on her jeans. Her left palm stung. She looked at it and saw she'd torn a callus.

Bailor sucked in his breath. Looking up she saw him staring at the scar on her wrist, the neat red line with the staple holes to either side, like the track of a lizard in the sand.

He met her eyes. "Listen," he said.

She shoved her fists in her pockets and shrugged. "Not your fault."

"Emily." A beat. "I won't ask you again." Another beat. "I promise."

They both knew he was lying.

But it was nice of him to say.

Originally published in On Spec Summer 2000 Vol 12 No 2 #41

Holly Phillips published her very first story in *On Spec* in 2000. Since then she has published more than 30 stories, including two story collections, as well as two novels. Holly lives in the Lower Mainland with The Two Esses (Steven and Savoy), and is nurturing a fledgling consultancy in technical writing and document design.

Closing Time
Matthew Johnson

Nep Gao stood on his tiptoes in the quiet garden to the back of the restaurant, working his small silver knife along the thinnest branches of the prickly ash tree, and wondered when his father's ghost would leave the party. He had died five days ago and was still holding court, entertaining all his old friends and customers.

It was just his luck, Gao thought, that his father had died in the middle of *qinshon* season, the few weeks when the tree's buds had their best flavour. Already, chewing carefully, he could detect a bitter note in what he had just harvested. At the rate things were going his father's ghost would still be around in a week, when the *qinshon* would be edible. This was usually their most profitable time of year, but so long as his father was enjoying the food and the company enough to stay on Earth, Gao was bound to provide food and drink to anyone who came to pay their respects. So far there had been no shortage of mourners, most of them just happening to come around dinner time and often even staying until past dawn.

With his basket full of tightly curled green buds clutched under his arm, Gao went back into the restaurant. Though it was only midmorning, someone in the room was playing a zither, shouting out parts of the *Epic of the Hundred and One*

Bandits. Louder, though, was his father's commentary on the action as it was sung, "That bandit's pretty clever, but not as clever as that butcher that used to try to sell tame ducks as wild. Nobody but me could smell the difference from the blood in the carcass!"; and, "I heard the great Xan Te play that verse once when I was on a trip to Lamnai. He hardly had a tooth in his head, but he ate two whole boxes of my pork dumplings."

Gao could not help blushing when he heard his father telling the same tales he had told a thousand times before. He had never done anything but run the restaurant, never traveled except to buy food or collect recipes, but to hear him tell it he had had more adventures than all the Hundred and One Bandits put together. Gao could not count the number of times he had heard his father tell the story of how he had gotten his trademark recipe—the garlicky duck from which he had taken his name, Doi Thiviei—from a hermit who had lived in a hut that was at the top of a mountain when he arrived in the afternoon, but at the bottom of a valley when he left at dawn. The zither player had fallen silent to hear the story, and Gao could see a half-dozen others kneeling on mourning stools, listening and chatting as they ate the leftovers of the previous night's meals.

"And then, just when I opened my eyes, I saw—nhoGao, is that you? Don't lurk in the doorway, son, come in and sit down. I'm just at the good part."

"I'm sorry, Father, but I must start to cook for today's mourners."

"Oh well, all right then. Bring us some fresh tea and some red bean dumplings, will you? Now, where was I? Oh yes—when I opened my eyes, I saw that the hut, which the night before had been on a mountaintop—"

Gao picked up the empty bowls, hurried on to the kitchen before his father could think of anything else to ask for. He could not help but notice that his father looked no more vaporous than he had the day before, and felt guilty for wishing it otherwise. For most people the mourning party was a formality, a way to make the spirit linger for a day or two at the most. It was supposed to be an expense—if it was too short, cost too little, there would be doubts about one's respect for one's father—but not a ruinous one. Sighing, Gao laid the *qinshon* buds onto a square of silk which he then tied into a bundle; any rougher cloth would rub their skins harshly and make them lose their flavour. That done he put a pot of water on to boil and looked around the kitchen, wondering what he could make as cheaply as possible that would not offend the mourners. He sipped the chicken broth that had been simmering since the night before, tossed in the bones from last night's dinner. He could put pork dumplings into the broth, make a soup with noodles and fava beans, top it with chive flowers from the garden. For the next course, he could deep fry thin strips of pork in batter; if he made it hot enough he might be able to use a pig that wasn't so expensive.

Feeling hungry now, he pried one of the stones in the floor loose, lifted the lid off the shallow earthenware pot that lay below, reached in and pulled out a pickled pig's knuckle. Looking carefully over each shoulder he took a bite. He had promised to give up eating pork when he and Mau-Pin Mienme had become engaged, but nothing calmed him down when he was nervous the way pork knuckles did. Her family were followers of the Southerner—her name meant Sweet Voice From the South—and so did not eat meat at all. When she had insisted that he at least give up eating pork it had taken him less than a second to agree. It had taken him only a day, following that, to realize that he could not possibly keep his promise, so he had bought a pot of pigs' knuckles one day while she and her family were at prayer and hidden it under the floor in the kitchen, so that she would never know what a dishonourable man she was marrying.

His mouth was now full of the sweet, salty, vinegar taste of the pigs' knuckles, and he could feel it easing his mind. It was true: he was a dishonourable man, dishonest and unfilial, breaking his word to his wife-to-be and wishing his father's ghost would leave him alone. He doubted that even Mienme, who, like all those of her faith had studied to be an advocate to the dead in the Courts of Hell, could convince the Judge of Fate to send him back as anything nobler than a frog. He sighed. It was only because he was due to inherit a good business that Mienme's father, a lawyer on Earth as well as the next world, was allowing her to marry him at all. He had always known how unlikely it was that he should be able to marry a woman like Mienme. She was beautiful and intelligent, while he was cursed with an overfed body and the doughy face that had made his father call him "Glutinous Rice." He knew better than to question the divine blessing that made her love him, though, and he had believed since they were children they would one day be married. In all that time he had never imagined it might be *his* father that would be the problem.

Thinking of Mienme made him want to see her, have her listen to his problems as she had so often done. Like other women who followed the Southerner she was allowed to go out alone, to spread His word, and he thought she would most likely be at South Gate Market this time of day. That would work out well enough; he could get all of the vegetables he needed there, and buy the pig later in the day when he was alone. Seeing her face, and hearing her advice, would be more than worth the extra trip. After carefully putting the pot back under the floor stone he opened a small jar in the shelf, took out a boiled egg marinated in soy sauce and popped it into his mouth to cover the smell of the pork knuckle. Then he poured boiling water into the large teapot, put a few of the red bean dumplings he had baked the night before onto a tray, took tray and tea into the front room where his father was still spinning his tales to a rapt audience.

"—of course, a chicken that laid eggs with two yolks would be worth a lot of money today, though we didn't think like that in those days. No, we only hoped she would survive the trip home so we could make Double August Sunrise for the Emperor—nhoGao, you've brought the dumplings. Won't you stay and hear this story?" His father was, if anything, more solid than when he had last seen him, the party more lively as noon approached.

"I'm sorry, Father, I have to go to the South Gate Market to buy food for dinner."

"Well, that's all right, I suppose. Do bring me back some of those preserved mushrooms, and some sweet beer for our friend here, whose throat must be getting dry." The zither player had not sung a word since Doi Thiviei started talking, nor was he likely to for the rest of the day, but Gao nodded dutifully before stepping back into the kitchen.

Once out of his father's sight he picked up the rag that held his shopping list and wrote "sweet beer" on it with a piece of charcoal. His father did not like him reading, saying every other

Closing Time

generation had learned to memorize their customers' orders, but on the other hand Mienme said if he were illiterate he would not be able to read the charges in the Court of Hell and his advocate would not be able to help him. He had to admit it meant he took fewer trips to the market, since without a list he always forgot something. He folded the list, strapped his grocery basket on his back, and went out into the street.

The streets between the restaurant and the market were crowded, even in the heat before noon, and the wind blowing from the west carried a heavy scent of medicinal incense. Someone in the Palace must be sick, he thought. As the massive iron pillars of the South Gate came into view the smell of the incense was met and quickly defeated by that of spices, sizzling oil, and a dozen different kinds of meat cooking. Pausing for a moment, Gao closed his eyes, tested himself the way his father had done when he was a child, making himself find his way around the market by smell alone. There, off to his right, someone was making salt-and-pepper shrimp, heating the iron pan until the shells cracked, releasing tiny gasps of garlic- and red pepper-scented steam. To his left someone else was frying *mat tran* on a griddle, making sure they would have enough for the lunch rush customers to wrap around their pork and kelp rice.

Satisfied, Gao opened his eyes again, scanning the crowd for Mienme's familiar face. He found her standing just inside the gate, handing out block-printed tracts to a family of confused-looking farmers. One, an older man with a white-streaked beard and a broad bamboo hat, was listening politely while the others kept a tight rein on the pigs they had brought with them. Gao waited until the farmer had accepted the pamphlet and moved on before approaching.

"You do your faith and your father honour," he said formally when she noticed him. Though they were engaged, there were still certain proprieties to be observed when they were in public.

Or so he felt; Mienme often seemed to disagree. "You know as well as I do that none of them can read," she said, shaking her head. "Our temple offers free lessons, but they won't stay in the city long enough for that. Besides, only the Master could convince a pork farmer to give up meat."

"And you try nevertheless," Gao said. "Such determination

will serve you well when you argue cases before the Judge of Fate."

"That's very sweet, nhoGao," she said, making him blush at the use of his childhood name. She was dressed in the brown cotton robe and leggings all her faith wore when preaching, and from a distance she might also have looked like a man. "But you don't have to reassure me, I'm not about to lose my faith—I'm just hot and tired, that's all. Why are you looking so glum?"

He shrugged slightly. He had not realized his mood was so apparent, resolved to better hide it from his father. "The mourning party is still going on today. If this continues my father's ghost will outlast his restaurant."

"What is it now, four days?"

"Five. My father is enjoying his party so much I think he is happier now than when he was alive."

Mienme put up her hood and extended her hand to him. With her face hidden anyone who saw them would only see a young man helping a monk through the crowded streets. "It's the food everyone's coming for. Couldn't you do something to it, put in something bitter so they won't like it so much?" she asked. "You could say it was a mistake."

"If I made a mistake like that, my father would stay another ten years just to punish me."

They stopped at a vegetable stand and Gao haggled with the merchant for beans and cabbage while Mienme seemed lost in thought. "I've got it," she finally said after they had put their groceries in the basket on Gao's back and moved on. "Remember the night my parents came to the restaurant and you made Temple Style Duck?"

"How could I forget?" Gao asked. "Your parents thought I was insulting them, making bean curd so that it tasted like duck. My father thought I was insulting the duck!"

"Exactly. Make him that and when he complains, say you're concerned about what the Judge of Fate will find if he keeps on eating meat after his death. That way it'll cool the party down, and you'll only be acting out of filial affection."

"That's true." Gao thought for a moment. "That's an excellent idea. You really are too smart to be wasted on a person like me."

Mienme laughed. "I know. I took an oath to defend the hopeless, remember?"

Closing Time

Five hours later Gao held his breath as he lifted the steamer basket's long oval lid. All around him lay the remains of the bean curd, sweet potato, arrowroot and other vegetables he had used. He did not make Temple Style very often—even most followers of the Southerner did not eat it; it had been created for high ranking converts who wanted their vegetarianism to be as painless as possible—but he enjoyed the artistry it involved, matching flavours and textures in a way that was almost magical. Gao, the youngest of his father's four sons, had mostly learned cooking from his mother, and she had been the vegetable cook. For that reason his father and brothers had been responsible for the meat dishes the restaurant was famous for and he had been left to take care of the vegetables and small items like dumplings. But his brothers had all left, one by one, to start their own restaurants in other cities, and for the last few years he had been doing all the cooking by himself, his father only planning the menus—menus he had changed, slightly, to include more vegetables and some of the things he had learned cooking for Mienme.

When the steam coming out of the basket cleared, he could see, inside, something that looked almost exactly like thin slices of barbecued duck, grayish-white with streaks of an almost impossible red. Getting it to look right was the easy part, of course; the flavour and the smell were harder, and much more important. He carefully lifted the slices out with a slotted spoon, and slid them into a waiting skillet full of oil and the sauce needed to complete the illusion. In seconds, the oil sealed the outside of the slices, browning them, and making the red streaks even brighter. He lifted the smallest piece to his mouth, burning his tongue slightly tasting it. It was perfect, better even than the cooks at the Temple made it. It had taken him months to duplicate their recipe, making sure he had it right before he could even invite Mienme's parents to dinner, but he had also improved it, giving it that crackling texture the Temple cooks had never managed. This was the dish he made better than anyone else—*Trianha Thiviei*, Temple Style Duck. This ought to be his name, not Glutinous Rice, something he had made every day for the poorest customers because his brothers were making more complicated things. He could not change his name while his father was still around, of course, but soon, perhaps...

Gao sighed, asking forgiveness for wishing his father gone, took the remaining slices out of the skillet then laid them on a bed of steamed and salted greens and white rice. He took the plate with rice, greens and "duck" in one hand, and a platter with ten small bowls on it in the other and went out to the front room.

"—so there we were, bound to make dinner for an official of the Fifth Rank and his family and all the salt brokers on strike— nhoGao, have you brought dinner?" The crowd of mourners had grown since the afternoon, with the new arrivals more than making up for the few that had left—word that one of the best restaurants in town was giving away free food had gotten around.

Gao nodded, not quite able to speak. For all of the justification Mianme had given him he could not escape the fact that he was giving his father something he would not like. Someone was rolling his stomach into dumplings as he spooned out the first bowl of *trianha thiviei*.

His father sniffed at the bowl. "Is this duck?" he asked, his brow furrowed.

No sense adding a lie to his long list of crimes. "No Father, it's Temple-Style. I made it because—because Mienme was worried about what will happen when you stand before the Judge of Fate."

"Is that so? What a kind girl she is." His father took up his sticks, brought a piece to his mouth and chewed thoughtfully.

"Yes, Father. She is very concerned about your trial." Gao felt like a red pepper pickle had been poured down his throat, wondering what punishments awaited him as a result of this.

"You know," his father said finally, "maybe it's because I'm dead, but I don't think I gave this stuff a fair chance last time. It's really quite good—and for my soul too, eh?" He laughed. Gao echoed him nervously. "Needs a bit more salt, though. Which reminds me, I was just telling them the story of the big salt brokers' strike—you know this one—it's a good story—"

Gao nodded, served the other mourners silently then went out the front door, leaned hard against the wall. He was not sure which was worse, that the plan had failed, or that he had hoped it would succeed. Either way things were no better—his father was enjoying his mourning party as much as ever, and the number of guests was only increasing.

As he stood in the cool, incense-perfumed night air, Nep Gao became aware of bells ringing in the distance. Not the familiar dull tone of temple bells, but a higher chime, three strokes, silence, three strokes. The palace bells, he realized. Whoever it was they had been burning incense for earlier—and from the number of bells it had to be an official of the Third Rank, someone in the royal family—had died. He had just pieced this together when he heard a voice call his name. He turned, saw coming down the dark street a man with two heads, one higher than the other. Gao squinted to see better but the second head was still there.

"Yes?" he asked, wondering if this was an agent of the Courts of Hell come to take him to his punishment early.

"We require a service of you," the man said. He stepped into the small pool of light cast by the torch above the door and showed himself to be two men, one riding in a basket on the other's back. It was the man in the basket, wearing the lacquered red headdress of an official of the seventh rank, who had spoken. Gao immediately dropped to his knees.

"How can your humble servant help you?" he asked, unable to keep from staring at the man's dangling feet in their white deerskin slippers. That was the reason for the basket, of course; the slippers, which had to be a gift from someone in the royal family, could not be permitted to touch the ground in this part of the city, but the street was too narrow for a palanquin.

"The Emperor's favourite uncle has died," the man said. "We are preparing the mourning party for him and have heard of the effect your cooking has had. The Emperor would like the honour shown to his uncle that has been shown to your father."

"I'm not sure I can—" Gao began, beads of sweat forming on his forehead.

"The Emperor would consider it an insult if the same honour was not shown to his uncle," the man said firmly. "Take this." The man handed a small jade token to the servant whose back he was riding, who then handed it to Gao. "This will let you and anyone helping you onto the palace grounds. You may keep it when you are done." Without waiting for an answer he gave his mount a quick kick in the thigh, making him turn around and head back down the street.

Minutes later Gao was lying on the mat in the back dining room, a bag of cold clay on his head and a dozen mint leaves in his mouth. He chewed the mint to control heartburn, but it was not helping tonight.

"How did it go?" Mienme's voice came from the window.

Gao stood up, opened the door. Mienme pulled herself through the window by her arms, still the adventurous girl she had always been. "Worse and worse," he said, and proceeded to tell her everything that had happened.

"Actually," she said after he had finished his litany, "this could work out well for us."

"How can this be good?" Gao asked, accidentally swallowing the mass of mint in his mouth. "The restaurant is already nearly broke, and now we have to serve food fit for an official of the Third Rank. We'll be ruined—I'll be lucky if I escape with my head."

"Just listen," Mienme said. "Your father can't complain if you give all the best food to the royal mourning party—imagine what that jade token on the wall could do for business at his restaurant. So you can't be blamed for just serving him simple food, and when you do that the mourners will stop coming and the party will be over."

"You may be right," he said slowly. He drew the token out from his belt pouch, ran his fingers over its cool, smooth surface. "Yes, of course. If we're cooking for the Emperor's uncle, he can't complain if we give him nothing but rice and millet gruel. Even the Judge of Fate couldn't complain." He held the token up against the wall. "I must have done a very good deed in my last life to deserve you."

"In that case," she said, grinning impishly, "come here and give me a kiss while you're still all minty."

Sometimes he wondered if her parents knew their daughter at all.

The next morning he was up at dawn, fishing carp out of the pond in the back garden. Once the fish were splashing in their wooden bucket, he took his small knife and cut a half-dozen

Closing Time

lilies from the surface of the pond to make into a sauce for the fish—fish fresh enough for the Emperor's uncle. These were the last two items he needed for the day's meals; after making sure the jade token was still in his belt pouch he went into the kitchen, put on his grocery basket, and went out into the front room. His father's ghost was regaling two or three sleepy mourners with his adventures, while several more lay sprawled on sleeping mats around the room.

"—of course, a pig that smart you don't eat all at—nhoGao, do you have breakfast ready already?"

"I can't cook for you today, Father, remember? I left a crabmeat and pork casserole in the oven, you can ask one of the mourners to get it out for you in a few hours, and I'll send you dumplings for the afternoon."

"Of course, of course—I'd almost forgotten. You'll do us proud at the palace, I'm sure—and what a story it'll make, cooking for the Emperor's uncle." Despite his words he did not seem very happy, and Gao wondered if he was finally starting to fade. Crab and pork casserole was not exactly gruel, but it was not the food Doi Thiviei was used to, either. He felt a sudden pain in his chest, hoped that if his father were to depart today it would not be until after he got back to the restaurant.

He had never been to the palace before. Despite the fact that it was at the centre of the city, few people ever received an invitation to go. Those who went without an invitation, hoping to poach the Emperor's white deer, usually wound up as permanent guests—or came home over the course of several days, one piece at a time. As he reached the gate he could not help worrying that the whole thing had been a colossal hoax, that the guards would take his jade seal and his groceries and send him away. When he showed them the token, however, they stood to either side of the gate, and one was assigned to lead him to the palace kitchens.

"How long ago did the noble official die?" Gao asked the soldier.

The man walked a few steps in silence before finally answering. "Yesterday afternoon," he said. Like most soldiers he had a heavy provincial accent, which perhaps explained his reluctance to speak. "Didn't you hear the bells?"

"I've been busy," Gao muttered. "Have you seen his ghost?"

The soldier again kept silent for a few moments, then spoke, no expression crossing his face. "No, but I hear it is very pale. He was an old man, and sick for a long time."

Gao cursed inwardly. Except for short, violent deaths, long illnesses were the worst. They left a person glad to die, and not inclined to hang around too long afterward. He thanked the guard when they reached the kitchen, and got to work unpacking his groceries. He had planned a light breakfast, fried wheat noodles sprinkled with sugar and black vinegar, in case the ghost was not too solid. Then he hoped that by lunch he would be able to serve the carp balls in lotus sauce and crisply fried eel to a receptive audience.

It was not to be. The Emperor's uncle was vaporous, not interested in talking or even listening to the zither. The mourning party was sombre, the guests mostly relatives and lower officials who were attending out of duty rather than friendship. They picked at the delicacies Gao served, leaving the rest for palace servants, who could not believe their luck. The ghost, meanwhile, ate only a bite from each dish, pausing neither to smell nor taste any of them.

By mid-afternoon, Gao was getting nervous. He had not managed to keep the Emperor's uncle from fading at all, knew that the official who had hired him would not be pleased. If he could have managed even two or three days, things would have been all right, but if he could only make the royal ghost stay a day and a night, it would look like an insult. He wished Mienme was there to help him.

Finally he resolved there was only one thing he could do: make the most elaborate, most spectacular dish he could, so that he would not be faulted for lack of effort. He settled on a recipe one of his brothers had found in a small village on the southern coast, *mau anh dem*—Yellow Lantern Fish. He sent a runner to the fish market for the freshest yellowfish he could find, telling him to look for clear eyes and a smell of seaweed. When the boy returned, he began to carefully cut and notch the scaled, gutted fish, and boil a deep pot of oil on a portable burner.

Minutes before dinner was due, he ordered the burner be carried into the room where the mourning party was taking place, followed behind carrying the fish himself. Though he

Closing Time

could not look at the faces of any of the guests he could tell few, if any, of them wanted to be there. The most enthusiastic of them, if not the wisest, were using this as an opportunity to get drunk. Even the zither player sounded almost as though he was singing in his sleep. At the middle of it all was the ghost, silent and uninterested in what was going on around him.

Gao had the burner and pot of oil placed in front of the royal ghost, waited a few minutes while the oil returned to the proper temperature. Then, with enough of a flourish to make sure all eyes were on him, he dropped the fish into the oil. In seconds it blossomed out like a paper lantern, its flesh turning golden and crispy. It was a dish designed to impress even the most jaded crowd, and it did not fail him: the guests pressed forward to get a better look and eagerly handed him their plates. Before the first bite was taken, however, Gao knew he had failed. Unlike the guests, the Emperor's uncle was still withdrawn, uninterested, not bothering to eat or even smell the fish.

My life is over, Gao thought as he walked home. If the Emperor's uncle had faded away by morning he would be blamed, and that was sure to kill business if it did not kill him. Just then he realized that in all of his worry about the Emperor's uncle, he had forgotten to send the lunch dumplings he had made for his father's mourning party. Without food that party was sure to have broken up by now, his father likely faded away. He suddenly regretted not listening to any of the stories his father had told over the last few weeks, too busy cooking and worrying about the restaurant. He had heard them all a dozen of more times, but now might never get a chance to hear them again.

When he neared the restaurant, however, he saw lights inside and heard voices. Creeping into the front dining room, he saw his father still holding court before a half-dozen mourners, the room strewn with empty bowls and teacups.

"nhoGao, is that you?" his father asked, spotting him as he tried to slink past into the kitchen. "How did it go at the palace?"

Gao shook his head slowly. "I am sorry I was not able to send you the food I made for the day," he said. "I was busy with—"

"Don't worry about us—we don't need food to keep the party going. Besides, I know where you hide the pig knuckles. Now, where was I—"

Watching his father, more solid than ever, Gao wondered what it was he had done so wrong at the palace and so right here. He had made dishes for the Emperor's uncle that were twice as elaborate as anything he had ever made at the restaurant, but had left the royal ghost cold. His father, meanwhile, looked likely to remain among the living indefinitely on a diet of pigs' knuckles. *I must be missing something*, he thought. *If only Mienme were here to help me think. She would say, if it's not the food—*

"Father, can you come with me for a few minutes?" he asked suddenly, interrupting his father in the middle of the story of the *seo nuc* game he had played against a beggar who had turned out to be an exiled general.

"I suppose," his father said, puzzled. "I can finish this story later. Where are we going?"

Without pausing to answer his father's question, Gao rushed back to the palace, flashing the jade token to the puzzled guard. The mourning party was down to just a few diehards, likely trying to win points with the Emperor. The royal ghost was hardly visible, a thin gray mist barely recognizable as once having been human.

"Please excuse me, noble officials," Gao said, dropping to the floor and bowing low. "I forgot the most important part of the mourning party."

A few seconds of silence passed as the guests watched him curiously, wondering what he was going to produce that might top the Yellow Lantern Fish. Finally his father said, "What a glum group. Reminds me of my father the day our prize rooster died, the one who would crow every time a rich customer was coming—" The guests looked at the chatty ghost in amazement, but Gao's father made straight for the Emperor's uncle. "Did he try to feed you that Temple Style Duck? I only ask because you're looking a little thin. The first time I met one of those Southerners I thought they were crazy, won't eat meat, won't eat fowl, not even fish. But I met one who was a wizard with rice—learned a few tricks from him—"

By the time dawn came, Doi Thiviei and the Emperor's uncle were chatting like old friends. The royal ghost was looking much more substantial and even accepted one of the sesame balls with hot lotus paste Gao had made for breakfast.

"Gao, I think I'll stay here awhile," his father said. "I hope it won't disappoint my mourners, but I've gotten a little tired of hearing my own voice. Take good care of my restaurant, will you?"

"Of course," Gao answered, ladling out the clear soup he had made from chicken stock and the last of the *qinshon* leaves.

"And I suppose you'll be marrying that Southerner girl and changing the name your mother and I gave you. I know you've never liked it, though it's a good story how you got it."

Gao frowned. "I always thought it was because—well, my face—and I always had to make it for the customers who couldn't afford anything else."

"No, no," his father said. "It wasn't like that at all. You see, when I first met your mother—but I suppose you don't have time to hear this story."

Gao sat down, took a sip of the soup, enjoying the fragile flavour of the *qinshon*. He only allowed himself one bowl a year, to be sure he would appreciate it. "I have plenty of time, Father," he said. "Only please, let me go get Mienme so she can hear it as well. We will both need to know this story so we can tell it to our children."

It turned out his father had lots of stories he had never told; or maybe Gao had just never heard them before.

Originally published in On Spec *Summer 2001 Vol 13 No 2 #45*

Matthew Johnson has published stories in such places as *Asimov's Science Fiction*, *The Magazine of Fantasy & Science Fiction* and *Strange Horizons*. A collection of his short fiction, *Irregular Verbs and Other Stories*, was published by CZP in 2014. "Closing Time" was the first story he ever sold.

fOSTER CHILD
CATHERINE MACLEOD

The baby came in the mail on Monday, arriving as Claire Warren's grocery bag tore. She marked its entry by screaming as marmalade mashed her instep. Claire yowled through her teeth, and made a fist, then realized she still had the mail in that hand.

"Uh, ma'am?" She turned back to the open door and managed a smile for the mailman. "You have another package."

"Oh. Thanks." She glanced at the postmark. Did she know anyone in Hastings, Kentucky?

"You gonna be okay, ma'am?"

"Yes, thanks." She shut the door behind him and flipped the box. The sender was *Starway Collectibles*. It took her a minute. Right—SF mail-order company. She'd sent the order last month. She hobbled through the groceries and opened the box with a steak knife.

The baby was *ugly*.

It was one of those gag alien embryos she'd seen advertised, wrinkled and gray, floating in a jar of sludge. Tendrils of something white and wispy drifted around it. She set it on the counter and dug through the box. Her receipt listed the contents as "Paperback: *Trust No One*."

Claire chalked another one up for Monday. She made a mental note to check *Starway's* returns policy, and maybe call them tomorrow. The embryo was from one of those novelty companies that sold "pickled" noses, fingers and eyeballs. Their appeal was beyond her. She turned away and promptly forgot about it.

She stacked the food in the cupboards and carried the crumpled mail down the hall. Application for cable TV; didn't want it. Flyer for Tracy's Hair Salon; didn't need it. She opened the phone bill, noting the minimal cost of an unlisted number. There were no calls. The only person who knew her address was the clerk who mailed her alimony. She slid that one in the nightstand drawer.

Having the cheques forwarded guaranteed her privacy, though she couldn't imagine her ex showing up—in meditating on her marriage, *Jason wasn't there* had become her mantra. The night the burglar smashed the bedroom window, Jason wasn't there. The day the dog got hit by a car, Jason wasn't there.

And the morning of her miscarriage, she knew he wasn't going to be.

Claire shucked her clothes on the way to the shower and grabbed the shampoo. The stubble on her head was long enough to be called hair now.

Jason said the baby's loss had unbalanced her, and she allowed there might be some truth in that. She'd cried at odd moments, making it hard to go out with his law partners. She'd stopped playing tennis with their wives—she was sick of their scrutiny. She didn't remember cutting her hair off. She did remember Jason asking her to leave. She took his alimony because it was be alone with money or be alone without, and she didn't lay blame. Divorce was too much like their marriage for that: she had comfort and means, and Jason wasn't there.

Claire thought of that as her time in the darkness, and felt herself traveling back to the light. She did the Saturday crossword. She slept late. She hung a bird feeder. She had hundreds of paperbacks she'd never had time to read. She read them now.

She carried one out to the kitchen, plugged in the kettle, and unlocked the glass door to the backyard. The sun was nearly down. The wind dried her hair in seconds, silver-blonde going silver-gray. The garden here was still half-wild. She was taming it slowly.

Claire liked the wooden fence no one could see over. She liked the neighbourhood where no one knew her nor cared to. She liked being among the missing.

The kettle whistled. She set tea to steep, and as she picked up *Stardance*, the embryo jar caught her eye again. It was ugly. Very. Claire shook her head in wonder at the mix-up. The doll was squashed and bent, folded at odd angles. Its eyes were large and set far back in its head. Their lids were almost transparent.

She nudged the jar, setting the fetus rocking gently in the murky liquid, and leaned close, watching it drift.

The baby opened its eyes.

"OH GOD!"

The baby stirred. Its tiny hands floated away from its body, pressing the side of the jar, halting its spin in the fluid. It hung there, facing her.

Claire backed away.

Maybe the doll was designed to do that.

She moved. The baby pushed on the glass with one hand and turned to watch her. She moved again. The baby tracked her. They looked at each other for a long time. Claire told herself not to jump to conclusions. An hour later she jumped anyway.

It was alive.

She lifted the jar carefully. It was warm. Had it been when she unpacked it? She didn't think so. She carried it to the table, wrapping her hands around it, warming it further. Her breath misted the glass. "You want me to take you to my leader?" The baby blinked. "You're right. It's a dumb idea."

But evidence of the existence of extraterrestrial life was sitting on her table in a damned Mason jar. She should call *someone*. The cops, the FBI—NASA?

Claire blanked. If they didn't believe her—and she was having trouble grasping it—nothing would change. She'd still be sitting in the kitchen with an alien in her lap. But if they did—

She would no longer be among the missing.

The baby would be among the dissected.

This was Monday with a vengeance.

Claire rested her head on her arms and watched the baby

bob. Maybe she'd read too many tabloid headlines, but suddenly it seemed dangerous to ask questions. No phone calls. She smiled tiredly. Not even to *Starway Collectibles*.

Now there was a thought. Her smile faded. Babies didn't grow in Mason jars. This one had to have been put there. Or maybe just fallen in: the jewel of all stupid accidents. Because it was a *baby*; its mother wasn't going to let someone just *mail* it.

And there was another thought. This was somebody's child and they were going to want it back. Claire remembered crying as the life-that-wasn't-quite fell out of her, and shivered.

She stroked her fingers down the jar. "Baby, if your mama handles loss the way I do, I'm in big trouble."

But she knew a way to guarantee her safety. Garbage pick-up was tomorrow, and newborns went missing every day. Plunk it in a can and run like hell. Let Mama find her then.

And let someone else find the baby and take a scalpel to it. Let the rats drag it home for brunch. Let Baby go screaming through a trash compactor.

Claire hoped Mama was a tolerant sort.

She fell asleep at the table, arms around the jar, and woke at dawn to find the baby's face near hers. It was watching her again. Its fluid had changed, becoming lighter, less dense. Maybe it was draining the nutrients out of it?

Claire thought that was a fine idea. She sat up and considered breakfast.

Baby tumbled as she rose, stopping her mid-motion. "What?" It stretched its arms over its head, then lowered them and rolled its eyes to meet hers. She whispered, "What?" It reached up again. Claire squinted into the jar. Her breath froze. It was pushing at the lid.

Baby wanted out.

Well yeah, bright girl, did you think it was going to stay in there forever?

The baby kicked weakly. Claire's hands fluttered helplessly for a moment, then grabbed the jar. Pre-natal classes hadn't covered alien birth, but she knew the signs of distress. It needed out. Perhaps, like a human baby, it could only exist in the waters so long. She rummaged a jar opener from the knife drawer. On the second try it gripped and the lid came free.

Claire peered into the liquid. What if it couldn't eat what if it couldn't breathe oh God what if it drowned in the air—

A small hand splashed out of the jar. Its long fingers wrapped around one of hers. The baby's head floated up out of the fluid. It looked up at her and—she couldn't help it—Claire smiled. Its eyes were midnight-blue, the colour of her own.

Its skin took on a dull silver sheen as it emerged from the jar. Its mouth opened and she waited for the usual indignant wail.

A sound like little bells came out.

The water was tepid now, with a faint smell of yeast. Claire dipped her fingers into the jar and very gently lifted him. He barely filled her cupped hands; he weighed almost nothing. Water dripped off him and puddled on the sideboard. She patted him dry with a fold of her housecoat, then eased him into the scoop neck of her nightgown.

Baby dropped his misshapen head in the hollow of her throat.

There was a flight of sweet notes as he yawned, exhaling vanilla breath. Claire brushed her chin across the top of his head.

"Be careful what you wish for," she said.

Because you might get it, she thought. She'd wanted a baby. She remembered a hectic day years earlier, when she'd wished for some time alone, and had been granted ten years.

All right, she hadn't actually been alone during her marriage, but she'd felt that way.

In the future, Claire thought, wishes would be more specific.

She made Baby's breakfast as she ate her own. "I'm working in the dark here," she explained around the toast. "I don't know if they have milk where you come from, but human babies like this stuff."

She stirred sugar into the warm milk, and washed the eyedropper. The baby gurgled most of it down. She waited to see if it came back up. When it didn't she punched the dropper full again, then tipped the pan over her coffee cup.

Clink ka-ching. A sound like zills.

"No, you're too little for coffee."

Baby squinted in the crook of her arm. She grabbed a tissue to wipe his mouth, but only discordant chimes came out.

"Oh God oh God okay you're chiming so you can't be choking oh God I've poisoned you—"

Human babies came with a built-in defence—whatever didn't agree with them, they disposed of. Who knew about this one? Claire drew breath and did the toughest thing possible: nothing. She couldn't call 9-1-1. Baby would have to shift for himself. She moved her fingers down his smooth body and encountered another question: how did Baby excrete?

She had an answer seconds later as she realized her hands were sticky and slick. Baby disposed of his waste through his skin.

Claire wrung out a facecloth at the sink. The faucet was still dripping as she landed on the floor. The baby jolted in her arms, chirping in protest.

"I'm sorry. My knees gave out." She reached up and groped the facecloth off the sideboard. Baby stuck a wet finger in his mouth. "Oh, you like that? Good—I'll get you a rubber duck."

She sniffed the facecloth: Baby didn't like the milk. She watched him suck his finger. Apparently he didn't mind the water.

Baby *clinked* again. Claire winced, but he seemed calm enough as he blinked up at her.

Ah. He'd just wasted his breakfast. He was still hungry.

Claire got on her feet with difficulty, and mixed a pan of sugar water. Baby drank and dozed off without incident. *Wise child*, she thought. She was stiff from napping at the table.

Sunlight slanted through the blinds in her room, making bars on the bed. Claire slid under the covers and eased onto her side, curling around the baby. She wondered how long he would sleep. After coming to term in a Mason jar, could he sleep safely in a horizontal position?

Baby snuggled close, his hands against her cheek, and hummed contentedly. Claire relaxed. If it was good enough for him...

She woke in two hours and fed him again, then wrote a list as he slept. Leaving the house was out of the question. She couldn't take him with her, couldn't leave him alone, couldn't bring anyone in. She'd have the groceries delivered. Baby food might be okay if she thinned it.

No, it wouldn't work. She'd ordered groceries before, but

never baby food. All it would take was one stray comment—
She smiled down into those enormous blue eyes, "Hey, sweetheart, guess who's getting paranoid? I used to just worry someone would find *me* here." She scribbled a few more notes. "We'll try fresh fruit. I can purée that myself. Don't worry, we'll find something you like."

Don't worry. Claire snorted faintly. She was in way over her head. But she caught herself rocking him, swaying as she wrote, and let it go. He wasn't interrupting anything.

She retrieved him from the bedroom after the delivery boy left.

"These are green beans. What do you think?" Baby wrinkled his flat nose as she held them up. "I used to feel the same way. They are an acquired taste. What about this?" She sliced the apple and held it under his nose. He fluted a couple of notes and rubbed his mouth across it. "Oh, is that good?" She crushed the slice into a thin sauce and fed it to him slowly.

That afternoon she learned he liked pear juice, barley water and strawberry tea, which he sniffed happily when she drank it herself. He was indifferent to bananas, which she'd never liked.

She carried him to the window at sunset. "This is my favourite time of day. I love watching the stars. If you have to love something that doesn't love you back, the stars are it. Aren't they beautiful?"

She glanced down and caught him staring at white moths beating their wings on the screen.

"Yeah, Baby," she laughed, "those are pretty too."

She wrapped him in her sweater, and cradled him close. Sometimes the journey to the light was hard. It might be nice to have company for a while.

The shower gifts had never been returned. That would've been her job, and before she felt up to it, Jason had packed them away. Even before moving day, when she'd found the box in the U-Haul, she'd known dealing with the miscarriage would always be her job.

Claire dragged the rocker into her bedroom. She found the Snugli under a musical crib mobile and took both into the kitchen. Baby was in the laundry pile. Her pantyhose were on his head.

"Don't even think about robbing a bank—you're too short to see over the counter. That'd be a heck of a disguise, though."

She fastened the mobile to a chair back and wound the music box. He liked the lullaby, and bounced as the plastic stars spun, She cried softly as he warbled, a liquid sound she knew by now. He warbled when he heard her voice.

It was the sound he made when he recognized something.

Does this make sense to you? she wondered. *Do the stars really sing?*

She wore the Snugli in front so Baby rode with his head on her collarbones. He squinted down in the bag as she loaded the dryer, poking his head into her shirt.

"I've got news for you, kid—that's not where dinner comes from." She slid a hand down to move him, then realized he'd gone still against her breast.

He was listening to her heartbeat.

Oh God, letting him go would be hard. He was stronger now, a bit heavier, an inch taller. Rolling on the floor was an adventure. He pulled himself up against the furniture like any child. She loved the way he cooed in his sleep, like the song of small birds. His eyes were so blue she thought moons glowed in them, and knew he preferred shadows because sunshine bothered them.

But moonlight didn't. He trailed his long fingers through it like a sparrow soaking up heat, and her heart ached even as it rejoiced that her favourite time of day was also his.

She'd have a couple of blurred photos she'd taken in the garden, and when he was gone, she'd have his Mason jar. Not much. She still wondered how he'd got in there. She'd wondered once if Mama might be dead, if she'd put Baby in the jar to hide him from danger. That notion had lasted until the six o'clock news. Claire sat Baby on her lap as she watched the update.

There were more reports of strange lights over Hastings, Kentucky. "Well, sweetheart, looks like Mama's hot on the trail."

Their first trip to the garden: fear. No one could see over the fence. There were no wandering cats to scratch him. But what if the soil was toxic to him, or the scent of the flowers poison?

Foster Child

What if the insects found him tasty? She had no way of anticipating. Any bump could be a disaster.

In the end, he decided. She found him leaning on the door, trying to push it open, and thought of his exit from the Mason jar.

Baby wanted out.

She gathered him up and opened the door. He sang as they went out, a single note echoed by the wren on the roof. He looked up and seemed to smile. He always looked like that.

Claire knelt and lowered him toward the grass. He patted it curiously. No sign of pain, no blistering from a chlorophyll allergy. She plunked him on the grass beside her and started to weed the daisies.

"Here, do you want one?" He ran a tiny fingertip over the soft petals. "That one is I love you, and this is I love you not—it's okay, it's just a game—and this is I love you."

She pulled a blade of grass from his mouth, and he chimed as she tickled his chin with a buttercup. No yellow, no surprise. He tracked a blue jay as it sailed overhead, and Claire realized suddenly how frightening this could have been. Was the sky a strange colour? Did he remember home?

Did he know this one was temporary?

Om. Claire knew that one: he wanted to be held. She obliged. He liked the tour of the garden. She'd cleared away the weeds and overgrowth, but hadn't planted much; the last tenants had left flowers of a dozen hues. She wondered what they'd felt, turning something they loved so much over to a stranger's care. She shivered in the June warmth and, without realizing she did so, Claire *omed*. Baby wrapped his arms around her neck.

He didn't fit in the Snugli now. He'd graduated to grape juice. She'd caught him standing by himself, and grabbed him before he toppled.

She wanted to see his first steps.

He trilled in protest as she turned for the house, but the sun was hot and her skin itched. She jerked back as sparks jumped from the door handle.

It wouldn't be long. The air was heavy, as though a charge crackled through it. There were more frequent reports of lights seen in Hastings. They were closer, moving in a rough line. The weather bureau couldn't explain them. The power companies claimed ignorance.

Claire waited until dark and went out on the step.

"Can you smell the rain coming? We can wait—I know you like to splash. I wish you could see a rainbow before you go."

And new snow and a circus parade. It wasn't going to happen. Claire hiked the baby up to eye level.

"You have to go soon. It's best for you." Her voice broke. She tried again. "I can't take you anywhere else and you can't stay with me forever. It's not as safe as it used to be."

He looked up at her seriously. *Clink.*

"Because this morning the delivery boy asked if I had a home office. Someone's noticed I never go out, and it's not normal for people to stay home all the time. We were okay until the questions started."

Claire smiled as Baby ran little fingers through her hair. "I don't want you to worry about me. I'll miss you, but I'll be okay."

Baby trilled softly.

"All right. I'll be okay *eventually*. I never intended to stay here; I still have my real estate license. That's how I met Jason—I sold him his house. I can go back to the real world. It's an interesting place. Yes, almost as interesting as those."

He was playing with her thumbs again. He didn't have any.

The clouds were blowing in fast. She looked down at the baby, squashed and bent at odd angles. She heard a crack of thunder and thought, *There goes my heart.*

"Once," she said, "in the middle of a fight, Jason asked me what I wanted. It was the only time he'd ever asked. I couldn't tell him I wanted someone to love and he wasn't it. I thought it would never happen. But we know better, don't we?"

He looked up and chimed briefly.

She said, "Will you try to remember me?"

Ching clink.

"I'll take that as a yes."

They sat for a while. He would leave with the memory of birdsong. There wasn't a lot left to say. Finally she took him out to dance in the rain.

And they were still dancing. Claire circled the kitchen to a country waltz on the radio. The rain stopped, and she considered the night sky in passing. Baby belonged in that icy Shambalah. She wondered which system was home.

He rubbed his head against her throat. It was a small movement, a sign of agitation. Claire's own skin felt tender, as though stroked with sandpaper. She could *feel* the people around them becoming edgy.

"Hang on, sweetheart—Mama's coming."

She wondered if she'd survive it. First contact with a Mason jar was one thing; Mama was likely to be another.

But first things first.

She trailed her fingers across his scalp. Her skin imprinted his warmth, his slight weight, his soft breath.

I will buy windchimes to echo your voice. I will hear the world differently. I will never again be too busy to look at the stars.

I'll remember you so clearly that a hundred years from now I'll still feel you in my arms.

Baby yawned an arpeggio. She waltzed him down the hall and settled in the rocker. Its motion lulled them to sleep.

The light woke them.

A freshet of alto notes blew out of the brightness. Baby poked his head through the crook of her arm and warbled. Claire found her feet and brushed her mouth over Baby's. She whispered, "Bye-bye," and wept as she held him out. Smooth arms brushed hers as they took him.

She forced a breath. She could be steady. She would be brave.

Her scream was horrible. Her grief was loud. But no—the scream wasn't hers; her throat would never make that sound without bursting. It was broken ice sliding off the roof.

It dawned on her, "Baby?"

He wobbled out and grabbed her leg. Claire tugged him free and offered him to the light again. He shrieked and clamped his hand around her thumb.

"I'm sorry please oh God I'm sorry Baby she's your *mother*."

A pale hand extended from the brightness. It slipped over Baby's arm and closed around Claire's wrist. *Clink chime.* Not

Catherine MacLeod

Baby.

Surprising herself, Claire smiled. She would continue to love the Baby. If allowed the time, she'd ask how he'd got himself mailed. She'd planned to go back to the real world; she'd never said whose. Specifics were everything.

Be careful what you wish for.

Claire stepped into the light.

Originally published in On Spec Spring 2001 Vol 13 No 1 #44

Nova Scotian author **Catherine MacLeod** spends too much time watching black-and-white episodes of "Gunsmoke" on youtube. Her publications include short fiction in *Black Static*, *TalesBones*, and *Solaris*, and several anthologies, including *Fearful Symmetries*, *The Living Dead 2*, and *On Spec: The First Five Years*.

More Than Salt
E.L. Chen

How sharper than a serpent's tooth it is
To have a thankless child!
— King Lear, Act I, Scene 4

The wino on the corner says he's my father. Ha. My father is some serial jerk who didn't stick around long enough to pick out baby names with my mom.

"Cordelia," the wino says in a bad English accent as I approach the crosswalk. Cordelia's not my name.

I eye the traffic lights. Still red. Great. I shift my schoolbag to my other shoulder and fake interest in the chipped black polish on my thumbnail.

"Cordelia," he says. "Do you not recognize your sire?"

As if I could forget a loser like him. Greasy tufts of white hair and a face sewn from faded red leather. Sprawled against a rusted three-wheeled shopping cart piled with empties, mateless shoes, blankets, and whatever else homeless alkies keep in shopping carts. His voice rising and trembling and dissolving into the dull buzz of afternoon traffic. "Cruel Cordelia," he says, "dost thou repudiate thy father, thy lord, thy king? O, unkind wench, as a serpent's tooth pierces an egg thou rend my heart."

"My name's not Cordelia," I tell him.

"What is thy name?"

I say nothing. I wish he'd ask me for spare change instead, even though what little cash I have has to tide me over until I get birthday money next week.

"If thou dost not know thy name, thou must be a Fool. Come, come, I have need for a Fool." His sunburned face stretches and splits, revealing front teeth stained a malt liquor brown. I wince. He smells like the time I went to Diane Rybcynski's party—back when we were still friends—and at least one person's fake ID had been accepted at the LCBO.

"I don't think so," I say, edging closer to the curb.

At the first glimpse of green, a desperate grip holds me back from the crosswalk as my fellow pedestrians surge ahead without me.

"Watch it!" I yank my arm away and turn to confront the old lech. "What do you think you're—"

The intersection bleeds and blurs before my eyes like a stain spreading on fabric. Only the old wino remains in focus—although he appears to be a different man, straight-backed and proud, his hair tamed by a circle of gold that must be heavier than it looks. I blink. "What—"

> FOOL: —saith my Lord? *(Bows.)*
> KING: Sweet Fool, make me forget that I hath like a trefoil leaf not one daughter but three. Would that I hadst pluck'd the green from the stem ere the rot touch'd me!
> FOOL: I shall make thee merry, Nuncle, and thou shalt forget. *(Pauses.)* Hey! What the hell—

"—is going on?"

I discover that I'm buried in a ragged sweater that appears to be made up of pieces of other ragged sweaters. I tear it over my head; it smells surprisingly clean, like fabric softener.

"Gentle Fool, be merry, make me forget that I hath not one daughter but three," the king says.

King?

I rub my eyes. The old man's wearing a frayed Maple Leafs toque, not a coronet.

Okay. I'm losing my mind. I chuck the fool's motley—the

sweater—into the shopping cart and sling my schoolbag over my shoulder so violently that my textbooks and binders bite into my back. If I don't walk away right now my head is going to burst with the impossibilities.

"Sweet, gentle Fool," he says, "wouldst thou forsake me too?"

"Good sir—I mean—"

I walk away.

The apartment door swings in a wide arc and bounces off of Mom's discarded sneakers. I kick off my boots and peel a crumpled form and a ballpoint pen from the bottom of my schoolbag. "I need you to sign this," I say, stepping into the kitchenette. "Or I won't graduate."

Mom looks up, one hand stirring a pot of spaghetti with a wooden spoon, the other holding one of her night school textbooks. She's still wearing her polyester supermarket smock. "Not again." She tucks the spoon under one arm, smoothes the form on the counter and scribbles her name on the dotted line. "I wish you wouldn't be so rebellious."

"Mom, rebellion is saying 'Screw you!' Not 'You couldn't care less about how we do in your class 'cause your pension kicks in next year.'"

"Is that what you said?"

"Yeah. To Mrs. Daniels. 'Cause it's true. She hates teaching English to us."

"Honey, just because it's true doesn't mean you should go around telling people."

I roll my eyes, anticipating her next words. One. Two—

"You need discipline," she says, pointing the wet wooden spoon at me. "If only I'd listened to Oprah and provided you with a father figure . . ."

Three.

". . . you wear those ugly black clothes, you covered up your pretty hair with that dye . . . I wish you'd wear something pink for a change. Why don't you go shopping with Diane?"

Because I'm tired of caring about what people think of me. Because I just want to finish high school and go to college, get out of the city. Because Diane's a bitch.

I say, in my best Diane voice, "Because, like, pink is so *out*."

"And honey, *call* when you're going to be late. I've got class tonight. I don't have time to worry about where you are."

"Mom..." The word comes out as two long syllables. "It's not my fault. There was this wino who wouldn't let me go—"

The spoon clatters onto the linoleum.

"Oh my God." Mom splays her book on the counter and picks up the spoon. "Oh my God. Are you all right? Did he—touch you? I'll call Jerry and—"

Me and my big fat mouth. I've unleashed Typhoon Mom. "No, he didn't *molest* me."

"What did he do?"

My mouth's open like Pandora's box, letting everything out. "... and the next thing I know, I'm wearing a Salvation Army sweater and treating him like a king."

Mom rinses the spoon in the sink and raps it against the edge of the pot. "Is this some kind of ploy for attention? Because if it is, it's not funny. I know you don't approve of me and Jerry..."

"No, it's not Jerry," I say. "Forget it."

"Forget it? My *teenage* daughter is spending time with some drunken *pervert* and I'm supposed to forget it? Hon, I don't think that's the kind of extracurricular activity that universities want to see on your application."

"Mom..." Two syllables again, buying me time to scavenge the right words to get her off my back. "He's just a crazy who thinks he's starring in *King Lear*."

"What, does he speak in iambic pentagram or something?"

"That's iambic *pentameter*. And he's probably just some middle-management guy who got laid off from his dot-com and then lost his marbles when his SUV got repo'd. He's harmless."

"Well..." She starts stirring the pasta again, which means that I've almost pushed her over the edge to my side. Almost. "I'd feel better if we talked to Jerry."

So I'm nonchalantly strolling down the street with an oh-so sticky cinnamon bun, a Thermos full of chicken noodle soup and a pocket stuffed with large-sized ZipLoc baggies. Courtesy of Officer Jerry, Mom's gentleman caller. They're not serious, thank God—but they've been "not serious" for four years now.

Sometimes I joke that she should run off to Niagara Falls

with him, but she says she has to think of me. Ha. I'm not a kid anymore; I'm almost eighteen. It's like she's using me as an excuse to keep Jerry at arm's length. Using me as an excuse for her ho-hum life of wasted chances. At least that's what I tell myself when I'm being optimistic—that it's an excuse. It beats being a *reason*. It beats the truth.

See? Can't even keep my mouth shut when I'm talking to myself.

"Cordelia!"

The wino who thinks he's King Lear raises a paper-bagged bottle in salute. "Hey there, Your Majesty," I say. "Got room on your throne?"

As I squat beside him on a flattened cardboard box, I realize that he's got the best seat in the house—a panhandler's-eye-view of one of Toronto's busiest intersections. People scurry past, like roaches flushed out of the shadows by a flashlight, ignoring everything around them except for some point in the horizon.

The old guy still smells like a house party, minus the pot. The mouldy sweat odour makes up for it, though. I don't know how Jerry talked me into this.

The bun, first. "I'm not Cordelia. I'm your Fool, remember? I brought you something to eat." I hand him the cinnamon bun. I expect him to tear away the waxed paper and devour the bun in a single gulp, but he eats with dignity, tearing off bite-sized pieces with his fingers and chewing each thoroughly and thoughtfully.

"My thanks, good Fool," he says.

"No problem."

The soup, next. I pass him the Thermos. His hand fumbles with the smooth surface; our fingers touch. The world splits and slides away, like parting curtains.

"Damn," I say. "Not—"

> FOOL: —again, Nuncle, what merriment shall I devise? I'll make a Fool of you yet, and embellish thy noble countenance with smilets.
> KING: (*Gesturing.*) Take up thy sceptre, Fool, and sound thy unruly bells. I would see thy exertions.
> FOOL: (*Rattles sceptre at passing maid.*) Good mistress, spare a coin for a wise man and a Fool.

KING: (*Chuckling.*) Who is the wise man, and who is the Fool?
FOOL: Why, thou art Fool, Nuncle. Art fool for believing thou wert cuckolded by a cuckoo, when the cuckoo is thy child.
KING: Impertinent knave! (*Boxes FOOL's ears.*)
FOOL: (*Dances out of KING's reach. Sings:*)
He who hath been grievously maligned,
With a hey, ho, the wind and the rain;
Must make amends lest he grow blind,
For the rain it raineth every day.
Nuncle, three servants approacheth.
KING: 'Tis my daughters' retainers. Speak, rascals. What saith thy mistresses?
[*Enter* SERVANTS.]
FIRST SERVANT: Oh my God, is this—

"—what you're doing after school now?"

Diane Rybcynski raises over-plucked eyebrows, her lip-glossed mouth curled in a mocking smile. Dylan, her on-again, off-again boyfriend, and her new best friend/flunky Brittany have similar expressions on their faces.

"That's like, *so* gross," Brittany says, wrinkling her nose.

I finger my jester's sceptre protectively—only to discover that I'm tracing the battered ridges of a faded plastic baby rattle. "It's, uh, performance art," I say, tossing the rattle back into the shopping cart.

"Yeah. Right." Diane snorts and struts away.

"You are *so* weird," Brittany says, trailing behind Diane, and I know that exaggerated accounts of my after-school activities will be scrawled inside a stall in the girl's washroom by third period tomorrow.

Dylan lingers like a bad cold. "Listen," he drawls, "if you need a place to stay, you can crash with me. My parents are out of town this week."

"I'd rather live out here on the street, thank you very much."

The leer crumples into disgust. "Freakin' dyke," he mutters, loping after Diane and Brittany. I have to laugh.

I watch Dylan's hand stray to Brittany's hip. She jumps and gives him a smilet—I mean, a little smile. Diane, of course, is oblivious. Some people only believe what they want to believe. Speaking of which—

"Arrogant, brazen rogues! They dare show such insolence to a king? I am not in my dotage! Like a ruthless plague my daughters' enmity hath infected them!"

I take a baggie from my pocket and pick up the now-empty Thermos. The bag makes a metallic, slithering sound as the flask parts the thin plastic walls.

"Farewell, Your Majesty," I say, scrambling to my feet. "Parting is such sweet sorrow."

"Christopher Melchior Barclay," Jerry says. "Retired English prof, drunk tank alumnus and one-time murder suspect."

"*What?*" The word flies out of Mom and me as one voice.

"Are you sure?" Mom asks.

"The fingerprints were pretty clear," he says. "Pulled up a recent drunk driving conviction. Name rang a bell, so I did some more digging." He hands her a sheaf of photocopies. "Last summer they fished his runaway daughter out of Lake Ontario. Her sisters said that before she left, she'd had a big fight with their dad over her boyfriend, so he was a suspect."

"So he's an alcoholic ex-con," Mom says in a pointed I-told-you-so voice.

"Not exactly. He's old, and the traffic cops nabbed him before he hurt anyone, so he got off with a license suspension and community service. And the judge recommended rehab and grief counselling."

"I don't think it worked," I mutter, peering over Mom's shoulder. Although the photocopy of Emma Barclay's newspaper picture is blotched and streaky, I can make out the dark lipstick, the heavily outlined eyes, the stringy black hair with pale roots, the pout that's just the right combination of boredom and contempt. She probably said a lot of things that people didn't want to hear, too.

"This Christopher Barclay didn't kill her, did he?" Mom says.

Jerry shakes his head. "Nope. It was the no-good psycho boyfriend. Was twice her age and had a history of domestic abuse."

Mom blanches. "Poor girl," she says, looking at me, as if

there's a lesson to be learned from Emma Barclay's misfortune. *This is what happens to teenage girls who dye their hair black and wear too much dark lipstick.*

I take Emma's photo from Mom. The youngest of three daughters, the caption says. The misfit, her sullen expression says. The youngest daughter in fairy tales, the one who's too smart and mouthy for her own good and tells her father that she loves him more than she loves salt. I bet that's what they were fighting about before she ran off.

Or maybe they were fighting over her appearance, like Mom and I fight over mine. Mom thinks that all I have to do is strip the dye from my hair and start shopping from brand-name lifestyle franchise stores, and then everything will be okay. Happily ever after. Like fairy tales.

Although now I know that the stories rarely end well. Even though the prince and princess get hitched, the stepmother dies a horrible death. Forced to dance in red-hot iron shoes until she drops dead. Or rolled through town in a barrel with spikes and nails driven into it.

Mrs. Daniels, my English teacher, says that comedies usually end in weddings because the loner protagonist becomes integrated into society through marriage. Think of outcast Rosalind. Fresh-off-the-boat Viola. The fugitive lovers of *A Midsummer Night's Dream.*

But one person's comedy is another's tragedy. Malvolio leaves town humiliated. Phebe settles for second-best because the love of her life is actually Rosalind in disguise. Demetrius never receives an antidote to the love potion, which I always found creepy. And all sorts of nasty, R-rated things happen in fairy tales to those who don't quite fit into the new status quo.

Bad things happen when you don't fit in. When you're too smart and mouthy for your own good. When your name's Cordelia and you refuse to suck up to your dad.

"Obviously Barclay's fixated on you because of the surface resemblance to his daughter," Jerry says. "But she's in no danger," he adds, turning to Mom. She's still looking at me. I duck my head and scratch at my nail polish. Little black flakes fall to the faded carpet like freshly ground pepper.

"The boyfriend definitely killed Emma," Jerry says. "Barclay's probably just mad with grief. I mean, can you imagine? You have a big fight with your daughter, words are said that you can't take back, she storms out—and you think that one of these days you'll forgive each other, but you never see her—"

Mom's gaze bounces off of me to Jerry. A stricken expression flashes across her face. Maybe she was remembering her own father, who died before I was born.

"Sorry," Jerry says, after an awkward silence. "I'm rambling. Now, your mom says you've been sharing hallucinatory experiences with this guy?"

The way he puts it makes me realize how crazy it sounds. "Uh—"

"Did Barclay give you anything?" he says in a patronizing voice. If his station interrogates suspects with the old good cop/bad cop routine, he must be the good cop. "Something he said would make you feel good? Open your mind? Make you *cooler* than the other kids?"

"Drugs? You think I'm on *drugs*?"

I look to Mom for help. She says, "Honey, you *have* changed dramatically this past year—changed your clothes, your hair, cut off all your old friends—"

"Take a urine sample if you want. Jeez." I throw up my hands, trying to think of a logical explanation to give them. Too much coffee. Late-teens crisis. Hereditary insanity. PMS.

All these explanations seem more ridiculous than a harmless old man whose grasp of reality is stronger than mine.

"I must've been imagining things," I say. "The school year's almost over. It's stress."

Jerry glances at Mom for her reaction. She looks sceptical.

"You know," I say, "it must be those all-nighters I've been pulling, studying *King Lear* for the English exam. I can't give Mrs. Daniels an excuse to fail me, after what I said to her."

He nods. "Well, be sure to get a good night's sleep. You won't be able to write your exams if you're tired."

Case closed, thank God. Mom says, "I'd better start dinner. You staying, Jerry?"

"Sure. Need help?"

He joins Mom in the kitchenette, leaving the details of Emma Barclay's life and death sprawled on the coffee table. I gather them up and chuck them back in their folder.

I almost believe it myself—the all-nighters spent poring over

E.L. Chen

King Lear—except we're doing *Hamlet* this semester.

I hate being a teenager. No one takes you seriously. Adults think you're a rebellious hipster who can't see beyond that festering microcosm called high school. They think you don't know anything, don't understand anything. And we don't. Because no one tells us anything, no one's straight with us. Ironically, the only adult who's been sincere with me is Barclay.

"Cordelia."

And yeah, sure, you can throw pop psychology at me. I've seen enough daytime talk shows to recognize that as the daughter of a working class single mother, I'm using Barclay as a father figure. But the truth is that I feel sorry for him.

"Hi, Professor Barclay," I say, stopping in front of his cardboard throne although I know that there's birthday cake waiting for me at home.

"Thou art mistaken, dear child," he says, tipping the contents of his paper-bagged bottle down his throat.

"Oh. Right." I pluck the baby rattle from the shopping cart and shake it above his head. "I'm not Cordelia, Your Majesty. I'm your Fool."

His face brightens. I drop the rattle back into the cart. "But I can't stay. I brought you something, though." I pull a sandwich and a drink box from my schoolbag. "It's not much. I'll buy you something better after I get birthday money." I set the food on the ground so our hands won't accidentally touch. "See ya."

"I prithee, my Fool," he calls out. I stop, turn. Slowly, because I'm not sure if reality is going to slip through my fingers again, even though Barclay hasn't touched me.

A homeless old man in ragged toque, grimy dress shirt and ill-fitting wool slacks squints at me with bleary eyes. "Dost thou believe that Cordelia shalt return? Her exit was ever so unnatural, so hasty."

"I don't know," I say. "I—I gotta go. See you tomorrow."

I give him an exaggerated bow and nearly knock the briefcase from a passing businessman's grasp. "Crazy teenagers," he mutters, scuttling off the curb and onto the crosswalk. I bow again and start for home.

"Break out the cake," I say as I fling open the apartment door. "The birthday girl's home."

I drop my schoolbag and enter the living room without bothering to unlace my boots. "I accept cash, cheques, and most major credit cards—what's *he* doing here?"

Jerry stands beside Mom, his arm around her shoulders. I think, *Oh no, this is it, they're finally getting married*, but then Mom says, "Honey, I have something to tell you," in a *really* shaky voice, like she's been building up the courage to speak to me for years. And she said *I*, not *we*, so I know that Jerry's only there as moral support. Which perplexes me even more.

Mom holds out a birthday card-sized envelope that's addressed to me in an unfamiliar, old-fashioned cursive scrawl. I take it.

"Who's this from?"

"My—your grandfather. My father."

A chill creeps slowly over my body with icy cold feet. "I thought Grandfather was dead."

Mom takes a deep breath and says, "He is to me." The resigned tone of her voice tells me that she's just burned all the bridges behind her.

"You told me Grandfather was dead." My voice curves upward, high and shrill. Jerry squeezes Mom's shoulder but looks at me, unblinking, unsurprised. "*He* knew—and not me?"

Their silence betrays assent.

"What about my grandmother? Is she dead to you too?"

Mom says, "Mama died when I was young, like I told you. That much is true. But Daddy—" She sighs, and to my surprise her mouth twists into a bitter, contemptuous line. "After all this time, Daddy wants to reconcile. I want nothing to do with him. But you're eighteen now. An adult. You can make your own decisions. You can pass your own judgment on that proud, stubborn son of a bitch."

I'm so shocked at Mom's harsh words that my mouth shoots off without thinking. "Ha. Look who's talking. Now who's the proud stubborn bitch?"

"Watch what you say to your mother!" Jerry barks. But Mom's one step ahead of him.

Her slap hits me so hard and fast that I drop the envelope.

"You don't understand," she says. "I loved him so much. He was my hero. I could always depend on him. After Mama died, Daddy was there to take care of things, take care of me, no matter what. And then he threw me out."

So that's why Mom got all freaked out the other day when Jerry started talking about fathers and daughters. "Because of me," I say, rubbing my stinging cheek.

"Yes." She closes her eyes. "Because I was pregnant with you."

"What about *my* father?"

Jerry says, "Go on. Tell her. She deserves the truth."

The truth. Ha. And Mom's always lecturing me about blurting out things that no one wants to hear. Because no one wants to hear the truth. Look what happens in fairy tales—the king kicks out his youngest daughter after she tells him she loves him more than she loves salt. Lear banishes Cordelia. Emma Barclay runs away.

I squeeze out a small smile. A *smilet*, as Barclay would say. And suddenly I understand what Mrs. Daniels means when she says that there's little difference between comedy and tragedy. No one likes the truth, so they laugh at it. They laugh because if they don't, they'll cry—or start screaming.

I say, "So my father's not a jerk after all, even though he ditched you when you got pregnant? And all this time I've been hating him when he's really a saint."

I stare in horrified fascination as Mom's eyelids flicker and a single tear escapes, running down her face in a thin rivulet.

"Honey," she says, "your father raped me."

Oh dear God.

"He took me home after a dance . . . Daddy was out, and—and—"

Oh. Dear. God.

"It was a small town, you know. Word got around. Everyone thought it was my fault, that I'd led him on. They didn't have words like 'date rape' back then. Good girls didn't do it; bad girls did and got what they deserved."

Emma Barclay's sulky, dark-lipped face flashes in my mind. The misfit. The daughter who's too smart and mouthy for her own good. Had Emma gotten what she'd deserved? Bad things happen to those who don't fit into the status quo, after all. Look what happened to Mom.

Does that mean *I'm* a bad thing?

Now that she's confessed the brunt of the truth, her remaining words flood out. "When Daddy found out I was pregnant he kicked me out and I haven't been back since."

Oh dear God, say something. For once in your life, can't you say something?

"You told me Grandfather was dead," I say.

"He is to me."

"You told me lots of things."

Jerry says, "She doesn't have to justify her choices to you! She was only trying to—"

Mom holds up her hand. Jerry shuts up.

"You were little," she says, "and wanted to know why other kids' drawings of families were different than yours. You couldn't understand."

Couldn't understand. How condescending. I'd expect that from Jerry, not Mom. "Please," I say, realizing helplessly that I'm about to be very cruel. But it's so easy to be cruel. Easier than swallowing pride and admitting to things that are better left unsaid. "Please, help me understand. You lied to me all these years. Or did you mean to tell me, but got caught up in the illusion that we were a happy family of two? The two of us, against him? Do you wish it had never happened? Do you wish that my f—"

I choke on the word, but then I wield it like a blade, as sharp as a serpent's tooth. "Do you wish that my *father* hadn't touched you? Do you wish I'd never been born?"

"Honey, that's not fair."

"*Do you?*"

She looks away, unable to give an answer. She looks away at the stack of night school textbooks, the polyester supermarket smock tossed over the second-hand sofa, the faded linoleum in the kitchenette. She looks away, but it's answer enough.

I'm eighteen now. An adult. I can make my own decisions. I choose to start walking without any direction save for the front door.

People laugh at the truth because if they don't, they'll cry—or start screaming. Surprisingly I haven't started laughing or crying or screaming yet. I don't know what I feel. I just know that I have to keep walking, or else the terrible truth will catch up to me.

"Cordelia, whither thou goest, child?"

"Hi, Professor Barclay," I say.

His face struggles with the name. "Thou art mistaken."

"Please," I say, wearily, "not now."

"Art thou ill? Thy wraith-like appearance distresses thy sire."

Barclay reaches for my hand. I pull away but it's too late. Our fingers graze each other. The world twists and tumbles. Turns upside down and inside out. I don't know if it's Barclay's madness or the weight of Mom's confession that's pressing down, overwhelming me, spinning me like a top.

And I remember that he's the only adult who has ever been honest with me, who has ever told me the truth—albeit *his* version of the truth.

"Father," I say. "Sire."

Barclay's hand trembles around mine.

"Sire—"

> CORDELIA:—'tis I, regretful Cordelia, thy once-beloved daughter. I beg thy forgiveness for my trespass.
> KING: *(Embraces CORDELIA.)* Nay, thou art a Fool. 'Tis I who must plead forgiveness of thee.
> CORDELIA: Sire, I... (Steps away.) No—I cannot—I can't—
> KING: Cordelia, daughter, thy vexation is unseemly.
> CORDELIA: I can't—no—

"—*no.*"

I break away from Barclay's grasp. This is no more real than my childhood, when it was just Mom and me united in the wake of my supposedly deadbeat dad. It's just another illusion. I squeeze my eyes shut, forcing out the vision of Barclay as King Lear. Two men dance in front of me, fighting for my attention: one with dignity, one without, both sad and tired.

Part of me wants to believe that this white-haired old man is my father, instead of the bastard who wouldn't take no for an answer. But the other part of me is brewing anger in a cauldron too small for its contents.

No. This is no more real than my childhood. "For the hundredth time, I'm *not* your daughter. I'm nobody's daughter." I push down the hurt; anger oozes and bubbles up around it, taking its place.

He grabs at my hand again. "Cordelia, daughter—"

"Let go!" I wrench myself away. *This is no more real than my childhood.* "Your daughter's dead! Your daughter's *dead*, old man. Don't you remember?"

He drops my hand as if it were a live snake and suddenly I'm left with the vision of one man. Barclay. Not the proud king, nor the delusional professor, but Barclay as he must have looked the second he heard his youngest daughter had been murdered. As I must have looked the second Mom told me that I had no father, only a history of violence and family scandal. The look of someone who has nothing—no hope, no love, no reason for living.

At least I have Mom, and as much as I hate to admit it, Jerry too. You've got to like a guy who loves your mom, without pressure, without ultimatums, without words, even though he's not getting laid.

Love without words. I want to tell Barclay I'm sorry, but for the second time in my life I'm speechless. This is what all those misfit girls—Mom, Cordelia, Emma Barclay, that youngest salt-loving daughter in fairy tales—must've felt that fateful day they were banished from their home. A terrible helplessness, an inability to think of the words that'll make everything all right again, the words that'll make their fathers love them again.

A deflated shell of a man sits before me on his cardboard throne, weeping uncontrollably. "Emmy," he says. He looks up at me and smiles sadly—one of those tragedy-defying *smilets*. There's a little bit of Lear in his eyes, but I know that the king is gone.

Barclay's delusions were no more real than my childhood. But they were real to him; hope was all he had left. And I took it away. Me and my big mouth. I take his wrinkled, sunburned hand in mine. Nothing happens—he's still Barclay, still weeping, repeating Emma's name over and over as if it'll bring her back.

I sit with Barclay until I can't watch his pain anymore—a mirror of my face half an hour ago—and then I retrace my steps back home in fierce, rapid strides.

So my happy childhood was a big fat lie, but it was real to me. Maybe Mom wasn't as happy, but I can see now that it took guts to raise me. She could've abandoned me, or given me up for adoption, or she could've let herself become overwhelmed with resentment. But she didn't. That took strength. And love. Like telling your royal prick of a dad that you love him more than salt.

Mom emerges from the kitchenette as I burst into the apartment.

"Honey," she says, her smile faint but firm, "you're just in time for cake. Happy birthday."

Her eyes are as red as mine but neither of us mention it.

"Thanks, Mom," I say. *I'm sorry and I love you,* I don't say. I give her a hug that breaks the world record for length and ferocity. Some things are sweeter, more honest when left unsaid. And sweeter still when understood without words.

She pulls a white envelope from between the pages of one of her textbooks. At first I think it's my eagerly anticipated birthday money, but then I see that the flap is torn and the front is addressed in a now-familiar, tear-stained, old-fashioned cursive.

"He sent me one too," she says, and I know that even though Barclay will never have his Cordelia, Mom's found her Lear. Exeunt all.

I adjust my grip on my duffel bag and pray that my good dress isn't too wrinkled under a couple weeks' worth of laundry. I hope my wedding gift surprises Mom; my roommate helped me strip the dye from my hair last night, revealing a natural brown.

The panhandler perched on the corner mumbles to himself, even though I'm fair game; a young student home from college for the weekend, sure to have change in her pockets. After all, she needs quarters to call her parents from the bus station. But the old man stares at the asphalt, knobbly knees pulled under his chin, his chapped lips opening and closing silently. He doesn't even look up at the well-dressed woman who stands in front of him, speaking in low tones.

I draw closer and realize that the panhandler is Professor Barclay, and the woman looks like—

"Emma?" I say, unable to help myself.

The woman turns, her eyes widening with shock and trepidation, and I see that the resemblance is only faint. She's a good ten years older. One of her sisters, then. "Regan," she says.

To cover up my embarrassment, I point at Barclay and say, "I thought he was in rehab."

She closes her eyes, briefly. "He was. Got him off alcohol, but they couldn't do anything about his stubbornness." Her smile is rueful. "He won't talk to us."

She bends over her father and tucks a twenty into the empty coffee cup at his feet. "See you next week, Dad," she says, walking away. He continues to mumble without acknowledging her.

I drop my bag and squat beside him. I have to lean in to hear his voice above the traffic. "*Actus est fabula*," he says. "*Actus est fabula*."

But even though Mom and Jerry are getting married, the play's far from over. Minor characters bleed off the stage and into the wings. Malvolio leaves town humiliated, swearing revenge. Demetrius never receives an antidote to the love potion. Barclay returns to the streets, and I'm the same misfit I always was, albeit with different coloured hair.

"Hi, Professor Barclay," I say.

He tilts his white head, noticing me at last. "Do I know you?" he asks.

I settle back on my butt and sit cross-legged. Mom and Grandpa aren't expecting me for another half hour. "My lord, dost thou not recognize me?"

He squints. "Cordelia?"

My smile wavers for a second. "No—'tis thy Fool, Nuncle."

"Ah. Good Fool. Loyal Fool." I can almost see the dignity seeping back into his bones. His back straightens. His chin lifts.

The baby rattle and shopping cart are long gone, so I pull my keys from my jacket pocket and dangle them from the key ring. The keys catch the light from the setting sun and make a thin, tinny jingling sound, like a handful of bells with stuck clappers. A passer-by drops a quarter into the coffee cup.

E.L. Chen

*Originally published in the Shakespeare theme issue of
On Spec, Winter 2002 Vol 14 No 4 #51*

E.L. Chen's short fiction has been featured in anthologies such as *Masked Mosaic* and *Tesseracts Fifteen*, and magazines such as *Strange Horizons*. Her first novel, *The Good Brother*, will be published by ChiZine in 2015. She lives in Toronto with a very nice husband and their young son.

Where Magic Lives
S.A. Bolich

"WHAT THE—"

It was the fourth time in five minutes Rayburn had dropped the pen while attempting to add up accounts, never his best activity, even when the pen cooperated. It rolled off the desk and struck the hardwood floor with a clatter. He spent several minutes scrabbling under the desk without success, scratching his hand in the process. Finally he gave up and straightened, sucking his hand. And there was his pen, lying quietly atop the day's schedule. He stared.

"I know it hit the floor," he muttered, somewhat spooked. He frowned and reached for it. It rolled away from his touch, skipping maddeningly out of reach. He snapped a word that would have shocked his clients, and slammed his palm down on it. Eyeing it suspiciously, he reached for the morning mail, at which point the pen slithered through his fingers like a greased eel and landed triumphantly atop the schedule again. Rayburn shook his hand, which felt queerly as if the thing had *moved* against his fingers, and glared, baffled. The rotten thing even seemed to have found the same resting spot, snuggling possessively over the last name on the list.

"All right! You win!" he snapped to the air, a habit he discovered himself indulging in more and more. But then

Rayburn Senior's spirit never seemed far, an oppressive nudge peering down at his son struggling dutifully to maintain the funeral home that had been the old man's pride and joy. Ray looked at the last column of the list, which stated the cost of the service, and saw CC in each block in Liz's neat hand. And *that* meant the fixed fee Clark County allowed for paupers.

He sighed, "Go polish your halo, Dad. Even you hated burying vagrants."

Ah, well. Business was business, even if it meant the best parlour would go unused today, its charm hidden away for more prosperous clients. That parlour was the only nice thing in the whole place, trimmed just so, not gaudy, no, but not gloomy either, a place of light from clever arrangement of windows, the slanting rays all congregating on the dear departed, lending thoughts of heaven to those left behind. A masterpiece, if he said so himself, though of course he never did. The last thing people wanted in a funeral director was enthusiasm.

Or red hair, and a terminally boyish face. Liz was the only one who appreciated those. Rayburn the Younger sighed and wondered idly if he could persuade this nagging ghost to just step in and run the place for him while he and Liz skipped out to Tahiti.

He shook his head. "Listen to yourself, Ray," he muttered. "Dad wouldn't get caught dead believing in ghosts."

Which struck him funny, and he started to chuckle, because certainly, his soberly proper parent had been too staid to accept supernatural phenomena. Or magic. Or fun, come to that. The pen was just a pen, and Ray's fingers were cold with January chill, and *of course* that explained why the pen refused to leave the last name on the list when he tried still again to pick it up. This time, it flat wouldn't budge, as if the ink had turned to glue and oozed out all over the barrel.

He stared, the hair lifting on the back of his neck. "All right. I'm looking now, okay?" he said, bending to the absurd.

Cautiously, he reached for the pen. Now he knew for sure it wasn't his father leaning over his shoulder, because whatever was controlling the pen was listening to him. It came sweetly away in his hand. He eyed it, and then cautiously picked up the list and read the name the pen had seemed so eager to point out.

No devils there, just an ordinary name that sounded vaguely

familiar. He frowned, trying to place it. This town wasn't so big that he didn't know all the people worth knowing. But it eluded him, and his frown deepened. "Eleanor Dancy," he muttered, over and over. "Who the heck was Eleanor Dancy?"

"*The Tale of the Oak*," Liz said behind him, and he jumped a foot.

"What?" He was so rattled he dropped the list. Liz bent to pick it up off the floor, brushing long dark hair out of her face as she handed it to him, smiling wisely. "*The Tale of the Oak*," she repeated. "You said once it was one of your favourite books."

"When I was about ten," he answered reflexively, and then his eye dropped again to the list she handed him. "Eleanor Dancy! I didn't know she lives here!"

"Used to live," Liz reminded him gently. "Not many other people remembered her either, it looks like." He remembered her then, the coroner's report that had arrived with the body, of how and where she had been found, huddled alone in a freezing apartment.

"Oh damn," Ray muttered, genuinely regretful. He had been enchanted for years by Eleanor Dancy's gentle books, full of wonderful, glowing characters who rode unblinkingly into danger for the sake of friendship and honour, and sometimes didn't come out unscathed. They had taught him a great deal about living one's life in a fashion *worth* living, and he had kept a tattered copy of *The Tale of the Oak* well into college, when he had let his roommate tease him into getting rid of it. He had regretted it for years, and finally forgotten it—until now.

A deep and abiding sense of shame took him. How could he have forgotten people who had helped shape his life: dashing Alan, laconic Guy, shy William, who had proved the bravest of them all? Or pretty, spoiled Isobel, or brave Anne, or fiery Meg? Or Peter? Lord, he had cried himself to sleep once over Peter, the lonely free lance who had discovered friendship too late. It had been years before he found the courage to pick up *The Winter Knight* again. How on earth could he have forgotten Eleanor Dancy's name, the incredibly gifted lady who had given them all life?

"Ray?" Liz was looking at him oddly, concern in her brown eyes. He shook himself and stood up, glancing at the clock. Elation filled him. There was still time to ready the best parlour before the first scheduled service. Thank God he prided himself on giving even paupers a proper send-off. Eleanor was decently dressed and her hair had been done yesterday by Nora Waters, whose only talent in life lay in her magical affinity for hair. His mouth quirked. *Magic . . . lives where it is welcome.* Hadn't Miles said that?

"Are you all right?" Liz asked softly. "You look like—I don't know. Kind of weirded out. Maybe you should let Jack take Ms. Dancy's funeral."

"No!" he snapped, and put out a hand to erase the instant hurt in her eyes. "I'm sorry, hon. I want to do hers. Her books were such magic, and no one remembers them anymore. She deserves to have one fan—one mourner at least, to honour her and say good-bye. I want to."

She looked at him straightly. "Some days I do remember why I love you," she said, and lifted on her toes to kiss him before marching out to deal with the phone ringing down the hall. "I'll tell Jack to set up Number One," she called over her shoulder.

He shook his head, grinning helplessly. She had read his mind, as usual. He glanced at the clock again and hurried out of the office and down the hall to the best parlour, let himself in and stood for a moment, savouring the wonderful atmosphere in this place. It was very much like a medieval cathedral in some ways, hushed and full of light and reverence, exactly the sort of place to pay last respects to a woman who had brought the Middle Ages to vivid life for thousands of rapt young readers. He moved down the aisle, noting reflexively that everything was dusted and tidy, though the flower stands were empty. *That* was no good. He strained to recall what was in today's flower order that he could filch—

"Excuse me."

The voice sounded tentative, echoing oddly in the hush. He whirled, prepared to be annoyed, and stopped at the sight of a young, red-haired woman peering uncertainly in at the door, just her face visible around the jamb. He halted, professional manners coming to the fore.

"Yes?" he asked politely. "Were you looking for Mr. Edson's service? Two doors down on the—"

"Oh, no! No!" she interrupted rather breathlessly. She had an odd accent, not quite British, not quite French. He couldn't place it. "I wanted El—Miss Dancy's."

"Oh!" It was his turn to be flustered. He had assumed from the fact that it was Ms. Dancy's landlord who found her, several days after the rent was due, that there would be no one to attend her service. "Of course," he managed. "You're in the right place. But you're a bit early, I'm afraid. It's not until eleven. You're welcome to wait, of course."

She came farther into the room, a slim figure in tight pants and tall boots, and some sort of long shirt, the colours and details all but lost in the dazzle pouring in the side windows. All he really saw was the glorious red hair tumbling loose over her shoulders. Not carroty, like his, but that deep rich auburn shade he had admired since he first discovered his own was never going to be that colour.

She slid into a pew. "Thank you," she said faintly. "I will wait. What is the hour now?"

"Um—" He peered at his watch, wondering again about her native tongue. "Five to ten."

She frowned a little uncertainly. "Thank you. Where—where is she?"

She sounded definitely ill at ease. Not an uncommon reaction. He was long accustomed to eyes peering about his establishment as if expecting to see embalmed bodies lying everywhere. He put on his most soothing manner.

"I'll bring her in shortly. Would you like an open casket?"

He distinctly heard her swallow. "N-no, I don't think so," she said faintly, and her accent was suddenly thicker.

"As you wish," he said courteously, and moved toward the side door. He hated wheeling in caskets with mourners already in attendance, but this time it couldn't be helped. Idly he wondered where this girl came from and what her connection to Eleanor Dancy might be.

He busied himself for half an hour, sneaking a few flowers from parlour three, provided by the house to brighten the sad and empty parlours of those people who truly would have no one to see them off. He gave them to Liz to install in Number One, and took himself into the back. He hesitated, eyeing the plain casket he had given Ms. Dancy from the county funds allotted to see her decently interred. Before he could change his mind he transferred her to an elegant mahogany thing no one in this town could afford anyway. It was his favourite, lovingly polished and dusted for the last three years, admired by all, purchased by none. She looked tiny in it, a gentle-looking old lady who had given so much to so many. He smoothed down her faded gray hair, looking down at her face. She had lived right here in his town, and he had not known. He had never even known what she looked like, and now he would be the last to ever see her.

The thought saddened him. Hastily he shut the casket lid before depression overwhelmed him. He wheeled it down the corridor and in at the side door of Number One.

And halted in confusion, staring at the packed pews in front of him. Where had all these people come from? The place was full from front to back, incredible for an unannounced funeral. And then anger overcame the shock, and he caught himself from glaring at them all. Where had they been, these friends of Eleanor's, when she died alone? Why hadn't they cared enough to call her, and discover her before a week had gone by?

Grimly, he wheeled the casket into place. It gleamed in the fall of sunshine, pierced by three long shafts of sun that brought the rich colour up out of the wood and set the brass glowing. *Like gold and jewels* he thought fondly, remembering the various ephemeral objects the heroes of her books had been wont to quest for. Things that had seemed so important until actually discovered, when invariably they had turned out less worthwhile than the friendships cemented along the way.

"Be ye starting soon?" a voice called behind him.

He blinked. A Scot? Here? Good Lord, how extraordinary. Instantly, his mind slipped sideways to *The Hidden Glen* and tall Jamie MacDougall, who had worn knives in his socks and used them once to save his worst enemy, because it would not have been honourable to let him drown in the magical flood conjured by evil Angus o' the Glen. They had set aside their hatred to survive, and ended up friends...

"Sir? Might we see m'lady?"

He frankly stared that time. For the first time in his life he cursed the strong sunlight in this place. Peering through it from behind as he was, he could hardly make out the shapes of the people in front of him, let alone faces, but surely that man over there in the corner was wearing a coat of arms? The colours blazed, red and gold, and however gaudy today's youth had grown, Ray could not think of one who was given to wearing dragons on his chest. *Dragons* . . .

His mind reeled. *Miles* had worn dragons. Sir Miles whose ancestors had been Kings of England back when the Saxons still ruled. God, it had to be a joke. And a rotten, cruel one, to come to a funeral dressed in costume. He took a step forward, a vague notion forming itself in his mind of throwing out the miscreant.

"Sir?"

He placed the voice that time, made out through the sparkle a pretty, earnest face peering up at him anxiously. A face he *knew*. He had seen it a thousand times, caught in living colour in the illustrations for *The Tale of the Oak*. Meg.

She stood up hesitantly, and he saw that she was wearing the same dress. Same flowing sleeves, same tight waist and demure bodice, same girdle emphasizing the slimness of her waist, a shimmer of blue and green beneath a gleaming fall of hair like spun sunlight. Lord, how had she come through downtown dressed like that? His mind groped for sanity and succeeded in building only more insanity. How could she be here at all? She had never existed.

"What?" he stammered feebly, because they were all looking at him now. Their eyes were intent and earnest and somehow more vivid than the eyes of modern people, as if the time they inhabited was so full of sudden death that they had learned in the cradle to pay attention, lest they miss any small aspect of the lives that could be snatched from them so suddenly.

"Might we see her, please sir?" God, it *was* Meg, bold Meg, speaking up for them all.

"Of—of course," Ray stammered, and somehow found his professional mask again. He turned and lifted the coffin lid, exposing the gentle face, which even yet showed nothing of the long days between death and discovery. Thank heaven it had been so cold in that apartment.

There was a stir behind him. Startled, he turned, and saw that the whole crowd of them were on their feet, the foremost craning their necks unconsciously to see past the dazzle into the casket itself. Meg drew in a slow, audible breath and slowly stepped up beside Rayburn, her eyes fixed on Eleanor's peaceful face.

"Oh," she said softly, and her voice was the musical lilt he had always imagined, gentle and kind as the one who made her. Her hand went up to cover her mouth, and her vivid blue eyes sparkled with tears in the brilliant light. Rayburn's training cracked; he half-moved to comfort her, and stopped as someone stepped into the space at his other elbow. He looked up, and saw Sir Miles of Etherby looking gravely down at him. Tall for his generation he had been, Miles, a quiet giant who still stood a full two inches taller than Ray himself, whose six-foot-plus went unremarked in the modern era,

"Might we have a bit of time with her?" the knight asked, his voice a mellow baritone.

"Certainly," Rayburn said, and stepped aside.

He watched, bemused, fascinated as one by one in orderly procession the mourners came forward. *So many*, he thought, *so many children come to pay their respects*. Old, young, children, greybeards—all of the rich and varied populace of a world dead six hundred years—but living yet in the depths of old bookstores, waiting patiently on library shelves for a small hand to turn a page and stumble into magic. Rayburn found his eyes blurring, and lifted a surreptitious hand that came away wet. He was forced to turn away when Peter—it could only be Peter, his grace marred by the limp left over from his last tournament—made his way to the front of the line and dropped lightly to one knee. "I've come, *ma mère*," he said softly, "to thank you."

Gently he touched Eleanor's still cheek. Miles, standing like a guard of honour at her head, reached out and dropped a big hand on the younger man's shoulder. Peter looked up and smiled, and Rayburn looked hastily away.

Presently he looked back, in time to see Peter lift himself to his feet again and stoop to set a light kiss on Eleanor's brow before turning away. Ray did not see who else came after that— did not see anything but a watery dazzle of light filled with shapes impossibly dressed.

After what seemed a very long time, silence descended again. The rustling of clothing and soft shuffling of feet ceased, and Miles' voice filled the parlour. "Good sir, were there words ye wished to speak?"

Ray jumped. His eyes slid reflexively toward the door, which somehow had gotten closed, and then to the minister's pew to one side. It did not greatly surprise him to find someone occupying it, a stooped scarecrow of a man in the plain brown robes of a monk.

"I—" he began, and gestured gracefully toward the monk. How well Rayburn knew him! So stubborn had Father Anselm been in his faith that the Devil himself had gone sulking away from his abbey, and so stubbornly righteous that Sir John and Isobel—there they were, in the second row, still nestling like turtledoves—had spent half of *The Rowan Tree* proving to him they were serious in their defiant quest for marriage.

"There are," he finished, "but I would like to say them after Father Anselm has spoken."

Row upon row of silent eyes assessed him for a moment, and then Miles nodded. "So be it." He turned to the monk, who stood. "Father Anselm. Our lady was no long-winded, so please be ye not, either."

A ripple of laughter ran through the parlour. Rayburn grinned along with them, a thrill of pleasure shooting through him at sharing that private joke. Anselm, as madly intense as ever, gave Miles a withering glare and took his place at the podium, peering at it curiously for a moment before losing himself in the matter at hand. His hand moved restlessly across the polished surface, ignoring the King James Bible that lay there. With another small thrill, Rayburn realized that for Anselm, the words were far older, and written in another tongue altogether.

Anselm lifted his head. His voice was surprisingly melodious, clear and strong enough to come back in echoes overhead. Rayburn looked up, startled, as chanting drifted back like birds from the vaulted ceiling, the beautiful deep chanting of a monkish choir, sounding the responses of the ancient service for the dead. He blinked. Vaulted ceiling? But the light was too bright; his gaze wavered and dropped to the dark figure wrapped in light, straight and unbreakable as the cross itself. The chanting went softly on, counterpoint to a long Latin prayer that Rayburn did not understand, during which no one in the audience moved a muscle. Eventually the monk fell silent, and heads lifted to meet his stare. Ray was shocked to see tears glinting on that ascetic face.

"I shall not speak to ye of the world beyond, or of the fact of

God's good grace with this gentle lady lying here. We know already she is at His knee even now, for sure and the evil one could have no power over her, and her sins so light her time in purgatory was but a breath, over before it was well begun. I shall say only that but for her this gathering could not be, and so let us rejoice in the memory of she who made us, even ye, Angus Blackheart, and a more wicked man I never met."

There was an inarticulate rumble somewhere toward the back, overlaid by a fierce and masculine, "Shush, Angus, ye crashin' bullock!"

"I'll not be shushed by the like of Jamie MacDou—"

"Both of ye shush or you'll both be recitin' paternosters until the Good Lord comes into his own!" Anselm bellowed. Profound silence fell again.

Rayburn fought a mad smile tickling the corners of his mouth. This wasn't really happening. Any moment now Jack the handyman was going to open the outer door and peer in, and find him daydreaming all alone in front of Eleanor Dancy's casket. Unimaginative Jack, whose very footfall would shatter Merlin's most puissant spell.

Stay away, he begged silently, and looked up at Anselm to find the monk watching him expectantly.

"Brother Gregory," the monk intoned, and he jumped, for not even Liz called him by his given name. He far preferred Ray.

"Will you say your piece now?"

Rayburn stood uncertainly away from the wall, nervous, now that it came to it, facing a crowd unlike any other he had ever encountered. The stock words of comfort that fell so soothingly from his tongue stuck there now as he moved into the place at the podium vacated by Father Anselm. What would these intense, deeply religious folk know of the glib lip service of his century to the god they kept at their elbow?

He looked out at them watching him so gravely, a host of people he had never seen—and yet he could name them all, even the red-haired girl who had been the first of all. Dear, hoydenish Anne, whose boy's breeks and boots and skill with a bow had once saved a prince. All at once he realized that if Liz had possessed red hair, she would look just like Anne. Was that why he had been so strongly attracted to her, felt so surely as if he knew her, like an old friend waiting to be? He had no doubts Liz could match any evil Duke ever born . . .

He cleared his throat hesitantly. "My friends," he began, faltered, and went on, deliberately. "Yes, I believe I can say that in all truth. You are my friends, the friends of my childhood and my growing up. For year after wondrous year I lived your adventures. I cried with you, and laughed with you, and ran in breathless fright with you, and stood on lonely hilltops and fought with you. You made my life rich in ways I never even understood until this moment. I am ashamed to say that at some point I forgot you. I forgot Eleanor Dancy. I forgot the elemental magic that created you. But you didn't. You remained true to your own world and to each other, as unchanging as the goodness that brought you forth. You taught me things I can never thank you for. *Eleanor* taught me. This wonderful lady, with her vast talent and imagination, made a whole world in her own image, a thing given to few to do—and fewer to do well. Yet the fact that she did do it superbly is attested to here, today, in the sight of all of you. I look at you, and I think I must be mad. I know you—and yet you never lived. Not really. Nowhere except in the minds and hearts of a million children—and a million adults who were better for the experience. Perhaps I'm dreaming right now, standing here in the dazzle letting myself be carried away by memories brought forth by a name on my roster of services today. Eleanor Dancy. I forgot her once. But I shall not again. And I shall not forget you. My friends. Thank you for coming."

His voice broke. There was a long, intense silence. And then a rustle filled it, and he looked up through tears to see them all on their feet again, nodding at him gravely as they filed past once more. Hands reached to touch him and moved on to trail lightly over the polished mahogany of Eleanor's last dwelling before they faded from his sight, blocked by flowing robes or glinting armour or the rich silks of another time. Gradually the room grew quieter; the faint rustling faded, and he looked up in a sort of panic to see the door at the far end standing open once more and the crowd passing through it one by one. *My God, what if someone sees them?* he thought dizzily. But—he could see the wall of the corridor beyond, despite the silent throng in the aisle. Meg passed through—and disappeared.

"No!" he cried softly, half reaching after her.

"We cannot stay longer," a voice said beside him, strangely compassionate.

He looked up into Miles' grave brown eyes. The knight nodded at him and started past. Ray suddenly could not bear to let him go so quickly. "Wait—please." He caught Miles' arm, and felt with a thrill through his whole body the mail beneath the velvet surcoat. The knight turned and looked at him calmly, but Ray felt his impatience to be gone. Truly his time was running out.

"Tell me—why did you come? *How* did you come?"

Miles gave him a surpassingly gentle look that nevertheless made Ray feel like a slightly retarded child. "She was our mother. How could we not come to honour she who gave us life?"

Ray swallowed hard. "Aye," he whispered, and never heard how he reverted instinctively to speech patterns he had outgrown years ago—the day he set aside these old friends for new ones. "I understand. But—how?"

Miles shrugged. "It is not my place to question the mind of God, good sir. I leave that to the clerics. I am but a knight, and ignorant of such matters. Suffice it that we wanted to come, and it was granted."

He inclined his head politely and moved on, to vanish like the others at the door. Ray stood alone in the sunlight, groping after reality. And slowly a grin started clear at his toes and burst upward through his body until his whole being felt like a smile. He wanted to shout, to dance, to turn handsprings over the pews like a child and run laughing down the halls, trailing magic like fizzing bubbles of joy. How had he forgotten where magic lived?

Softly he leaned down and kissed Eleanor Dancy's faded cheek. "Good night, my lady," he whispered, and gently closed the lid of the casket. An instant later the sun climbed beyond the window, taking the dazzling sunshaft with it. The medieval cathedral vanished along with the faint chink of Miles' mail shirt.

But away up toward the ceiling, sounding softly in quiet defiance of the strictures of adulthood, rang a faint, silvery shiver of notes, like the distant horns of the Faerie hunt, drifting up from 'neath the roots of a great oak . . .

Originally published in On Spec, Summer 2002 Vol 14 No 2 #49

"You kept me up all night!" is something **S. A. Bolich** hears a lot. She is the author of five books, with a new series of six launching in 2014. Her first short story was published in *On Spec*. "Where Magic Lives" was an honorable mention for the Year's Best Fantasy and Horror that year. Her first novel, *Firedancer*, was a finalist for the 2013 EPIC Award for Fantasy.

THE BLACK MAN
A.M. ARRUIN

The suburb of Bergamot View was well-known as a progressive and enlightened community. Many of its inhabitants supported Greenpeace and other radical organizations, whose bumper stickers they affixed to their SUVs and minivans. One neighbour, Ed Czechuk, had in his younger days been a member of a socialist discussion group, when he was still articling for the law firm in which he was currently a partner. He still had much of the literature, stored in an antique trunk purchased at a garage sale put on by the bankrupted farm families; the trunk sat next to a rack of punk rock CDs and a bookshelf containing Marx's *Das Capital* and Guzman's *Living Simply*. Ginger Goodings, who lived at the end of Poplar Lane, had one summer painted the interior of her house in overlapping shades of lime and purple, an eccentricity that was not only tolerated, but lauded in the community as a shrewd resistance to the sterility of commodity culture. Many of her neighbours supported starving children with a monthly allowance sent to Africa or Asia. And almost all agreed, over red wines or double lattes, with just enough irony to soften the guilt, that consumption was not the answer to life's trials and boredoms, and that richness and satisfaction lay mainly in the spiritual and communal. "After all," said Ginger Goodings, "though it is a cliché, money cannot buy happiness."

"Or paint," said her son, Robbie, dead-smash in the middle of his adolescent smartass stage.

"Which reminds me." Doug Smolz, the accountant, checked his Rolex. "I'm late for my meditation class." Doug hated both golf and lawn bowling, which he claimed were potent twin symbols of human alienation and environmental disaster, an argument for which he marshalled an impressive array of facts about fertilizers and water consumption, and which had already convinced half the neighbourhood, though not enough to make them give up watering their lawns.

After many years of charity and goodwill, the community association at one meeting was shocked to realize that the neighbourhood contained only two families of visible ethnicity—the Shimozowas and the Mohranrajes, both with dentists as primary breadwinners. So Tom Hawkins, the association president, stood and moved that the problem be addressed immediately, and the duration of the meeting was devoted to a plan. With funds originally earmarked for the organic garden, they purchased a small, brightly lit flat above the old Chinese grocer's, and decorated it with tasteful furniture and a series of classic novels. Then they sent out a summons, by newspaper and worldwide web, which said:

> *Wanted: one black man to receive free lodging and sundry benefits in the community of Bergamot View. Please apply in person to the Community Association (evenings).*

That evening, the hedge that ringed the woods at the end of Dinger Crescent parted its leafy curtains, and a devil stepped through.

"But you're not quite the kind of black man we're looking for," said Ginger Goodings, the volunteer of that evening. She leaned forward, oddly attracted to this apparition, who put her

The Black Man

in mind of her *Myths to Live By* classes with Guru Babi Cromwell. "You look more like Pan than anything."

The black man did not smile. He said nothing, but pointed again to the summons. So Ginger phoned Gwen Packer, who phoned Doug Smolz, who cell-phoned Tom Hawkins, already on hole seventeen at the local par-four. They gathered for an emergency meeting and interview, at which the black Pan-man said nothing, but continued to tap the summons with a finger. Finally, because even Doug Smolz could not think of a compelling argument otherwise, they agreed to let the black man live atop the Chinese grocer's and become the community's latest and most innovative symbol of political activism. And they threw a block party at which they cooked and ate hotdogs with cheap soda and a modicum of irony, and the kids winged by on skateboards, with stuffed cheeks and dirty mouths, and somebody suggested a volleyball game, and others suggested a speech, but the black man himself said nothing and did not eat.

This was a disappointment that multiplied almost exponentially from day one. Not that anyone wanted their newest neighbour to "jive talk" and "hustle," as Robbie Goodings said. That would be cartoonish, and racist for that matter. But why didn't he speak at all? Why didn't he say thank you, at least?

Soon the black man began to play a violin late into the night. He played well, but it was ludicrous and ungrateful to keep everyone awake, and even the politest suggestion that he close the window or watch the clock was greeted with stony silence. It was also clear, from the dust on the shelf, that he read none of the great literature provided, not even *Othello*, or the poetry from the Harlem Renaissance. Soon a myth sprang up around him, at least among the more charitable folks in the neighbourhood, and it became generally agreed upon that he had been the victim of some trauma, perhaps in his childhood. As Doug Smolz pointed out, just before rushing off to pick up his son from soccer practice, "People who do not conform to white standards of beauty are often subjected to traumatic experience, which we, as the empowered, must try to mitigate."

Still, the disappointment turned to outright resentment for some, on occasion of the three month anniversary celebration of the black man's arrival. He ate three hotdogs at the barbecue, surprising everyone, then proceeded to display a prodigious set of basketball skills in an energetic game of hoops with the kids, followed by a stunning and varied performance of dance moves and rhythmic intelligence which continued through most of Robbie Gooding's funk collection.

Keeley O'Keefe, who taught Celtic Studies at the university, shook her head in disgust. "That's offensive. A catalogue of clichés that serves only to perpetuate the stereotype."

"And it's a stereotype we invented, as the people who have the power," said Doug Smolz. He ordered his sons not to watch.

"Should we take the hoops down?" said Ginger Goodings, at the next community association meeting. "Can we forbid funk?"

Tom Hawkins shook his head. "That would be an overreaction."

Ginger sighed. "I guess you can't force people to have compassion and good values. God knows I've tried with Robbie. He only gets worse."

No one could think of a solution. When the sweet familiar sounds of the black man's violin began, they simply shut the window and decided to go over the community association's books and accounts. They found them completely out of order, and not even Doug Smolz could make sense out of them.

Despite the neighbourhood's percolating disappointments and resentments, a considerable number of women began to get crushes on the black man, first in secret, then more openly.

"He's gorgeous," said Atlanta Bowkers, a doctor at the Women's Medical Centre. "The way his hair goes, almost like he's got horns underneath."

"Makes me horny," Debra Gentry said, a bit hoarsely. "Why I bet he'd really—"

"What?"

Debra Gentry giggled, then coughed. "Said he makes me horny."

She flushed, but they all laughed at the pun, which went a long way toward displacing their isolated embarrassments, and inaugurated an immediate sense of shared secret. Within days, there was an almost virtual community of black man admirers, who recognized each other on the street, and nodded gently, and smiled, and sometimes winked.

"He's a babe," they would say, in the vernacular of the preceding decade. "He is babe-a-licious."

"No doubt. I'd love to see . . ."

At which the conversations would inevitably dissolve into chuckles, and mugs would be sipped, and low-fat bagels bit, and in some cases, though not many, cigarettes lit.

Things might have picked up for the black man, with his growing coterie of secret admirers, had he not one day walked unannounced into the community association offices, sat down without a word, and balanced all the accounting. It took him five minutes. When he was done, he simply rose, closed the books, and brought them to Ginger Goodings, who had been watching and fantasizing about his long ebony fingers.

She phoned Tom Hawkins immediately.

"He's brilliant." She could barely breathe. "He fixed everything. It took him about two minutes."

But Tom Hawkins was not impressed. Neither was anyone else on the committee, nor anyone else who heard the story.

"We could have done it ourselves," said Doug Smolz. "We just didn't have the time."

"I was going to do it this weekend," said Gwen Packer.

Keeley O'Keefe, who had never attended a committee meeting, let alone been in the building, had her own take. "The light is feeble in there. He could simply see the columns more clearly. They have some genetic advantage with their eyes. Good night vision."

"Common among hunter-gatherers," agreed Doug Smolz. "One of the things that makes them superior to those of us in the civilized world."

"My daddy says he's an asshole," said little Dylan Hawkins, at which his father glared, and said, "Who taught you that word?" while everyone else gazed at the floor or their fingernails. Even Ginger Goodings finally disapproved of the black man's accounting, and suggested that Doug Smolz go over the work and correct it in time for the next meeting, to which Doug Smolz agreed, with the qualification that he was quite busy that week, and wouldn't have the time to do it to his complete satisfaction.

Word spread quickly; resentments grew. Only Atlanta Bowkers still admitted to wanting to, as she put it, "take a bite out of the black man." In fact she followed him to the basketball court at the Gwynn Hunter Elementary School one night, just as the moon was peeping through the lattice of poplars on the hill. He had been hitting shots with such accuracy and consistency, and leaping so high, that it looked to be some kind of devilment, and Atlanta Bowkers found a heat flushing down from her belly button, and splitting to sizzle the inside of her thighs.

"Listen, honey." She blocked his way off the court. "I'm a doctor. But that doesn't mean I can't be a nurse."

He returned her gaze with neither interest nor puzzlement.

She went for broke. "Will you tie me up? Toss me around?"

"I'd prefer not to." It was the first time anyone had heard him speak.

Atlanta Bowkers felt such an anger rise in the hollows of her skull that, for a moment, her eyelids went completely dry, and she could not see at all. When the moon misted her eyeballs once again, the black man was halfway across the schoolyard. His legs blurred in a rising mist cloud—droplets breathed from the field's moist belly. Suddenly the sprinklers gushed, floating him up on moonlit rainbows. His feet did not touch the ground again, and he sailed into the night on a chariot of blue mist, looking for all the world like an angel.

The next day, Atlanta Bowkers told everyone she met that the black man was the devil himself.

"I doubt he's the devil," said Tom Hawkins, at the emergency meeting of the community association.

"No." Doug Smolz chewed the tip of his pen, staining his lips blue. "The devil is part of an old Christian myth that has licensed enough misery in the world, thank you very much."

"Yes," Keeley O'Keefe, who had recently found within her a latent activism, agreed. "The crusades. Slavery. Colonialism. The list is long and bloody. No, let us not reactivate the Old World tales of the devil. Let us look for a less incriminatory myth."

"I heard," said Gwen Packer, "that the whole edifice of Christian beliefs is actually built on an older stratum of Pagan mythology."

"You heard that in my class," said Keeley O'Keefe.

"I never took your class. I've never even been to university."

"Then you heard it from one of my students."

"I read it in a book by Guru Babi Cromwell, someone twice as knowledgeable about other cultures as—"

"Ladies," Doug Smolz held up a hand, blue-stained along the fortune lines. "You're both right. There are older models to look at here. We need to give indigenous peoples their due, and recognize where we have stolen their lifeways."

"Were the Celts indigenous?" said Tom Hawkins. "Wasn't anyone there before them? Because those are probably the people we should recognize, the people that had the roughest go of it."

The meeting lasted for five hours, only one of which was actually devoted to practical solutions. Of these, there were only three, soon whittled to one: to find and hire an expert in indigenous pagan mythologies. But this was no easy task. In fact, in the week after the ad was placed, only a few herbalists and chiropractors from the nearby suburb of Hummingbird Hills showed up, and, after their interviews, were all dismissed with a perfunctory "thank you."

"Good lord." Tom Hawkins rubbed his sinuses, after the last chiropractor was gone. "What is the colour of evil anyway?"

"White," Doug Smolz said without hesitation. "Moby Dick was white. He was evil. Batman wears black, he's a good guy."

"What does Robin wear?" said Gwen Packer.

"Green. He wears tights too." Tom Hawkins saw the look on Doug Smolz's face, and quickly added, "Which doesn't mean that he was gay. Or that there's anything wrong with being gay. Not that it's wrong not to be gay. Or not wrong to not be . . ." He rubbed his head.

They made no headway over the next week. Meanwhile, many of the neighbours began to show up in growing congregations beneath the black man's window, where they proceeded every sundown to beat drums to drown out the despicable wail of his violin. Those who didn't own drums either went to buy them at the African Drum Shop, or resorted to rhythmic household items—gonging pots, panging pans, snipping scissors.

"What colour is God?" yelled Keeley O'Keefe at the crowd.

"No colour!" they yelled back.

The drums throbbed. There were phone calls from adjacent suburbs, inquiring into the racket. The *Six O'Clock News* showed up. High school cheerleaders arrived to lend choreographic support, and nobody quite caught the irony that the Bergamot High football team was nicknamed The Devils. Not until Robbie Goodings, who seemed to enjoy the chaos, pointed it out. "Why not make the black man the team mascot?"

He suggested it sarcastically; it was received seriously. "Yes," folks said with a great deal of enthusiasm. "Why not? That's the best thing the neighbourhood could do under the circumstances."

The drums throbbed. Through it all, no one noticed that one evening the black man himself quietly packed up his violin and left by the back door. No one noticed, not for weeks, until one evening Atlanta Bowkers burst sobbing from the front doors, mascara smearing her cheeks in salty stripes, and cried, "He's gone!"—then collapsed to the lawn, while behind her Debra Gentry forgot that the doors opened inward, and, in her roaring hurry to second the news, flattened her face on the glass like a bug on a windshield.

The drums stopped. There was a grand moment of silence, a collective indrawing of breath. Somewhere in the neighbouring suburb of Hummingbird Hills, a police siren unwound itself.

"After all we did for him," said Keeley O'Keefe, finally. The sentiment was echoed in an instantaneous and almost mystical outpouring of collective rage, in which everyone's self-awareness vanished, and the drums pounded again, and the usually composed citizens of Bergamot View began to dance madly, and wailed, and smoked cigarettes materialized from nowhere, and pulled each other's hair, and, perhaps, though it was not substantiated, engaged in unspeakable varieties of sexual commerce with each other's spouses, behind bushes, inside faux-fountains, atop picnic tables.

Next morning, no one was completely clear on what had happened. Tables were overturned. There was mustard everywhere. And the black man—the devil, or djinn, or whatever he was—had truly gone. Robbie Goodings suggested that, if the devil had been watching the night's shady spectacle—already so vacant in collective memory—he had probably decided to leave for good.

"Well, fine," said Robbie's mother. "He was not what we were looking for in the first place."

Days later, Robbie, himself, disappeared. The police found nothing but a cold trail through the woods at the end of Dinger Crescent, where the moon pooled in silver hollows, and the detectives grew sleepy, and emerged hours later with only a hushed memory of violins. They said the boy had likely run away. There was no foul play. There was nothing anyone could do. Ginger Goodings cried for days, and could not sleep at all, not even with the aid of gentle herbs. She spent nights repainting her walls in fauvist greens and yellows, and only came out of mourning to practice yoga and deep breathing on the boulevard.

After several weeks of embarrassed nods and perfunctory hellos, the community association regrouped to organize damage control and a new plan, for the suburb of Bergamot View did not take lightly its responsibilities to social justice and world citizenship.

"We need to get back on the horse," said Tom Hawkins. "We need to address, once again, the imbalance of racial diversity in our community. We need to get someone into that apartment again."

Everyone nodded. Ginger Goodings nodded off.

"But what kind of tenant?" said Doug Smolz. "We need to do it right this time."

"A Celt?" suggested Kelley O'Keefe.

"Not indigenous," said Tom Hawkins.

In the end, they prioritized a list of visible ethnicities, and decided that, in context, a Native American—not an Indian, they were from India—would make the most suitable tenant for the flat above the old Chinese grocer's, given that they were here first, and that they had a beautiful mythological system which could really teach everyone a lot about taking care of the earth, if not the lawns.

The new plan, while not foolproof, was a measurable improvement over the last. Its possible ramifications were thoroughly discussed and specified, its margins for error finessed through a software designed originally by Aruna Mohanraj, one of the suburb's dentists, to track the hygienic maintenance of her patients. So the community association sent out a new summons, by newspaper and worldwide web, which said:

> *Wanted: One red man to receive free lodging and sundry benefits in the Community of Bergamot View. We are very firm on our criterion: you must be a red man. Please apply in person.*

That evening, the hedge that ringed the woods at the end of Dinger Crescent parted its leafy curtains, and a devil stepped through.

Originally published in On Spec, Winter 2003 Vol 15 No 4 #55

A.M. Arruin lives in an abandoned hotel in the Porcupine Hills, with a crow who talks, a cat who wishes he could, and a fish who thinks she can. He was once the author of *Crooked Timber: Seven Suburban Faerie Tales*, along with many published short stories and poems.

PIZZA NIGHT
LAURIE CHANNER

There's a slam like a gunshot going off, makes you and Lesley both jump a foot on the couch, nerves instantly on edge. You look across the clutter of the big loft, to see Tim, electric and alone, near the door, his date nowhere in sight. "Shut up!" he yells over. "She's gone, all right?" He whirls and punches the door, hard, twice, and that shakes you, too. "FUCK!" he blares. Of course he hurt himself. "FUCK!" again. Of course it made him madder. Past the plants, bookshelves and entertainment unit, he kicks at something you can't see, and you hope it's nothing of yours or Les's. You know he's acting out, but it twists your guts to see force applied like this.

He bounds over to his area and turns up his thrash metal. Slipknot or Tool or one of those bands whose name adorns most of his T-shirts. That's not usually a problem, after all; you like Hole.

It's getting harder to hear the movie you rented, but you bite your tongue before daring to say anything. Even before tonight, you've been finding it harder and harder to confront him, because of the ensuing hassles. "C'mon, Tim," you try, more wheedling than decisive. You want this to be a nice night for Les, who's had a bad week with pain. "What's the rule about volume?"

He turns his too-bright eyes toward the two of you. It's well-lit over where he is; he switched on his track lighting a while ago, and Les turned your lights down to watch the TV screen better at the start of the movie. It's like he's showcased in spotlights for you and Lesley, the audience, in the near dark, side by side on the sofa over in the other end of the loft. Tim waits just long enough to make you think he's going to ignore you, which might actually be a relief in itself, but then he hops over to his stereo and dials it down to the marker you all agreed to six months ago when he moved in. It's a line at 6 in red-black nail polish. It's his, from a night he went to see Marilyn Manson. Les threw all her nail polish out years ago, and you've never owned any. Six is still kind of loud, but the loft is big enough that you're supposed to be able to hear the TV in your end while he plays his music in the other end, near the door, no one disturbing the other, especially Lesley now that she's on disability. You wondered when he moved in what you and Les would do if he didn't respect the volume arrangement, what kind of trouble that would be. Those were the days.

Hyperacuity has set in now, though, and you're sensitive to the slightest noise from Tim's end. And the noise is more than slight. He's still pissed, and he's not done showing it. He wants to be noticed, of course, so you and Les avoid so much as glancing his way, the same reason and the same way you've made it a practice to determinedly stare away from stretch limos when you see them gliding through the centre of the city. You don't want to give him the satisfaction of attention.

It's *Lawrence of Arabia* on the DVD player, four hours of it, your pick because you've never seen it before and it's supposed to be stupendous. It's wasted, though, because with all Tim's slamming around, you can't concentrate, haven't picked up on who the characters are or what's going on. Every scene is newly disorienting. Les has had to explain to you nine times who Alec Guinness is playing. You can think of him only as Obi-Wan Kenobi, a calm and comforting presence from *Star Wars*, and

Pizza Night

you wish he was here. Instead, he looks so different in this picture, and it unsettles you more than it ought to. It's only a movie. You reach for the remote, ready to bail on the whole thing, but Les takes it from you. "This is what we do. Don't let him win."

You know what she means. It's Friday night: date night, movie night, pizza night. It *is* what you and she do together, and have done since you met. You do it even though she's barely mobile any more with her fibromyalgia and her wrecked back. It's the highlight of her week now that she can't teach anymore.

The movie's meant nothing to you now, though, since the first half hour. The pizza's sitting cold on the coffee table in front of you, barely touched. Tim *has* won, even though his beef wasn't with either of you. The more he bangs things around in his end of the loft, the more he enlarges his own angry sphere. He's constricted yours and Lesley's two-thirds of the loft until it feels like the two of you are sitting together on a little life raft the size of this couch, this table and this TV screen, exposed and adrift in his turmoil.

Tim is puttering slightly less noisily on his side of the loft. You sneak a look and see he's rummaging through desk drawers, in the manner of a Muppet, even down to tossing the stuff he doesn't want willy-nilly back over his shoulder. He moves to the kitchen, does the same through the utensil drawers.

"I can't find the big scissors!" he yells. "Where's the big scissors? I need the GOOOOOOD scissors!"

You stop looking. You know the sound each drawer makes, though, and can follow his path by listening, though you're trying not to hear.

"SOMEONE HAS TO HELP ME FIND THE GOOD SCISSORS!"

You sit up straighter on the couch and start to open your mouth to holler back when Lesley puts a hand on your arm. She shakes her head wearily, her meds draining her. This is old news. Tim venting out loud. This is what *he* does. And what it always does to you. It's always the same amplitude whether it's something major like spilling coffee on his computer, or minor, like a pen that won't write. But tonight you don't know why it's especially menacing. Maybe you and Lesley don't need his share of the rent *that* badly.

"Are you just going to sit there, you great fat puddings, or is someone going to help me?"

Lesley shakes her head again. "Don't take the bait," she says, not taking her eyes from the screen. "Don't give him the satisfaction."

Sharing a loft is an exercise in *not* hearing. Your friends always ask, "Sure, maybe you can tune out somebody else's TV or phone conversation, but what about, you know . . . *sex*?"

You actually *can* ignore the noises of him with a girl. In fact, it sounds so embarrassingly clumsy, you'd rather not listen in. And he's had to tune out you and Lesley. He hasn't said it's a problem. In loft-living, when you can't help but hear, the unspoken rule is to at least pretend you don't. Despite the insinuations some people have made about him listening in, you seriously doubt he's been getting off on the sound of two overweight, middle-aged dykes getting at it, as infrequently as it happens. It's not what twenty-two-year-olds salivate over when they think of girl-on-girl scenarios.

But it's why you don't really know what's gone on here tonight. You've gotten so good at tuning out that by the time you actually *did* hear the commotion, the sharp sounds, voices and that final slam, they were already vibrations dying away on the air. And then you weren't sure what you'd heard. And it's *that* and what you have or haven't done about it that's the real problem. Not Tim.

He's still bashing around in his end, muttering away to himself, occasionally tramping back and forth to the bathroom, and you feel small in the face of it. You finally say to Les what's been bothering you the most. You say it very quietly, sunk down as you are on the couch, partly so Tim can't hear, and partly because you're ashamed. It's over an hour too late. "I think he hit her."

Lesley's answer is quick. She's not as zoned on her medication as you thought she was. "No, he didn't. He wouldn't. We were sitting right here."

"We heard something."

Les is firm, "That was a door slam."

"You don't want to believe he hit her because we didn't do anything." All the things you and Les have stood for, marched for, spoken out about, the rainbow of ribbons you've worn. But that was years ago, before you both got so tired. Take Back the Night? Hell, tonight you can't even Take Back the Loft.

"It wasn't the sound of flesh hitting flesh," Lesley says, "It was something hard. She slammed the door on her way out or he slammed it after her. She's not here anymore, is she?"

You cast your mind back to that one specific moment, the first minute everything changed. There were raised voices you hadn't been properly aware of except in retrospect, and the one loud sound that drew your attention to the fact that *something* had been going on. Les is right, it wasn't a smack on skin, nor even a fist to soft flesh. It had been harder, sharper, woodier. It could have been the door. It could have been a body hitting a wall or something. But there was only one slam. The girl was gone now, so it had to have been the door. If she'd been slammed first, there'd have been two sounds. You take some consolation from that.

You know, however, that you're rationalizing. Whatever the details, something happened tonight, under your roof, and the more it sits with you, the worse it sits with you. Something that caused Tim's date to leave so abruptly was maybe something you and Les should have stepped in on. You are more uncomfortable than ever.

Eyes on the screen, you wish the movie was shorter, because you can't bear the thought of sitting here, miserable, unable in your current circumstance to comprehend a word of it for another two hours plus. It might as well be a foreign movie with no subtitles and no dubbing, as you stare dumbly at it, not seeing. At the same time, you wish the movie was longer, because as soon as it's over, you will have to move, speak, interact. Something more will be expected of you and you're afraid of what that will be, or what effect it will have. For now it's cover to hide behind. *This is what we do on Friday nights.* Instead of watching the moving images, all you can do is watch the digital counter on the DVD player tick over slow seconds.

"SHIT!" It's another gunshot. You jump a foot, your nerves jangled all over again. Tim spikes at full voice over on his side, and throws something into something else with a loud metal clang. Lesley takes another piece of pizza. You don't know how she can. The last bite you had tasted like you were eating the box. Tim works away at something on the other side of the loft, his back to you at his desk. You guess he's found the scissors, or a suitable substitute.

In a few minutes, he canters cheerfully over to in front of your screen.

"Do you mind?" Lesley says, her irritation plain, craning to look around him. You have to look at him. To do otherwise would be to behave differently, exactly what Lesley told you not to do.

Tim doesn't look like a Muppet now. He used to, his baby face with the short white-blonde hair and goatee framing it top and bottom. He's got his pizza box, the other half of the two-for-one deal you phoned in for at the start of the evening. The orange and white box is greasy and red-smeared, as is his shirt. "Want this?" he asks. "I don't." He doesn't wait for an answer and flings it onto the table, showering crumbs all over, knocking the remote onto the floor and spilling your Diet Coke over the magazines which slide off in a slow cascade, taking the pizza boxes with them.

"Tim, you idiot!" you cry out and jump up reflexively. Now you're alive, Coke dripping onto your socks. But oddly, you're shaking too. "Look at the mess you made!" you say, trying to hold on to the indignation even as your spirit drains away. How many times have you said that?

"Understatement of the year," Tim laughs, unfazed, and bops off.

You don't know what's gone on in the movie, but suddenly, there's Peter O'Toole at a bar, leaking blood in wet stripes through the back of his khaki shirt. Something has happened there, too. You lose it and start to sob tearlessly. "Don't," Les says quietly to you. "It's okay. Just stay in this minute. Get through this minute." She moves to get up. "We need to wipe this up."

"No," you say. Her back is bad tonight, more than usual,

Pizza Night

which is why it was supposed to be a quiet night in, not worrying about lumpy movie theatre seats, or hard chairs in the pizza place, just the couch and the heating pad she needs. "I'll go get a cloth."

"Wait," she says, "just use these." She hands over the orange and white napkins that came with the pizzas. "Don't bother going all the way over there. Stay here."

You get it. The kitchen is over by Tim's space, near the door. You'll have to go past him to get there. For the first time you realize that maybe Lesley is rattled by him tonight, too. You start mopping up.

Lesley slides awkwardly onto her knees on the area rug, picking up the crusts and crumbs that spilled off your plates. She's moving so painfully. "You shouldn't be doing that," you say.

"No," she agrees, but carries on.

You pick up Tim's pizza box. "It feels like they didn't even eat any." You flip it open and it looks like you're mostly right. Someone's eaten all the outer crust and toppings off, leaving the entire soggy white middle crust underneath, redded over with the remnants of sauce. Maybe *that's* what they fought about, Tim snarfing all the toppings. A word floats into your brain out of nowhere, half-heard and half-remembered. *Pizza-face*, said a woman's voice. It was part of the fight at the door, the part you hadn't registered before. This makes you smile.

"Gloria." Lesley's voice is tight. She has opened the box after you put it down, to throw the crumbs in. The crumbs are still in her hand as she stares in. Now you see what you didn't before. What's in the box is flat and round and wet, but it's smaller than the large you ordered, not the twin to yours and Les's anymore. And it isn't sliced, like pizza.

What's in the box isn't pizza. It's something bad and it's something to do with the girl, and you don't let yourself think any further than that. This is your mundane life, not a horror movie. Your mind won't go there.

"Glo, this is bad," Les's voice is really strained.

This time it's your turn to deny. "Don't," you say. "He couldn't have done anything. We were sitting right here. Right *here.*" But you realize now that Tim never said his date had *left.* He just said she was *gone.*

But you know this is *not* how young pretty women get murdered. It's supposed to happen in dark alleys, or on remote pig farms. It doesn't happen at eight-thirty at night in an urban loft while two aging lesbians eat pizza twenty feet away *in the same goddamned room,* and watch Peter O'Toole and Alec Guinness playact in their Arab robes and hope the roommate keeps the noise down to a dull roar.

Lesley reaches into the pizza box and picks the thing up out of it. The not-pizza thing turns slowly as it dangles between her fingers, and it's as bad and worse than you thought. It's flesh, limp like fabric. You can't make out details, nor do you want to, but your mind fills them in. It's the girl's face, stripped off her skull. Pizza-face. Oh Fuck. Lesley drops it back into the box, breathing hard.

Your brain won't go all the places it needs to at once. This much you know: with the two of you studiously ignoring him, Tim has already had an hour to do what he wants.

You have trouble wrapping your brain around the thought: Tim did this. Not just to his date, but to you. He brought the box over to show off, and to send a message. *This is what I can do.* Implicit in that is a message about what you *can't.* You both need to get out of here, right now, both to notify someone and to escape him. But to leave, you'd have to go through his space and past the kitchen and bathroom and who knows what other horrors lie there. Also, you do not have a way out of here with Lesley, who needs assistance to walk. And you are not going anywhere without Lesley.

But it's Lesley who acts. She rises slowly and grimly, like a swell on the ocean.

"TIMOTHY!" she thunders.

His head pops up above the back of his futon across the big room. He smirks, knowing he's achieved an effect.

"DID YOU DO THIS WITH MY GOOD SCISSORS?"

The smirk fades into a look of surprise. Lesley's in full-volume teacher-voice now. "I WANT THOSE SCISSORS OVER HERE RIGHT NOW AND THEY'D BETTER BE SPOTLESSLY CLEAN!"

Tim's head disappears again. You gasp and hold your breath.

Pizza Night

Will Lesley's teacher-tone just set him off again? How many times can a grenade go off in one night?

"Grab the phone," she says quietly and urgently to you, while Tim isn't quite looking. He's now in the kitchen, running water and rubbing at something.

You look blankly at Les, your mind whirling. "Just get through one minute at a time," she says. "Get the phone," she repeats.

You try to go there, grateful not to have to think back, or ahead. The phone. It's a cordless, and hardly ever where you want to find it. "The phone," Lesley says again, looking at the end-table where it usually sits within her reach while you and Tim are at work. It's not there. "Where is it?"

You have to think back for this. You remember. "It's charging." It started beeping when you phoned for pizza. You also can't help but remember something else: that this was when Tim was still getting along with his date and they both chimed in on the order. You start to shake and try to get back into this minute and only this minute. Where is the charger? In the kitchen. His end.

Tim reappears with the big shears in hand. It is not a sight that gives comfort. He approaches. *Oh God what was she thinking?* He's going to hurt you both because you know what he did. He made sure you knew.

"There!" he says. "Happy?"

Lesley, like she doesn't know enough to be afraid, grabs the scissors right out of his hand. He's half-turned to go.

"Timothy!" Lesley says warningly.

Big, aggrieved sigh, like a kid. "Whaaat?"

"If I go into that bathroom, is it going to be a pigsty? Because if I go all the way over there with my sore back, and it is, there's going to be hell to pay."

He snorts. "You can't walk. You need a bedpan. You can't do anything."

He's summed it up. This is why he could be obliging about the scissors. He's in charge of everything else. Les is, or seems, oblivious. "And you better not have made a mess of Glo's nice clean kitchen!"

"It's a whole fucking week since Gloria cleaned, you stupid cow!" he yells back.

"Then it's your turn now," Lesley says calmly. She shoves the pizza box at him. "And keep your goddamned messes off our side of the loft! What have you been told about that?"

Tim pulls the limp, fleshy mess out of the box, takes a bite out of the middle of the forehead, and spits it at Lesley. Then, as he stomps back to his zone, he turns and hurls the entire pizza box through the bathroom door.

You don't know how, or if, this will end. It feels like it's been forever since it started, but it's maybe been only another hour. Peter O'Toole is still on the screen, anyway, though you and Lesley aren't making any pretence of watching anymore. Tim is restless in his end of the loft. He doesn't seem to know, either, what happens next. You all know what the standoff is. If he leaves, you and Les will contact the authorities. If you try to leave, he has to do something about you. Until then, you're all trapped in this limbo. You're frightened, but also pissed off that he hasn't thought it through, that you're all stuck like this. He still has his music on and sits on his futon swiping through his ipad, where he can see you and Lesley and the door. You notice that somewhere along the way, he has taken the phone from the kitchen.

From where you sit, it looks like an ordinary Friday night again, as long as you don't think about what you can't see from here. And, since Lesley told him off about the mess, it's played like an ordinary Friday night, almost like you're all pretending nothing has happened. It's too surreal.

Not everything is frozen in time. The Diet Coke you guzzled earlier with your pizza is killing your bladder now. You can't hold it anymore, and you say so to Lesley. "I don't want to go in there, but I have to. Think he'll let me?"

She shrugs. "When you gotta go, you gotta go," she says, trying a supportive smile. She squeezes your hand.

Tim's head pops up when you walk as nonchalantly as you can over there. He glances at the phone, beside him on the bed, just to make sure. For your part, you try not to look at anything but the bathroom door. If only you could all pretend nothing had happened. Smears on the floor and the furniture over here catch your eye, though, and you know that isn't possible. The

Pizza Night

worst of it is probably around the next dresser, or in the kitchen. You're glad the bar-height counter and stools keep the floor out of view for now.

Once in the closet-sized bathroom, added by the developer as an afterthought, you close the door, wincing at the splayed pizza box and its contents ploughed against the far wall, under the sink. And suddenly, it's just you in the tiny room, gasping at what's been dumped in the shower stall. It makes you gag and almost vomit in the sink. You can't look.

And now you're certain: none of you is getting out of the loft. It's an almost calming thought, because it seems right punishment for your failing to stop it. Tim's date didn't make it out, why should you?

You still need to pee, more than ever, and you turn to the toilet while avoiding looking at what doesn't even look like a person anymore. But even then, you don't pull the shower curtain to hide her—it wouldn't be right. She shouldn't be put out of mind like that. You're ashamed that right now you can't remember her name.

When you're peeing, you hear Les's voice, sharp. "Tim!" There's a long scraping sound. "Gloria!" she shouts urgently. You stop, mid-stream, jump up, dripping onto the floor, and immediately try to push the door open, but of course you can't. The handle turns, but he's pushed a wardrobe in front of it. Lofts don't come with closets. "Tim!" You pound on the door. "Lesley, are you okay?"

So he has thought it out. He's just been waiting for you to move.

"Kill yourself already," you hear Lesley say. "You know you're going to."

Then— "Glo—"

It's cut off by another sound, and this time you know it's the sound of a fist on flesh.

You yell and pound. You go berserk, bouncing off the door in your own panic. It's a long time before you stop to catch your breath. And then you hear something—a faint voice, way off.

"*Lesley!*" you scream.

Yelling to each other, she tells you what you need to know. Tim has tied her to a radiator in the other end of the loft, in your bedroom area. He hurt her some, enough that she probably couldn't move even if she was free. She won't tell you more, because it doesn't seem to matter now. Neither of you is getting out of the loft.

"Did he leave?" you call.

"You could say so," she says. "He's on his futon." After a second's pause, she adds, growing fainter, "He used the good scissors."

Despite everything, you actually laugh at that.

It's hot. You finally remember that the bathroom has a window, head-height, that you open, but it's tiny. You'd never fit through it. You wouldn't even have fit through it twenty years ago. It overlooks the alley, but no one's out there now. It's a garment factory on the other side. No one coming to work now till Monday. First break at 9 a.m. when all the immigrant Russian workers go out to the alley to smoke.

Monday. You holler out encouraging things to Lesley while you rummage around the little cupboard in here. She doesn't answer, but you know she's saving her strength. You can make it to Monday, and she can too. And if you're too weak to speak for yourselves, you can drop out a note.

The only paper, though, is t.p., which will flutter away in the breeze. Then you see the pizza box. Miracle of miracles, it's the one with the receipt for the order still taped to the lid. Yours and Les's phone number, address, everything. You could add a note on the cardboard. But a grungy pizza box in an alley won't attract any attention, so you need something else.

And then you see it. For real this time. It's spilled out on the floor under the sink like an abortion, a couple of feet away from where it used to belong, on the body in the stall. You very, very gingerly reach out, with a tentative finger and spread the flesh out on the tile.

It is her face. It looks wrong, but still real. It's disturbing, which is what you want. Someone will see this. Someone will point and stare. Someone will call out to others. It will attract attention, disrupt the shift, result in authorities being called. Someone will look at the pizza box, and then, someone will come to investigate.

You're suddenly struck by what you're about to do. You didn't help her. But surely she'd help you if she could. You stroke the skin of her cheek lightly. Then you put her in the box, and force the box out the tiny window, praying.

You tell yourself you won't think about how it could all go wrong. You should have waited to shove the box out on Monday morning. Stray dogs sniffing it out, an early snow that covers it up, or it simply lands without spilling its contents.

You tune those thoughts out the way you learned to tune out sounds in the loft.

You call out to Lesley. Someone will come. You sit and wait.

Originally published in On Spec, Summer 2004 Vol 16 No 2 #57

Laurie Channer is a Toronto writer. She won second prize and an honorable mention in successive years in the Toronto Star Short Story Contest and has had her debut novel *Godblog* optioned for film. She is currently working on a mystery/thriller series of novels.

Boys' Night Out
Rob Hunter

Sally Schofield was new to Sur la Mer and with the soccer mom's requisite formula family: minivan, flaxen-haired children only moderately overweight, large hairy husband with pattern baldness. The invitation was for cookies and conversation. It had been Hilary Braunstein's turn to break the news.

"Did I ever tell you about David, my first husband?" The two women were seated in a suburban kitchen, an American icon: coffee and cookies and a carafe of freshly cut daisies formed a barricade across the centre of a polished granite countertop, defining their spheres. The newcomer was seated near the door—an easy exit.

"Sorry? I didn't realize you had been married before." Sally's cookie was dipped, tentatively, held under the steaming surface, then removed. *Well, we're cutting right to the chase, aren't we?* thought Sally. The cookie was not eaten, but studied.

No collagen here, thought Hillary Braunstein. Sally's cookie was held poised at lips too full, too young, too moist and sensuous to be anything but the genuine article.

"He wasn't . . ." began Sally. Had David died in the war? Unlikely. The cookie's fate hinged on Hillary's answer. The question and the cookie hung between them.

"A gated community like Sur la Mer should be the ideal place to raise a family," said Hillary.

Evidently, whatever had or had not happened to David was on hold for the time being. Hillary's veering off topic was considered endearing by her friends. "You never know where Hillary is headed next," they said. Sally found it irritating.

"You know—as far from New York as you can get and still be in it," said Hillary. "Ocean bathing surrounded by water on three sides . . ." She made a needless adjustment to the perfectly arranged daisies. ". . . and that nonpareil view of the lights on the Verrazano Bridge. At night, of course."

Five blocks.

The year before their move to Sur la Mer, Jim Schofield had leaned into the wind and pulled his chin lower into his coat collar, shoulders hunkered up against a March wind scuddering in from the Jersey piers.

He should have stayed in Wisconsin. It was five cross-town blocks to where he'd parked his car—five *Manhattan* cross-town blocks, the better part of a mile—in the rain, sleet, snow and the pounding heat of high August.

An exquisite pain took that moment to drive a rusty cavalry sabre into the pit of his stomach. That second martini at Lloyd's Bar. Or was it the third? He'd have to cut back. Jim gagged at the curb. He bent over with his head between his knees and vomited in cascading waves. He felt immediately better but his eyes were now blinded by tears. He felt for the curbing with his heel, but it wasn't there; he tripped and stumbled. In a yellow arc, a medallioned taxi swerved past in a tight uptown turn, its driver leaning on the horn and screaming curses in a foreign language.

Yeah—from here on out, one drink then home. He should have stayed on the farm in Wisconsin.

Sally Schofield was a pretty blond woman who still looked good in a flowered spring frock. *The luxury of bare arms, not a wattle or a saddle bag on her*, thought Hillary. Sturdy legs—well-shaped, tanned, shaved and moisturized.

"You shave your legs." It was a statement.

Sally looked surprised and re-crossed her legs, a defensive posture. "You'll have to forgive me if I'm a little antsy. I don't do interviews well. That's what this is, isn't it? An interview, the ice-breaker, the Welcome Wagon?" *This was all so very TV-Land*—The Andy Griffith Show, Leave it to Beaver, *just like on cable.*

"Of course, you are in denial."

"What?"

Hillary hummed a slight tune as she dithered with the daisy-painted saucers, sugar bowl and creamer that formed the *cordon sanitaire* between them. She reordered a stack of paper napkins. "We try to keep all this *entre nous*, strictly between us girls. Lycanthropism has enjoyed a, an, uh . . . *unfavourable* public image. Too much goddamned TV. That is why newcomers get the tour and the lecture. You know the drill: peasant cunning on the rampage, ozone filled air from Tesla coils and Van de Graaff generators. Great lolloping hordes of shopkeepers and railway clerks come panting up rocky switchbacks to Doctor Frankenstein's castle with their pine pitch torches—burn and destroy, kill, ravage, extirpate, their answer to the *outré*—quivering with dread at anything outside their daily grind."

Five blocks.

The walk should have helped with the spare tire hung carelessly at his midriff, but the day's end martinis Jim Schofield allowed himself at Lloyd's negated all the walk's good work. The homicidal taxi had by now disappeared into the traffic at 42nd Street, its horn a descending Doppler ringing between the walls of buildings. He shuddered as he crossed an empty 39th Street against the light. Behind him the light turned to WALK and the smell of freshly savaged flesh, steaming and bloody, filled his nostrils. A red haze splattered across the insides of his eyes.

Cow slaughtering. Eight-year-old Jim Schofield rolled on the blood-wet ground with the yard dog: any other day a Wisconsin farm boy playing with Ol' Shep. At one particularly tempting chunk of offal, the yard dog snapped at him. Jim bit the dog's ear off. Jim spat—dog blood was different, somehow forbidden. He stood to throw up, then scrambled into an empty silo with his trophy as the yard dog whimpered under the swaying corpse of Barbie AB619.

His aunt Irene had stood, sauced-eyed, in shock. "Jim . . . no." Deep in the hollow, ringing silo they pulled him clawing and howling off the cow's entrails. After that Jim was watched. The family did not speak of the business of the cow killing ever again.

From an alley stuffed with trash, one of the city's derelicts beckoned to him. This was one of those alleyways of permanent twilight prowled by drunks, junkies, building supers and the homeless. The man was curled up on a ventilation grate, knees under his chin. He looked pretty well beat-up, but then they all did.

Home, he had to get home.

Jim turned to go. Another moan, weaker, brought him back. The guy was hurt, maybe by those gangs of wilding teenagers he had heard about. He had to help. He steeled himself to the likelihood of mouth-to-mouth resuscitation as he crouched over the man.

The man was having trouble breathing. Jim tore at the man's clothing, exposing his chest. The man's throat was russet-ripe, a sun-swollen fruit full to bursting. As the taut skin popped, hot blood burst into Jim's mouth and dribbled past his lips to cover his face. Where it clotted and dried.

"Penises," said Hillary Braunstein. "Seal penis bones. David, my first husband, cut and polished them for amulets. In Alaska. The sexually challenged wear them: Sid wears one. He rode away on his motorcycle to homestead in Alaska—David, that is. He left me for subsistence farming and penis polishing. That was 1988. He said he was going for cigarettes."

"Oh," Sally's cookie hovered, unmoving. Sally was silent. The ball was still in Hillary's court.

"How did you two decide on Sur la Mer?" Hillary asked.

"Oh, I thought you knew. It was your husband, after all." Sally entered her comfort zone; the cookie was eaten. "Jim met Sid at one of those boys' sports nights they have after work. It was in a bar . . . In the city? Sid didn't tell you? After that it was every month like clockwork for about a year. All Jim could talk about was moving out here."

"Ah . . . yes."

Sid Braunstein aimed his remote at a wide screen plasma TV. "You into baseball? I'm a Red Sox nut. Had to sign up for satellite service to get the games."

The two husbands sat out on the deck in white painted wicker chairs with cushions whose bright oversized daisies echoed the motifs of Hillary's kitchen. Sid Braunstein was a jovial, hairy man with a tightly packed body, a college jock who hadn't let himself go in middle age. His paunch looked solid enough to have genuine muscle behind it. Sid worked out. Jim surreptitiously touched the bulge at his own midsection. Sid noticed.

"Don't let it get you down. Free weights."

"Huh?"

"Free weights. I have a mini gym in the garage. And the girls watch our diets. This . . ." Sid held the bowl of clam dip aloft like a druid holding a chalice high to catch the first rays of a dawning solstice, ". . . is a plenary indulgence. *In durance vile here must I wake and weep and all my frowsy couch in sorrow steep*—Robert Burns. It's about getting banished to the outer darkness, as it were . . . while the girls chat up the neighbourhood amenities."

"Yeah, Burns." Jim had read Robert Burns in high school.

"Mmmm . . . don't know how she does it, Hillary," said Sid Braunstein. "Armed with but a simple blender and a whack of cream cheese, spices and clams, she can create ambrosia. Help yourself to another beer. We're not shy here."

"Uh, yeah . . ." Jim scoured his memory for Red Sox statistics.

"Jim met your Sid in Manhattan," said Sally Schofield.

"A sports bar. Lloyd's on Madison Avenue," said Hillary. "Sid's baseball hangout. I know. He was on his way to the train and caught your Jim in an alleyway off 39th Street making a shambles of a homeless man. It was too late for the derelict, but Sid got your husband sedated and back to the clinic." The older woman crossed and then uncrossed her legs. The legs were marvellously long, tanned and slender. "Your Jim wouldn't remember. None of them do; that's why the wives have to be in charge."

Limousine legs thought Sally. *And doesn't she love to show them off.* She blushed at getting caught staring at her hostess' marvellous legs.

Too young, too pretty, thought Hillary. And *dumb as a post. Let's toss her a bone.* "David did come back, eventually, but by then it was too late." Hillary waited while Sally reflected on this last tidbit.

"Oh . . ." A neat change of subject. *But she was the one who brought it up, the missing first husband*, thought Sally.

"I know this because he sent a postcard once. One postcard: 'Dogs run free, why not we?'"

"There are huge national parks in Alaska," said Sally.

Maybe not so dumb. "He was tired of feeling confined? He needed room to roam. All this was before Sur la Mer, of course. The mere suggestion of a gated community would have driven him right up the wall."

She's doing the legs thing again, thought Sally. She couldn't pull her eyes away fast enough.

Gotcha, thought Hillary.

"There is a forgetfulness—a mild amnesia, you might call it. The lacunae are sometimes . . . ahh, embarrassing. Like this?" Sid pulled what might have been a medallion from inside his aloha shirt. A polished disc reflected opalescent gemstone hues. It was fastened around his neck by a leather thong.

"Hmm . . . nice? What is a lacunae?"

"Sort of like an alcoholic blackout. Not the blackout itself, but the hole where your missing time went. A *lacuna*, singular— Latin, first declension, assigned gender feminine—appropriate as the girls cover up for us."

Sid held the dangle in front of Jim's nose. He gave it a gentle tap so it swung like a pendulum. *He's trying to hypnotize me*, thought Jim.

"From the penis bone of a seal." Sid dropped the amulet back inside his shirt. "David, Hillary's first husband, made it in Alaska. David made a run for it, but he came back. Before he left, he bit me. But, like I said, he came back. Overland. He must have followed the railroad tracks. There were news reports. His trail pointed right here. Anyone with the brains God gave a tree could have figured things out." Sid upended his can of beer and reached for a replacement. "Thank God for narrow-minded chauvinism. Nobody would have believed it even if they had caught on. Which they didn't. Derek Lowe and Pedro Martinez. The Sox have a decent bullpen at last."

"David left on a motorcycle; we don't allow motorcycles here in Sur la Mer. One of the rules. Here, have another." Hillary pushed the platter of cookies across the centre line back to Sally's side. "We went the Lysistrata route—Aristophanes? Withholding sex, that got their attention. First we tried threats and confrontations about those *things* they will keep on dragging home to bury in the yard—the boys can't recall anything of their midnight rambles or so they say. Dear, please don't let your mouth hang open like that."

"But . . . Jim?"

The woman is a born ingénue, thought Hillary. "And the answer was right there all the time. We simply had to get some protection."

Sally thought of condoms and Allstate, the good hands people. "You already have the gates. What's left, guard dogs and sentries?"

"From the government. Our husbands were threatened, therefore Section 4—CFR 17.11 could be brought into play."

"Seventeen-eleven. That's not the convenience store . . ."

"No, that's the U.S. Fish and Wildlife Service. The Endangered Species Act of 1973."

"Oh. Yes . . . ?"

"We are an aging population here in Sur la Mer. You have children," said Hillary. It was a statement, not a question.

"Yes."

"In the play, Lysistrata—and it's a comedy—the women go on a sex strike. They got fed up with their husbands always charging off to war. We supplement the husbands' treatments with herbs."

"Isn't that dangerous?" Sally had seen a TV report on the perils of self-diagnosis. "There was that diet drug—*ephedrine* . . .?"

There was a squeak from the legs of a high-backed colonial reproduction chair as Hillary stood and collected the cookies and the cups. "For thirty years the doctors slapped hormone treatments to women and called it 'enhancement.' We pointed this out—their maleness would be 'enhanced.' It's only fair," said Hillary Braunstein. "And we got the cancer and the strokes. I figure if a woman loves her husband . . ." She absently dumped the plate of cookies into the garbage disposal. "We don't compost," she offered by way of an explanation. "Makes the ground too easy to dig in. I have an herb garden."

Hillary walked out of the room. They would view the garden.

"Yes, I'd love to," said Sally.

"Here, help yourself . . ." Sid Braunstein passed the bowl of clam dip. "Ambrosial. The girls, God bless 'em," said Sid. "They have the top hand and they appreciate that. We acquiesce. Since the Lysistrata thing."

"Lysistrata," said Jim Schofield.

"Lysistrata. Don't ask; Hillary will tell Sally and Sally will tell you—that's how it works. Durance vile on the patio. Heh heh. Beer and chips beats bread and water.

"Lysistrata. Isn't that a play by Aristo . . ."

"Yep. The girls needed a rest. And the hormone treatments did it. No more unchaperoned midnight impromptus; we all get hairy and horny at the same time. Impotence puts a strain on the best of marriages." Sid gave Jim a nudge with his elbow. "Come home with a wet willie and the girls like to know where it's been . . . Heh heh."

At the back door, Hillary slipped into a pair of garden clogs. "Since you are the new girl, you get to patrol the wire. Fence maintenance. It's only three nights a month and not too demanding. Here's a set of rubber wellies. I think they'll fit you, Sally. They were David's; he had small feet."

"How did you meet your second husband?"

"We even had a skateboard park built. For the kids?" Hillary had changed the subject. Again. "Turns out we can't have kids. None of us. Something about the treatments. Oh, you mean Sid. Well, David and I were living in Jersey at the time; Sid was a veterinarian with a midtown clinic. On Madison Avenue. All very upscale and glitzy. The doctors couldn't find anything wrong with David. One of them made a chance remark..."

"Is this what all the secrecy is about?"

"My, Sally, but you are fast on your feet. Excellent. See, David was a werewolf. We have made some, ahh, understandably tentative feelers to the government as to endangered species status for the husbands. But so far..."

"Then Sid is...?"

"And so is Jim. And that is why you and I are here today going on a tour of my dumb, totally useless herb garden while our husbands swill beer and natter man-talk on the deck. Ow!" A blue spark arced from a wire fence to Hillary Braunstein's finger. "It's only 24 volts but it packs a wallop if you forget your rubber wellies."

"You have an electrified fence?" Sally was aghast.

"The picket wire. That's what we call it from the days when Marshall Dillon gave the trail bosses till sundown to get their unruly cowhands out of Dodge. We do the same, only in reverse. The husbands tend to roam."

"Dodge?"

"Ah, the generational difference. *Gunsmoke*—an old TV show. Marshall Dillon strung barbed wire around the perimeter of the town. To keep the cows off the streets?" Hillary held a finger poised near the wire. It was strung tight between self-anchoring metal posts and twisted onto yellow plastic insulators. "It shouldn't be much longer and we can turn the damned thing off."

"Was. You said David *was*. And Jim..."

"No, dear, there's no cure; don't get your hopes up. Sid put him down. An overdose of morphine, quite painless. David couldn't change back, but David was a rare case. Sid and I had discovered feelings for one another. And David bit him before running away to Alaska, so Sid was a goner. Even with belladonna poultices."

"Hence the herb garden?"

"Sharp girl. Even with his medical knowledge, Sid was caught short. Belladonna is a specific for werewolf bite. Lacking belladonna, Sid improvised with the available members of the family. Deadly Nightshade: potatoes and tomatoes. French fries and ketchup. We were the talk of the Madison Avenue Burger King that night."

"So just how did you come to Sur la Mer?" asked Jim Schofield.

"Well, as it happens, I'm a veterinarian and Hillary came to see me about David. See, he'd killed the newspaper delivery boy."

Jim froze on the edge of his chair. The blue corn taco chip in his hand dripped clam and sour cream dip onto his slacks.

"Strike a nerve, did I? Hey . . . get a handle on that. Ruin your crease." Sid pulled a paper serviette from a stack folded into a decorative wire holder, "Any trouble back in Manhattan? Beyond chasing cars and peeing on policemen's legs?"

As Sid leaned to wipe the fallen splotch of dip from Jim's pants he spoke urgently as if they might be overheard. "You know the kind—folks usually end up here on the run from some mess they have to get away from. Not the full of the moon, that's all bullshit. Hundreds of thousands of years ago, the moon was closer, much closer to the Earth. And the months were shorter. There is a hormonal rhythm. Antibodies in the blood release a timed catalyst that triggers a hormonal shift. Really fast and nasty. But you would know all about that. That derelict I caught you with in the alley? There, that should do it." Sid wadded up the napkin and dropped it on the floor. He leaned back and fondled his remote. "Once a month the girls fire up the electric fence and lock the gates."

A weak arc of crackling blue curved from the fence wire to Hillary's outstretched finger. "It all depends on where you stand." She played the spark like a yo-yo, pulling her finger in and out. "There's a formula—inductive capacitance, something like that. See, no shock."

"You like touching the fence, don't you?" said Sally. The electric blue followed Hillary's finger but never seemed to make contact.

"Like I said, I just moved a little. It's all in where you put your feet. And the rubber wellies too. Give it a try."

"No thanks."

"Whatever. Being a soccer mom . . . I almost envy you, Sally—the ballet lessons, soccer practice, fencing, Boy Scouts. When the men developed their—ahh, *problem*—and we applied hormone treatments, they became sterile and lost all interest in sex, and I mean *totally*. No more Mom's Taxi; our kids aged and went off to school. You will have the only children in Sur la Mer. Of course if you get caught outside the wire after curfew, you'll have to fend for yourself. But it's only two days every month. And they're horny as hell." Hillary smiled a wide, suggestive smile.

Sid reached to scoop up a mighty dollop of clam dip with a taco chip. "Like I might have said, lycanthropism is, or has been for most of us here, transmitted through the bite of an affected individual. I'd say you are a natural." Sid gave Jim a meaningful look.

"Meaning . . . ?" Jim remembered his aunt's eyes when they caught up with him in the silo.

"Meaning some folks are born with the talent. We call it a talent. It is, you know, a talent. But there's nobody to show off for. Neat party trick except you don't get invited back." He stuffed the dip-freighted chip into his mouth. A blob clung to his nose. "Yep. You're a natural."

Jim uncomfortably shifted his weight on the patio cushion.

"Childhood memories? Got the fidgets?"

"Yes." Sid appeared happy with that and Jim decided not to belabour the point.

"I envy you. Hormonal," said Sid Braunstein as he reached for another Coors. "You gotta hand it to them, the girls, they got it all doped out . . ." Sid was enjoying a mild beer buzz ". . . Vatican II, the rhythm system as applied to lycanthropy. Really cool stuff and Hillary figured it all out for herself. Got the idea from the hormone replacement therapies—you know, after the birth control pills scare? I just did the grunt work, contracted with the manufacturing laboratories and all."

Hillary led Sally down a manicured path of white polished pebbles. "It's not easy being different. Ever try to slip a werewolf past a condo board? They even hire private eyes; would you believe it? OK, so the men are normal most of the time. And no amount of electrolysis would explain away the—ahh . . . *artefacts*. Things they bring home to bury. They're just like big kids, really. But who knew when they would get all hairy and feral?"

Sally slipped in the oversized rubber boots. "Oops. Sorry." A wounded *mandragora officinarum* hung dejectedly where it had been snapped off. White milky sap oozed.

"Careful. This little patch represents two years of work. The occasional organ—a little something for later—that we could have put up with. But the yards were a mess. Who's to know how a man's mind works? Oh yes—the condo boards. After the twelfth try I was willing to chuck it all and buy outright. Always some old bat in a bouffant wig and her pet poodle humping Sid's pants leg. We formed a non-profit corporation. Investment capital was lean after the dot-com bust and we picked the whole place up for chump change."

"It must have cost millions."

"A million-five, actually. Sid was a celebrity veterinarian. He performed surgery on Meg Ryan's pussy. Twice. That's one of Sid's jokes. We had references. There's nothing a condo board won't ask—they leave you stripped and drained. One time I said I wanted to grow patio tomatoes on the roof, for emergencies. But I didn't tell *them* that. Remember the French fries and ketchup? Well, it was like I peed in the communion chalice."

"Oh, are you Catholics? With a name like Braunstein, I just naturally assumed . . ." Sally fell silent. The insides of the borrowed boots were sweaty and her face felt flushed.

"Tomato red."

"Huh?"

"Tomato red is the colour I would have turned if I had made a gaffe like that one. You are forgiven; it is really quite attractive on you, Sally. Tomato red, I mean. Tomatoes are called the 'wolf apple' by the way. At least that's their name in Latin: *lycopersicon esculentum*—the 'wolf *peach*,' rightly."

Sally looked at the herb garden. "I don't see any tomatoes."

"No, no tomatoes. Ketchup is more concentrated. We buy it by the case at the Pick'n' Pay."

"Clap for the Wolfman; he's gonna rate your record high . . ." The TV was off and an Oldies CD now blared from Sid Braunstein's patio boom box.

"The Guess Who. A favourite," said Sid. "Clap—*clap* for the Wolfman . . ." Sid laughed heartily; he did not look like a man who laughed a lot. His eyes bulged, and his face turned beet red. "Sorry. *Sorree.* Woo, hee. *Whoop-whoop, hack hack hack.*" Spit flew as Sid bent double over the bowl of clam dip. He recovered, still choking from the unaccustomed laughing fit. "Snorted . . . beer . . . up my nose. Ahh . . . hmm. Actually, sexually transmitted diseases are not a problem here in Sur la Mer as they are out in the normal world—the *civilians*, we call 'em. Leptospirosis, distemper and rabies, though . . ." He grew thoughtful, pulling on his beer. "Gotta lay off the rabbits and the squirrels. Cats, too. Stick to your own kind, that's my motto. Disease-wise, the baddest actors are always the species jumpers. Gotta keep it in your pants—if you're wearing any, that is. Pants cramp your style when you're chasing a cat up a tree."

Sid beamed. Jim beamed back, this was another laugh line—*clap for the wolfman*, yuck, yuck. Jim Schofield smiled and felt more at ease. He wondered how Sally's interview was going. Sid ignored Jim and fiddled with his TV remote. The game was back on again.

Sally and Hillary had reached the garden's far perimeter where a large cement toad crouched under a spreading ornamental yew tree. The toad was the size of a Harley-Davidson motorcycle fallen on its side.

"Don't you just love him," said Hillary. "He has a very knowing look when the light is right."

"Very . . . *large*," said Sally.

"Big is good," said Hillary, "He came with the place. And he's sitting on some of the boys' more incriminating, ahh . . . trophies."

Sally had lagged behind. She was scraping at a suspicious clump adhered to her foot.

"Step in something? Let's have a look-see,"

Sally held up the afflicted rubber wellie.

"Nope. Just dog poop," said Hillary. "Wipe it on the grass. It's easy to tell the difference when you've raked up enough of the stuff—the boys get a high fibre diet. They tend to fat so we watch what we feed them."

Sally sat on the toad to clean her boots.

"I called up the agricultural extension service. Bet you didn't know New York City had county agents. Anyway, that is how I met Everett Castelnuovo. There's something about a man in uniform. He was very attentive. At first I thought he had the hots for me but he smelled a research paper. You know, publish-or-perish, something for a scientific journal. Sur la Mer was going to put him on the map, career-wise."

"He wore a uniform?"

"Well, a sleeve patch and a twill serge bomber jacket. He was quite handsome, a Mark Trail type filtered through Chiquita Banana, what with the bolero and all."

"Was."

"He came in over the picket wire on a bad night, intruder-wise. The boys' night out."

"Oh."

"I'm expecting his replacement any day. From the Fish and Wildlife Service, an expert on 'chemical ecology,' whatever that is." Hillary toyed with a sprig of bittersweet nightshade that had been broken off by another misstep. She looked accusingly at Sally and held the wounded herb under her nose. "*Solanum dulcamara*—the potato family, would you believe?"

"You mentioned Lysistrata?" said Sally, trying for a diversion.

"Going without was as hard for us as it was for them. But we were willing to sacrifice for the greater good. Now that we have them back, they are totally limp, but at least we have them home nights. Most nights . . ."

"Ahh . . . YES!" A crowd roar issued from the TV's stereo speakers. Sid looked expectantly at his company.

Jim felt he should contribute something. "Hey . . . how's about that Manny Ramirez?"

"Thirty-seven homers and 104 RBIs last season, but that's not why we're here. We are self-policing." Sid zapped the set with his remote and the screen went black. "This is important. I'm supposed to be vetting you on life in a gated community. You're here for a reason, you know. In Sur la Mer? Hey, that's good!"

"Huh?"

"*Vetting*—I made a pun. I didn't mean to—*veterinarian*—my profession and all. Have to tell Hillary about it, she'll get a chuckle. Basically I'm not a humorous guy."

"Oh, I wouldn't . . ."

"Yes, you would. Baseball and animal autopsies are my area of competence, period. No stand-up. Anyway, I thought Hillary was having an affair. Some guy from the government. Now Hillary, I just love her to bits. I was hurt, chagrined, humiliated, all of the above. And I lurked. I caught him coming over the picket wire one night. He was packing a sensitive microphone— you know, the kind with a tripod and a parabolic reflector—a laptop, night vision goggles, the works. I buried him in the mandragora patch. When I was back to normal I confronted my wife. Boy, did I get an earful! The girls had to dig him up and plant him under the garden toad. Seems I had made a mistake."

"But here we were talking about having the husbands declared a threatened species . . ." Hillary had been idly poking with her toe at a mounded planting of *atropa belladonna*. A human toe was exposed. "Oh shit. *Simply shit!*" She knelt and brushed away shredded cedar bark. A severed foot protruded from the mulch. It had been gnawed. Hillary poked the toe and its foot back under cover and patted the shredded bark flat. "Well! I thought he was late returning my call. A steep curve in their learning processes, these government men. Your tax dollars at work. Everett's replacement, the man from the Fish and Wildlife Service. He brought it on himself—I told him to call first. He should have checked his voice mail."

Rob Hunter

Hillary directed Sally's attention to a particularly attractive grouping of daisy-like flowers. "*Arnica Montana*, of the aster family, actually. The popular name is 'wolfsbane,' good for headaches. I think I feel one coming on."

Originally published in On Spec, Summer 2005 Vol 17 No 2 #61

Rob Hunter is the sole support of a large orange cat and the despair of his young wife. He does dishes and windows and keeps their Maine cottage spotless by moving as little as possible. He has been a newspaper copy boy, railroad telegraph operator, recording engineer and film editor.

Mourning Sickness
Robert Weston

The conference floor was so awash with noise that Suvinder thought he'd misheard. "Sorry?" he said. "'Sarah'? I don't think I know any—hold on, are you from Home and Garden? Actually I've been meaning to call you guys about our—"

"No, no," said the voice, "Suvinder, it's Sarah. U of T Sarah. Remember?" She paused. Then as if it was necessary, she added, "Peter's wife."

Suvinder wasn't sure of his expression, but he was grateful for the physical anonymity of the telephone. "Sarah Bateman. Or I guess I mean Milligrew, don't I? Sarah Milligrew. I have to admit, I hadn't heard from either of you in so long, I'd written you off. So, um. How are you? Well, I hope."

"Actually no, I'm not so good." She said something else, but the HBO demo started nearby and her voice was lost.

Suvinder hollered into the phone. "What? Look, I can barely hear you. I'm at this TV convention and there's a—"

Sarah spoke slowly. "It's Peter, Suvinder. He had a stroke."

Suvinder had nothing to say in response. He stared at the wall of monitors that lay beyond the independent producers' booth—a massive barricade of promotional light and sound.

"Suvinder? Did you hear what I said? Peter had a stroke, and then—and we lost him."

"Lost him? Wait, that doesn't—we're not even forty. Sarah, he couldn't've—"

"It was his condition. He lost his father only last year."

"His condition?"

"The funeral's tomorrow morning. I'm sorry, Suvinder. I'm sorry I couldn't find you sooner."

As abruptly as she had appeared—as an unidentified number on his cellular phone—Sarah was gone. The details of the ceremony and the news that Peter had suffered all his life from a congenital heart disease came from Peter's older brother, someone Suvinder had never met.

The moment the phone was back in his breast pocket, Suvinder's vision swam. He was forced to steady himself against a chunk of the feeble pasteboard that was everywhere.

"Hey, how'd it go with the Food guys?" It was Bill, Suvinder's partner at Up-Start Productions. Bill had been off on another pitch—trying to sell a collection of skiing accidents to Xtreme TV—while Suvinder had met with two buyers from The Food Network. Up-Start's first and only pilot was called *Street Chefs*.

Suvinder couldn't answer. His legs wobbled, the pasteboard gave way and he crouched to the floor to keep from falling down.

To Bill, collapsing anywhere was unthinkable, bad for business. Nevertheless, he managed to make sense of it. "So it went pretty badly, huh?" he said, eyeing the HBO display. "Yeah. Me too."

Suvinder shook his head as if he needed something dislodged.

Bill pursed his lips. "No?" he asked, his voice rising optimistically, "You mean, 'no, it didn't go badly?' C'mon Vinnie, don't fool around. Are you serious? They actually wanna buy it?"

Suvinder kept on shaking his head. Finally he said, "They didn't buy it."

"So what happened?"

"I got a call from a friend, an old friend. She called to tell me about another old friend of mine. Who died."

"Died?"

"I have to go to the funeral."

Bill put a hand on Suvinder's shoulder. "Sure, buddy. As soon as we get back."

Suvinder stood up and tried to moisten his mouth. "No," he said. "The funeral's tomorrow. And it's in Vancouver. I'll just have to change my ticket."

"Yeah, okay, maybe. But listen, we still have two days here and what if—"

Bill was interrupted by three enormous security guards. They surrounded Suvinder. All three were monstrous, but they were dwarfed by the great thing that loomed behind them. "Excuse me, sir?" one of them said to Suvinder. "But is this your elephant?"

The beast's ears flapped against its head. Suvinder looked up and remembered what his mother had told him, about seeing it for the first time. Serenity—that was her word for it. There would be serenity, she'd said. He told himself he'd have to call her and admit she was right. Oddly, he found himself smiling at the security guard. It was a listless, tight-lipped grin, but a smile nonetheless. "Yes," he said. "I suppose that's my elephant"

Bill backed away, holding his hands up in apology. "Sorry, buddy," he said, "I didn't realize it hit you so hard."

One of the guards took Suvinder firmly by the arm. "Sir, I'm afraid we'll have to ask you to leave. On behalf of the Las Vegas Convention Centre, we'd like to express our sincerest regret for your loss."

January in Las Vegas was hardly the height of the tourist season. Standing outside the convention centre in nothing more than a business suit, Suvinder could see his breath, puffing out of his mouth in short-lived clouds.

He hurried back toward his hotel—the dilapidated and oft-neglected Riviera. His elephant loped quietly behind him. At the hotel, he tipped the bellhop five dollars to watch the animal while he checked out and retrieved his luggage. He swooped indoors, past the sirens of god-knows-how-many slot machines, and found the woman at the front desk to be suitably rueful and obliging, but as she handed Suvinder his receipt, he caught her gazing warily over his shoulder.

Outside again, he tried to reason with the elephant. "Listen," he said, whispering up toward the beast's ear. He hoped the thing would understand if he spoke clearly and with a gentle timbre. "I need to catch a cab to the airport. It'll be a bit of a chore with you standing right beside me. So please, just wait here until I find one. Can you do that?"

The elephant blinked.

Suvinder coaxed the beast around the corner, away from the twinkling lights of the Riviera marquee. He raised his hands to the elephant's face, a gesture any domesticated animal would comprehend. "All right? I want you to stay. Right here, okay?" Suvinder backed toward the street and thankfully his elephant remained in the shadows.

When he flagged down a cab, the driver was all smiles. He graciously got out and hefted Suvinder's battered luggage into the trunk. "To the airport?" he asked.

"Yeah, that's right."

As they pulled away from the curb, the driver whistled along to throwaway pop that hissed from the radio. On the dashboard there was an ornamental word—JESUS—moulded to resemble a fish.

"How you holding up?"

Suvinder only half heard. "Sorry, what?"

"You okay?"

"Uh huh."

"You sure?"

"I'm fine. I just—I don't want to miss my plane."

"You sure that's all?"

"Yeah. That's it. Why?"

The driver tapped the rear view mirror and Suvinder turned around. His elephant was lumbering along the shoulder of the road; a few of the other cars were forced to swerve to avoid it. The woman in the next car back glared through the windscreen. Suvinder slumped in his seat.

The driver chuckled. "You never been through any kind of loss before, have you?"

Suvinder shook his head.

The driver nodded. "That's what I thought," he said, "but count yourself lucky. My first time was when my dog died. I was only a kid and I was dumb enough to think my folks'd gone and bought me a new pet. In the end it was just like going through the whole thing twice."

Suvinder grimaced. "That's awful."

"Oh yeah. I loved that dog more than my own mother. Since then, I've had more elephants than I care to remember. I tried outrunning one or two of them, but really, the only thing you can do is work through it."

"That makes sense."

"Anyway, if you're like me, ol' Jumbo won't stick around more than a few days."

Suvinder sighed. "Oh," he said, "a few days." It was longer than he'd anticipated.

"Sure, a few days, no more than a week. 'Course sometimes you hear about chronic cases, but those folks have problems, serious problems—psychological problems, y'know? That's not you, right? You look pretty put-together to me."

"Maybe. I don't know." Suvinder looked out the window. He could see the long shadow of the elephant, flitting over the roadside cacti.

"It always helps to talk about it. If you like. With this traffic, we'll be on the road at least another—maybe ten or twelve minutes."

"You want to know what happened?"

"If you feel up to it."

Suvinder looked at the back of the driver's head. Was this man genuinely concerned or simply morbid and curious? Suvinder decided it didn't matter either way. "It was my best friend," he admitted. "The funeral's tomorrow."

The driver looked in the rear-view again. His eyes moved from Suvinder and then to the elephant that trailed them, several car lengths behind.

"We were best friends at university," Suvinder went on, "Right from week one. We did everything together. We both studied film and we produced a few shorts together—good stuff, too, considering the shitty equipment we had to work with." Suvinder took a deep breath. "It turns out he had a heart disease, something serious. He had it all the time and he never told me. Nobody ever told me."

"Geez," said the driver, whistling a single descending note, "no wonder you got yourself such a big fellah. Almost there now, by the way. You know which terminal?"

The Las Vegas airport loomed ahead. When the taxi slowed

to climb the entry ramp, Suvinder's elephant closed the gap.

"Doesn't matter which terminal," Suvinder commented darkly. "International, I guess. I'm flying with Air Canada." When the driver didn't ask for any more information, Suvinder went on with his story. "There was a girl. Her name was Sarah and she was a drama student, an actress—or at least she aspired to be. Peter and I—man—we clawed over each other tooth-and-nail to get her in every one of our shitty little movies. More than likely, she was the only reason they were remotely bearable."

"You don't say," said the driver, turning around in his seat.

Suvinder hadn't noticed the taxi had stopped. "She dated us both. After we graduated, we agreed things would stay on the level. We'd all remain friends—just friends. But then, well," Suvinder paused to knock his head lightly against the glass. "Then they both moved across the country and I stayed put in Toronto. I guess I thought I had something good going at the time. With my work, I mean."

The driver opened his door and popped the trunk and Suvinder finally caught on. His elephant was loitering at the entrance to international departures, and a man in an orange vest was madly waving his arms, urging the cab driver to drive away.

Changing his ticket to Toronto-via-Vancouver wasn't as expensive as Suvinder expected. Air Canada offered a generous bereavement discount that was a tenth of the price, plus the usual service charges and airport tax. The airline's charity was less surprising, however, when the clerk informed Suvinder that the cargo plane charges for simultaneously shipping an elephant would be triple the cost of a standard fare. Suvinder whispered a prayer and handed over his AMEX card. After producing the unsalable pilot for *Street Chefs*, his charge account was fast approaching overdraft. Miraculously, the tickets cleared, but the first available flight didn't leave until the middle of the night.

When his plane finally set down in Vancouver, Suvinder was already too late to attend the ceremony. Instead he would go straight to Peter's burial. He rented the cheapest car on the airport lot, briefly consulted a roadmap and sped recklessly toward West Vancouver with his elephant struggling to keep up.

Mourning Sickness

Capilano View Cemetery was a gorgeous expanse of greenery cut through by winding roads, evergreens and bare oak trees. The north-shore mountains loomed across the bay, and the Vancouver air was like a moist sponge, a welcome change after the desert cold of Nevada. The cemetery grounds were so large they seemed derelict, and it took Suvinder some time to locate the plot.

Chairs—thirty or forty of them—were set out in rows and most were already occupied. Suvinder was relieved to find that his was neither the largest nor the smallest elephant in attendance. When he joined the group, his animal took its place among the others, milling around an idle bulldozer, presumably the one used to excavate the grave.

He found a seat at the rear. Beside him was a man of girth, dressed in a suit that was comically small and ill-fitted. He wore a thick moustache and his eyes were deeply bloodshot. "Go ahead," he said, a moment after Suvinder had already sat down, "There's no one sitting there."

"Thanks," said Suvinder, leaning forward in an attempt to catch the man's eye.

But the man didn't look up from the ground. He only said, "I was his secretary."

"You worked for Peter?"

"Two years. Almost two years. I never would have thought—" he trailed off and threw a backward glance over his shoulder, toward the herd. "That's mine over there. That big old African. Who'd have thought, heh?"

Suvinder looked over his shoulder. The man's elephant was even larger than his own and Suvinder felt his cheeks colour with an unexpected pang of shame.

The large man sniffled and cupped his mouth in his hand. "Never in a million years. Never—never, ever—would I've expected to show up at the guy's funeral. He was so damn young."

"I guess it was a surprise for a lot of people."

"Yeah. How'd you know him?"

"We went to school together."

Peter's secretary slung a heavy arm round Suvinder's shoulders. His grip was stifling; his breath smelled of rye whiskey. "You go way back, hey? Looks like you're holding up pretty well."

"I'm coping."

"Good for you." The man used a thick finger to draw an invisible circle in front of his face. "What's all this blubbery get you? Not a goddamn thing. Honestly, I only feel worse. And I'll bet the damn African's ready to dog me for weeks and weeks." He blew out a syrupy breath and the strength of his embrace faltered. Gently, like a drowsy child, he placed his head on Suvinder's shoulder and closed his eyes.

An uncle Suvinder had never heard of spoke at length. Only when he made reference to Peter's "adoring wife and family," did Suvinder catch sight of Sarah, who until then had been just another dark figure among many. She was sitting at the far end of the front row, evidently between Peter's mother and the brother Suvinder had spoken to on the phone. When the uncle's eulogy had deteriorated into tears, the minister took over. He concluded the ceremony just as a light rain began to fall. To bring him out of his stupor, Suvinder slapped the secretary's meaty thigh.

"Sorry," said the large man, wringing his hands.

The coffin was lowered into the ground and the mourners began to leave. A number of them filed between Sarah and her husband's grave. Hands were reassuringly squeezed; soft words were exchanged; Sarah and her mother-in-law were kissed lightly on the cheek, again and again.

Peter's secretary didn't bother saying goodbye to anyone. He rose suddenly and lurched toward the cars.

"Are you sure you're okay to drive?" Suvinder called after him.

"I'm fine," he replied. "Tell them I'll skip the reception. I'm going home." The man found his car—a rusted Mazda—and puttered away with his elephant thundering alongside. Suvinder kept his eye on the vehicle as long as he could. Just before the car moved out of sight, it veered drunkenly toward the shoulder. Responding quickly, the man's elephant trumpeted forward and the secretary swerved back on course. Suvinder smiled. He imagined the secretary would arrive home in one piece, just as long as he didn't get over Peter's death before he got there.

When Suvinder turned back, most of the mourners had left the gravesite. When he saw Peter's brother help his mother out

Mourning Sickness

of her seat and lead the old woman away, Suvinder moved forward.

When he was still a few feet behind her, Sarah turned. "I didn't think you'd made it," she said.

"It was a hassle getting here," Suvinder explained. "When you called I was in Las Vegas."

"Working?"

"Yeah."

"How's everything going for you?"

"It's going okay." Suvinder looked around at all the empty chairs. The cemetery's custodial staff was already clearing them away. "I certainly wasn't doing as well as Peter."

Sarah nodded. "Peter did pretty good for himself. But you know, Suvinder, he only ever ended up a moneyman. He never got his hands dirty and he never really produced anything. Not like you."

Suvinder almost laughed. "Never anything worthwhile, Sarah, believe me." He took a seat beside her—the place where Peter's brother had sat through the ceremony. Sarah's hair, pulled up from her face in an austere bun, smoothed her features and made her even younger than he'd remembered. Then he made out the lines in her face, the dark patches under her eyes. But no, those were always there, weren't they? It was as if she hadn't aged at all. "Who cares about what I'm doing?" he said, "What about you? How've you been, Sarah? How're you holding up?"

"It's difficult, but I guess I'm okay. I knew about Peter's health right from the start, but like I said on the phone, it was still—"

"Sarah!" Peter's brother was calling from the last car still parked nearby. "Are you coming with us?"

Suvinder nodded to the man but the gesture went unacknowledged.

"I'll stay a bit longer," Sarah called back. "You take Mom back to the home. I'll meet you there soon."

Peter's brother climbed back into the car. When he pulled away, two of the biggest elephants Suvinder had ever seen—twins, it seemed—followed the car down the path. Suvinder returned his attention to the grave. "He's really gone, isn't he?"

Sarah stood up abruptly. Suvinder felt compelled to do the

same. As he rose, she threw her arms around his waist and burrowed her face in his chest. "I'm awful, Suvinder. You must think I'm a monster."

"What? No, don't say that, Sarah. You're not a monster."

"I'm a terrible person."

Suvinder squeezed her. He stroked her back. He rested his chin on the top of her head. They were all motions he'd made once or twice before, years and years ago. But then he saw what she meant. There were only two elephants left on the grounds—his and hers. Sarah's elephant was small and frail. It moved with a crooked gait. It was sickly. And worse. It was walking away.

"Don't you see?" she said, her voice trembling and tight. "I told you. I'm not fit to live. It should be me in that box."

A moment later, Sarah's elephant hobbled into the evergreens and vanished. Suvinder watched it go. Part of him wanted to call after it, but what good would it do?

"What happened?" he asked. "Did something happen between you guys?"

"There's not much to tell. There's no 'big thing.' We just went in different directions. And we drifted." As if to demonstrate, she pushed Suvinder away. "You know what we did the week before he died? We talked about a divorce." She gestured to the open grave and laughed wretchedly. "I guess he was pretty serious about it, hey?"

Suvinder didn't know how to respond. He saw that now, with the chairs cleared away, his elephant was the last one on the grounds. It approached and stood a short distance off, its dark skin gleaming with rain.

"I'm quitting my job," he said.

"What?"

He sat down again and stared into the grave. "I'm gonna sell my half of the company—to my partner. He's wanted to have his own thing for a long time anyway. Besides, it's not all it's cracked up to be, Sarah. It really isn't." He looked up at her. "I was thinking I might move back out west, start again."

She offered him her hand. "Maybe now's a good time to start again."

"Maybe," he said. He put his hands on his knees and stood on his own. He walked to his elephant and touched it for the first time, running his fingers over the flank. The skin was warm and wet and rough. He turned back to Sarah. "C'mon," he said. "I'll give you a lift to the reception."

Originally published in On Spec Fall 2005 Vol 17 No 3 #62

Robert Paul Weston is the author of several award-winning novels for children and young adults, including *Zorgamazoo*, *The Creature Department*, and *Blues For Zoey*. His short fiction has appeared in *The New Orleans Review*, *Kiss Machine*, *Postscripts*, and others. He lives in London, England.

Sticky Wonder Tales
Hugh Spencer

Hey Squiffy:
Sorry to hear about the bowel infection. Even sorrier to hear that it's one of the intelligent ones.

Just how intelligent do you think? If you've got one of the stupider batches I've heard that you can sometimes pacify them by watching sitcoms from the 1960s and early 1970s. Not *Dick Van Dyke* or *Green Acres*, because there's some hidden smart stuff and surrealism in some of those.

No. Try the blandest thing imaginable—like *The Brady Bunch* or *The Partridge Family*. That ought to settle 'em down. No, scratch *The Partridge Family*, I hear it's a bit dangerous if the bugs go totally comatose.

Otherwise, how is the mutation coming along? Not too fast (because we'll miss you), I hope. Not too slow either (because that would be boring).

Everything is such a question of fucking balance these days.
Cheers,

Andrew:
I agree with you on your last point. You have to keep on evolving but not so much that they don't know where to send

the bill for the Science Fiction Book of the Month club.

Can you believe that such a quaint institution still exists?

Anyway, to answer your main question: the process seems to be moving along pretty well. The bacteriological route is uneven and kind of painful, but what can I say? The price was definitely right.

Maybe I should have done what you did and gone the technological route.

Have they moved you on to any new simulators?

Best,

Hi Squiffer:

They put our whole team into the most advanced model of our oldest and most obsolete simulators. I think that's better than being assigned to the least advanced model of the middle-range systems. But you know what a dangerous optimist I can be.

I can be realistic too. Which is why I know there's absolutely no way some guy from the suburbs of Steel Town is going to get hold of any exotic tech. At least not this fast.

Our trainer explained that could be some kind of an honour. "An unusual challenge for advancement." Which is boss-code for "this job is going to be so boring that it will fossilize your brain or so dangerous that it will melt your gonads."

Maybe both.

Anyway, the "unusual challenge" is trying out some Super Culture chatter that might be some technology teaching software. Of course, it could be random eruptions of interstellar gas. Our team gets to figure out which.

No problem, it only ought to take twenty, maybe thirty years.

Even if it does turn out to be something meaningful, it doesn't necessarily follow that the information will be anything particularly important. It could be blueprints for the intergalactic equivalent of those little plastic tabs for bread bags.

Then again, it really might be some profound existential insight. Real meaning of life stuff. We're talking at least 80 million civilizations and a shit load of space and eternity.

Profoundly yours,

Andrew:
I had a great dream last night.
I was back in our old house in Saskatchewan. It was the dead of January; snow everywhere, about three in the morning. You know, one of those unbelievably black, bleak and frigid nights.
I really miss them sometimes.
Anyway, I turned away from the kitchen window for a second to take a sip of cocoa, and when I look out again, there's this amazing shifting wall of aurora borealis everywhere. Along with the electrical crackling in THX sound and it's like high noon with an ultraviolet sun. Then the effect fades and it goes back to night again. But it's hardly black out there now. I'm looking at some planets—gas giants—floating over the snowdrifts. Five different variations of Jupiter out there—the multicoloured bands of gas take up over a third of the sky.
Which makes a striking contrast to the outline of the old Greek Orthodox church on 105th Street.
Un-fucking-believable . . . as I believe the Bard once put it.
I suspect the dream was some kind of psychic compensation for a longstanding disappointment that we never got any *Big Ships*.
The dream also helped me not worry so much that I'd completely forgotten Annie's eighth birthday yesterday. I can understand how you can evolve beyond some old friendships, but forgetting about your kids? Another downside of this Process, I suppose.
Speaking of which, I've got to go now. The bacteria have reached a developmental phase that makes me extremely flatulent. I'm still connected enough to my family to notice that they dislike it if I don't deal with this problem in the bathroom.
Got to pass some gas on my way to the stars.
Bloatedly,

Squiffoid:
Sorry about your fart-attacks. Hope you got around to fixing the bathroom fan before all this started.
Are you still ticked about the lack of Big Ships? *Get over it, guy!*

Hugh Spencer

Maybe what I'm about to tell will be a bit of a consolation. Probably not, because it's happening to me and not you, it's just likely to tick you off even more.

But what the hell, I'll tell you anyway. The software we're using to drive the simulators is indeed meaningful. It seems to be some kind of mission programme in a solar system that we've never heard of.

Holy shit! The graphics! The sounds! The motion commands!

Sweeping, swooping, blasting our way through multi-coloured rings of interstellar dust, crashing through the core of an exploding sun.

Hate to say it, but these shows make your Saskatchewan dream-scape sound pretty lame.

It's not quite a fleet of UFOs hiding behind the moon or Gort on the White House lawn, but I'm definitely living some kind of a classic sci-fi movie here.

Sorry, I know this must sound really insensitive. It's just that we're having so much fun here and I'm sure once Central Administration finds out that we've got something interesting here, they're bound to take it away from us.

With apologies,

Andrew:

Thank you. I really appreciate how you're trying to help me hang on to my basic humanity by annoying me as much as possible. It's almost working.

You helped me to remember that I really, really still want those Big Ships. I want to see them *personally*. I'd even settle for getting goofy sunburn like Richard Dreyfus in *Close Encounters*.

Any kind of Significant/Transcendent Experience would make me feel better about what's happening in my real life.

I'm becoming a serious asshole.

I'm pretty sure it's a side effect of the Process.

God, I hope this is a side effect of the Process.

I know all the books say you shouldn't use your emerging abilities without training and in particular you shouldn't do so with family and friends present. But these things creep up on a person.

At first it was small stuff, subconsciously implanting a desire in my oldest's mind to finish his homework and go look for a summer job. Then you start suggesting that broccoli is actually a Slurpee from 7-Eleven. Eventually you're levitating your kids to bed at 9 p.m.

Harmless, right?

Not really.

Yesterday my youngest left all his Power Rangers stuff scattered all over the floor of the family room. It was bath night and I went in there looking for him.

What happened next was all my fault. I shouldn't have gone in there with just my bare feet.

Those action figures have a lot of pointy bits.

Well, my enhancements just snapped on and I melted all the toys in the basement.

Just like that.

The books do say that some "powerful affect-based manifestations are likely to occur," but I always figured that my advanced mental powers would be a very calm and cerebral thing. Think about it, the Process is supposed to come from some higher civilizations somewhere in the Galactic Core. I mean to me that implies thought, rationality, reason.

To me, it does not suggest that I would suddenly lose it and reduce the proceeds of the last three Christmases to smoldering pools of plastic.

Maybe my deduction was more of an assumption.

The next thing that happens is that my eight-year-old is standing in the doorway. He saw the whole thing. You can imagine the waterworks that Pat and I had to deal with.

Could you imagine if Derek had actually been in the room when I did that?

I could have melted him!

The next time I go in for more prescriptions, I'm going to ask for more than something to deal with the flatulence.

Take care,

Squiff:

I don't know about those Big Ships, but I'm pretty sure we're dealing with some damned *fast* ships here.

Hugh Spencer

I'm still having a lot of fun. I seem to have mastered the speed and directional controls for whatever kind of vehicle this is supposed to be. Last week we got a memo from the Lab, telling us that they *think* that we're running training software for some kind of spacecraft.

Well, *duh*!

Then they went on to tell us not to be alarmed if the instruments on our consoles started to change. The alien software is making some suggestions to our sim hardware.

This is just so cool.

Do you remember that old MG Roadster that I fixed up for your old girlfriend? The red thing that had the running boards?

It was a loud and beautiful pig of a machine and if you stroked it right and said nice things it would do anything for you. (A lot like your old girlfriend, as I recall.)

Whatever craft we're simulating is a lot like that old MG. Except that it's capable of moving faster than light and I think it can travel through time. Which means that if you steer it just right, the chronometers will tell you that you've arrived before you left.

This is so much fun that I really don't mind that I'm not flying the real thing.

I've never loved a job this much. I really am the happiest when I'm in the motion capsule tugging at the control-tendrils and scoping out all the 3D imaging.

Do you remember Sue's youngest and how he was with his old Nintendo system? How he would bang away at the controller for hours on end? Silly kid used to cry and scream like they'd just pulled his teeth out if he couldn't move up to the next level. And when he did finally beat the game it was like he'd just found out that he was a junkie who just won a lifetime supply of morphine from the Lottery.

I told the kid that the cube was just a simple computer and what happened in the game was really just how you were interacting with the game programmers.

"No way!" the kid yelled at me. "It's all about how *good* you are, *how much you believe in the game!* The game knows you are trying your best, and it rewards you!"

That really creeped me out. The only thing that was creepier was the way the kid started lying in the dark all day in his room.

Waiting for the time when Sue finally gave up and said he could play some more.

You were at school so you probably don't remember how Sue had a yard sale a few months later and the game system mysteriously disappeared. The two weeks of withdrawal symptoms were a bit rough but I hear the kid turned out okay eventually.

I'm a bit like that kid these days. I lay around my room waiting for the next sim-run. What's really creepy is the fact that I love that part too.

Shivering and sweating here.

Andrew:

I got some new medicine and I'm feeling better.

The Process continues.

I can now see lower frequency sound waves and I don't need solid food any more. This makes grocery shopping a little more complicated but the family hasn't complained too much.

At least there's enough of my original physiology operating that the Prozac-like capsules I'm taking still work. There are no more outbursts of domestic telekinesis or spontaneous combustion. But I'm still obsessing about how everyone managed to miss first contact.

First Contact.

Remember when people used to capitalize those letters? Seems rather silly now.

I agree with those sociologists who finally decided that we all just "kind of noticed" that alien concepts and information were seeping into the collective (un)consciousness of the human race.

I also remember an interview with that Carl Sagan wannabe who said that this had probably been happening for quite some time but only recently had the phenomena reached the "cosmological tipping point" where we could now expect an "exponential increase in these intellectual manifestations."

Billions and billions of weird new ideas, all raining down on us.

Fuck, that was pretty good television.

I remember the interview because I felt so sorry for that astronomer and all his buddies. They'd had all those antennae stretched out all over the planet and the aliens weren't using radio signals to communicate with us.

They weren't even trying to communicate with us.

"The Vgotsky Effect" is what they eventually called it. I looked it up on the Internet if you actually care.

God, I'm ranting about nothing here. Must be the pills.

Anyway, we discovered that we were picking up the alien civilizations through "sublingual mental processes." Which apparently is the only way that information can be conveyed on a faster than light basis. Which is pretty handy if you're running a vast Galactic Super-Culture. (Ah, more obsolete capitalization.)

When I was younger I used to think all of this was pretty monumental stuff. Why doesn't anybody care about this kind of thing anymore?

Maybe it's like computers. You probably don't remember how exotic and exciting they used to be. Then we all got one, then we all had to start using them—so computers went from being a part of The Amazing World of the Future to yet another boring thing in everybody's pain-in-the-ass job.

So what's the outcome, I write in my drug-addled state.

Well, we are a very practical people. If alien concepts are seeping into our minds, then the best thing to do is to try and put them to some kind of commercial use.

In addition to the pills, I've been drinking quite a bit lately. Therefore, I'm pretty drunk right now. I'm sitting out on the porch, and my youngest is next to me building towers with Lego. Cost quite a bit to replace.

I'm trying to get some fresh air to help the bacteria breathe. The little buggers have penetrated the walls of my stomach and now there're rows and rows of little flesh valves in my gut, struggling hard to suck and push the air.

Isn't that a great conversation starter for my neighbours as they walk their dogs past the house? My youngest doesn't seem to notice, bless him.

It's about five in the afternoon, and the fact that I look so bloody horrific is one reason that I'm knocking back gin and cream soda so early in the day. Another reason is that I'm not sure how much longer my body will let me get drunk.

Now, how unfair is that?

Sorry about all the tedious free association, it won't happen again.

The next time I write, I'll be a genetically evolved super-being with the capacity for more coherent communication.

Toodles,

S—

Toodles?

Breathing through your gut? Are your abs just a big balloon now? Did you do all those sit-ups for nothing?

Sorry, guess I shouldn't make fun; it's just that I've had a hell of a week. Not exactly bad, just very different from what I was expecting. And since I spend most of my days exploring a simulation of the outer fringes of an unknown quadrant of the galaxy, that's saying quite a lot.

Things were going great until Wednesday. Just coming up on noon. Middle of the week, middle of the workday. Good time for something extreme.

I was steering out of a really complex five-sun solar system with 18 gas giants, when I noticed that I couldn't let go of the direction controls.

It felt like the skin on my fingertips had fused into the hardware. Did I mention that something had happened to the console? No, well, now it looked a lot softer and it was throbbing.

That just didn't seem right. I was still on a high from my hot piloting, so while I was interested at the intellectual level, I was more than willing to carry on with the mission profile.

"What the fuck is going on?"

That was what the shift controller was screaming. Which, I guess was a good thing. I mean it was nice that somebody out there was actually paying attention.

Anyway, the controller hits the master switch and shuts down all the sims. So I'm sitting there waiting for the techs to show up and unscrew me from the capsule. Meanwhile I sit there and watch the console kind of sigh and shudder, like somebody had just let all the air out of the electronics. (Yeah, I know that makes no sense!)

Then I pulled my hands away from the controls and saw the

Hugh Spencer

gooey pink tendrils that linked the insides of my fingertips with the wiring of the sim's hardware.

Definitely one of those Cronenbergian moments.

What was even stranger was the fact that while this hurt like ten simultaneous root canals, it also felt quite wonderful. Hard to explain, really.

So they used some tiny lasers to cauterize the tendrils, and wheeled me off to the medicos. Once we got there they jammed sensor probes up every orifice you can imagine, and put us on 24/7 monitoring.

So I lay there with a wire up my ass until Sunday. The good news is that they say we get to go back to the sims tomorrow.

Toodles to you too . . .

Andrew:
I guess this is a big week for transformations.

My skin has wrinkled up, turned green, and my eyes are all puffy and yellow. I look like one of the Incredible Intergalactic Turtle People.

Maybe that's not a joke. Maybe I really am one of the intergalactic turtle people.

Hard to say these days.

My doctor says that my Evolutionary Transformation Process has pretty much spiked, and very soon I'll be comfortable with all super-human abilities.

I don't know what qualifies him to make a statement like that, but I actually think he's right. Every time I have a bowel movement, I spontaneously factor quadratic equations while experiencing powerful flashbacks of the last time my neighbours had sex.

Which I'm sure will come in handy in the office environment at some point in time.

Best,

Stephen:
I received my official briefing today. Here's the short version:
The software we've been running in our simulators is turning me into an alien organism. Not just me, the whole team on my

shift.

You can imagine, as I watched the new tendrils slither out of my fingertips, what a big surprise that was.

Gosh, doctor, I said (the gill slits in my cheeks made my voice really wet and sloppy), I thought it was just a case of the flu.

No, they aren't that stupid. There must be some legal reason they gave me the news in this way. Sure enough, the medico opens up my file and takes out a document that I must have signed when I accepted the job.

"It's important for you to understand that, even though this is an unexpected development," the guy says, "you gave us full consent at the outset of the project."

That's an interesting medical opinion.

The chair in this office is making what passes for my ass these days really uncomfortable. All terrestrial furniture is bad these days. I only feel good inside the sim. I really don't care what the Company doctor is telling me. All I want to do is get back to my mission runs.

"We're shutting down the project," the doctor says. "We're just not sure what directions these transformations are taking."

Shutting it down? No runs?

Shit. Shit, shit *and shit*.

The doctor peers at some notes. He sounds a little uncertain because this communication was written by people who went to different schools.

"Apparently the missions you've been training for seem to be for some part of the galaxy that we're not likely to access for another two or three millennia."

I should have said something at that point. Raised some objection. But I didn't.

Maybe my mutant lisp was making me feel self-conscious.

"We just don't see any practical applications."

Bullshit. They just don't feel like spending any more money.

At that point, I do remember standing up really fast. Then I remember the flash of the doctor's needle, and the last thing I remember was noticing how quickly the floor was approaching my face.

The tranquilizer must have worked very fast. Guess my physiology hasn't changed that much.

Take care,

Andrew:
Sounds like we had some very similar days.

At least as far as needles and the lecture on "informed consent" were concerned. They have a better case with me. Unbelievable as it sounds to me now, I actually signed up for all this nonsense.

They called me up from my cubicle, on yes, a *Wednesday*.

I was doing lateral data matches from different Company divisions, and I was doing some good work. I didn't appreciate the interruption.

It's hard to get back on track when you're on a good telepathic roll.

Elwood was waiting for me. He was waiting in an office with a window.

Big domed forehead, brain the size of twelve supercomputers, bulging purple bloodshot eyes. As I recall, Elwood had those ugly eyes before he underwent the Process.

I never liked Elwood. I didn't like Elwood when he was an intern in human resources, I didn't like him when he had xenoplasmic goo oozing from his ears and nose, and I didn't like him on that particular Wednesday.

Even though he was a highly successful super-being.

It's interesting to discover what changes in a person and what doesn't.

"Stephen," Elwood spoke very quietly, very carefully. "We've been accessing your Actualization."

Yeah, tell me something that wasn't completely obvious, you ultra-craniated moron, I thought.

Then I briefly wondered if empathic telepathy was one of Elwood's evolved skills. Oh well, he might as well know the truth.

"We feel that the synergy between your potentialized self and our corporate objectives . . ."

This was not going to be good.

". . . isn't yielding the sorts of benefits we had hoped for."

Like you, maybe I should have said something. I could have tried to argue this point. Maybe I wasn't as smart as Elwood but my task-functional I.Q. was probably pushing 350 and I had been charted as a much more creative thinker than he'd ever be. So what, if I had slimy grey skin, a perpetually running "nose," and breathing pores up the sides of my body that emitted gasses that made me smell like a dead raccoon most of the time.

Small price for progress, right? I was one of the courageous few who had accepted the challenge of the (apparently) slimy, sticky and smelly space beings.

None of these revelations were going to help with my discussion with Elwood. Alas, he was the one with the astonishingly advanced bean-counting abilities. If I had dropped .00015% below some arbitrary performance criteria, I'm sure that chrome-dome here would know all the math behind it.

"We're going to have to terminate, Stephen."

Could be worse, I thought. With all my brainpower and creative genius, I could go freelance. Become an amazingly irritating and rich consultant.

Then it was my turn to get a piece of paper. It was something that I'd signed back when I was a lot dumber.

"You do understand that because we paid the costs for your intellectual improvements, we can't allow anyone else to profit from them."

It just got worse.

Here's an interesting historical factoid: do you know that they will use the same substance to burn out my mutagenic agents that they used to treat venereal disease? I mean before they discovered penicillin.

Mercury.

That's right. They're going to inject me with heavy doses of brain-killing, blood poisoning mercury. It will definitely sharply reduce my intelligence, it might make me go blind, but at least it won't kill me. Which, by the way, was the other option that Elwood mentioned.

I can even go home eventually. I wonder if there'll be anybody there waiting for me.

Maybe they've already started with doses in my food. I feel stupider these days. I'm watching a lot more sports on TV.

They say that eventually I'll get to come visit you at Fort Fuck-Up. Did you know that's what they call the containment facility for Unplanned Evolutionary Manifestations? Okay, at least my vocabulary isn't shot yet. And do you notice that we definitely capitalize those words?

We'll make quite a pair on visiting day. I'll never be so far gone that I won't be happy to see my baby brother.

You can tell me about the wonders of the universe and how you dreamt of visiting all those fantastic civilizations that drift beyond the stars.

And I'll just be wondering what stars are.

Love,

Originally published in On Spec Fall 2006 Vol 18 No 3 #66

Hugh A.D. Spencer has written for magazines, anthologies and radio. *On Spec* was instrumental in Hugh's writing career by publishing "Why I Hunt Flying Saucers" (which was nominated for an Aurora Award), "The Triage Conference" and "Sticky Wonder Tales". His first novel *Extreme Dentistry* was released in April 2014.

Emily's Shadow
Al Onia

The secluded little shop looked too inviting, and customers came in no matter how hard the lone proprietor tried to discourage them. This morning, the California sun gleamed through the windows. Silhouetted onto the rear wall, fuzzy letters read *Sandy's Sickles – Your Classic British Restoration Specialist*. A short man balanced on a ladder leaning against the wall. Alex "Sandy" McGuigan fussed with a screwdriver, installing a small sign.

Finished, he backed down the ladder. On a shelf eight feet above the shop floor rested a black and chrome Black Shadow. Sandy wiped his hands on the ever-present rag hanging from his overalls. The "Not For Sale" notice would save him from the constant offers to buy the bike. He looked at the larger sign he'd taken down. *If You Value Your Life Like I Value My Shop – Don't Touch Anything*. He turned it to face the wall then heard the mail drop.

"Ach, more bloody bills, nae doubt." Sandy squinted into the sunlight and went through the letters. One was heavier. He lifted his cheaters to his veined nose and saw the return address was the Department of Motor Vehicles. He dropped the rest of the mail on his counter and quickly opened it.

"Ah, there it is." He held the vanity license plate and traced the five-letter name with his finger. Sighing, he reached into his pocket and pulled out a set of mounting bolts. Sandy climbed up the ladder again and installed the plate onto the motorcycle. "Emily," he whispered. Sandy gave the fender and the new plate a quick wipe of his rag. Had it been nearly two years since he'd met her?

"Hello? Mr. McGuigan?"

Sandy had not heard her come in. He continued the task at hand. He torqued the last head bolt to his preferred spec, then rolled his stool from behind the BSA single. A woman, much younger than he, but still at least thirty, stood cradling a cardboard box. She glanced in the direction of the noise. "Hi. Are you Mr. McGuigan?"

"Aye, I'm Sandy."

"What a great place you have here." She came over to him. "A Shooting Star, right?" She peered under the gas tank and walked around the machine, still clutching the box.

Sandy nodded and watched her, ready to scold. Many lookers wanted to touch before anything else. She was different. Someone had taught her well.

She completed her circuit. "I've heard you're the best. At tuning and stuff. And restorations."

"I enjoy a challenge."

She set the box down on a vacant bike lift. "My name's Emily. I've brought something I'd like you to see, if you can spare a few minutes."

Sandy nodded. "It will take much of the afternoon to get this one running smooth, judging by the wee difficulties I've had wi' her so far." His special touch with machinery worked best when he was alone. And the rest after to rejuvenate needed solitude as well. He'd humour her, then lock the doors after she left.

Emily said, "It looks brand new."

"Oh, that it does. There's looks, and there's what's underneath. Ye never know until you run it in." He pointed at the bins of plastic-wrapped engine parts lining the wall behind him. "I can assemble any two engines with the same parts and to identical tolerances. One will tick over first kick, but its twin could take me a week to fettle."

"You must love your work. Your tools are spotless. I'll bet you have a tough time finding mechanics to work with you." She gave him a smile and a wink.

"I work alone," he said, then was sorry he snapped at her. She seemed to take no offense.

She nodded. "I understand. Another person would be in the way of you putting a bit of yourself into each project."

Sandy doubted she knew how close that was to the truth, but not in the sense she intended. He changed the subject. "So what is it I can do for you, Miss, uh, Emily?"

She opened the box she had brought in and began removing balls of crumpled paper. "This is what I have to show you." She lifted out a black and gold petrol tank with the letters H.R.D. stencilled on each side. Like an enchanted sword or hallowed talisman, it gained presence in the light of day. It glowed, befitting the untarnished aura of the legendary marque.

"A Vincent," Sandy breathed. He cleaned his hands on a fresh towel. "May I?"

"Of course." She handed it to him.

Sandy felt the energy leap to his fingertips before he touched it. In his hands, it smoldered. This would tax his ability and his stamina to a limit he'd never dared.

He cleared his throat to speak. "Excellent respray." He carried it over to the window and turned it in his hands. "Done a while ago, I'd guess. Most chaps use lacquer now. This was done in enamel." He handed it back to her, letting his fingers rest against the metal as long as he dared. "A lovely piece, nae doubt, but I still don't know what I can do for you. I don't buy pieces that I dinna have a customer for. They're quite rare."

"I know. I have the rest of it in my truck. I brought it all." She glanced around his shop. "I want you to help me put it together."

Sandy felt the air rush from his lungs. The rest of it? A Vincent Black Shadow, the *ne plus ultra* of post-war British motorcycles. He hadn't worked on one since his apprenticeship in Scotland as a teenager, nearly forty years before. His tuning magic was undisciplined then. He could now sense and exploit the natural energy in a bike, where it was efficient and where it was lost. This would test how far he had progressed. "I don't tolerate people 'helping' in my shop. I work alone." His eyes went back to the tank.

"Let me show you, Mr. McGuigan." Emily placed the tank back in its box. She grabbed his arm and escorted him outside. Her intense vitality surprised him. In the space of a few heartbeats, he felt Emily wax and wane like a building storm. Like the Vincent, she was a rare find.

She lifted the topper door on her truck and opened more boxes. Like the tank, pieces were carefully wrapped and organized. The frame bits gleamed black at him. Polished timing-covers sat atop a box marked "Engine." It was beautiful. The opportunity of an ever-shrinking lifetime had just walked through his front door. He said, "Where did you get this?"

A small frown appeared on the girl's face. "My ex-husband. He brought it back from Scotland ten years ago. He was a roughneck on the North Sea rigs. One of his co-workers needed cash, and Gerald bought it. We were going to build it together, a project to share." She opened another box and cleared away the paper. She pulled out the headlight nacelle. "I love the dials. They're like faces."

Sandy admonished, "Gauges, not dials."

"Gauges, got it. Thank you." She handed it to him and continued, "He tired of it and me. I let it sit in my mother's garage for the last three years." She blew dust from another box. "More than anything, I want to get it on the road. I need to have part of me in this motorcycle, to prove to myself I can do it."

She levelled her green eyes on him. In that moment, he could forgive her anything, even if she turned out to be Irish.

She said, "I'll follow whatever rules you demand. I came to you because everyone I talked to said you were the only person who could make this bike live. I had to meet you first, though." She touched his arm again. "I can't take it to anyone else. Please?"

The passion in her voice tightened his gut. He could not bear to see this machine leave here except under its own power. He said, "First of all, I don't build trophies. Do you ride?"

"I have begun to." She drew out the handlebars and turned to face him. She placed her hands where the grips would go and sat on a make-believe saddle, shoulders forward in a racer's crouch. "I will ride this motorcycle, Mr. McGuigan."

"Good. If you're going to be in the way, you'd better call me

Sandy. Come, lass, let's get it inside and start inventorying what we've got. I'll need that to give you a price."

Emily said, "I saw your sign about *Delinquent Accounts Will Be Sold*. I can assure you I have the funds."

He said, "Ach, that's just for the ruffian trade, don't you worry about it."

She said, "Thank you, Sandy."

She passed him a box from the truck. Their hands touched. She and the Vincent shared a contagion. And he had just been infected.

Sandy shouted over the roar of the engine. "D'ya remember how we smoothed the inlet castings? Now, I'll have to change the air screw settings a wee bit from factory spec." He hunched over and performed the operation in sequence, front to back. His ear was more exact than any mechanical synchronizer. The girl, as always, watched him, ready to follow his next order. She tilted her head, listening, then turned away. There was something different about her today.

He took advantage of her momentary inattention to comb the Black Shadow's corona in a uniform direction. Sandy passed his hand up the forks, across the frame, then made a second pass from the cylinder heads to the crankcase and back over the chain to the rear hub. Nary a rough spot, he thought. Not on the bike anyway. Emily didn't notice. He wondered if she was reaching the stage every customer experienced during a project: anxious to complete, yet bored with the endless detail. He called it "the restoration wall." Sandy shut off the ignition.

She snapped her head back. "It sounds good to me."

"Aye, she's as sweet a runner as I've had. I wish those damn tires would arrive."

Emily perked up, "Really, that's all we need?"

He sensed she was struggling to show interest. He couldn't put his finger on it. He put his hand on her shoulder. Her energy was low. He gave her shoulder a light squeeze. "Well, they will help. Tires, final wheel truing, light harness. Did you take the seat to the upholsterer?"

"I meant to do it yesterday. I got delayed. I *will* take it in tomorrow. Today, I'm bushed."

He said, "When it seems like there are too many frayed ends to pull together, that's when you've got to persevere. America was not founded by weak-willed Scots."

"I thought the British and French had something to do with it."

He waved his hand in dismissal. "Ach, propaganda; there's nae a village nor a river nor a mountain peak that does nae have a Mc- or Mac-someone-or-other in its history."

"I'm sorry, Sandy, I've just been really tired lately. It isn't the bike. You've been wonderfully patient with me and it. I'm struggling with details right now." She drew herself up and saluted him. "The seat, tomorrow."

Sandy didn't see Emily for a week. He pressed on with the bike as far as he could, wanting to finish, yet wanting more to share it with her. Ach, you old fool, he rebuked himself, what would she want with a curmudgeonly oatmeal savage like you?

When she didn't show up for a second week, he tried her phone. The message stated she was unavailable until further notice and to call her mother if necessary. Sandy waited two more days. He lowered the petrol tank into place and secured the mounting bolts. It was the focus of the machine. A pedigreed steed ready to conquer the steeplechase. He ran his hands lightly over the lettering for the umpteenth time. He hooked up the fuel lines, but resisted starting it without Emily. "I need the seat. Where is the girl?"

He dialled the number on his clipboard. "Hallo, is this Mrs. Breem? This is Sandy McGuigan. I'm helping your daughter with her motorcycle. Emily's what? No, I didn't know. Is she all right? Can I visit her there? Just let me write this down. Room six-twelve, yes I've got it. No, thank you verra much. Good day."

Sandy stared at the note. He tried to lift it from his desk but it weighed too much. How could she not have told him?

Sandy entered room six-twelve. His knees buckled for a moment. He didn't like hospitals. It was the smell, he decided. The smell and the negative energy. Emily lay by the window, looking out. He cleared his throat, not knowing what to say.

She rolled her head, "Sandy, am I glad to see you. Come here and give me a hug."

Emily's Shadow

He clutched his cap and walked over to her, sidestepping the tubes and wires running from her bed to the wall.

"It's great to see you, Sandy." She squeezed him tighter than he expected. He didn't know how hard to squeeze back.

She said, "How are you? Should you be away from the shop? I'm not paying for travel time, you know."

"I'm fine. How are you? I spoke to your mother. You did nae tell me."

"About this?" She lifted an arm and dangled the IV tubes. "I am sorry, Sandy, I'm supposed to be in remission. Working with you is positive therapy, but I'm having a bit of a relapse. They're going to drain some fluid tomorrow, and I should be up and about by the end of the week. I took the seat in and told him to call you when it's ready. How is the bike coming? Did the tires arrive? The Avons, right?"

Sandy couldn't stop examining all the hookups. "Emily, I don't know much about medicine, but all this malign machinery canna be good for a body."

"We can rebuild her," Emily said in a stern voice. "Make her better than she was." She laughed. "And you better have that machine ready for me to ride when I get out."

Sandy accepted her hand and felt the vigour trying to will its way through her muscles to her fingers. "What's wrong with you, then?"

Emily rolled her eyes, "Well, I have refused to ask for the prognosis, and won't hear of the odds one way or the other. It's called Hodgkin's disease, and I know that Mario Lemieux beat it and so will I. That's all there is to say about that. Did you bring pictures?" She wiggled her fingers at him.

Sandy was overwhelmed by her tenacity. "No, but I will take some this afternoon and I'll call on the seat. She'll be ready in a week, I promise."

"I will hold you to that."

A nurse bustled in to change IV bags.

"I better be getting back to the shop."

"Thanks for coming, Sandy. Can you forgive me for not telling you?"

"Why should I need to?"

"Because you are my very special friend. You have shared your shop and your talent with me, and I didn't share this with you. This means a lot to me, you coming here. Give me a hug before you go. Never mind about her." Emily winked at the nurse.

He bent over and put his arms around her. She said, "I won't break, you can hold me tighter than that, ya wiry devil."

He did pull her closer and squeezed. "That's more like it, Sandy," she said and kissed his cheek.

Even if he could have thought of the right words, the lump in his throat wouldn't let him speak.

True to her word, the following Monday, Emily was waiting for him to open up.

True to his word, Sandy had the Vincent ready. He said, "I haven't fired her since we static tested her last month. I was waiting for you."

They pushed it out into the morning sun. "Are you up to starting her?" he asked.

Emily swung her leg over the saddle. "Try and stop me. I believe the routine is, fuel on." She turned the tap like he'd shown her. "Choke full, carb tickle, switch on, and . . ." She lunged up in the air and dropped her entire weight on the kick-starter. He smiled approval as her right wrist twisted in coordination with the kick. The V-twin engine rumbled to life. They were both grinning like kids.

He said, "Let her warm up without revving the throttle. When she'll idle without the choke at just over one thousand rpm, she's ready to ride."

Emily donned her helmet and gloves. Sandy ran inside and came out with his camera. "Give me that smile again," he ordered.

She grabbed the handlebars with both hands and stuck out her tongue as he snapped the picture. She released the choke and studied the tachometer. She looked at him and he nodded. Emily engaged first gear as he'd told her and let out the clutch, her eyes fixed down the road. He saw the woman and bike as one graceful entity for the first time. She accelerated away from the shop. He heard her upshift once, and then again. Ten minutes later, bike and rider were back.

Emily was still grinning. She shut off the ignition, closed the fuel cock and grunted the Vincent up on its main stand. She undid her helmet, shook her hair loose and coughed.

"Are you okay?"

She smiled, "I am in love." She hugged him. "Sandy, it's wonderful. I'm so pleased. You should be proud of what you've done. I have only one question."

"Go ahead."

"What's a ton?"

"Ye nae did a ton?" Sandy exclaimed. "She's hardly run in." He began to fuss around the machine, feeling for signs of stress.

"I don't know. What *is* a ton?"

"One hundred miles per hour. A Black Shadow will easily do the ton, but neither it nor you are ready."

"Admonishment accepted. No, I only had it up to fifty or so. A half-ton, just like my truck."

"A good first ride. I want to check my clearances and torque settings. Was the clutch okay? It seemed to grab just a wee bit early."

"The clutch was fine for me. I read these vintage bikes are difficult to shift."

Sandy said, "They can be, for some. But you have a natural feel for timing your throttle and clutch coordination. You're a gifted rider and I don't say that often."

"Thanks. Coming from you, that is a great compliment. And you're a gifted, no, a *magical* mechanic. I shall celebrate by taking you out for dinner this evening. You will close early, and I will pick you up at seven o'clock."

Sandy stammered, "I'd better get her inside. Do I need a tie?"

"For supper? I hope not. But no overalls, either."

Dinner was at a little place overlooking the river. They watched in silence as the sun set over the arid hills to the west of town.

Sandy couldn't avoid the obvious question any longer. "When do you want to collect the bike?"

Emily put down her wine glass and looked down for a minute before responding. "Could you keep it for a while longer? You said you had to check the torque settings and such."

"Aye, I'll do that tomorrow, and she'll be finished. I've never had a project come together so painlessly. I'll miss her. And you. Around the shop, I mean."

Emily said, "Why Sandy, I've never seen you that color. I didn't think you could be any redder. It's quite becoming."

"It's warm in here, I'll admit with no shame."

"I'd like you to keep her for now. I may not be able to enjoy her immediately." She coughed into her napkin.

"What's wrong, lass? Is it the Hodgkin's?" He felt insensitive as soon as the words left him.

"They found a shadow on my lung in the last x-ray, but there is treatment I can undergo depending on the diagnosis."

"It's their damn machines. They manufacture problems. You take a motorcycle. If it does nae run proper, you eliminate the potential trouble spots logically. You tell them that you won't have being sick anymore. Hold out your arms."

He moved his hands from her shoulders down to her fingers, as close as he could without touching her skin. "Ya feel that? That is your energy." He repeated the process two more times until the rough spots were eliminated. "As long as you can marshal it in one direction, you'll be right."

"I do feel it, Alex. I will fight this and win. There may be the odd setback along the way. So will you keep the bike?"

"Of course. I'm planning to go back to Glasgow in a few weeks and the Vincent will be safe in the shop."

Emily brightened. "You're going to Scotland? How marvellous." She squeezed his hands. She bit her lower lip for a moment then asked, "Can I go with you, Sandy? I'd love to see Scotland again."

Sandy was dumbfounded. "What would your mother say? And she's *my* age."

"How long have you lived in America? My mother can say that her *adult* daughter is in Scotland, fulfilling a dream with a true gentleman."

"I will always be a gentleman in the strictest sense with you."

"I know, I would not ask you for more; it would jeopardize what we have."

"What about your treatments?"

"Don't you want me to come?"

It was Sandy's turn to cough. "I would enjoy your company verra much, but I don't want the trip to be the last thing you do."

"Sandy, it won't be. Neither will it be the last thing *we* do."

Three weeks later, they stood in line to board their plane. Emily said, "Sandy, I have a going away present for you."

"Your coming wi' me is present enough, surely."

"This is something special." She pulled a paper out of her handbag.

"My reading glasses are stuffed at the bottom of my pack," he protested.

"I'd love to read it to you. It says I am in remission. I just have to check in every month or two, but that's all. Bonnie Scotland, get ready for me.

"Sandy, I've never known you to be at a loss for words."

"If I say too much, I'm afraid I'll choke up." He ran his hands along her sleeves. Her energy was in unison. He continued to comb her aura.

Emily whispered in his ear, "Softie. If you're still too choked, I'll eat all that haggis myself."

Sandy shook himself. "That you will *not* do, young lady."

Sandy dismounted his BSA and walked over to where Emily and the Vincent were parked.

She pointed at the Pacific Ocean hundreds of feet below. "The fog filling all the inlets reminds me of the Scottish coast, remember?"

"Aye, a wee bit warmer here though." He sat on the guardrail, savouring the moment and the company. They had spent the last two months riding every weekend, following Emily's quest to see every bit of northern California, on two wheels.

She pointed to the map on her tank. "The bed and breakfast is another hundred miles. No need to rush but I am tired."

She started her bike. It coughed and quit. She gave a second kick. It caught, but she had to keep revving the throttle.

Sandy took off his helmet and knelt down. "Stay seated. Keep it running."

He listened and ran his hand down her back. He passed over the engine. Rider and machine were ill. It was more than he had the reserves to mend. He made his choice. Sandy stood behind the bike and caressed both hands down Emily's spine and legs.

He repeated the ritual from her shoulders to her hands until he was drained.

He said, "You'll ride my Beezer back home. I'll wrestle with this beast."

Emily nodded, "I feel better, but I think you're right."

Back in the shop, Emily wrung her hands, "I knew it! I went too fast and broke it."

Sandy shook his head, "It's nothing you've done, lass. She's a stout machine; and as near as I can tell, she's nae broke." He ran his hands over the engine, listening to the rough idle and trying to smooth it out. "I don't understand it." He stood and wiped his hands then turned the ignition off.

Emily put her hand on the seat. "I have to tell you something, Sandy." She hesitated then continued, "It was over a month ago. I did it."

"Did what?"

"The ton. A hundred miles an hour." She grinned. "I couldn't help it. She just purred and I thought to myself, *Emily, if you don't do it now, you'll always wonder what it feels like.* So that's why I thought I'd broken it."

"Nonsense, she was meant to be ridden, not sit here looking prideful. You run along home. You're still tired from the trip. I can tell. We'll right her tomorrow."

"Okay, I will see you in the morning." She gave his cheek a peck and walked slowly to her truck.

When she had gone, he solemnly placed both hands on the tank. He closed his eyes and willed the energy to flow but there was no magic. He had lost his gift for the Vincent. He walked over to the BSA and tried it. Not just the Vincent then, he concluded. His talent now flowed only to Emily.

Twelve months later, the Vincent still sat in Sandy's shop, its only movement by hand, to keep out of the way of the other mundane projects. Sandy covered it, turned out the lights of his shop, and resigned himself to a visit he did not want to make.

He knocked on the door, his cap gripped firmly in both hands. Emily's mother opened the door to Emily's room. "Hello

Sandy, she's expecting you. I'm going for a bite to eat."

"I'll stay as long as you want and Emily can stand."

She said, "Don't you ever think that. You gave us all so much more time with her."

He squeezed her hand and went inside.

"This is better than the last time I was here," he said. There was no machinery. Emily lay in bed by the hospital window, the lone medical instrument an IV tower and bag.

"Sandy," her whisper was hoarse.

"You're wearing that wig we found in Sonoma." He brushed the bronze hair back from her forehead.

"It was always your favourite." The low sun cast shadows through the window across her bed.

Sandy said, "It's turning red under the sunset."

"Never as red as your face that night I asked you to take me to Scotland, do you remember?"

"Aye, that's a night I'll ne'er forget. Nor the other trips we made."

Emily said, "I liked Santa Barbara the best."

"Santa Cruz," Sandy corrected her.

"Of course. The painkillers confuse me." She raised an arm an inch above the bed and waved the IV tube. "I don't even recognize Mum some days. I never knew there were battles a body isn't meant to win." She coughed. Sandy held her until the spasms stopped. "How's the bike?"

"I fuss wi' her regularly. I'm not ready to give up on her yet."

"Don't let it eat you up. The Vincent served its purpose."

"Aye," he said, staring out the window at the lengthening shadows. "It gave you life, Emily."

"It gave *us* life, Sandy. You're a different man than when I met you."

"Only around you," he said.

"No. I see you smile more often and you are unaware of it. It's who you are now."

He held her and whispered, "I found purpose." He could feel Emily's aura fleeing her body. He held her tighter, trying to corral the energy that could no longer be contained within her. He stared at the tube running into her arm. There was nothing to silence his pain.

Sandy took a final look up at the Black Shadow, lifeless in its repose, the only "trophy" he'd ever built. Every bit of his magic had gone into it, but he did not regret that loss. It had freed him. And Emily, she had freed him and exhilarated him.

He shuffled to the front window of his shop and picked up the other new sign he had ordered. It slid out of the packing, and he placed it facing toward the street. He stepped outside and checked it in the dying sun. *Apprentice Wanted. Apply Within.*

Originally published in On Spec Summer 2009 Vol 21 No 2 #77

Al Onia is a geophysicist living in Calgary, Canada. In addition to *On Spec*, his fiction has appeared in *Ares, The Speculative Edge, Heroic Fantasy Quarterly, Spinetingler, Marion Zimmer Bradley* and the anthologies Body-Smith 401, North of Infinity and Warrior Wisewoman 3. Al is a two-time Aurora Award finalist in the short story category. His first novel, *JAVENNY*, will be published in August 2014 by Bundoran Press.

The Resident Guest
Sandra Glaze

Between the ages of sixteen and twenty-one, I was a part-time front-desk clerk at the Edwardian Hotel. In that time, I also graduated from high school, learned to drive, had my appendix out, lost my virginity and nearly finished a degree in history. But when I see my appendix scar, still white against the flesh made pink by the heat of a bath, it isn't nearly dying that I think of, but staring out into the darkness of the lobby at midnight supported by four massive pillars.

A hotel lobby is a whirling eddy of humanity. You can never step into the same lobby twice, to paraphrase the philosopher. To a girl from the suburbs, the lobby was a well of experience by proxy—a lot of it cynical and tawdry, in fact, so much the better. It was a shabby place that had known grander times, but I was a new woman, at least in those hours away from parents and school friends. Each guest was an audience for whom I could rehearse my new self.

Standing behind the desk—we could never sit no matter how empty the lobby or how late the hour by edict of Mr. Herschel, the general manager—my duties were to file keys, take messages, advise housekeeping which rooms needed to be made up, register guests, and very occasionally, turn guests away. Mr. H had also decreed that we could not register guests of opposing sexes who wished to share a room, if they could not provide proof of "benefit of clergy." This decree was embarrassing to uphold and faintly ludicrous, the year being 1973.

So, it is 1973 and I am standing in the lobby of The Edwardian Hotel around midnight on Remembrance Day. My absent appendix is throbbing. I get some relief by shifting my weight from foot to foot. My feet, curiously, do not bother me at all, despite seven-inch platform heels. Nietzsche said something to the effect that a woman who was aware that she looked good would never catch cold, despite the inadequacies of her dress. In those days my feet never pained me so long as I stood stylishly. This is no longer so. Nietzsche also said that what didn't kill us made us stronger. Two proofs that Nietzsche is of limited application, but I digress.

The lobby of a hotel is a public space. The public, provided they are presentable and solvent, are welcome to visit the lobby and even linger if they are on their way to a function or the bar. The Edwardian had two bars, each one named for London squares: the Leicester, and the Trafalgar. The Leicester Square had a theatrical theme and was a favourite with the D'Oyly Carte Opera Company when it was in town to perform at the Royal Alex Theatre. I never learned to like Gilbert and Sullivan, but I loved being in the passing company of those world-weary actors. I didn't mind when they compared the Edwardian unfavourably with other hotels they stayed in, because learning the name of a better hotel in New York or Tokyo added to my own varnish of worldliness.

The Trafalgar Square had a naval theme, complete with the *de rigueur* denizens of a port. Dan Gregson, chief of security, his bald head the shape of a bullet, would sweep these ladies out every night. After which they would drift back, not drawn by the possibility of trade so much as borne back by an irresistible tide.

For hotel guests however, a lobby is also a private space, an extension of their room, where they are free to linger as long as they like. Mr. Leslie treated the Edwardian's lobby as his parlour. It was where he read the newspaper and socialised. He never had visitors, of course, and he never spoke to the other guests. He only spoke to the bellmen, myself and Rose, who ran the switchboard. She was a tiny sparrow of a woman who loved the ballet and who seemed held to earth only by the weight of

The Resident Guest

her luxuriant hair, which she wore in thick braid to her waist.

Another contradiction contained in a hotel is the idea of the resident guest. Mr. Leslie was our resident guest. How can someone be a resident, that is to say, occupy their home and be a guest there at the same time? Mr. Leslie said it wasn't so strange when you thought about it, because we are guests in our own bodies. He was a small, thin man, always dressed in carefully-pressed grey trousers and a blue jacket, with the left sleeve carefully pinned in place, so that his phantom hand pressed against his heart in a perpetual pledge. He was a veteran of Vimy Ridge. It was rumoured among the bellmen that he had won the Military Cross, but he only spoke of the war to amuse you or invite you to think him a fool.

When I asked him about his Military Cross, he explained that he was assigned to a regiment of Dr. Barnardo's Boys. All of the men in his unit were orphans who had been dispatched to Canada to be fostered or enslaved, depending on whose care they had the luck or misfortune to be handed to. Mr. Leslie had been sent to a tobacco farm outside of St. Mary's. "That farmer thought hisself hard done by, being sent a pair of tiddlers like me and my sister. We worked hard, but he were fair to us and didn't do my sister no wrong, which was more than could be said for many, I can tell you. I often think it were the hard work in the clean air on that farm what made me fit fer trenches." Despite being sent to Canada as a boy and decades spent in a shipping office of the Canadian Pacific Railway, his Yorkshire accent endured like a dry-stone wall.

To promote *esprit de corps*, the men of the First World War were often assigned to regiments by some commonality, "Pal Brigades" they were called. They could be lads from the same village or town. There was a brigade made up of professional football players, and another of coal miners all drawn from the same pit. Mr. Leslie said all of the Barnardo boys were on the small side, most having nearly starved before coming out to Canada—and many starved here.

To hear him tell the story of his medal, a general stopped by for an inspection. Having done the rounds of the barracks, he said, "Here are some medals lads, a VC and a Military Cross. They're all the King can spare today," and threw them to the troops. Being one of the tallest of the shortest, Mr. Leslie said he caught the Military Cross, but he only ever wore his general service medal, "a sign of comradeship," he said, and nothing more.

My first night back after my operation, Mr. Leslie appeared out of the darkness, smiling broadly and advancing upon the desk so rapidly, his medal beat time on his chest. He leaned into the desk enthusiastically like an invading ship making the beachhead a little too fast. "E lass, thou were that close, but thou look well on it now."

I almost wondered if he'd visited me in the hospital in my delirium, even though I knew he never left the hotel. It seems Freddie, the bell captain, had told him what had happened. "Thee's lucky thou didn't have my surgeon," he chuckled, "I went inta' infirmary with trench foot!" He turned to where at least one bellman should have been waiting with Freddie for me to call "front" and carry up the bags of late arrivals. Tonight, however, there were no late arrivals: there were no bookings at all, except a small airline crew who were expected around three a.m. So, there was only Freddie, but no other bellmen in sight. They were probably in the labyrinth of service corridors, smoking, or giving the hookers the all-clear.

Freddie was a tall, well-padded Italian with wiry hair who tugged regularly at the sleeves of his slightly-too-small uniform jacket—a gesture that somehow suggested he was getting ready to throw a punch. Despite Freddie's daunting size, the bellmen collectively reminded me of mice. They would disappear when there was nothing to profit them in the lobby, and would reappear before a new guest had set down his suitcase.

The bellmen knew the hotel intimately. They knew the view offered by each room, the quality of the bed, whether the bathroom had a tub or only a shower, and also the history of each room and its lingering effects. Room 728 faced east towards St. James Cathedral. In 1929, a despondent stockbroker had hanged himself in it at the stroke of midnight. Guests in that room often claimed to have been kept awake by the church-bells tolling twelve every hour. A woman had given birth in Room 430, and her pangs often infected subsequent guests, who would call down asking for sodium bromide or even the house doctor we didn't have.

The bellmen could be quite unkind to difficult or miserly

guests, for though as front desk clerk I assigned the rooms, if they contradicted me, guests inevitably opted for their seasoned choice over mine. I never asked the bellmen when, or in what room, Mr. Leslie had died, because he was still so firmly with us. In the half-light I could see little patches of grey stubble that he had missed. "A one-armed barber is more useless than a one-armed paper hanger and that's the truth of it," he said, as if he'd read my mind.

"Today must be a very special day for you," I said by way of distracting him, in case he had in fact read my mind. I nearly began to tell him about the Remembrance Day assembly we'd had that morning, but that would remind him of the girl I was at school, a person I determinedly left behind when I punched the time clock inside the staff entrance off Dalhousie Lane that always smelt of garbage and onions.

"Aye, hard not to think of my mates today, but you know lass, when I think of 'em, it's the living, not the dying I remember—the good, not the bad.

"There been lots of talk about how cruel the officers were. My captain were kindness itself. He checked all the lads' feet as regular as possible. Trench foot were no joke. If he found a man getting into trouble that way, he bathed his feet his self, just like our Lord. He'd dry and powder 'em and he'd give 'em a pair of his own socks, knitted by his own gran', who were a duchess no less. Made us promise not to let on if we ever came to dinner," and he laughed. "About as likely as finding a strawberry in Hartley's jam! Now the food, that was terrible! I haven't had rabbit since I left France, nor will I ever again, so help me." He grew quiet. "That's how I came to lose my arm, did I never tell thee?

"Now you might think I should be grateful to that rabbit, because he was how I came to finally be sent home, but that coney didn't think to cross my path until August 1918, so I think I would have rather taken my chances. Your history books might have you believe that it were constant noise and shelling down there, but it weren't. There were lulls where you could actually hear the birds singing. Where you could stop being scared long enough to realise you were soaked to the bone, aching cold, hadn't had a letter in weeks and were hungrier than you'd ever imagined you could be and still draw breath. E, in some ways the lulls were worse than the fighting, but they were a chance to forage.

"Some of the boys would set to rat bodies, not for valuables, but for food, what were more valuable than anything. That I couldn't do. A mate offered me a share of some bully beef he'd found, but the thought of eating rations meant for another man, I can't say why, made me gag. I said to him, how do you fancy some fresh meat? There were some woods just to the south of us. I set my snares, just like I did on the farm. It took an hour or two, but I caught myself a large jack. By then it were almost dark, and would you believe it, I fell into a foxhole and broke my arm on a gun emplacement. Just an unlucky tumble. I had a green stick break. So much for lucky rabbit's foot."

"They amputated your arm because it was broken?"

"Nay, nay lass 'course not, but then the shelling started again and the triage officer put clumsy lads like me with only a broken arm at the back of the queue. By the time I got to front'a queue, it'd gone gangrenous, so no choice. Things like that, they happened all the time, one them quirks of fate. Leastways, it was me left."

I wanted to know why he wasn't angry, but the sudden appearance of Dan Gregson, meant I didn't get to ask.

"Hello, beautiful," Gregson said, filling the desk space with his bulk and the smell of sweat. "You wanted me to do a room check."

I had paged him three hours before, when I came on duty. The Vice-Regal Suite had been vacated late, but there was no record of whether it had been made up, and it was reserved for an early check-in. Dan was one of those men who thought all women preferred being called various adjectives or generic endearments. At the same time, he made a point of tacitly asserting his power by never doing what you asked him to when you asked him to do it. "Yes, I wanted to know if the Vice-Regal was made up," I told him, even though he already knew this.

"I don't know, I'll check it for you," he said looming up, "but first you'll have to hold my hands for five minutes." I realise that you are probably as disturbed by my compliance as I was at his request. His fee for service had never risen beyond 300 damp seconds of my hands in his. Though it was not pleasant, it was no worse than waiting for a bus in the rain, and considerably

The Resident Guest

less frightening than finding out what he would have done if he'd been denied. The five minutes ended. "OK cutie, if you don't hear back from me, it's made up."

Mr. Leslie, who had vanished into the depths of a wing chair at Gregson's approach, reappeared. "Doing a double back?" he asked. A double back was when you worked two shifts separated by less than twelve hours. If you were assigned a double back, it usually meant staying the night at the hotel. I said I was, and because the hotel was so quiet the night manager was letting me have one of the better rooms. "Make sure you put the chain on't door, won't you, lass?" he smiled encouragingly, and disappeared.

My airline crew had just arrived, each one of them thin, bronzed, weary, and by their faces, instantly disappointed by their accommodation.

I put the chain on the door that night, more because it seemed sensible than because Mr. Leslie had said to do it. "One of the better rooms" featured foil wallpaper that reflected the light that crept around the corners of the psychedelic curtains that didn't quite cover the window. I slept fitfully. My side ached, and I wasn't used to the cathedral bells tolling the hour. At least that was what I thought woke me at first. Then I realised it was the rattle of the door against the chain. I waited for a thick damp hand to attempt to reach in, but there was only laboured breathing and a few more impatient jangles, before a voice humid with menace said, "Bitch," and pulled the door shut with no thought to preserving the quiet.

The next day, Mr. Leslie passed by the desk on his way to the cafeteria in the basement where staff also ate. "Sleep well lass?" Yes, I nodded, and started to speak, when he cut me off with, "Mulligatawny soup today, and rice pudding," and winked. I never told him what happened, or thanked him. Somehow it seemed we each understood.

Over the following months, Mr. Leslie took to keeping the watches of the night with me. I can still see him with his back to me, leaning onto the desk with his surviving arm and commenting on the flow of people through the lobby, especially the ladies. "Now that's mutton dressed as lamb and no mistake," or, "I've seen better legs on a table."

He took the complaints of other guests to heart. One couple

insisted on checking out only an hour after checking in when the wife found a mousetrap under the bed. "E, but there were nowt in it, and if there were, the matter were dealt with, were it not?" He shook his head and let out a heavy sigh.

I asked him about Vimy, but he would not be drawn out on the subject, even when I said I was doing research for school, although he took great interest in my academic career. "Never look back lass, that's my motto. Every time I've looked back, I've got in trouble."

He also took an interest in my fledgling love life. When my boyfriend of four months gave me a necklace for my birthday, he asked to see it. I leaned forward, but he said, no, to take it off, he wanted to hold it. He clutched it for a few minutes, looking away before handing it back. "Aye, e's a good enough lad, but not quite good enough, lass, and he's bound for far away. You've no call to give him what you can't call back." I didn't always take his advice, but I always regretted it when I didn't.

Remembrance Day drew near again. "I'll tell thee why I joined up," he said suddenly one night, as if he was announcing he was stepping out to get a paper. He cocked his head, inviting me to speculate. To fight for King and Country was my obvious guess. "Nay. Same as a lot of lads: to impress a lass."

"And did you?"

"Not so's you'd notice," and he laughed, but it sounded like an empty tin can tumbling on concrete. "She lived two farms over. Lovely she were, chestnut hair and blue eyes. A voice like when you chime a toast on a crystal glass. Katie Boldwood, she were then.

"When we lads signed up, the farmers all about there clubbed together and threw us a great supper. There were so many folk you'd have thought it were Harvest Home, except the ladies put their best tablecloths on the trestle tables, and them that had china put it out, and all the local grandees drank our health. They told us we was brave and we'd come home heroes. That's where I got my keepsake of Katie Boldwood."

Once again I guessed the obvious: her picture, a lock of hair?

"A spoon. When nobody were looking, I stole the spoon she'd used to eat her pie. Maybe that's where I went wrong. Taking that spoon were wrong, and I took it with me all the way to England—terrible crossing—and then all the way to France. I ate some terrible muck with it, I can tell you. With every horrible mouthful, I told myself, this spoon has touched the lips of Katie Boldwood, and if I get through this, I just might too.

"My best pal in the unit was Charlie Fielding, cracking lad. He joined up 'cause he were that homesick; he thought if he made it through, he could go back to L'unun for keeps and maybe find his sister.

"We were having what passed for breakfast when the shelling started. It's a wonder we could hear the whistle sounding. It were the signal we were to go forward to the assembly trench. I don't remember being afraid. I just remember grabbing my rifle with left hand and racing ahead of Charlie, the spoon in my right. I must o' thought I'd shove it somewhere safe before we went ov'r top. Except I dropped it. I stopped to pick it up. I bent down. The bullet that were meant for me killed Charlie." There was a long silence. "So he never saw L'unun again," he said by way of a conclusion. In the Leicester Square bar someone broke a glass and laughed.

"And did you ever see Katie Boldwood again?"

"Nay, lass, nay, and it's Mrs. John Baldwin now, or so I heard last. That'd be a good match, uniting two farms side by each. I heard tell them made a pot of money selling them two parcels to developers.

"When there were enough of my regiment to gather round a table, we used to meet up once a year o'r the Royal York—the boys liked that one, closer to Union Station. Couple them went back St. Mary's way and married local girls, like I allas intended, but there you go. I weren't fit for farm work no more, so I ploughed a desk. It weren't a bad life.

"Silas Campion told me the Edwardian were where Katie and John came before setting out on their honeymoon journey. After I retired, they tore down the building my flat was in, and by then the Edwardian was, well, what polite folk would call affordable. And, yes, I imagined that maybe one day Katie would take a sentimental journey and I might catch a glimpse." He looked up and saw my face flooded with pity. He smiled adding, "And return her spoon." His laughter echoed strangely up in the atrium and lasted far longer than the sound that bore it.

"Do you really still have it?" I asked when the terrible moment had passed.

"Indeed I do," and he patted his left breast pocket, but didn't take it out to show me. He'd already let me see too much.

Days and nights went by. Mr. Leslie was in a jaunty mood. He strode through the lobby on his way to dinner. He saluted me with his newspaper and whistled "I'm the Man Who Broke the Bank at Monte Carlo." Other guests in the lobby looked around, trying to see where the song came from.

My first job when coming on duty was to ensure that if any reservations had requested a particular room, that the room was ready. A Mr. J. Baldwin had booked a suite for two nights for him and his wife. The manager had given the room at the regular double rate because it was for their golden wedding anniversary.

As I filed keys in their cubby-holes I wondered if Mr. Leslie knew, had known, that the girl his young self had so desperately wanted to impress, the girl he went to war for, would soon be a guest at his hotel, and that was why she had been on his mind. A quick scan of the lobby confirmed that Mr. Herschel was not about. I went around the corner to where the switchboard operator was secreted. I wanted to talk to Rose, who had known Mr. Leslie longer than I had. But Rose wasn't there. Instead Astrid was on duty, chattering to a friend about a party she had been to. She beckoned me to approach without pausing for an instant. I retreated back to my post.

Later that night, an older couple came striding across the lobby. Freddie was not far behind, managing their three large bags with great professionalism. Mr. Baldwin was tall in a pinstripe suit that was vaguely out of date; handsome, but not as handsome as he clearly had once been before his frowns had become permanently etched in his forehead.

She was still stunning, just as Mr. Leslie had said. Her hair was still chestnut brown, not like I'd imagined, cascades of curls, but swept up in a glamorous way that drew attention to her periwinkle-blue eyes. Her clothes were absolutely *au courant*, yet dignified. I could imagine her surrounded by suitors. I couldn't imagine her eating pie with a spoon in the open air.

"Miss, I believe you have a room for us, Mr. and Mrs. John Baldwin. I can't believe you don't have parking."

"It's not on site, no, but we can take care of your car."

The Resident Guest

"I'll be happy to park your car for you, ma'am," Freddie said carefully putting their bags down.

"This used to be a remarkable hotel," Mrs. Baldwin observed, "and now you have people who can do two things at once. You will take care of our bags," she said to Freddie without looking at him, "and you," she indicated Ted the bellman behind her with the slightest tip of her head up and backwards, "will take care of the car." Her voice cut through the lobby air like a blade made of frozen honey. It hurt, but you couldn't say why.

It was my turn. I hadn't moved. I could see Mr. Leslie by the fireplace, underneath the picture of Edward the VII, craning his neck for a better view. "Apparently he can do two things at once and you can do none. Eyes front, young lady. We would like to check in."

"Yes, of course, I'm sorry," I handed her the registration form. Mr. Leslie moved closer. He was standing by one of the two pillars closest to the desk.

"Pen, you ridiculous girl!" Her irritation was accelerating. I felt caught between it and Mr. Leslie's approach. I hastily found a pen and handed it to her. She began to fill out the registration form, pressing ever harder in order to make the pen work, tearing at the three-part form with the pen as if it were a dull knife. "Bring me another form and a pen that works," she ordered. Mr. Leslie seemed to hesitate.

"I'm terribly sorry about the pen. I'm sure you'll like the room: it's one of our best. Do you have any special plans for while you are in town?" I was babbling. I knew it, but it was all I could think of to try and sweeten her mood. "I see you are here for your golden anniversary. Congratulations, that's quite a milestone. My parents just separated. It's wonderful to see such commitment."

Mr. Leslie took another step forward. She was nearly finished with the form. Without looking up, she quietly told me, "Stop being pious," Mr. Leslie was within earshot now, "and take off that poppy you sanctimonious chit; Remembrance Day was two days ago."

I handed the suite key to Freddie, tough Freddie, friend of whores, procurer of drugs and after-hours alcohol who, like me, had tears in his eyes. Mrs. Baldwin turned on her expensive heels and motioned for him to lead the way.

All experience is gained at a loss. Where Mr. Leslie had stood there lay a small pile of dust.

Between the ages of sixteen and twenty-one, I worked as a front-desk clerk at the Edwardian Hotel. In that time I also graduated from high school, learned to drive, had my appendix out, lost my virginity, nearly finished a degree in history and saw a ghost die. Torontonians are notoriously indifferent to their local heritage. When time came for the Edwardian to make way for condos, there was a whimper of protest outside and a couple of articles beside the electronics ads in the newspapers.

I was not sorry to see it come down.

Originally published in On Spec Summer 2009 Vol 21 No 2 #77

Toronto born **Sandra Glaze** attended Brock University, after which she has been scribbling out a living as a business writer, journalist and blogger. The author of a children's book, *Willobe of Wuzz*, her ghost stories have been published in Canada and the U.K.

Come from Aways
Tony Pi

Madoc was a striking man in his thirties, his eyes bluer than the sea. I could well imagine him as an ancient prince.

I sat next to his hospital bed and smiled. "*Siw mae*, Madoc."

He paused, the way I would whenever I heard a phrase in Newfoundland English to make sure I hadn't misheard. Then he sat up and spoke excitedly, but I couldn't understand what he was saying. Contrary to what people believe, linguists don't all speak twenty languages or pick up a new language instantly. Where we excel was figuring out linguistic patterns.

Doctor Liu smirked. "Did you call him *pork dumpling*?"

I understood the confusion. *Siw mae* sounded like *siu mai* in Cantonese, which meant *pork dumpling*. "It means *how are you* in modern Southern Welsh. Madoc would have been from Snowdon, Northern Wales, so I should have said *sut mae*."

Two weeks ago, on December twenty-sixth, a strange ship had drifted into the Harbour of St. John's. Found aboard the replica of the Viking longship were four dead men and one survivor. Will Monteith from the Royal Newfoundland Constabulary contacted me to help him pinpoint the man's origin through his language. Analyzing the tapes of the man's speech, I came to the strange conclusion that the man who called himself Madoc had been speaking two archaic languages:

Middle English and Middle Welsh.

To be certain, I asked Will to arrange a face-to-face interview. Sometimes linguistic evidence was visual. For example, the *v* sound in Modern Welsh was produced like in Modern English, with the upper teeth against the lower lip, but the *v* in Middle Welsh was produced with both lips, like in Spanish.

I turned on the tape recorder and pointed to myself. "Kate." I indicated Detective Monteith and Doctor Liu. "Will. Philip. *Meddic.*" Doctor, in Middle Welsh. The double *dd* sounded like the first sound in the English word, *they*.

He repeated the names and grinned.

Madoc was a puzzle indeed. The theory that made most sense was that he and the other men were trying to recreate the Madoc voyage. Prince Madoc of Gwynedd was a Welsh legend, believed to have sailed west from Wales in 1170. He returned seven years later to tell of a new land of untouched bounty across the sea. Intending to settle the new land, he set out with a fleet of ten ships of settlers, and disappeared from history.

This man could be a Middle Ages scholar with damage to Wernicke's area. Wernicke's aphasics had no problems with articulation, but their utterances made little sense. For the most severe cases, sounds were randomly chosen, spliced together to sound real, but contained few actual words. "Madoc" might be suffering from a similar jargon aphasia. However, the MRI and PET scans showed no such damage to his brain's left hemisphere.

But how authentic was Madoc's command of Middle Welsh? I had two tests in mind.

I gave Madoc two poems I had found, one by Gwalchmai ap Meilyr, another by Dafydd ap Gwilym, both printed in a font called Neue Hammer Unziale. The font seemed closest to Insular Majescule, the script a twelfth-century prince might have been familiar with. "*Darlle,*" I prompted him to read.

Madoc read the first poem easily, but tripped over some of the words in the second.

Will raised an eyebrow. "Shouldn't he be able to read both poems?" he asked, his detective's instincts coming to bear.

"I made it difficult on purpose," I explained. "The first poem was by a court poet who lived around the same time as Madoc. The second poem, however, was poetry written in the fourteenth century, and is usually designated as early Modern Welsh. I expected him to have more difficulty with that one. It's like Chaucer trying to read Shakespeare, or Shakespeare reading Tennessee Williams; different time, different language."

"You're trying to trip him up! Police work and linguistics are a lot alike," Will said. "Patterns and mistakes."

"I've never quite heard it put that way, but you're right." Will and I shared a smile.

Second test was a production task. I took out a colour pictorial of England, and opened it to a photograph with nine men in a pub.

"*Gwyr. Pet?*" Men. How many?

"*Naw.*" Nine.

I shook my head. "*Naw wyr.*" Nine men. I prompted him to use compounds, as I wanted to test a phenomenon called lenition or mutation. In Welsh, if a word came after a number, the first sound sometimes changed or was dropped, as in the case of *gwyr* to *wyr*. Mutations appeared elsewhere as well, but seeing as I was only dabbling in Celtic, I kept it simple for myself.

Madoc caught on fast; we went through the book counting people and things. When we came to a picture of a boat, Madoc pointed to it, then himself. "*Gwyr. Pet?*" How many survived from his ship?

I cast a sidewise glance at Will.

"*Un*," I answered. One.

A shocked expression overtook Madoc's face.

"That's enough for today," I said. I gave him a bottle of ink, a sketchbook, and a seagull feather I had cut into a quill pen, and mimed writing motions. I wanted to analyze his writing.

Madoc took my hand and drew it close for a kiss.

Will smiled. "He might not be able to say it, Kate, but I think you're after making a friend for life."

A week of interviews later, at Detective Will Monteith's request, I presented my findings to the other experts at the R.N.C. Headquarters downtown: Doctor Birley from the Provincial Coroner's Office; Rebecca Shannon, a lawyer working *pro bono* for Madoc; and Professor Connon from the

Tony Pi

Department of Anthropology at Memorial University.

I had reservations about coming. My linguistic analysis had led me to a strange and inescapable conclusion: there was no doubting Madoc's native fluency in Middle Welsh. Even if a hoaxer had learned Middle Welsh, he might pronounce words wrong, or not know the words for common things. Madoc never tripped over syntax or vocabulary, except when it involved a modern object. Could he *be* the genuine Madoc, lost at sea over eight hundred years ago, found at last in St. John's?

Was it a mad fancy? Perhaps. The academic in me scoffed at the idea. But the romantic in me wanted to believe. Here in Newfoundland, it seemed like anything was possible. I didn't know how to describe it, but there was something magical and mystical about this place. I wouldn't be surprised to find a leprechaun at my house, for instance. Time had stopped this winter, snow falling every day like the weather was stuck and couldn't move ahead to anything different. I felt like I was living in a snow-globe, and the same guy kept turning it upside-down and shaking it. In his world it was only five minutes of playing; but inside the snow-globe, an entire month passed.

But could I convince the others?

"He's a native speaker of Middle Welsh, with some training in Middle English," I said. "He did quite well on the reading passages, and the way he pronounced his vowels and consonants were consistent with my expectations. The written evidence further supports it."

"Preposterous!" Connon said. "A good scholar could learn a second language well enough to fool you. It's a hoax by someone in the Society of Creative Anachronism, I wager."

"We spoke to the Seneschal at Memorial University and contacted everyone on their Shire Roll, but no one from their group is missing, and no one heard about any re-enactment of the Madoc voyage," Will said.

"I hear he's learning English," Connon continued. "How do we know that it wasn't his plan, fake the Madoc story long enough to ease back into English?"

"You can't stop someone from learning a new language. He's a human being, not an artefact from some dig!" I said.

"'Ang on, 'Arry," said old Doctor Birley. He had that Newfoundlander tendency to drop his *h*'s and add them back on words that shouldn't have them. "It might be plausible that h'one man didn't 'ave vaccination scars or dental work. I meself was vaccinated in '72, but I don't 'ave a scar. But h'all *four* bodies, plus Madoc? The h'odds of that are right slim. Unless they were h'all raised in the backwoods, of course. But a person who 'as the wherewithal to pull off an 'oax like this wouldn't be so isolated from society. Or do you think someone planned this for forty years?"

"I'll admit the boat is the work of a meticulous forger." Connon passed out some photographs of the ship and items found aboard. "The design's consistent with what we know about twelfth-century ships. A Viking longship with a high prow, carved with a lion's head. That's an interesting point. You might have expected the red dragon typically associated with Wales, but the Lions of Gwynedd were in use in the Gwynedd arms, up until the time of the Tudors."

I set aside a picture of a twisted iron nail and studied the weather-worn red lion's head that Professor Connon described.

"I was expecting a coracle," Philip Liu interjected. "I was reading Severin's *The Brendan Voyage* about the seaworthiness of ox hide boats, and whether they were used to reach North America."

Connon shook his head. "That was sixth-century Ireland. By the twelfth century, the Welsh made alliances with Norse raiders, and there were Norse settlements in Wales. Legend has it that the *Gwennan Gorn*, Madoc's ship, was made from oak, but held together with stag's horn instead of iron. The seafaring myths of those times warned of magnetic islands, which would have spelled doom to ships built with iron nails. The ship's authentic in that respect. Nice touch, that. However, I have concrete proof that it's all an elaborate hoax." He showed us a photograph of a pipe. "One of the artefacts recovered from the ship. Note the five-petal white rose on top of the five-petal red, stamped on its heel."

Philip recognized it. "A Tudor rose."

"Right! Henry the Seventh created it to symbolize the union of the red rose of Lancaster and the white rose of York. But the Tudors didn't begin their reign until 1485. If Madoc's from the twelfth century, where did this anachronism come from?" Connon asked.

"Maybe he stopped off to have a smoke," Rebecca joked.

Everyone laughed, but an intriguing idea came to mind. "Why not?" I said. "We're thinking a single trip. Maybe it's not his first and only trip through time?"

Connon snorted. "We're *scientists*! The very idea of time-travel..."

"It's not impossible," Philip said. "Einstein's theory of relativity allows for time-travel in the forward direction. Time dilation will keep a man from aging as fast, if he's too close to a serious gravity well. Who knows? I'm starting to wonder if he isn't the genuine article!"

Connon shook his head. "You're on your own. I won't jeopardize my reputation with a cockamamie time-travel theory. I'm denouncing him as a fraud, Detective Monteith. Good day." He grabbed his photos and stormed out.

Connon's departure left us all in a state of unease. Will sighed. "He's right. If we announce that Madoc is a time-traveller, they'll call us crackpots."

Rebecca, Will and I went for muffins and coffee at Tim Hortons after the meeting. The line took forever. The girls at the counter made one thing at a time, but by George they made it right. People didn't hurry here.

"Linguistics is the best evidence we have, Kate. Without you, Madoc will look like a fraud," Rebecca said.

I picked at my partridgeberry muffin. "I know. His future's in my hands. Where does he stand, legally?"

"If he's a fraud, he could be charged with public mischief," Rebecca answered. "Maybe breaking immigration laws, if we can establish that he isn't Canadian. If he's a real time-traveller, well, I don't think there are laws that are applicable. But as a Newfoundlander, my instinct's to welcome him to the Island, not lock him up."

"The press will eat us alive," Will said.

"I know a way to appease the press. A screech-in," Rebecca suggested.

"What's that?" I asked.

"You don't know what a screech-in is?" Will asked. He laughed. "We'll have to initiate you too, Kate!"

"It's a grand old Newfoundland tradition," Rebecca explained. "It's a ceremony to initiate a CFA to honorary citizenship. CFA stands for 'Come-From-Aways,' or people who aren't from Newfoundland. Like mainlanders and time-travellers."

"What do you do at a screech-in?"

"We drink screech—that's Newfoundland rum. Kiss a cod, dip your toe into the Atlantic. Good fun for all," said Rebecca. "Then you become a proud member of the Royal Order of Screechers, and get a certificate to prove it."

"Kiss a fish?"

"Don't knock it till you try it," said Rebecca, with a wink.

"What you said, about Madoc's multiple trips in time?" Will said. "Maybe this isn't the first time he's been to Newfoundland. Maybe he stopped in Avalon."

"Avalon?"

"You might know it as Ferryland, a historical site about an hour-and-a-half away, half way to Trepassey," explained Rebecca. "It's a tourist stop, but I go out there to collect rocks, sometimes. The beach is amazing. Lord Baltimore set up the Colony of Avalon there in 1620, before he moved to the States because of the cold."

"Maybe he'll recognize the area? Will, can we bring him to Ferryland?"

"If my superiors say it's fine, we can go tomorrow. But I think Professor Connon should come along," Will said.

I didn't like the idea, but we did need a historian. I nodded. "Tomorrow."

On our way to Ferryland, Harry Connon went on and on about Sir George Calvert, Lord Baltimore. I sat with Madoc in the back of the car. Will had taken him to a barber and dressed him with modern clothes, so he wouldn't look out of place. Madoc watched in wonder as we passed cars and trucks on the highway. I had half-expected him to react with fear and horror at the strange technology, but he seemed fascinated instead. He truly had the soul of an explorer!

Madoc was skimming through time like a skipping stone, and I wanted to know how he was doing it, and why. I had cobbled together some simple questions in Middle Welsh.

Did he know where he was? *Yes.*
Did he know what year it was? *No.*
Did things change when he sailed? *Yes.*
How many times did things change? *Eleven.*

Eleven! Assuming he first set sail around 1179, and that each trip shunted him forward the same number of years, that would average seventy-five years per journey. His sixth stop would have been 1629, around the time of the Colony of Avalon.

What was he looking for? *The end of the whale-road. To learn. To see if it takes me back home to my people, my brother*, he said.

I recalled that in the legend, his brother Rhiryd went with Madoc to settle the new land.

How did he travel through time? *Storm comes every eighty-three days. Help me, Kate.*

I checked my datebook. Madoc arrived on Boxing Day. Eighty-three days from that would place the next storm on March eighteenth.

Poor Madoc! I thought my first winter in Newfoundland was long, and I'd only lived a couple months of it. He arrived from each journey in winter, only to leave at winter's end for a future winter. That was at least two years of fog and snow.

"Will, is there any significance to March eighteenth in Newfoundland?" I asked.

"The day after Paddy's Day? Yeah. Sheila's Brush. That's a big snowstorm that always happens on or around St. Patrick's Day. Not quite the same as Paddy's Broom, another storm that also comes around then. Sheila is Patrick's wife, see. She's always mad at him, chasing after him with her brush and painting everything with ice. Why?"

"Because that's the day the time portal opens again, to seventy-five years in the future," I said.

The dig was closed on weekends, but Connon had research privileges here, facilitating our visit. To my surprise, the anthropologist was getting along with Madoc. As we traipsed through the snow at Ferryland, he spoke to Madoc in English, taking for granted that he would understand. Madoc was animated, pointing to places, speaking to me in Middle Welsh, but I caught only a few words. Clearly he had been here before. Frustrated, Connon put a pencil in Madoc's hand, and made him draw in his sketchbook.

Madoc led Connon through the dig, sketching out a map of Avalon as he remembered it. "His sketches seem consistent with the buildings we know to be in the Colony at the time. These buildings he drew are the bakery and brewhouse, which don't exist today. They tore them down in 1637 to build Kirke House," Connon explained. "You've done your homework, Madoc."

Will and I left them to their explorations for a quiet stroll along the shore. Like Rebecca said, the rocky beach had some beautiful stones. I knelt and picked up a smooth green stone. I showed Will the lovely lines in the rock.

"That's what we call a 'salt water' rock," said Will. "Rounded and smoothed by the sea."

A tall, elderly gentleman down the beach waved at us. "You two look like a charming couple," said the man, smiling.

Will furrowed his brow.

Embarrassed, I corrected him. "Thank you, but we're not together."

"Take it from a man who's seen much in his lifetime. You two belong together." The old man tipped his hat and continued along the shore.

"Did you know him?" I asked.

Will shook his head. "He reminds me of my father, is all."

"What will happen to Madoc?"

Will sighed. "He has no money, no citizenship. Kind folk like you'd find anywhere in Newfoundland will help him out, but he'll be a burden unless he learns some English. Maybe he could sell his story; I don't know. But he'll end up in limbo, without Canadian citizenship."

"I have an idea about that, but I need to discuss it with Rebecca first," I hinted. As Madoc's *pro bono* lawyer, she would know whether the legal loophole I saw would actually work. "But in the end, wouldn't it be simpler to let him go back on his ship? Imagine finding out what the world would be like in seventy-five, a hundred-and-fifty, three-hundred years from now. See how future generations live!"

"He'll be adrift and alone."

"No one needs to be." I took a risk and took Will's hand. He didn't pull away.

"Have dinner with me tonight, Kate?" he asked sheepishly.

"I'd like that."

"Come in, Kate, and shut the door." Professor Claudia Seif had recently been appointed the Chair of Linguistics at Memorial.

I knew why she wanted to see me.

"I had a call from Harry Connon," she said. "When I recommended you to the detective, I was expecting diligent, responsible analysis. Instead, you've made yourself a laughingstock of the field. It reflects badly on the department."

"I stand by my judgment, Claudia. It's not the orthodox answer or the safe answer, but it's what I believe. I won't lie."

"Watch what you say to the press, Kate. Think about your future."

I sighed. "What future? I've been paying my dues for the last five years, moving from city to city, and I've yet to make any short lists for tenure-track positions. "

"Kate, you're a good linguist." Her voice was softer now. "The breaks will come. Drop this 'Madoc' madness."

There would be no convincing her. "Thanks for the talk, Claudia. You've given me much to think about," I said, and left.

O'Reilly's Irish Pub was packed for the screech-in/press conference, and the journalists were chattering excitedly among themselves. Claudia stared daggers at me from the back row.

Will introduced himself, then began, "On December twenty-sixth, a Viking longship was discovered in the Harbour of St. John's. Five men were found aboard, but only one was alive. Autopsies by the Coroner's Office indicate that the men died of hypothermia. The survivor was in quarantine for fourteen days as required by the Quarantine Act, but showed no signs of disease. However, when the man regained consciousness, we discovered that he didn't speak English, French or any other modern language.

"Several experts examined the body of evidence about our

mystery man. The ship and his language point to the man's identity as Prince Madoc of Gwynedd, a twelfth century Welsh legend." The journalists whispered and chuckled when they heard this. "Whether this is a hoax or a case of time-travel remains in dispute among our experts. At this point, I'll yield the floor to them: but please save your questions until they all have had a chance to speak."

We each took a turn presenting the evidence. Connon expounded on the hoax hypothesis, while the doctor and the coroner expressed ambivalence. When it was my turn, I glanced at Claudia. What if she was right? Was I throwing away my career by standing behind what I believed?

I looked at Madoc, wondering what would become of him. He smiled.

I was as alone as he was. My feeling of being disconnected wasn't because of the fog and the rain. If I really looked, that sense of not belonging stretched back for years. We were two of a kind: I too wanted to see the future and start afresh. I knew then that I couldn't hedge like the others did. I *had* to be Madoc's voice in this matter, even if it meant my career. I took a deep breath, and spoke.

"Based on the linguistic evidence, I must conclude Madoc is truly a man out of time." I went on to discuss why it was nearly impossible to fake pronunciation and grammar as consistently as a native speaker. "Given his native fluency in Middle Welsh, I must conclude that he is, indeed, from the twelfth century."

Claudia stood, shook her head in disappointment, and left.

All eyes were on me. I felt like The Fool on a tarot card, about to step off a cliff.

Rebecca saved me from the press. "I'm representing Madoc *pro bono*, ensuring that his rights aren't being violated. Currently, we're unable to ascertain his nationality. But suppose that he really is Madoc. He would have been among the first Europeans to settle in Newfoundland. There's no disputing that he's Welsh; all the evidence pointed to that. But is he *Canadian*? Ah.

"The legend tells that Madoc set out with settlers to a newly found land across the sea. We know he was at the Colony of Avalon. Even Professor Connon admits that Madoc knew things about Avalon only an expert would know. And later this spring, archaeologists will begin excavations at a previously unknown site, to see if Madoc was right about a hitherto undiscovered building that existed in Calvert's time. If he lived in Avalon, then by the *Newfoundland Act* that admitted Newfoundland to Confederation in 1948, that would also make him a citizen of Canada."

"But he wasn't alive at Confederation, was he?" a reporter shouted.

"Well, he certainly wasn't dead." Laughter. "He truly is one of the first immigrants to Newfoundland. I say we, a people known for our hospitality, take him in with open arms. To that effect, we're throwing a 'screech-in' here at O'Reilly's, and you're all invited!"

The question period was chaotic. I thought I handled most of the questions well, but the ones that asked if this was all a joke were frustrating. Will finally announced it was time for the screech-in. As a native-born Newfoundlander had to perform the ceremony, Will would do the honours. They dragged us to the center and crowned us with yellow, plastic sou'wester hats. Then, we were given a full shot of screech rum.

"Hold your screech up high and repeat after me. *Long may your big jib draw!*" shouted Will.

"*Long may your big jib draw!*" I yelled, even though I had no idea what that meant. I only knew I needed a stiff drink. I squealed when the rum hit my taste buds and gut.

"That's why they call it *screech!*" someone shouted. The crowd laughed.

They prompted Madoc to repeat the same. "*Long mei ywr bug si'ib dra'?*"

"Close enough! Bring out the cod!"

I woke in my bed with a hangover and an upset stomach, not remembering how I got home. Rum and fried baloney definitely didn't belong together.

I found Will asleep on my couch. He must have driven me home.

Not wanting to wake Will, I went into the bedroom and called Rebecca. "I think we need to help Madoc back on his journey. And I'm seriously thinking about joining him."

"You mean, going to the future?" Rebecca asked. "Kate, think it through! What would you do there? End up like him, a living museum?"

"I'll find something," I said. "Imagine, a chance to put theories of language change to the test!"

"What about your classes?"

"I doubt I still have a job." I twisted the phone cord. "I'd like to leave instructions to take care of unfinished business."

"Kate, give it more thought! People *died* on that last voyage."

"I thought of that. We can stock up on supplies, prepare ourselves better."

Rebecca sighed. "You're serious about this? What about a crew? And a ship?"

"I'll think of something."

After the call, I gently woke Will. "Good morning, sleepyhead. Thanks for looking after me."

"My pleasure," he said, rubbing his eyes. "Can I make you breakfast?"

I smiled to hide my troubled thoughts. "Know how to make peach pancakes?"

I told Will about my plan as we ate. "We need to give him back his ship, Will, by St. Patrick's Day."

"What? We can't."

"It's his property. His destiny. His journey doesn't end here, I know it."

"The brass will never allow it!"

"One day, that's all I ask. Call it a re-enactment of the Madoc voyage, a heritage moment, something. If it doesn't work, you can repossess the boat, and us."

"Us? What are you saying?"

"I'm going with Madoc."

Silence hung between us.

"I'd like you to stay, Kate," Will said at last, taking my hands.

I squeezed his hands. "Come with us."

"'Now' is enough for me, Kate. Is it for you?"

"A chance like this comes once in a lifetime. I think there was a reason I met Madoc, here and now. He's the adventure I've been looking for."

"Not stability?"

"That, too," I admitted. "Perhaps I can't have both, not yet.

Maybe there isn't a bright future seventy-five years from now. But to give up a chance to experience something extraordinary? I don't think I can."

"Isn't that what love can be?"

I looked into his eyes. He was the sweetest man I had met in a long time. I didn't want to break his heart. "Help us."

Will sighed. "You're a stubborn one, Kate Tannhauser. Very well, the future is yours. But for now, the present is ours."

He leaned over the table and kissed me. It was a long, unhurried kiss, just as I imagined.

The media frenzy that followed in the weeks after was not unexpected. Our time-travel theory was portrayed as ridiculous by most, praised by few, and always controversial. I had a spate of invitations for television, newspaper and radio interviews, and I agreed to the reputable ones, but ignored the sensational ones. The consensus was, *this could only happen in Newfoundland*.

Rebecca and her husband opened their guest room to Madoc, after he was discharged from the hospital. I met with him to discuss joining him on his journey. "*We will return you to your ship, to your storm,*" I said in his language. "*I am coming with you.*"

There was a look of surprise and joy on Madoc's face. "*I am honoured, Lady Kate. But we need more men.*"

"*I will find them,*" I said.

Madoc nodded. "*Bring no iron. Mistake. Danger.*"

As far as I could tell, the phenomenon that allowed him to travel through time was based on powerful magnetic fields. Passing through such a gateway with ferrous metals over a certain size either disrupted the field, or made the transition dangerous. He had discovered it on his first journey, finding that objects made of iron aboard their ship burned with *canwyll yr ysbryd*, "spirit candles" or what we called St. Elmo's Fire, followed by a sudden snowstorm. Although they tossed all their iron off the ship, he still lost two men to the waves. On his last journey, someone must have accidentally brought iron aboard the *Gwennan Gorn*, a theory supported by that twisted iron nail found aboard the ship.

We still needed a crew.

I met with the Society of Creative Anachronism Seneschal of the Shire of *An n-Eilean-ne*, which was Scots Gaelic for "an island of our own," and gave him the details of my plan. "Imagine, a chance to see the future, a one-way trip. I know it's a lot to ask, leaving this time behind. But I need people who are willing to take a risk, and soon."

"It's an unusual request, but let me send out a notice. You never know, with us lot. We mostly look to the past, but some of us also look to the future. After all, what could be more appealing than becoming anachronisms ourselves?" He smiled. "But it seems to me, you could do a great deal of good for people who have lost hope."

"What do you mean?"

"There are some diseases modern medicine can't cure, but what about future medicine? Some people don't have seventy-five years, but they hang on to hope."

He was right. There might be new cures in the future. Then again, there might not be. All I could promise them was a gamble.

Slowly, the calls and emails came. People had heard about the opportunity through the SCA. I told them it might be a dangerous, one-way trip, but the journey would be the adventure of a lifetime. I never heard back from the majority again; but to my surprise, some were serious about joining the crew.

Though he disapproved of my plans, Will helped weed the jokesters and the dangerous from the list of volunteers. "It's not cheap to fly to Newfoundland. Only the serious ones will come," Will said. We whittled the list to twelve, ten men and two women. Four had sailing experience, and one was a Welshman who offered to expedite translations with Madoc.

The crew arrived a week before St. Patrick's Day. They were a diverse crowd: fisherman, physicist, historian, ex-marine, writer, student, trucker, doctor, and more. They all had their own reasons to come with us.

We prepared provisions, avoiding ferromagnetic materials altogether. The SCA rallied and made period clothing appropriate to Madoc's time. We chose the four lions of Gwynedd for our symbol, stitched onto white and green cloth.

Madoc and I continued teaching each other our languages. "*It's not too late, Lady Kate. You can stay with good Will. I promise to see them safely into the future.*"

I shook my head. "*It's what I want.*"

Alas, St. Patrick's Day came all too soon. Tomorrow, we would set sail.

I spent that night with Will, cradled in his arms.

I asked him one last time. "Come with me."

He held me tighter. "I need certainty." He reached for his coat by the bed, and took out a small black box from his pocket. My heart pounded. A ring?

No. Inside the box was a golden necklace, its pendant adorned with the salt water rock I had so admired at Avalon. He put it around my neck and fastened it. "It's not iron, so it's safe. Something to remember me by. I love you, Kate."

I couldn't hold back the tears anymore. "And I you. Remember me, Will."

The next morning, the harbourfront was packed with students, strangers and friends who came to see us off. Most of them expected the whole thing to be a publicity stunt. I saw Rebecca, Philip, and Harry Connon, but there was no sign of Will. Was it too hard for him to see me off?

It had been Will who convinced the Coast Guard to return the *Gwennan Gorn* to us temporarily. High-prowed, she creaked as we set foot aboard her. The sound was strangely reassuring. This ship had survived many journeys and the test of countless years. She would serve us well.

What would the world be like, seventy-five years from now? Would Newfoundland be exactly the same as now, as though no time had passed? I didn't know. All I knew was that the Will I loved would not be there, waiting for me.

I distracted myself from that thought, focusing on our preparations. We loaded food and other supplies onto the ship, within the roofed enclosure built into the center. We checked and double-checked the manifest, and we swept the ship and crew with a metal detector, looking for forgotten iron. The last crew might have been lost because of a nail. I didn't want to make the same mistake.

When we were fit to launch, I stood at the head of the boat with a hand on Madoc's shoulder. "Fellow travellers!" I shouted. "I trust you've said your goodbyes. We might go into the storm and go no further than today. We might meet with disaster. Worst of all, we sail into uncertainty. But throughout history, haven't there always been men and women with adventurous souls, who have left behind loved ones to find new horizons? In the future, men will build ships to the stars. They will choose to do as we do today, to leave behind everything we love to explore the unknown."

I paused and met the eyes of my shipmates. "It's a frightening prospect, I know. But I know if I never took this chance, I will regret it for the rest of my life. I hope you all feel the same. Let's *make* history!"

My crew cheered.

The snow began to fall, and the wind picked up. Sheila's Brush was on its way.

Upon Madoc's signal, the crew began to row. The *Gwennan Gorn* glided through the harbour waters past the ice floes. I looked for Will and spied him pushing through the cheering crowd, an old man following behind. It was the gentleman Will and I had met on the beach at Avalon.

Will waved from the docks, wearing civilian clothes. "Kate! Wait!" He leapt onto the ice floes, the pans, between the docks and the ship.

"Stop rowing!" I cried.

Will leapt from pan to pan, ignoring the danger. He clambered into the boat, took off his watch, and dropped it in the water. "My last piece of iron."

I embraced him. "What made you change your mind?" I asked.

"Madoc convinced me," Will said.

I looked at Madoc. Had he learned enough English from me to talk to Will? Or had he been a fraud, all this time?

Will saw my confusion. "No, not him. The man we met at Avalon? Madoc Monteith. Our son."

It took a while for it to sink in. "How?"

He showed me the golden pendant he wore beneath his

clothes. The stone was identical to the one he gave me, striations and all, but old and worn. My hand flew to my neck. Mine was still there!

"They did find another way back. Remember I told you about Paddy's Broom, the other storm that comes around the same time as Sheila's Brush? Our son came back through that gate, and gave me this as proof. It's the certainty I need. Let's face the future together, come-what-may."

I understood.

Madoc hollered. Ahead, a rainbow halo appeared in the whiteness of snow and fog. The gate!

There was no turning back. Into the storm and into the future.

"Come-what-may," I said, and kissed Will.

Originally published in On Spec Spring 2009 Vol 21 No 1 #76

Dr. Tony Pi is a linguist with a Ph.D. from McGill University. A 2009 Finalist for the John W. Campbell Award for Best New Writer, he has met two purported amnesiacs in his career, which inspired this story. Visit **www.tonypi.com** for a list of his works.

STILL
GREG WILSON

A lot of my stories aren't true, but this is a true story . . .
Once upon a time, there was a young puppet named Still. She wore black and white and eight shades of green, and had a happy, smiling face. Every morning, she went to school to study reading, juggling, arithmetic, and history. At recess, she and her friends chased each other around the playground pretending to be gargoyles. If the teachers weren't looking, they tied bits of string to each other's arms and legs and staggered around as if someone was pulling on them until whoever was pretending to be Key the Cutter set them all free.

Still's favourite thing wasn't school or games, though—it was her violin. It had been carved out of the same piece of wood as she had been, and she never went anywhere without it. She loved its sweet young sound, and played everything on it, from tingly little nursery rhymes to the slow song of the canals at night. She even took it to bed with her, so that she could sleep with her arms around it.

Her parents smiled at one another when she did that. Her father, Elbow, was a paper folder, and made the crispest, straightest creases you have ever seen. Her mother, Ramble, was a painter. Every day, puppets came to her and said, "I've just been given a very important job. Can you please give me a serious face?" or, "I'm feeling blue—can you please put a happy face on me?" Hour after patient hour, Ramble gave her customers the faces they wanted.

One day, Elbow brought home a big box full of old papers. "The mayor found these in the basement of City Hall," he told Ramble and Still. "And she wants *me* to fold them all up so that they can be put away properly. It's going to be a hard job. See?" He held up one of the pieces of paper. It was yellow around the edges, and crackly-stiff from having been damp and then dried out. "If I make even the slightest mistake, the paper might tear, or the crease might not be straight!"

"Well then, we'd better stay out of your way for a while," Ramble said. She kissed his cheek. "I'll go and grind up some lemon peel and amber for my paints. Still, why don't you go up and clean your room?"

"All right," Still said. Up the stairs she went. Her room was a mess. There were socks on her bookshelves, and books curled up asleep on her desk, and pencil shavings spilling out of her drawers.

"Hmph," Still thought. "This will be a *lot* of work. I wonder where I should start?" She sat down on the bed to puzzle it out. As she thought, she tucked her violin under her chin and began to play.

"Still," Ramble called. "Are you cleaning your room?"

"Ye-ess," Still called back. She couldn't put her books away until she moved her socks, but she couldn't put *them* away until she tidied up the pencil shavings, and she couldn't do *that* until she moved her books . . . As she thought, her fingers picked out a little tune on her violin.

"Still!" Ramble said loudly. Still jumped. Her mother was standing in the bedroom doorway, her shoe going *tap tap tap*. She hadn't bothered to pencil a frown on her forehead, but Still could tell that she was exasperated. "Elbow needs to concentrate. If you want to play your violin, why don't you go outside?"

"Can I go to Mister Leaf's?" Still asked. "He told me last week that he thought I was ready for some special lessons." *And music lessons are* much *more fun than cleaning,* she added, but only to herself.

Ramble's shoe went *tap tap tap* a few more times. Then she

nodded. "All right. But you have to clean up your room when you get home."

"I will!" Still promised. She gave Ramble a hug, then clattered down the stairs. The front door went *bang!* behind her.

The sky was blue, and the air had that clean, damp smell that comes after rain. Still skipped along the cobblestone streets, playing little tunes as she went. She went straight to Mister Leaf's house—except for one little detour to slide down a brass handrail in the park, and another to wave at a big passenger balloon that was taking off for the moon.

Mister Leaf's house stood next to a little square park full of trees and benches. It was a nice part of town. There were no glass rats creeping half-invisible across the stones to gnaw on her legs, or pirates in red and gold lurking in the bushes, waiting for a chance to bundle her up inside a roll of carpet and smuggle her onto a ship and haul her halfway across the ocean to sell her to a pride of lions so that she could scratch them under their chins when they were finished hunting. It was a nice house, and a nice summer-sunshine day. There was no way Still could know that it was going to be the worst day of her life.

A single drop of rain went *plop* on the cobblestones. Another drop plopped beside it, then another. "Oh, bother," Still said crossly. She didn't mind the rain (although Ramble always made sure that she got herself completely dry, so that she wouldn't warp), but it put her violin out of tune. She looked up at the fat, gray clouds, then ran *tik tik tik* across the cobblestones and rang Mister Leaf's doorbell.

A moment later the door opened, and a deep, warm voice said, "Why, what a pleasant surprise! Please, please, come in."

Mister Leaf wore blue and orange and a polka-dot hat. He had black curls painted on his forehead and a big smile painted on his face. His eyes were made of tiger-orange topaz. They were so friendly, they almost seemed to shine.

He stepped out of the way and waved her in. "To what do I owe this unexpected pleasure?" he asked.

"My father has some very important work to do," Still told him as they went upstairs to the music room, "so I was hoping that I could get a special lesson."

"Ah," her teacher said. "Very good. Very good. But look, your violin is wet. Here, you should dry it off." He took a tea towel from on top of the piano and handed it to her.

Still brushed a few drops of water off her violin, then handed the towel back to Mister Leaf. As she did so, their fingers touched, and his eyes suddenly seemed to sparkle.

Still felt as though she had a blush painted on her cheeks. She turned around to face the window and tucked her violin under her chin. The rain was darkening the red bricks of the houses across the street. "Shall I start with scales?" she asked.

"Of course," Mister Leaf said. "And remember, not too fast. The most important thing is to hear the music as you play it."

Still played a G scale, then a B scale, and then a C-sharp scale, which was the hardest scale she knew. Mister Leaf nodded his head to help her keep time, and said, "Good, good," or, "Slow down—try to smooth the notes into each other."

"Very good," he said when she finally finished. "Now, would you like to play a song for me?"

"If you'd like," Still said. She laid her bow on her violin's strings and drew it down. The sound was as sweet and as thick as chocolate syrup, but as clear as the purest ice. She closed her eyes and played a slow, sad gypsy waltz.

When she was done, she opened her eyes. Mister Leaf had stepped forward, so that he was standing just inches away from her. "Ahhh . . ." he breathed. "That was beautiful. May I try?"

"Try what?" Still asked.

"Your violin—may I play it?"

"Oh my," Still said. Her clockwork seemed to be whirring double-time inside her. "I—I've never let anyone else play my violin before," she said. "I don't know if I should."

"I'll be careful," Mister Leaf promised. "We can keep it a secret if you want." He held out his hand.

Suddenly, Still felt guilty. He was being so nice, giving her an extra lesson like this. What harm could it do?

"Here," she said impulsively, holding it out to him. "But please be careful."

Mister Leaf took the violin and bow from her. He gazed at them for a moment as if they were the most precious things in the world. Then he brought the violin up to his cheek and laid his cheek against its bottom side. "It's perfect," he whispered. "The varnish . . . the polish . . . It's the most beautiful thing I've ever seen."

Suddenly he turned the violin right side up and tucked it under his chin. He thrust the bow across the strings. *HRING!* He pushed the bow back across the strings, then drew it down again, *HWAH-HWING!*

"Wait, stop!" Still said. "You mustn't play so hard!" But Mister Leaf didn't listen. He began to fiddle furiously, faster than Still had ever seen anyone play. The bow flew back and forth across the strings. The violin sang, then shrieked, then howled as he played high notes and low notes, chords and *pizzicato* and trills that ran from one end of the scale to the other.

"No, wait, stop! Stop! Oh please, stop!" Still cried, but Mister Leaf just played on. Still grabbed his arm and tried to pull the violin away from him, but he was too strong. Faster and faster he played, until suddenly the strings went *PLINK! PLINK! PLINK!* He had cut right through them!

But even then Mister Leaf didn't stop. Before Still's horrified eyes, gray wisps of smoke began to rise from the body of the violin. He was playing so fast that the violin was catching on fire!

It must have been the smell of smoke that made him stop, because there is nothing that puppets are more afraid of than fire. Mister Leaf raised the bow with a flourish. Then, to Still's horror, he began to chuckle. The chuckle turned into a laugh, and the laugh got bigger and bigger. "Ah hoo hoo hoo," he chortled. "Ah hee hee hee. Oh, th-th-that was fun! That was *fun!*"

As he laughed, Still began to cry. "What have you done?" she wept. "What have you done to my violin?"

Mister Leaf laughter subsided. He blinked at the violin. "Oh my," he said softly, "what's this?" He peered at the violin as if he had never seen it before, then pushed it back into Still's arms.

"You broke it," Still sobbed, clutching the violin in her arms.

"Sh, sh," Mister Leaf said. "It's not that bad. We can fix it."

"But what will I tell Ramble?" she wailed. "And Elbow?"

"Oh, you mustn't tell them anything," Mister Leaf said hastily. "Why, if they found that you'd let this happen, they'd—they'd—why, they'd put strings on you, that's what they'd do! They'd screw little eyehooks into your elbows and knees, and run black silk strings through them, and they'd never let you move your own arms and legs again, just to make sure that this could never happen again. Do you want that? No, I didn't think so. Now, the rain has stopped—I think it's time for you to go home."

Afterward, Still couldn't remember how she had found her way home. She must have fallen, though, because by the time she recognized the streets again, she had an ugly dent in her cheek. All she could think about was her violin—her poor, scarred violin.

Her joints and limbs were aching with the damp and cold by the time she reached her front door. She practically fell through it into Elbow's arms.

"Still!" he cried out. "Still, honey, what's wrong? What happened?"

"I—I fell," she sobbed. She held up her violin. "And I—I—"

"Sh, sh, sh," he said, rocking her in his arms. "Come in here where it's warm. Ramble! Ramble! Come quick!"

The two puppets sat their daughter down on the couch in the living room and gave her a cup of warm linseed oil to drink. "Here, let me see that," Ramble said gently. She took Still's chin in her hand and turned her head from side to side to look at the dent in her cheek. "Oh, it's not so bad," she said after a moment. "A little bit of putty, and some careful sanding, and you'll be as good as new."

"Why, it'll even make you look more grown-up," Elbow said. "Just like the dimples in my cheeks. I wasn't carved with them, you know. I got this one when I fell out of a tree, and this one when—"

"But what about my violin?" Still interrupted. She had wrapped three thick blankets around herself, but she still felt cold, cold, cold. Even with a big gloop of honey, the linseed oil tasted like ashes. All she could think about was the black scorch on her violin.

"We'll take it to the shop tomorrow and get it fixed, I promise," her mother said gently. She took the violin from her daughter's stiff hands and laid it aside. "Now, why don't we put you to bed? You can clean up your room tomorrow."

Still lay in bed a long time the next morning. Her window grew brighter as the sun rose, then dimmed as it passed overhead. Her mother and father came in to see her a couple of times, but she closed her eyes and pretended that she was sleeping.

Finally her mother brought the doctor to see her. He had narrow shoulders and a beaky nose, and wore wire-rimmed glasses without any glass in them. He put his stethoscope on Still's tummy and chest and forehead and listened to her clockwork go *tick, tock, tick, tock.* Then he sighted along her arms and legs, one by one, to see if they had been warped by the rain.

"There's nothing wrong with her wood," he said to Ramble. "She's as sound as the day she was made. And that dent in her cheek isn't as bad as it looks—I'm sure you'll be able to fix that up in no time."

"Then what is it?" her mother asked. "What's wrong?"

The puppet doctor shook his head. "I don't know. Perhaps her clockwork got a bit jumbled up in the fall. I'm sure it will sort itself out if you give her some time."

So Still got to stay home from school that day, and the day after that. Each morning she lay in bed until her mother or father came to get her up. She brushed her teeth and oiled her joints and got dressed, then went down to the couch and sat under the blankets, staring out the window at the carts going past on the street and the balloons going by in the sky. Sometimes her fingers twitched, as if she was playing the violin, but she never mentioned it, or wondered where it had gone.

But all the while, Still felt like she was floating in dark, still water. Whenever she caught a glimpse of herself in the mirror, the dent on her cheek made her look like someone else. She stared into her eyes, and saw a stranger. "You mustn't tell," she whispered. "They'll put strings on you if you do."

On the third day, her father came into her room with a big smile painted on his face. "If you'd like to get up and get dressed, there's something waiting for you downstairs," he said.

"All right," Still said. A moment went by. She didn't move.

"Oh, come on, daffodil," Elbow said. "It'll cheer you up, I promise!"

"All right," Still said again. Somehow, being cheered up didn't seem to matter very much.

When she came downstairs, a big box wrapped in brightly-colored paper was waiting for her on the kitchen table. The creases were as sharp as the edge of a knife, and the folds were so clever that her father eventually had to show her how to get the paper off without tearing it.

She set the paper aside and took the lid off the box. "Well?" her father asked. "What do you think?"

Her violin lay inside the box. Fresh strings had been put on it, each one a different color. Its body had been sanded down smooth and re-varnished. There was only a faint, shallow groove to show where—where—

"What do you think?" her father asked again. "Doesn't it look just as good as new?"

"I guess so," Still said. "Thank you."

"Well all right then," Elbow said jovially. "Now, if you hurry, you can still get to school in time for juggling."

"I guess so," Still said. She stood up and began to walk toward the front door.

"Aren't you going to take your violin?" Elbow asked.

Still stopped, then said, very softly, "I guess so." She picked up the violin and walked out into the street.

Still trudged along the cobblestone streets to the school. The sky was a warm, clear blue, and little clockwork birds were chirping in the trees. The puppets she passed chattered to one another as if it was just another day. She ran her thumb back and forth over the faint groove in the top of the violin that was the only sign of—of— She pushed the thought out of her head.

Still didn't stop when she reached the school gate. She just set her books on a bench very carefully for anyone who wanted them and kept walking. She didn't pay any attention to where she was going—she just let her own weight carry her down, down, down.

As she walked, the streets grew narrower, then dirtier. Gaps began to appear in the cobblestones, and tendrils of fog began to fill the air around her. They grew steadily thicker until Still could barely see from one side of the street to the other.

And as she walked, the puppets around her started to change as well. Their faces became cracked and worn. Some of them had so little paint left that it was impossible to tell who they were, or how they might feel. None of them looked straight at her, and she was careful not to look straight at them.

Finally Still reached a dead end. She was too tired and

hungry to think. An old banana crate full of newspapers lay on the ground beside her. She climbed into it, curled herself around her violin, closed her eyes, and fell straight into a deep, dreamless sleep.

She woke up once, in the middle of the night, when something cold and hard scampered across her leg. "Tee hee," it giggled. She hugged her violin close to her chest and shivered. She'd never seen a glass rat, not for real, but other puppets had whispered stories about them at sleepovers. What they wanted more than anything was oil to stop them squeaking, and if the only place to get it was from a puppet, well, "That's why they have diamond teeth," everyone would whisper in unison.

It took her a long time to get back to sleep.

She woke up hungry the next morning. She hid her violin behind an old sign for a watchmaker's shop at the end of the alley, then trudged up through the fog to a small market.

Still folded a piece of newspaper to make a box (now, who had taught her how to do that?) and set it on the sidewalk. She stood there for a moment, as still as her name. The wind felt like ice water on the dent on her cheek. Slowly, she ducked her head down, as if she had a violin on her shoulder. Slowly, very slowly, she raised her arm as if she held a bow.

And then she began to play. A few puppets stopped to watch, and then a few more. They stared at the strange sight of a young, beautifully-painted puppet playing a violin that wasn't there. Still didn't make a sound, but the puppets around her would have sworn that they could almost—almost—hear music. It made one puppet think of black butterflies fluttering among blood poppies under a full moon. It made another think of a hawk circling patiently over a snowy field in winter, just waiting for the rabbit's clockwork to run down.

When Still stopped, the puppets around her sighed. A peg-legged old puppet in a soldier's uniform pulled a grimy green gumdrop from his pocket and tossed it into Still's paper box. *Plop plop plop* went a few other pieces of candy. Still bowed gracefully, then picked up her takings and trudged back into the fog.

And so began the pattern of her days. Every night she found a box or doorway, and curled up with her violin in her arms. Every morning she hid the violin somewhere safe, then walked into the market to play her silent music. She forgot to remember that she had once slept in a warm, dry bed, or that the puppets who had made her had loved her. The worn-out puppets who worked in the markets on the edge of the fog wondered about her for a while, then found other things to wonder about. In no time at all, she was just another nameless toy.

From time to time, though, properly-painted puppets from the heart of the City wandered through. The nice ones came to buy old, broken-down things to mend—chairs with wobbly legs, flutes that were missing a few notes, or picture frames that didn't hang straight. The others, who weren't so nice, came for the smell of the fog. They walked around the market in groups, making jokes with one another and staring at everyone. Some of these puppets pointed at Still and laughed, but there were always a few who would give her licorice or even some chocolate if she would pretend to play for them. A few even asked her to come back with them and give them a private concert, but Still looked at their bright, shiny eyes and shook her head.

As the weeks went by, Still got to know a few of the other puppets who lived in the fog. She told them that she had been stolen from a far-away villages by lions, and sold to pirates who had brought her across the sea to work as a slave in the glue mines. "How did you escape?" they asked. "Oh, that's a secret," she said. "If I tell you, you might tell them, and then if I'm ever caught again, I won't be able to get away." They didn't believe her, and she knew they didn't, but they pretended right along with her, just as she pretended to believe that the one-armed puppet who pasted leaves on the trees had once been a princess, or that the twins who boiled scraps of canvas in an old black kettle to get the oil out were really magicians in disguise.

From time to time, though, Still heard Elbow's or Ramble's voice, very faintly, calling her name. Whenever that happened, she whispered, "*You* don't belong here anymore," and hid herself until the voices went away.

And once, just once, she saw a puppet she almost recognized. His clothes were blue and orange, and he wore a polka-dot hat. He had black curls painted on his forehead, and a warm smile painted on his face. He was with a crowd of other puppets, all of them so painted and polished that they looked brand new. As she watched him, he pointed at the little cans of fish scales that one tired old puppet was trying to sell and laughed, "Ah hoo hoo hoo . . . Ah hee hee hee . . ."

Still hid behind a pile of old dreams until the puppet was gone. When she finally ventured out again, she played her silent music faster and more furiously than she ever had before. Her arm practically whirred as it flew back and forth. No one gave her any candy that day, and even a few of the puppets in the market's stalls muttered about her under their breath.

And so the days passed, each colder than the one before, until one morning Still woke up to find a faint dusting of snow on the dirty streets around her. She wrapped her violin in newspaper, then climbed up a drainpipe so that she could tuck it under the eaves of a warehouse whose windows had been boarded up. She walked the long way around to the market, just so that she could see how the snow made the city look. She played all day, but only a few puppets went past, and none put any candy in her paper box.

As the sun began set, Still trudged back down into the fog, circling the block once to make sure that no-one was following her before climbing up the drainpipe to get her violin.

It was gone.

Still felt around under the eaves. It wasn't there. She leaned out as far as she could so that she could grope around the next section. It wasn't there either.

Panic grated in her gears like sand. The dent on her cheek seemed to throb. Where was her violin? Where had it gone?

Still was just about to start whimpering when a grating voice above her said, "Is this what you're looking for?"

Still was so startled that she almost fell off the drainpipe. She looked up. The voice had come from a beaky gray head that sat atop a short, barrel-shaped body. The figure had long arms, and wings folded up against its back. It was a gargoyle!

"Some crows saw you hide it this morning," the gargoyle said in a voice that sounded like bricks being scraped together. "You know what they're like for taking things, so I thought I had better keep it safe for you."

"May I—may I have it back?" Still asked. She felt as though her mainspring was about to snap.

"Of course," the gargoyle said. It handed the violin back to her. Still snatched it from him and hugged it close.

"Will you play it for me?" the gargoyle asked. "It's been a long time since I heard any music."

"I—I don't play it any more," Still said. "But if you'd like to come down to the street, I can give you some of my gumdrops. For keeping the violin safe," she added, seeing the gargoyle's frown.

The gargoyle shook its head. "No thank you," it said. "Even if I *could* come down to the street, I don't have much use for candy." It shrugged its wings.

"Why can't you come down?" Still asked. "Are you guarding the building?"

The gargoyle's voice scraped, *skrrk skrrk skrrk*. It took Still a moment to realize that it was laughing. "No," it finally said. "I can't come down because I *can't*. Look!" It pointed at its legs. Still gasped. They were carved out of the same stone as the building. The top half of the gargoyle was alive, but the bottom half was part of the building.

"I was made this way so that I would always be on guard," the gargoyle told her. "That's why I'm called a 'guard goyle.' And for years and years, that's what I did. But then everyone stopped coming, and the shops all closed, and only the fog and I were left."

Some little piece of machinery inside Still ticked over for the first time in a very long time. "Well, if you're not going anywhere," she said shakily, "And if you don't have anything else in particular to do, would you mind looking after this for me sometimes? Because I keep worrying, every time I hide it, that someone might find it and take it away, and I—I just don't think I could bear that." Slowly, very slowly, she held out her violin.

And so Still and the gargoyle became—friends? Perhaps. He told her stories about what the streets had been like years ago, when all the lanterns were lit and puppets on stilts swished back and forth waving signs for different shops. He told her about hearing cheers the first time puppets had gone to the moon and back in a balloon, and about the weeping when the city had woken to discover that Key the Cutter was gone.

That was when Still realized just how old the gargoyle was. "Don't you ever wish you could see the rest of the world?" she asked one evening. She was sitting beside him on the roof, kicking her feet gently against the icicles that hung down from the eaves. Every once in a while she would kick a little too hard, and an icicle would fall to the street below and go *tink* like a little bell.

The gargoyle was quiet for so long that Still thought it had fallen asleep. But then it rustled its stony wings. "Don't you?" it replied.

"Oh, I've already seen it," she said. "I grew up far, far away, in a village on the edge of the desert. When I was little, I was stolen by lions. They sold me to pirates, and *they* put me to work in the glue mines. It took me years to escape."

"Do you think you'll ever escape from here?" the gargoyle asked.

Still opened her mouth, then closed it. "I don't know how," she finally whispered. "I wouldn't know where to start."

"Well, what would Key have done?" the gargoyle said. "Key the Great, Key the Cutter, Key who snipped strings and walked where she wanted to, and then showed other puppets how to do the same. What would she have done?"

"I don't know," Still said with a shrug.

"Well, why don't you ask her?"

Still forced a laugh. "Ask *her*? But she's been gone for ages! She must be sawdust by now."

The gargoyle shook his head. "Not Key," it said. "As long as there are puppets in the world, there'll be a Key to help them cut their strings."

"But I don't have any strings," Still protested. She waved her arms. "See?"

"Sometimes the strings are inside," the gargoyle said. It reached out a long arm to touch the dent on Still's face. She jerked her head back. "See?" the gargoyle said. "*Something* pulled you away. And something keeps you from playing your violin, even though you look at it every morning the way a squeaky puppet looks at oil."

They spoke no more that night.

The next morning, though, Still decided that she would get the gargoyle a scarf as a present. The midwinter eclipse was coming up, when families gave each other gifts (had she ever done that?). "He probably hasn't had a present in years," she thought. "Maybe never." She had saved up half-a-dozen gumdrops and a big piece of licorice. Another couple of gumdrops and a few sugar sprinkles in change, and she'd be able to get him a scarf that would reach right down to the ground.

But Still knew that gumdrops would be hard to come by in the market now that winter had arrived. If she wanted to earn that kind of candy, she would have to go higher up in the City, up where the puppets' shoes matched and their stitching was done with silk thread. Up where—where— She shook her head so hard that the thought fell out and rolled away.

Still walked until she came to a tidy little street full of tidy little shops, then chose a corner where puppets were getting on and off bright red streetcars. She found a newspaper on a bench that was so fresh, the ink still smelled faintly of cinnamon. She folded the comics page into a neat little box and set it at her feet, then bent her head and began to play. The fingers of her left hand fluttered in the air, sliding up and down on strings that weren't there. Her right arm was as graceful as the neck of a swan. Even though she wasn't making a sound, she was playing as beautifully as she ever had.

Which is why she was so surprised when an old puppet with frizzy white hair sniffed, "I *never!*" as he walked by. "Out here in the street like that!" he said to the puppet walking beside him.

"It's shameful!" the other puppet agreed.

Still kept playing. Some other well-dressed puppets sniffed at her as well, but a few dropped sugar sprinkles into her box. Just before lunch time, a strawberry gumdrop went *plonk* into the box. Still kept playing. As the shadows grew longer, the sugar sprinkles began to pile up. Finally, just as the shopkeepers were taking in their sandwich signs, a tired-looking puppet wearing a turban and big black boots tossed another gumdrop into her box as he strode by. She had enough to buy the gargoyle a scarf!

Still scooped up her box and turned. And froze. And ducked into the doorway of the shop behind her. She pretended to read the sign—*Microscopes and Tweezers, All Kinds, Finest Workmanship Only*—until the reflections of a handful of puppets went by. Most were her age, but one was older. His clothes were blue and orange, and he wore a polka-dot hat. He had black curls painted on his forehead, and a big smile painted on his face.

The younger puppets all had instruments tucked under their

arms: flutes, trumpets, glockenspiels, and midget tubas. Still recognized some of them from—from—

"You're all playing quite nicely," she heard the older puppet say warmly. "Especially you, Mustard." He put his hand on one puppet's shoulder and gave her a friendly squeeze. "I think you're just about ready for some special lessons."

"Thank you, Mister Leaf," the young puppet said, "But I don't know if my parents can— I mean—"

"Don't worry about that," the older puppet said. "I'm sure we can work something out."

The streetcar arrived with a rattle. The puppets got on. Still waited until she stopped shaking, then walked slowly back into the fog.

She was so quiet that evening that the gargoyle finally said, "Are you angry with me for what I said about strings?"

"What? Oh, no, I'm not angry," Still replied. She shook her head. Her thoughts rattled around for a moment, but were just as jumbled when they came to rest as they had been before. "I just heard something today . . ."

"Something bad?" the gargoyle asked.

Still nodded. "Something horrible," she said. She hugged her legs to her chest and put her chin on her knees. "What would you do if you knew someone was going to do something awful—something really, really awful?"

The gargoyle shrugged his stony shoulders. "I'd whistle as loud as I could until the police came," he said. "Then I'd tell them everything I knew."

Still raised her hand to her face. The edges of the dent in her cheek had worn smooth, as had the other nicks and scratches that life on the foggy streets had given her. "But what if they'd put strings on you if you told?" she whispered. "What if they'd screw eyehooks into your elbows and knees, and run black silk strings through them, so that you could never move your own arms and legs again?"

"I'd do it anyway," the gargoyle said. "If you let something bad happen, that's almost the same as doing it yourself." He shrugged his stony shoulders once again. "But you have to remember, I'm not a puppet, I'm a gargoyle. Maybe the last steadfast gargoyle left in Key's City. If I—"

"Key . . ." Still whispered. The whirling thoughts in her head fell into place, *clunk clunk clunk,* like the pieces in a jigsaw puzzle. "She'd know what to do!" She leapt to her feet. "And you said she was still here, didn't you? Oh, where can I find her? Please, please, tell me!"

The gargoyle looked at her with love and sadness in his stony old eyes. "I can't tell you how to find her," he said.

"Why not?"

"Because you have to figure it out for yourself." The gargoyle held her violin out to her. "Here. Follow this, wherever it leads. That's all I can tell you."

Still snatched her violin away from him. It had a few nicks and scratches too, from the places it had been hidden, and her thumb could feel a faint groove from—from— She shook her head angrily. She had just managed to get all her thoughts to fit together—she was *not* going to shake them up again, not when something so important needed to be done.

"But how can I follow a violin?" Still asked. "It can't float through the air like a balloon, or run like a clock. What am I supposed to do?"

The gargoyle just bowed his head. Still begged and wheedled, she blustered and raged, but the gargoyle wouldn't say a word.

"Fine!" Still shouted. "Be like that! I thought you were my friend, but you're really just a horrible old piece of stone. You don't care at all!" She spun around, grabbed the drainpipe, and slithered down to the street. Little drops of oil welled up in her eyes as she ran through the street, down, down, deeper into the fog than she had ever gone before.

She ran and ran past the grimy walls and bent-over lampposts. Suddenly she slipped on a dirty patch of refrozen snow. Her violin flew from her hand and tumbled end over end through the air. "Noooo!" Still shrieked as it vanished over a low brick wall. She heard a faint *kersplash.*

Still scrambled to her feet and chinned herself up on the wall. Two stories below lay a canal full of cold, dark water. Her violin bobbed gently up and down in its middle. Even as she watched, the current was pulling it away.

Still gulped. She would float too—after all, she *was* made of wood. But how would she get out? There were no ladders on the side of the canal, no docks or stairways that she could see. And it was getting dark . . .

Still

She pulled herself up onto the wall. It was only half as wide as a sidewalk, and splashed here and there with treacherous patches of ice, but she walked as quickly as she could, glancing down every few moments to keep her violin in sight.

She was trying so hard not to lose sight of her violin, and not to slip on the ice, that she was almost on top of the stairway before she noticed it. The steps were worn and icy, but she clattered down them two at a time. At the bottom, they turned into a narrow footpath running along the canal's edge. There was ice here too, and frozen slime, and some of the stones were loose. And it was dark, even with the moon coming up—so dark that she wondered if the tiny patch of stillness in the middle of the canal was really her violin, or just her imagination.

Up ahead, Still could hear an echoing, gurgling sound. "Now what?" she wondered wearily. The answer turned out to be a round-roofed tunnel big enough to swallow a coal barge, its mouth covered with a heavy iron grill.

Still gasped in despair as the current swept her violin between its bars. They were too close together—she could reach an arm through, but couldn't squeeze past them. And her violin was disappearing into the darkness!

Still looked around wildly. There wasn't a gate. There wasn't an alarm bell for her to ring, or any sign of a secret door. There was just the pale moon above her, the blank walls of the canal, and the broken stones of the narrow path beneath her feet.

The stones! She bent over and picked one up, staggered to the edge of the canal, and jumped in.

Without the stone, she would have bobbed up and down like a cork. With it in her arms, she sank straight down into the cold, dark, dirty water. She squeezed her eyes shut so tightly that little bright patterns of light danced on the backs of her eyelids. The oil in her joints felt like it was freezing solid. She could end like this, she realized. She could be snagged on some thrown-away piece of machinery under the water, and trapped in the darkness until her clockwork rusted solid and she ended, and no one would ever know.

Still hung on just a moment longer than she could bear, then let go of the stone. *Whoosh!* She shot up like a clown fired out of a circus cannon.

"Pfaaah!" she spluttered as her head broke through the

surface. She looked around wildly. There was the grill—and there was the sky, on the other side of it! She'd done it! The current had swept her beneath the grill!

That same current was still carrying deeper beneath the city. Misshapen patches of fungus glowed the roof of the tunnel like moonlit clouds. A side tunnel led away from the one Still was in. She couldn't see her violin any longer. There was no way to tell where the current had taken it.

"I can't just stay here," she fretted. "What should I do?"

As if in answer, something giggled softly behind her. She whirled around with a splash. "Who's there?" she called. No one answered.

"Please, can you help me?" she said loudly. "I'm lost."

"Tee hee, tee hee." The giggles seemed to come from all around her. "She's lost . . . she's lost . . . tee hee . . ." Still whirled around again in the water, peering into the darkness. Suddenly she heard tiny feet scamper across stone, and saw one of the patches of fungus on the wall ripple slightly.

Glass rats! Glass rats, with diamond teeth and sharp little appetites. Another patch of fungus rippled, and another. There must be dozens of them, all around her!

"What do you want?" she cried out.

"Tee hee," the rats giggled. "Why, oil, of course," one rat squeaked. "Slippery puppet oil, and crunchy puppet wood."

Still floated in the water with rats all around her. "I'm afraid I don't have any wood or oil to give you," she said as calmly as she could.

The little ratty voice spoke up again. "Well, if you won't give it to us, we'll just have to take it," it squeaked, which made the other rats giggle, "Tee hee, tee hee," once again.

"But what if I don't want to give it to you?" Still asked.

"Give it to us?" the rat squeaked. "Tee hee, tee hee! Why, it's already ours! Everything that comes down here without a good reason is ours."

"But I *have* a reason!" Still said. "A very good reason!"

The giggling stopped. "And what reason is that?" the rat squeaked.

"I'm looking for something," Still said. "Something I lost. Something very important."

"Really?" the rat asked suspiciously.

Still

Still hesitated. If she told them the truth, they might eat her violin! "Yes," she said firmly. "I'm looking for Key the Cutter. I have to warn her about something."

There was a moment of silence, then the rats began giggling again. "That's not why you're here," the little voice squeaked. "We can tell. Rats can *always* tell. Now, perhaps if you give us your arms and legs, we'll let the rest of you go."

"All right!" she said. "All right, I lied. I'm looking for—I'm looking for my violin. It fell in the water, and I have to get it back."

There was another moment of silence, a longer one, but then the rats began to giggle once more. "Still not the truth, still not the truth," the little voice said with glee.

"All right! All right!" Still shouted. "I'm not looking for Key. I'm not really looking for my violin! I'm looking for—for—for me! That's why I'm here! I put myself somewhere, but now I can't remember where that was, and I'm trying to find me again. Now, if you want to eat me up, then come and eat me up and get it over with!"

Silence filled the tunnel. It stretched and stretched until Still thought she would scream, and then the little voice said, "Rats, she figured it out." Little feet scampered away in the darkness.

Still waited a moment, then paddled over to the side of the tunnel and pulled herself up onto the walkway. She was safe now, but what did that matter? She had no idea where she was, or her violin either. Drops of oil welled up in her eyes and ran down her cheeks. All of a sudden she felt too weak to keep looking, too weak to walk, too weak to even stand. She slumped down in a heap.

She had no idea how long she lay there—minutes? Hours? Her next thought came when she realized that something was bobbing up and down in the water in front of her. She blinked. It was still there. She blinked again, then picked it up.

It was a tiny boat made out of neatly-folded white paper. Neatly-folded paper—now what did that remind her of? She shook her head. Something was written on the side of it. She couldn't read it—the light was too faint. She stood up wearily and held it up close to the nearest patch of glowing fungus.

Someone had painted a picture of a puppet on the side of the boat. Written underneath it were the words, "Have you seen our daughter?" Still peered at the picture. The puppet looked familiar somehow. She was wearing black and white—

"And eight shades of green," Still whispered, there in the darkness. The paper boat fluttered like a bird trying to escape from someone's hand. Still realized that she was trembling. She knelt down and gently set the paper boat back in the water. "Go ahead," she whispered, pushing it out into the current with one finger. "You go ahead, and I'll follow you."

The little boat bobbed up and down as it floated gently away. Still followed it, lost in her thoughts. Black and white, and eight shades of green . . . Eight shades of green . . . She *knew* that puppet, she was sure of it. But what was her picture doing on the side of a paper boat?

When the boat reached the split in the tunnel, it turned right. Still followed it around the corner, and stopped dead. A whole flotilla of little paper boats lay in the water in front of her. She knelt and picked one up. The same picture was painted on its side. "Please help us find our daughter," it said. She picked up another. "If you see our daughter, please tell her that we love her."

Her hand was trembling as she picked up a third boat. "Still, please come home," she read aloud. Suddenly she hugged the little boat to her chest. "Ramble . . ." she whispered. "Elbow . . . Oh, where have I been?"

She pulled the boats from the water one after another. They spilled out of her arms onto the walkway, but she didn't care. She was sobbing, but she didn't care, because she knew what she was going to find.

And there it was—her violin. The current that had carried the boats to this backwater had brought her violin as well. She picked it up and hugged it close. "Time to go home," she whispered.

Still walked out into the dawn with her violin in one hand and the little paper boat in the other. A bird chirrupped nearby, then fell silent, as if embarrassed.

The streets around her were broad and clean, and the houses were as tidy as Elbow's creases. Her fear lay in her belly like cold soup, but she kept walking. The streets began to fill with puppets on their way to work, or school, or just out to enjoy the crisp, cold day. A few stared at Still as she strode past, but she paid them no heed.

The park next to Mister Leaf's house was just as tidy as she remembered, and the steps leading up to its front door were just as square. The high, hesitant sound of a flute floated through the air from the second-story window.

Still set the little paper boat on the sidewalk in front of the steps, laid her violin on top of it, and bowed her head. Slowly, she raised her left arm, bent at the elbow. Slowly, so slowly, she tilted her head to one side, and brought her right arm up, the wrist and elbow loose, just as she had been taught. Slowly, silently, she began to play.

The wind rustled the last few paper leaves on the trees around her. A squirrel with a squeaky tail scampered across a branch. A child's balloon blew by. All of them were louder than Still's music. It was as silent as deep snow, and it spread out in waves around her. First the puppets in the nearby houses heard it. They set down their gossip and chores and stared at one another. The streetcars fell silent, and then the children in the playgrounds. Even the roustabouts working on the balloons overhead stopped their chatter and bluster.

Passersby began to gather around Still. "What's she doing?" they asked one another, but no one had an answer.

Finally a police puppet rode up on a shiny blue bicycle. He leaned it against a tree, straightened his serious hat, and scowled. "What's going on here, then?" he asked. Still just kept playing.

"Excuse me, miss, but I asked, what's going on here?" the police puppet repeated. He took a step toward her.

"Perhaps I can explain," a warm voice said. Still opened her eyes. Mister Leaf was outside his front door. His student was standing beside him, her flute in her hands, her eyes big and dark. Mister Leaf's hand was on her shoulder. She looked straight at Still, and Still looked straight back at her.

"Well, I'd be grateful if you would," the police puppet said. "It's a mighty strangeness to me, it is."

"This poor thing was one of my students," Mister Leaf said. "She had an accident—look, you can see the mark on her cheek. She ran away from home several months ago. Her parents have been very, very worried. I'm sure that—"

But no one ever got to find out what Mister Leaf was sure of.

The young puppet at his side shook off his hand and walked down the steps. As Still kept playing, the young puppet set her flute down on the paper boat beside Still's violin, tucked her elbows in at her sides, raised her hands, and began to play silence as well.

Someone gasped. "Tsk tsk," said Mister Leaf, striding down the steps himself. "You really shouldn't encourage her. She needs—"

But no one ever got to find out what Mister Leaf thought Still needed, either, because a puppet in the crowd stepped forward. Wiping away the drops of oil on her cheeks, she raised a ghostly trumpet to her lips.

The silence was deafening. Together, the three puppets played Still's song all the way to its end. When they were done, Still lowered her arms.

"I didn't fall," she whispered. The world was so quiet that everyone around could hear her clearly. "I didn't have an accident. I had *him*."

The moment was broken by Elbow and Ramble pushing their way through the crowd. "Still! Oh, Still!" they cried. They hugged her between them.

"Oh, daffodil," Ramble finally said, gazing at the nicks and scratches on her daughter's face. "You're all grown up now. Are you all right?"

Then, finally, Still began to cry. "No," she said, hugging her parents close, "but I will be."

It took Still a while to get her story out. When she was done, the police took Mister Leaf away. "Strings are too good for him!" Elbow said harshly as the three of them walked homeward. "After what he did—your violin, that poor girl's flute, that woman's trumpet . . . Chains are what they ought to put on him!"

"Strings will be enough," Still said quietly.

It was several days before she could slip back to the little market on the edge of the fog. She bought the biggest, brightest orange scarf she could find, then walked down into the fog. She took three wrong turns on her way to the gargoyle's warehouse. Finally, she spotted the familiar drainpipe. "Hello," she called out as she climbed it. "Are you awake? I've brought you a present."

But when she reached the top, all she found was a worn old statue with the remains of a fierce look carved on its face. She stared at it for a long moment, then wrapped the scarf around its neck, climbed back down the drainpipe, and went home.

Originally published in On Spec Summer 2010 Vol 22 No 2 #81

Greg Wilson is a programmer, teacher, and author who lives in Toronto.

THE ASHEVILLE ROAD
COREY BROWN

Her father had been a railman, cut down in his thirty-fourth year by a castling bent on the £86 cargo on board. Elaine had been eleven, old enough to remember everything about him, but not mature enough to see him as anything less than the ideal man. She had not wavered in her determination to never again attach herself to anyone who rode the rails.

Lord knew, Devin had tried to sway her.

He thought of her often on the long pulls from Charlotte to Greensboro, drifting away from the drumbeat of the timer at the front of the engine. He would imagine them walking in the woods near her home in Thomasville, looking out across the village made white by blooming dogwoods. He could always persuade her to give up her resistance in these dreams, and the two of them would sit on a hillside and hold each other close until the foreman's whip came down across Devin's shoulders, spraying sweat, and stinging like mad.

"Get back in time, damn you!" Herman would shout. "You pull your weight or I'll dump you with the rest of the bastards!" He would point to the sodden glades by the side of the track where the castlings lived, and Devin would shudder despite the heat.

The mercury rose as high as one hundred on summertime

runs, with nothing to stave off the sun but the engine's tin roof. The breeze blew through, but the summer wind was not one that cooled, and its most valuable function was to keep off the bugs. The plague worked fast under these conditions, and men dropped at their handbars, slumping to the ground while the bars cycled on, up and down, up and down, while a man lay dying below.

On the King's birthday, Devin's team lost two men to sickness. The train was large, with a sixteen-man Walter engine, the *Lady Wales*; but to lose two men on one pull was rare indeed. Some of the crew muttered prayers as the second man was laid on a stretcher and carried to the rear of the train.

"The plague's comin' back," Devin's friend Alan whispered. He had the bar to the right of Devin. Two years older than Devin, Alan was still a hauler too, but would probably never be elevated to railman. He was strong of back but simple of mind, and had never mastered the mechanical skills a railman needed on the road alone. "The plague's been gone two years," Devin said, watching over his shoulder as the sick man was helped up into the caboose. The hearse car, it was called by the railmen. "And if it was comin' back, we'd be the first to know." News reached those who served the road first, since they roamed the length and breadth of the colony. "Those boys got yellow jack, more'n likely."

"I've heard of whole crews gettin' it on one shift," Alan said. He held his head low so Herman would not see him talking. "They find the train next day with the dead men still on it. They bury 'em right there beside the track." He looked at Devin with wide eyes. "That could be us."

But the sun dropped, and the mercury fell, and by the time High Point fell in their wake they had regained the steady pace of the timer's drum-beat, pushing their bars up and down, driving the train through wide fields of cotton. Signal towers, maintained by the railroad for the King's government, appeared every mile, occasionally whipping out some message in a flash of red flags, speaking in a language only the signallers understood.

The tracks came over the top of a gentle rise, and the bulk of Greensboro station loomed before them, a black octagon with a peaked roof like a witch's hat. Smoke from a thousand chimneys in the town beyond glowed in the setting sun. It would be dinner time for the villagers, sitting down with family and recounting the day's events by lantern light. On board the *Lady Wales*, the whip cracked again, and Devin and his mates swung harder at the bars.

Herman rang the bell at the head of the engine. A second later, an answering bell came from the station, and the double doors blocking the track swung open, casting a rectangle of yellow on the darkening ground. Beyond could be seen the frantic activity of railmen and mechanics, and here and there, the glint of torchlight on brass. A spider-web of tracks converged on the station, coming from Raleigh, Charlotte, and Durham. Even now, trains headed downhill from the east and north. Devin let his grip on the bar slacken as the *Lady Wales* slipped through the doors into the heat and light of the station.

Herman led his charges by hand signals now, as his voice could no longer be heard in the back. The *Lady Wales* slowed to a crawl, guided to its platform by a yellow-jacketed station boss. The minute she stopped, labourers converged on the flatcars, unloading the cargo onto carts that would soon be on the streets of the town.

Devin rubbed his aching shoulders and arms as he dropped to the plank floor of the station. A cantina crew ran up, bearing trays of water and food, and Devin snatched an orange.

"Look at 'em," Alan said, nodding to the two sick men being carried from the train. "They got it sure. They'll be dead by morning."

"Maybe they didn't drink enough water," Devin said, peeling the fruit with aching fingers. "It could be heat stroke. Have you got to be so damn negative?"

"Devin Barefoot?" The voice brought Devin and Alan up short. A man in a twill suit and spectacles stood before them. This was a manager, one of the men in the offices that overlooked the station floor. Devin swallowed hard and nodded.

"Yes sir, that's me," he said.

"Will you come with me, please?" The man turned on his heel and walked away. Devin and Alan exchanged a wary look, and Devin followed after.

The man introduced himself as Appleton—no first name—and led Devin upstairs, from the noisy floor to the quiet offices.

The smell of the air changed from the sharpness of machine oil and sweat to the mustiness of old paper and dust. Devin grew aware of his grimy road-clothes, and looked at the floor whenever one of the other managers passed by.

When they finally arrived, the office was surprisingly plain. Appleton's stern demeanour softened, and he motioned Devin to a chair. "You need it," he said. "You work a lot harder than I do."

Devin smiled and eased himself into the chair. Appleton sat behind the desk and tapped a folder lying in front of him. "We've got a job that's come up," he said, "something of an urgent nature. We need to get a train to a little village called Thomasville."

Devin started in his chair, and Appleton gave a little smile. "You've heard of it."

"Yes, sir."

"Been there before?"

"Lots," Devin said.

"The road has an arrangement with the King," Appleton said, "that provides free transportation to people with relatives that are seriously ill or dying."

Devin had heard of the provision, and nodded.

"There is a young lady in Thomasville who has requested our services. Her situation is more extreme than most, so we've agreed to meet her at noon tomorrow." Appleton pulled a slip of paper from the folder and pushed it across the desk at Devin. "Her name is Elaine Pittman."

Devin's heart pounded. He saw Elaine's name on the paper, but did not move to pick it up. "Is she sick?"

"It's her mother," Appleton said. "She's dying."

Devin remembered now. Elaine's mother was a consumptive, and had been taken away not long after her husband's death to a sanatorium in the mountains. Devin looked at Appleton. "But she's all the way up in—"

"Asheville," Appleton said. "We want you to take Miss Pittman to see her mother."

Devin blinked. "What crew am I on?"

Appleton pulled another folder from his desk. Devin could see his own name written on this one. Appleton left the folder on his desk, unopened.

"How long have you been with the company, Mr. Barefoot?" he asked.

"Five years," Devin said. He looked at the folder on Appleton's desk. *But you already know that.*

"Long time. How come you're not a railman by now?"

Devin felt his face redden. "I don't know. Just hadn't done well enough to move up, I guess."

"Your foremen say you're smart. Smarter than most, even. You can read and write."

"Yes, sir."

"You understand how a rail car works, how all the parts operate?"

"Yes, sir. Sure I do."

"Well, what else do you think a railman needs?"

Devin sat in the chair and chewed the inside of his cheek, pondering the number of times he'd been reminded how old he was for a hauler. "I don't know. I guess if I had figured it out, I would've been a railman by now."

The corner of Appleton's mouth twisted up into a smile. He pushed a brown paper envelope across the desk. "We need you to go to Thomasville and pick up Miss Pittman. It'll be your second consecutive run, of course, so you'll get time-and-a-half, plus mileage."

Devin ran his finger under the envelope's flap. The contents fell out into his lap, and his heart skipped a beat. It was an octagonal patch of sky blue, with gold trim around the edges.

"We'll get one of the ladies downstairs to put that on your uniform," Appleton said. "You can pick it up in the morning."

"Yes, sir." Devin fingered the rough fabric of the patch. "Thank you."

"One of your foremen heard about this job, and thought it was time we gave you a chance," Appleton said. "Herman Turner, as a matter of fact."

Devin gaped at him. "*Herman?*"

"He thinks very highly of you. He said he figured you had wasted enough time with the grunts, even if you didn't think so."

Devin thought of Alan. "They're good boys," he said. "Even if some of 'em aren't too smart, they work hard."

Appleton smiled. "I know." He handed Devin the job folder. "Good luck, Mr. Barefoot. Show us you've earned it."

Devin walked to the hauler's quarters in a daze. He was a *railman* now. He could not even bring himself to speak the word, and signed in at the desk as a hauler, just as he always had. He took a candle from the bored clerk and trudged up the narrow staircase.

Devin's room was small and musty, like all the hauler's quarters. He threw a blanket over the dirty ticking that served as the mattress and heaved himself onto it without even kicking off his boots. A cool breeze blew in through the window, tapping the shutter against the outside wall. The clack of a horse cart on cobblestone drifted up on the wind, and Devin caught a few snatches of drowsy conversation. Out there, the people of Greensboro were slipping off to bed, secure in the knowledge that another day much like this one waited on the other side of the night. By dawn, Devin would be long gone.

He woke to the sound of a heavy fist pounding on the door.

Devin caught the 5:15 out of Greensboro, bound south to High Point. For the first thirty minutes he and his mates churned the bars in darkness. Then the gray glow in the east turned to pink, and Devin saw the silhouette of a church steeple. As the train grew closer, he noticed gaps in the structure where sunlight came through, and then the tall grass in the churchyard. The plague had been here, and the village had been abandoned. Devin turned away and focused on the rails.

In High Point he transferred to the 10:20 to Archdale, a four-bar Remington on which the foreman drove the bar along with the haulers. The load behind the Remington was light, two flatcars of cotton, and not twenty minutes out of High Point the train came to a junction. On the spur line heading west sat a single-bar Dawson, gleaming in the sun like a newly-polished rifle.

Devin shouldered his pack but did not step off the car.

"Okay," the Remington foreman said. "This is it."

"Yep," Devin said, tugging his pack's strap tighter over his shoulder.

The foreman's puzzled expression softened into something like a smile. "Need help with anything?" he asked.

Devin shook his head suddenly, as one waking from a dream.

The Asheville Road

"No thanks," he said, and hopped down onto the gravel rail bed. "Thanks for the ride."

The Remington's foreman waved as the train moved away. "Good luck! Watch out for that first hill!"

Devin turned to the little Dawson, and the lump in his throat grew larger. In a kind of trance he stepped through the pre-run checklist—gears oiled, flywheel rotating freely on its bearings, brakes smooth and unblemished. Then he climbed aboard, put his feet on the iron footplate, and gently let off the brake.

The track sloped downhill, and the Dawson drifted off without a sound. Devin gripped the oscillating handbar and gingerly added his own force. Soon the Dawson was sailing along at ten miles an hour, and Devin allowed himself a hint of a smile.

No sooner had he done so than the track rounded a bend and plunged down a five percent grade. Devin felt his stomach lurch as he pulled back on the brake lever. Try though he might, the Dawson's speed dropped only a little by the time it reached the bottom of the hill. Devin gritted his teeth as the Dawson swung around a tight corner, wheels screeching.

"Stupid. *Stupid*," Devin said as he brought the car to a halt. He breathed deep and wiped the sweat from his palms. "You know you're supposed to read the top first."

He withdrew the map from his pack and spread it on the barpost. There, marked by a tight convergence of contour lines, was the hill he had just come down. It was even labeled with red letters.

"It won't happen again," he said, and studied the rest of the route until he could see it in his mind.

The country through which he passed was one of rolling hills, requiring no more than a 3 gear for a single-bar like the Dawson. The soil was rich, but the plague had been here twenty years before, and the human population had yet to return. The only sounds Devin heard besides the whoosh of the Dawson's mechanism were the blue jays and the wind in the oak trees. For half an hour he saw no sign of another human being. Then he rounded a turn and saw three columns of smoke rising into the morning sky. He had arrived.

Devin brought the car to a stop at the Thomasville landing. It was hardly more than a plank floor, without even a roof to keep off the rain. Devin set the Dawson's brake and looked around the little glen.

"Hello?" he called out. "Is anyone around?" Then Elaine stepped into the clearing.

Devin knew he was staring, but he could not take his eyes from her. The last time he had seen her, she had been a skinny adolescent, with the giggly carelessness of youth. Now she had become a woman, and carried herself tall and upright. Devin swallowed hard and wondered if he had matured as much.

"Elaine," he said, reaching down to take the basket she carried. She climbed aboard without returning his acknowledgement, lifting her skirt to clear the grease-covered workings of the Dawson. "You can sit here," he said, indicating one of the two passenger chairs at the front of the car.

"Thank you," she said, arranging herself on the seat. Devin contemplated her solemn expression, trying to find even a hint of recognition. He set about preparing the Dawson for the next leg of its journey, switching the direction of the drive gear and oiling the machinery.

"I'm real sorry about your mother," he told Elaine. "I hope she'll be all right."

Elaine nodded. "Thank you," she said. When she did not speak again Devin let off the brake, gave the bar a good shove, and the Dawson glided off in the direction it had come.

She remained silent all the way back to the main line. Devin paused at the junction and leaned into her field of view. "It's me," he said, "Devin. Remember?"

She turned to look at him, as calmly and dispassionately as a surgeon might regard a patient. "I know," she said. "I want to thank you for coming. The railroad answered faster than I thought they would."

The chill of her gaze made him feel even more childish, and he fished for something to put him on an even footing. "I'm a railman now," he said, touching the blue insignia on his sleeve.

It had been the wrong thing to say. Outright hostility replaced the coolness in her expression. "How nice for you," she said. "Enjoy it while you can."

Devin cursed himself silently. He kicked off the brake and pushed the Dawson forward again.

The sun rode high in the sky now, filtering through maples

and oaks to shed a mottled light on the rails. The scent of honeysuckle was in the air, mixing with the fragrance of the pines that crowded the track. Occasionally they would pass a signal tower, and Elaine would crane her neck to look up at the red flags waving in the breeze. At ten, they passed to the south of Salem and pushed on west toward Hickory, paced by the steady beat of the bar.

The hills grew steeper here, with the occasional crossing on the stout oaken bridges the Royal Engineers had thrown up over creeks and rivers. Devin used a number 4 gear, a medium ratio with enough power to get up hills but enough speed to make good time going down. The Dawson's flywheel absorbed a great deal of the energy on downhill stretches, giving it up when the track sloped upward again. With a good railman at the helm, the speed of a train did not vary more than a few miles an hour. The Dawson glided along, barely making a sound. "Is Asheville a very big place?" Elaine asked suddenly.

Devin thought for a moment. "No," he said. "It's not much bigger'n Thomasville. The mountains is a hard place to make a living."

She made a little motion that might have been a shudder. "My mother's written me from the sanatorium. She says there are crowds of men in the streets at all hours of the day and night, without any work to do, and without any families. She says none of the patients are allowed in town after dark."

Devin remembered seeing groups in the streets of Asheville, but could not recollect feeling threatened. *Some of those boys are railmen*, he thought, *blowing off a little steam.* "It's not really so bad—"

"They won't let me stay in the hospital," Elaine broke in. "They say I'll have to stay in town, and walk to see Momma." Her expression was imploring. "I don't know anyone there. I don't know if there are any places to stay, any hotels or inns—"

She broke off and turned away. Devin stared as she worried the lace edges of her handkerchief and darted little glances out at the forest.

"I'll walk you into town," he offered. "There's a couple of places to go. You won't be the only lady."

"I've never been so far from home," she said. "When Momma left, I didn't think I'd ever see her again. Asheville seemed like it was on the other side of the world."

Devin pushed the bar, thinking of the great spaces beyond the mountains but saying nothing.

"Nothing much ever happens in Thomasville. People don't fight, they try to help each other. The only bad thing is when the plague comes."

Devin thought of the two men on the train the previous day and bit his lip. "Asheville's got some good people too," he said. "You'll see."

By mid-afternoon they had reached Hickory, and Devin called a stop to eat. They sat atop a small rise, from which the surrounding countryside rolled away in rippling hills that were only a hint of what Devin knew lay over the horizon. He chewed the sandwich he had stuffed in his bag and looked out to the blue sky in the west, shivering a little as the sweat dried from his arms.

"Do you ever think things might have been different?" Elaine said. She too was looking out at the horizon.

Devin hesitated. "You mean . . . for us?"

"That maybe the plague would have never happened, and so many people wouldn't have died." She looked back at Devin. "What kind of world would we live in?"

Devin shook his head. "I never thought about it."

"Really? You never thought about how our lives would be if we didn't spend so much time burying the dead?"

Devin shook his head again and smiled sheepishly.

Elaine laughed. "Of course not. You wouldn't think of such foolishness. Men have to be so *practical*."

Devin laughed too, and ducked his head to hide his embarrassment. It was the first time she had ever called him a man.

After they finished eating Devin set about preparing the Dawson for the long climb into the mountains. He struggled with the heavy iron machinery, lifting the armature to switch the drive from the 4 gear to the 5. He climbed aboard and breathed a quiet sigh of relief as the bar moved easily in his hands, and they ascended again, slowly, into the hills.

The North Carolina mountains were deceptive in the approach. Unlike their younger counterparts to the west, they did not rear up suddenly from a flat plain. Cloaked in a soft-

The Asheville Road

looking carpet of trees, they hid behind row after row of foothills, each one only mildly higher than the last. It looked easy on the map, a succession of not-too-high peaks through which the road wound like a snake. A railman starting out in confidence from Salem would arrive in Asheville utterly spent, arms shaking from the endless row of hills. Devin knew this danger, having been to Asheville twice. He let the pace of the bar slacken, saving himself for the final push.

"Is it hard?"

Devin looked down to find Elaine watching his struggles. He blew off the drop of sweat dancing at the end of his nose and grunted out, "Yes."

"I'm sorry."

It had been the easy thing to say, but he could see in her face that her pity was sincere. He shrugged. "It's my job."

Elaine scowled. "Everyone says that."

In two more hours they reached the mountains proper, and the track took them along the side of a steep cliff, from which they could look down on the waving tops of maples and pines. The sun rested in the shallow bowl between two rounded, ancient Appalachian hills. In a few minutes it was gone, and the shadows crept up from the valley to swallow the track and the little car moving along it. Devin struck a match to light the oil lamps hanging at the front and rear of the car. Elaine sat in a circle of yellow light, shuddering at the chill in the air.

"It's going to be dark when we get there," she said.

Devin knew it would be midnight by the time they reached Asheville, and said so. He got a woollen blanket out of the supply box at his feet and gave it to her.

"Do you have much problem with . . . people harassing the train?" she asked, wrapping herself in the blanket.

The castlings, Devin thought. "Sometimes," he said. "They don't much like to mess with little trains like this. They wait for big ones that carry a lot of cargo. Besides, we got some protection." He patted the iron box attached to the barpost. A six-shot pistol rested inside.

"I'd just as soon not see anybody till we get to Asheville," Elaine said.

Devin knew this part of the country had been decimated by the plague. The graveyards were full, and the towns almost empty. "You might get your wish," he said softly.

Darkness came on in earnest now, and the grade reached one in eight, the steepest the road would build. Devin clambered beneath the Dawson and changed the gears once more, to the sixth and last, but still his muscles screamed. Sweat poured from his forehead and spattered the deck. The bar grew slick in his hands, and his knuckles turned white with the force of holding it.

At last, when he thought he could push no longer, the Dawson crested the hill and the track levelled off. Devin blew out a sigh and let the bar cycle without him, massaging feeling back into his shoulders and arms.

"Are you all right?" Elaine's voice sounded far away, as though the thin mountain air could not carry her voice.

"I'll be all right in a while."

"I don't want you to get hurt. I don't know what I'd do if something happened to you." She pulled the blanket more tightly around her.

"It's beautiful here in the daytime," Devin said. "You'll see tomorrow."

"We could die up here," Elaine said. "We could fall right off this mountain and not stop till we got to the bottom."

The wind gusted, a cold breeze that lifted the sweat from Devin's brow. He became aware of how quiet it was, not a single cricket or frog to be heard. "It's beautiful," he said. "I'd hate to go my whole life and not be able to see it. Lots of people do."

Elaine's fists were two lumps clutching the inside of the blanket. "There are so many bad things in the world," she said. "You've seen more than I have. How can you stand to think of it?"

He shook his head, seeing her dismay and not comprehending it. "I don't," he said.

The train hit something hard. In the next instant the Dawson was up and off the tracks. Devin heard Elaine scream. Then he hit the ground, and the air was knocked from his lungs.

The Dawson's oil lamps went out, smashed against the ground. A half-dozen figures appeared in the moonlight, hunched over and moving with the jerky gait that identified them to Devin immediately.

Castlings, he thought.

The Asheville Road

Devin rose and ran to the Dawson, lying on its side next to the track. The castlings quickly encircled him, careful to keep outside the range of his grasp. One by one they lunged in toward him. He batted away first one attacker and then another, moving ever closer to the box where the pistol was stored. Before he could reach it he felt the sting of a blade catch his arm from behind. He cried out, and with a flood of anger spun and grabbed his assailant by the waist. Each castling accounted for perhaps half Devin's body weight, and with muscles developed through five years of hauling, Devin hurled the man squalling down the hillside.

Devin found the strongbox on the side of the overturned Dawson, and fired two shots straight up. A tongue of flame flared out from the barrel, and in the brief light Devin saw the castlings scattering into the woods. One looked back at him, and he saw the pinched features, more canine than human, of a young woman no more than three feet tall.

Devin leaned back against the Dawson, breathing hard. "Elaine? Elaine?"

No answer came. Devin searched the ground near the Dawson, scrabbling in the gravel with his hands and finding nothing save a boot left by one of the castlings. He found one of the oil lamps, relit it with shaking hands, and went to the edge of the hill.

He saw her right away, lying at the base of an oak a hundred feet down.

Without feeling the branches tearing at his skin, he tumbled down the hillside, half running, half falling. She was lying face up, eyes open, staring at the sky without blinking. Devin grabbed her hand and called her name, but she did not move. He felt her body with his hands, and there were broken bones, and blood that stained his hands and mixed with the blood from the wound on his arm. He tried to find a pulse, a hint of breath or some other sign of life. Then he sat with her and rubbed her still hand for a long time.

At last he rose and carried her—how light she was, compared to the heavy load of the bar—back to the track. He found the woollen blanket and wrapped her in it, as if to keep the failing warmth within her.

The Dawson was not to be moved, since not even Devin's

arms could budge the heavy iron machine. He rested in the lee of the deck, out of the cold wind, until the first glimmers of dawn lit the opposite hillside. Then he rose, stiffly, and walked half a mile down the track to the nearest signal tower. With the red flag every railman carried he sent the distress signal Herman had taught him, repeating the motions until the sleepy signaller noticed him and repeated the signal in confirmation.

The tower's big signal flag went up, a slash of red on an oaken boom. Almost immediately it was answered by its fellow on the next hill, and soon the message went spinning away over the mountains. Devin walked back to the Dawson to await the rescue crew. He slumped to the ground next to Elaine and let his eyes close at last.

The birds were just beginning to sing.

The Dawson had been damaged beyond using, so the road mechanics hooked it to a ten-man Witherup and hauled it up the mountain to Asheville, still bearing Elaine's body. Devin did not need to concern himself with alerting Mrs. Pittman, he was told. The railroad had men who did such things, usually for the families of railmen or haulers killed on runs. Devin argued, but he was tired, and the steady insistence of the Asheville manager wore him down.

Devin was outfitted with a single-man Walter, an old model no longer used outside the mountains, for his return journey to Greensboro. The old engine squeaked and clacked; but the road to Hickory was downhill all the way, and Devin hardly needed to do more than squeeze the brake. Now in the daylight he could see the empty villages in the valleys, desolate houses with broken windows and sagging porches, where the sun shone through and lit the debris that always accumulates in abandoned buildings. Twice he saw castlings scurrying away from the tracks. He thought of the pistol in the iron box, but did not move to get it. The car rolled on, with Devin's eyes fixed on the rails that rolled beneath him.

He stopped at the place outside Hickory where he and Elaine had eaten the day before. Such a rage overtook him that he tore the railman patch from his sleeve and flung it into the woods. He screamed and yelled, though no one was around to hear,

The Asheville Road

until his anger was spent and he slumped to the deck of the Walter, too tired to do anything but coast downhill to Greensboro.

At seven in the evening he sighted the peaked roof of the station. Some part of his mind remembered to ring the bell, and the station door opened like a great mouth, swallowing him up into the din and chaos inside.

Devin had gone perhaps fifty yards when he noticed several figures following his car. He recognized friends from his old crew, and saw with some astonishment Alan waiting at the end of the line. Devin forgot to push the bar, and the men following him pushed the Walter with their hands.

Devin hit the stop at the end of the line with a light bump, and looked down at Herman standing before him.

"Take him," Herman said, and hands reached up to help Devin from the car. He found himself standing before his old foreman, wishing he could be anywhere else. He waited for the inevitable rebuke.

"The plague is back," Herman said.

Devin looked from one man to the next, finding confirmation of the awful truth in each face. Alan had been right, after all.

"It started in Durham this time," Herman said. "The road is stopping all commercial runs to take doctors and medicines into the city. You'll be going to Hillandale. They've lost three there already."

He motioned to one of Devin's old crewmates. "Find the manifest for Devin," he told the man. "He needs to know what time he's leaving."

Devin stared at his old boss. "I'm not going out again," he said. "I'm done with the road."

Herman regarded him closely, and for a moment Devin was sure the big man would strike him. "Wait," Herman called to the crewman he had sent away. The man turned, eyes questioning.

"Get Devin a new patch," Herman said. "He's lost his."

Devin opened his mouth, but Herman shook his head. Devin did not protest when they took his coat to sew on another patch.

"Come on," Herman said, flipping through the papers of Devin's manifest. "We don't leave until morning."

They took him to the railmen's quarters, where there were strong drinks waiting, and they stayed up singing and telling stories of the road until the small hours of the morning. In the haze of drink and exhaustion, the men's faces blurred together in Devin's vision until they looked like the same man, the Railman, who had felt this pain before and would bear it again. They were all incarnations of the same thing, and Devin knew he was that thing too, and would be for the rest of his life.

At eight the heavy fist came to pound on his door. Most of the other crews had already left when Devin reached the station floor, groggy and with an aching head, but Herman and the *Lady Wales* were there. Devin nodded to them across the floor. Herman returned a solemn wave, and then cracked his whip, cursing at his charges to get the *Lady Wales* moving. Devin heard the *Lady*'s bell clang as he turned away.

Devin boarded the single-man Walter again, taking the brake key from the mechanic on duty. There were four large boxes in the cargo cage at the front of the engine. Devin signed his name in the log book, and the great door opened to let him out into the daylight.

The car was heavily loaded, much more so than the Dawson had been when it carried Elaine, but Devin was strong, and he drove the car across the flat ground with ease. Soon he could only see the thin trails of smoke from the houses where breakfast was being cooked, and the people of Greensboro were waking to another day.

By midday he was miles away.

Originally published in On Spec *Summer 2010 Vol 22 No 2 #81*

Corey Brown is a mechanical engineer residing in the sunny climes of South Florida. Originally from North Carolina, he used his native land as the setting for "The Asheville Road." In addition to *On Spec*, Corey's work has appeared in *Electric Velocipede*, *Space and Time* and the 23rd *Writers of the Future* anthology.

Buddhist Jet Lag
Christian McPherson

I was living
in the now
but then I fell
a few seconds behind

I would just miss
the elevator
the bus

and before I knew it
I was living
in the 30-minutes-ago

I would
burn my rice
be late for work

then things got worse
I started living
in the two-hours-ago

I was missing
doctors' appointments
lunch dates

it crept up on me
and all of a sudden

Christian McPherson

> I was living
> in yesterday
>
> I sang Beatles songs
> and got fired from work
>
> I became depressed
> hit the bottle
> ended up living
> in the past
> babbling on my couch
> about the good ole days
>
> then came the intervention
> people said "you can't live in the past"
> people said "you need to think about the future"
> the men in white coats came
> as did the pills
> the rubber rooms
> the drooling
>
> now I'm all better
> now I'm back in the now
> now I might actually be a few seconds ahead
>
> I catch things before they fall
> people think I'm just moving things around
> but I know the future
> because I live there.

Originally published on On Spec Winter 2011 Vol 23 No 4 # 87

Christian McPherson is the author of *Cube Squared, My Life in Pictures, The Sun Has Forgotten Where I Live, The Cube People* (shortlisted 2011 ReLit Awards), *Poems That Swim From my Brain Like Rats Leaving a Sinking Ship*, and *Six Ways to Sunday* (shortlisted 2008 ReLit Awards).

A Taste of Time
Scott Overton

The tinkle of the bell announced a customer.

That was unusual—there weren't many customers anymore. Gabrielle had owned the Shop & Smile *dépanneur* for thirty-five years, and in the early days the bell had rung like a wind chime on a March day. But no more. Most of the people on the concession road now shopped at the new Price-Well—even the ones who smiled to her face and wished her a good day as they drove quickly past.

It took an effort to rise from the old chair in the backroom, but she tried to hurry. The bell-heralded arrivals might be some of those young smart-alecks who stole her candy.

Not this time. It was Mrs. Simm from the neighbouring farm. Marjorie. And she had a little girl with her: eight or nine, with dark hair and a short sun dress that was covered in a print of some odd-shaped orange blotches. No, maybe a cartoon character? There was a single word that looked foreign.

"Hello, Gabby," Marjorie said. "Amanda, this is Miss Dufour. She owns the store."

The girl gave a polite curtsy and said, "It's nice to meet you," making Gabrielle smile in surprise. Not many children were taught such manners anymore.

"Amanda's come to visit us for the summer," Marjorie said. "From the States. Her mother—remember our daughter

Sandra? She lives in Michigan now."

Gabby used to hear a lot about that daughter, especially when Sandra went off to university, but that was before Marjorie got the job at the library in town. Since then she'd been too busy to drop by for gossip. Her husband, Edgar, had to handle all of the chores on their small farm himself, dawn to dusk. How did they expect to look after a child for the summer?

Marjorie said, "Amanda's looking forward to roaming around the farm, but I've told her she mustn't go anywhere else on her own. Except maybe here, if we send her to pick up a few things."

So that was it. They expected Gabby to be a part-time babysitter. She ought to say something to quell that notion *tout de suite*.

But the girl spoke first. "Gramma says you know lots about the farm property. And the town that used to be there. Gramma says it's covered with *blueberries*." She said the word the way she'd speak a magic spell, her smile revealing small teeth that were just a little crooked, but sugar-white.

"Blueberries. Yes, there are blueberries," Gabby huffed. "You can hardly walk without stepping on the things."

"Don't you like blueberries?"

"Everybody likes blueberries." Her grandmother patted her shoulder. "We just dropped in to pick up some flour and brown sugar and butter."

"Blueberry muffins, I bet. You'll need baking powder, too," Gabby said. "It should be fresh."

"You're right. I haven't baked in a few months. Better give me some, please."

Gabby made up the order and accepted the money.

The child was fascinated by the whole process. "Everybody loves blueberries," she repeated, as she and her grandmother waved goodbye and made the bell ring again.

But that wasn't true—Gabby didn't love blueberries. Had not since she was a girl herself, perhaps about Amanda's age. Her father had hurt his back and couldn't work. They had no money. So the family spent the month of July picking blueberries, and ate them for months afterward. Little else.

Blueberry muffins, of course, but also pancakes and porridge. Fritters and frying-pan bread. Buckle and grunt. Chutney. Cobbler. Even blueberry soup and blueberry shrub made with vinegar watered down for drinking.

That was long before the days of itinerant vendors selling berries from the backs of pickup trucks along the highway.

Blueberries tasted like poverty to Gabrielle.

She dusted a few shelves while she was up, and made sure the mousetrap was fully hidden behind some cans of celery soup that nobody ever touched. Then she hobbled back to her magazine, surrendering once more to wastrel Time.

The next day was Sunday, a day for the Simms to be home with the little girl. She didn't visit the *dépanneur* Monday or Tuesday, either. It wasn't until Wednesday morning that she appeared, wanting more muffin cups and shortening.

"Amanda. Do people call you Mandy?"

"At home, and at school. Gramma and Grampa don't. Gramma had a cousin named Mandy, but they don't talk about her."

Gabby nodded knowingly. Then the silence became awkward. She didn't talk to children very much anymore. "So . . . what have you been doing with yourself? At the farm."

"Exploring. And eating blueberries." The bright crescent smile was all the more winning because it wasn't perfect. Soon her parents would take her to an orthodontist and some of her childhood would be sacrificed. "There are so many blueberries. Everywhere. Just like you said, Mrs. Dufour."

"It's Miss, and you can call me Miss Gabby. You be sure not to eat any other berries there. The other kinds could make you sick."

"Gramma told me. There's a big bush with juicy red berries. Near the bottom of the hill. I won't eat them."

Gabby nodded, remembering. That would be where the great pin cherry tree had stood in the churchyard. The tree burned to the ground in the fire that took the town. Pin cherries wouldn't hurt the girl, but other shrubs had grown up around the spot. "There used to be a church right there," she said.

"I know. Beside the post office, and the li . . . livery stable."

Gabby's head snapped around. How could . . . ? Oh, but there were probably some remains of the foundations still left, overgrown by weeds. Maybe the Simms had tried to plough there and were stopped by the blocks.

It had been a fine church–the steeple stretching skyward as if competing with the hilltop to be closer to God. The pastors who came and went every few years eyed the crown of higher ground with envy.

"The hill *would* have been a good place for the church," Mandy observed.

"Yes. Yes, it would." But the hill had belonged to the Laclé family for generations, and young Armand Laclé . . . well, he'd had very special plans for that hilltop, once he could finish his studies as an architect.

Plans he'd meant for Gabby to share.

She coughed and dusted invisible flour from her skirt as she hoisted herself to her feet. It took a few moments to find the muffin cups. Then she fetched the shortening, took the money, and sent the girl on her way.

When the tinkling call of the bell beckoned her from the back room on Friday, Gabby stopped cold in the doorway.

It was the girl again, a red scarf at her neck, tied in just the way old Mrs. Landry had worn her scarves, and no one else Gabby could ever remember: the knot pulled to the left side, and the ends spread apart with the upper one pinned to the top of her shoulder. Silly, some thought. *Distinctive*, Mrs. Landry had insisted.

"Where did you get a scarf like that?" Gabby asked, without even saying hello.

"Gramma helped me with it," the girl announced proudly, pivoting from side to side, cross-eyed from trying to look at the scarf. "I thought it looked . . . distinctive." She smiled as if pleased with the grownup word.

Gabby found herself reaching toward the countertop for support. "And what do you want this time? Sugar? More muffin cups?"

"No, thank you. I just wanted to show you my scarf."

"I suppose you're going to wear it blueberry picking. You'll catch it on the bushes, you know."

"I'll be careful. I found an old one like this under a bush yesterday. But Gramma said it was too faded, so she gave me hers."

"There could be bears out there. Maybe you should leave the blueberries alone for a while."

"But they're *so* good. I like the light blue ones best. As if they're painted with blue Jell-O powder. Those are sweet. The others—the ones that are almost black—they're kind of pasty. If you use them for jam you need more sugar. They're better for chutney." She nodded her head wisely. "You get to know blueberries. The little crunchy ones. The fat juicy ones. Some with just a few berries in a clump. Others in clusters, like grapes. Sweet in the sunshine, fatter in the shade. But the tangy ones are good, too—maybe they wish they were oranges or lemons. A few bushes grow next to pine trees, and you can taste that in the berries."

"My, you've become quite the expert." Old Mrs. Landry had sounded just like that sometimes, too, showing off with the things she knew about food. She had been the best cook in town.

The child took the words at face value, and beamed, running her hands down her shorts to smooth them. Gabby felt ashamed. She reached for the jar of toffees behind the counter, took a couple, and held them out.

"Here. Just for a change from berries. And be careful around the farm. Those old buildings could have root cellars. You might fall in."

"I know where they are. I won't fall." Mandy turned with another smile, and the bell tinkled overhead as she went out. Gabby looked up at it for the first time in years, and was surprised by its whiteness, and the blueberry motif she'd painted on it by hand. She'd forgotten about that.

The girl didn't come again for nearly a week. Maybe Marjorie wasn't pleased that Gabby had given the child candy. No, that was silly. It was only because the weather was so fine. A sun-dappled day offered better things to do than hang around an old woman in a lonely store. Like picking berries. It was good picking weather. She hoped Mandy wouldn't get into any trouble with snakes or wasps. Perhaps Gabby should look for her to make sure she was all right.

Just then the door bell chimed, and sunshine poured in.

Scott Overton

"*Bonjour, Mademoiselle Gabby. Crème glacée, s'il vous plait. Et . . . Ah, oui. Du sucre, du pain, et du lait. Merci.*"

"*Bien sûr!* Your French is very good, Mandy." She stepped toward the ice cream freezer. She knew the Simms weren't French, but then all the children learned it in school these days, she supposed. With such a good accent, though. That was surprising.

"*French*, Miss Gabby?"

"Yes, it's very good. Well done."

"I don't know what you mean."

"What you just said. About the ice cream and everything. *Très bien.*"

The puzzlement in the child's eyes was genuine. Gabby felt a knot of fear in her stomach. Had she only imagined it? Translated the English words in her head, somehow. Was her mind starting to play tricks on her?

The next Thursday was wet. Mandy sat in a chair near the front window of the *dépanneur* with a small pad of paper on her lap, sketching in pencil. Old stock—not worth charging for. It kept the child occupied while Gabby worked. There was a ledger to update and new stock to order, even with so few customers.

When her back became too sore to bend over the counter anymore, she yielded to her curiosity and hobbled toward the front of the store. As she looked over the child's shoulder, her hand flew to her mouth.

It was a sketch of a house. So familiar. And so *good*—where could a child of nine have learned to draw so well? Long, grey boards with swirled grain and dark knots. The portico that was too fancy for a frame bungalow, with a tell-tale of peeling paint on the crosspiece. Filigree in the window curtains.

She knew that house. Gustave Houle's house.

Gustave Houle, who was a painter twice. For money, he would paint homes, whitewash fences, stain barns. For his own pleasure, he made canvases of the landscape, the simple buildings, and the simple people of Manqueville. He helped Armand learn how to draw for his architecture courses.

God in Heaven. The child was recreating Gustave's house— with Gustave's own skill!

How was it possible?

"Where did you see that house, Mandy?"

"In my head. I thought it was pretty. I was eating some blueberries down by the creek, where it slows down and gets a bit marshy. It's a nice place. Lots of flowers."

There would be, yes. Gustave had also been a devoted gardener. Some of the seeds must have lived to try again, the hardiest ones that didn't require care. The daffodils and day lilies maybe. The hostas—they'd spread like weeds if the deer didn't get them.

"Eating blueberries. Always the berries," Gabby mused. The low bushes were at home throughout the rocky expanses of northern Ontario. They had a special fondness for burned-out clearings, where forest fires left behind acidic soil and shade-free spaces. They'd laid siege to Manqueville and then consummated their victory in its ashes.

The berry plants drew nutrients from the earth. Could they draw other things, too? Essences of things long lost?

The ringing above the door broke into her thoughts. It was Marjorie, come to fetch her granddaughter for dinner.

"Thank you so much for looking after her, Gabby. I hope she hasn't been any trouble."

"Oh, no. Not at all. She's a very nice girl. And talented. Look at the sketch she made."

Mandy proudly displayed her work. Marjorie looked at it and gave Gabby a conspiratorial smile. "Yes, it's very good. And it was nice of Miss Dufour to help you with it."

"I didn't . . ." But Marjorie had turned away to pick up a few things in the grocery aisles. Some Hamburger Helper, Gabby noticed. Home cooking was disappearing, even here in the north country. People had other priorities. She hobbled to the cash register.

"Amanda's French is very good, too," she said tentatively.

"French?"

"She learns it in school, does she?"

"No, Gabby. Amanda lives in the States. They don't teach French in the schools there. It's too bad, really." Too bad. Was she talking about the lack of a second language? Or an old friend who might be starting to slip a little, and imagine things? The look on her face was hard to read.

When Mandy came again, Gabby was gruff with her. She'd been brooding over the things she might have only imagined, and over what people might be saying. All because of one little girl.

People already talked behind her back when she went into the new town for nails or newspapers or notions. Or just to see a fresh face or two. *Old maid* was one of the kinder names they used when they thought she didn't hear. But now it might be even worse. Because of a little brat and her damned blueberries!

As soon as the thought came to her, she regretted it. Mandy had turned back to the door, disappointment like a brand on her face.

"Wait, child. I'm sorry. Come. Sit with me." There was a stool behind the counter—the girl mounted it with a little help. Gabby dragged her chair from the back room. They sat together, not sure where to look.

"Tell me about the fire," Mandy said.

Gabby's eyebrows lifted. Did she really want to do that? What should she reveal? Especially to a child.

Manqueville had been a thriving town then, small but robust. Mostly lumberjack's families and mill workers, but some others. The fire had sprung on them out of the night, sweeping in from the bush on a sudden change of wind, so there'd been no forerunner of smoke, no warning. Just hungry flames that found a feast of wood far drier than the forest, and wanted it all.

Most of the victims had died in their beds. Or behind parlour windows, staring at the flames that entrapped them until they were overcome by smoke, if they were lucky. Women and children—the husbands were away at lumber camps. Like Papa. Gabby and her mother had been lucky because Soyer's Pond, behind the house, was just wide enough, just deep enough. The flames arced over their heads through the dark sky as they hunched in the water up to their noses, submerging frequently to keep their hair wet.

Armand wasn't a lumberer. But he wasn't killed in his home, either. One of the survivors had seen him pull his mother out of the house and run into the night, but their bodies were never found. Like so many others, they were part of the ash and rubble. The fire was so hot it consumed everything.

That he was dead, Gabby had no doubt. Otherwise he would have come for her.

She shook her head slowly, aware of the child watching.

"It was bad, very bad. A lot of people died. And a lot of dreams. Let it go at that."

They were memories she hadn't wanted to relive. They tasted like dust. Like blueberries.

Day after day Gabby expected to hear the bell at the door and see Mandy's picket fence smile again, but she didn't come. Gabby made an excuse to drive into the new town and dropped in to the library. Marjorie looked surprised to see her. And something more. She said Amanda hadn't been feeling well—probably too many berries—but her smile wasn't quite comfortable on her face.

Gabby thanked her and left. She knew what had happened. Marjorie had kept the little girl away, afraid to entrust her any longer with a lonely old woman who might be going senile. And maybe she was right. It wasn't sensible to believe that things like knowledge, or language, or talent could be ingested like sugar and salt. The sign of an unsound mind—it had to be.

So she felt the summer slip away. The blueberry plants would soon be barren once more, their profusion of tiny pointed leaves turning rusty at the edges. Good riddance. Maybe that was the real message: that it was time for Gabby to be going too. Perhaps she should sell the store and move south. Somewhere. Anywhere. As she'd wanted so desperately to do all those years ago after the fire, but hadn't. Was it simply life's inertia that had held her back? Or because, by then, going anywhere at all had seemed so very pointless?

Then suddenly Mandy was back. With a jingle like a fairy's laugh, she appeared as if she'd never been away.

"Gramma said I shouldn't come here and bother you so much. You're busy. But I didn't think you'd be busy all the time. Are you?"

"No, child. I'm not busy at all. How have you been? How are the blueberries?"

"Not so many anymore. You have to look for them. I ate a lot this morning from some bushes at the farthest corner of the farm, where the fire didn't go. There are some very old trees there."

"Yes, very old."

"I was thinking it would have been a wonderful place to put a library and town hall. With a beautiful clock tower. Grand and tall, with a clock face you could see from anywhere in town. And especially from a house on top of the hill. On a fancy porch with carved posts and a wrought iron railing, you'd look across a sea of rooftops under a starry sky, and catch a glimpse of the clock face in the moonlight just as the bell chimed twelve." Her brown eyes shone with the vision.

Gabby gasped. The child sounded just like Armand with his lofty dreams. Armand on the evening before the fire, holding her in his arms on the porch of his mother's house and talking, talking with the fervour of the true believer. Just before Gabby had finally confessed that she didn't *want* to stay there, in a house on the hill or anywhere else in Manqueville. That she felt trapped in such a small town with its small minds. Hated it, and begged for God to free her. Begged to God.

She looked at the child in wonderment.

"Amanda," she said. "Do you remember where to find those bushes you ate from this morning? Could you take me to them? I . . . I have a craving."

"Sure." The girl held out her hand and Gabby took it gratefully.

The tinkling bell fell silent as the door closed behind them.

Originally published in On Spec Spring 2012 Vol 24 No 1 # 88

A radio broadcaster for more than thirty years now living in Sudbury, Ontario, **Scott Overton's** short fiction has been published in *On Spec, Neo-opsis, Penumbra* and several anthologies including *Tesseracts Sixteen: Parnassus Unbound.* His first novel *Dead Air* (a mystery/thriller about the radio industry) is published by Scrivener Press.

Penultimate
F.J. Bergmann

You can't understand the words, of course, but you feel it
singing, one note that lasts beyond remembrance.
You will preserve that thought, decant it in the years to come,
when you are old and wooden, when you are at rest.
This is a good day; it will be like sweet juice from ripeness
that you can savour again and again after it has fermented
inside your brain, long after you forget who you are.

Your pension and savings would only go so far; the
health plan informed you there was still no fix in sight
for some of the iffy genes you carried, making rebodying
or rebooting "unachievable at this time." You envisioned
the unfinished autobiography inscribed inside your skull
erasing itself page by page. Already there were tunes
you could not finish, unexpected sputters of silence.

You kissed your world goodbye. Said farewell to shadows
cast by your native sun for the last time. Lovers had left
you years before, moving youthward like leaves unfalling,
spiralling back up to greening branches and an absence
of seasons. So what if they had become nothing more
than collections of altered molecules, the organic bolted
to the mechanical, in a slurry of fuel and volition?

F.J. Bergmann

You learned to live in the moment, to travel light. Always
there was room in the immense star freighters for another
useful, small creature to disappear. Bells rang, summoning
you to service, as the ship caromed between planets
with names you couldn't pronounce, a cosmic pinball,
silver shifting to red. Beings with unimaginable capabilities
for kindness excused your frailties and failings.

They asked to hear your music, wanted to know everything
about you. Their choral harmonies encompassed and joined,
a metaphor for communion turned into sound. As you stand
on the glassy beach on the far side of a distant galaxy,
listening to something like a vast chime create its tremendous
resonances, you realize that the journey is endless,
its destination a place where you have not yet been born.

Originally published in On Spec Summer 2012 Vol 24 No 2 #89

F.J. Bergmann writes poetry and speculative fiction, often simultaneously, appearing in *Black Treacle, Lakeside Circus, Silver Blade,* and elsewhere. Editor of *Star*Line* and poetry editor of *Mobius: The Journal of Social Change*; recent awards include the 2012 Rannu Prize for poetry and the 2013 SFPA Elgin chapbook award.

Pilgrim at the Edge of the World
Sarah Frost

The sun sat on the horizon like a fat red egg. Kaainka squinted into the light, trying to fix every detail of this moment in his mind. Wings folded and spread. Long beaks stabbed the air. Feathers painted yellow and red burned in the sunset. This could be his last night among the People. The camp's elders danced, singing the Song of the Ancestors. Tomorrow, Kaainka would leave the People and walk north. He would return as an adult, or not at all.

That night, after the camp had finished singing the sun down from the sky, Kaainka found a place to rest by the campfire. The People walked all around him, dark and graceful shapes in the firelight. No one spoke to him. A red-dyed twist of antelope gut tied loosely around his neck set him apart: No longer a child, but not yet an adult, Kaainka would leave before dawn while the People slept. Until then he was only a traveler resting for the night.

Kaainka looked up at the sky. Even dimmed by the firelight, the stars were glorious. His eyes traced the great arc of light that hung over his head. The stories said that shining path was made by the River of Death where it spilled out into the sky. He spotted one of the wandering stars as it glided by, slower than a falling star but faster than the moon. It faded as he watched, flashed, and faded again. Kaainka looked away. A wanderer was an unsteady omen with which to begin a journey.

Footsteps brought his mind down out of the sky. Eikss walked up to Kaainka where he sat by the fire. Fire-light shone on the scales of her legs and the fine blue skin of her face. She held a waterskin in her beak, the last of its stitching still undone. Eikss set the waterskin down and pulled her needle free of the tough goat hide. Holding the skins together with her feet, she stitched up the side with quick, even strokes of the needle.

"The desert is fierce and wide," she said as she worked. "You will need to carry as much water with you as you can, and drink sparingly. Walk in the cool of the morning, and in the evening as the sand loses its heat. Do not walk in the dark, or you'll fall and break your leg. Then you will never come back, and I will owe Airk the entrails of my next kill."

"He thinks I won't come back?" Kaainka said. Eikss had made the journey last year. When she returned, she had been wiser, full of stories and unexpected stillness. Kaainka longed for her, but dared not say anything. He would think about courtships when his journey was over. He couldn't afford the distraction, and children couldn't go courting in any case.

"He thinks I will be impressed with the guts of the next slimy thing he pulls from a mud-pool." She laughed, and tied off the last stitch on the waterskin. Eikss took the skin in her beak and proffered it to Kaainka. He took it, and tucked it under his wing.

"Thank you," he said. Then, on impulse, he added, "You shouldn't be talking to me."

"Mind how you speak in my camp, traveller." She snapped, and then laughed. She turned her head to the side, fixing him with a one-eyed stare. "Walk in the Ancestors' footprints," she said, and then huddled down by the fire to sleep.

Kaainka set out under the night's last stars. The waterskin hung around his neck, next to a new grass bag for his fire-saw and his food. He had packed some *chok*, a hard, oily seed that would not spoil and would fill his belly when food was scarce.

Pilgrim at the Edge of the World

They tasted like fat and dung-dust, and he hoped he would not need them. A slim stone knife rested in a sheath tied to his leg.

The stars guided him north. As the sun rose, Kaainka beat his short wings mightily to reach the top of a termite mound. The savannah stretched away around him, broken here and there by thorn-trees and other termite mounds. A warm breeze ruffled his feathers. This was his land, the land of the People, and he must leave if he was ever to take his place among the People and add his voice to their songs.

That night, his first night alone, he made a small fire and sang the Song of Beginning. He told himself that he would not be afraid until he came to truly unfamiliar lands. Thus reassured, he squatted down, resting on his ankles and tucking his beak under his feathers.

As his fire died, the night filled with sounds unbroken by the rhythm of the People's footsteps. Something cried, and it sounded like laughter. Kaainka's head snapped around. Eyes stared out at him from the darkness, eyes that would not have dared to come so close to a proper camp. Kaainka tucked his head back against his wings but kept his eyes open, watching the night.

He woke before dawn, somewhat surprised to find that he had fallen asleep and even more surprised that he hadn't been eaten. Kaainka shook the sleep from his feathers, then sang the Song of Chasing Stars to the sun as it rose. The songs of the night insects ended and the daytime songs began. In the distance, he thought he heard a lion roaring a challenge to the waking world.

Kaainka walked north. Walking the savannah was no real challenge. Kaainka had done it all his life. Day followed night, and Kaainka walked, leaving all his familiar landmarks behind him. His skin prickled with excitement, and not with fear, or so he told himself. He scavenged when he could and hunted when he had to. Soon, Kaainka came to the edge of the desert.

Camps of the People seldom came this far north. Grass grew in clumps around bushes that had the bad grace to be poisonous as well as thorny. Between the huddled plants, the ground was cracked and barren. There were no lions here, no half-eaten carcasses to rob from the lesser scavengers, and no easy kills. Kaainka enjoyed chasing the brittle lizards and too-clever insects that were his only prey here, but it took a lot of them to fill his belly.

Kaainka woke. A low, loud sound vibrated up from the ground and into his breastbone. His fire was out, and high clouds made dark rents in the starry sky. He stood up, flipping his wings in annoyance, and peered into the night.

The first elephant nearly stepped on him. Gray mountains padded by on feet as wide as Kaainka's outstretched wing. "Ahi!" he shouted at them. "Ahi! Ahi!" A camp could turn a herd with their cries when necessary, but he was alone. He looked around, but saw nowhere to go in the forest of legs; no tree or termite mound within reach. Kaainka huddled down and tried to be as small as possible, convinced he would be trampled and killed before his first glimpse of the true desert and what lay beyond. He moaned, slicking his feathers down hard to his sides, and closed his eyes.

Something soft poked him in the back, dragging up through his feathers and over his head. Kaainka opened his eyes. A trunk dangled in the air before him, pausing long enough for him to draw a panicked breath. Then it swung away into the darkness. Another one came down, delicately stroking his back, then another. Kaainka looked up and up, all the way to the elephant's face. He thought he saw the flash of a dark and knowing eye. Then the herd vanished into the night. The bone-shaking rumble of their singing faded, and the world was still. Kaainka lay on the ground, panting.

For many nights after that, the elephant herd haunted Kaainka's dreams. By day he walked, and foraged, and sang. Soon the savannah gave way to true desert, and he had more pressing problems.

When he came to the top of the first dune and looked out over the desert's vastness, he found himself doubting the old stories about sand-lizards and other desert prey. Surely nothing could live in this emptiness. Sharp-edged hills of yellow sand marched away to the horizon, arranged like rows of feathers, utterly barren. Kaainka could only stare.

Eikss's advice to move only at dawn and dusk saved him. The sun's fierceness grew as it climbed in the sky, glaring down at him from above and burning the sand until he was scorched from both sides. Sand blew in his eyes, and the only shade came from outcroppings of golden stone.

By the third day, Kaainka became convinced that the desert hated him personally, and he hated it in return. Sand wore away the scales on his feet and what little prey he could catch tasted foul. On the fifth day, he couldn't find even the meagre shelter of a rock. He abandoned his search when the terrible face of the sun heaved itself above the horizon. Finding a patch of firm sand, he dug himself in as he'd seen the sand-lizards do, flicking his wings until he was half-buried. Then he tucked his head under the shade of his own spread wings, and waited out the day.

Walking again at twilight, Kaainka felt terribly exposed. He imagined what he must look like: a lone black-feathered form on the empty sand. Night fell in the desert. Kaainka sang the Song of the Sun, then prayed quietly for clouds, if not rain. He ate his *chok*, happy to have any food when the sand-lizards evaded him once again.

Kaainka's water ran out before the desert did. He cursed the glutton he had been at the start of his journey and sang openly under the sky for rain. His feet were heavy and his tongue lolled sideways out of his beak. The sun pressed down on him like a white-hot stone.

At noon on the second day after his water ran out, Kaainka's mind touched the thought of giving up. Huddled in the dwindling shade of a boulder, he wondered whether he could just stop, just let the drifting sand bury his body. Perhaps it would be better, if he were truly lost and had no hope. Then he thought of Eikss's laughter, and the inscrutable kindness of elephants. As twilight fell, Kaainka got to his feet and walked on.

Three days after his water ran out, Kaainka reached the river. At first he took it for a mirage, just another cruel illusion dreamed up by the sand. Thick, wet stalks of grass crunched under his feet before he believed the evidence of his eyes.

Kaainka flung himself headlong into the first puddle he saw. He landed in it belly-first, then he ducked his head low and splashed water up over his back with his wings, washing the dust and misery out of his feathers. He laughed with delight, got water in his nose, sneezed, and laughed some more. He ate fruit and grubs and drank until he sloshed.

As the sun set, the night sounds of a strange land rose around him. He shivered. In his joy at his salvation, he had forgotten the path he was on. At the heart of this green country lay the River of Death, the path from the lands of the People to the home of the Ancestors, and from there to the stars. Kaainka lifted his head and sang, for the first time, the Song of the River.

His voice faltered when he got to the part about the great river-lizards, whom even the lions feared. Kaainka wondered how far the lizards wandered from their river. According to the stories, they had to stay near the water, but the stories never said how near. Kaainka thought of his reckless dive into the pool, and shuddered.

His path turned north again, following the river. The stories said that far, far to the north, beyond the great nesting-mounds and the House of the Ancestors, there was a place where the river fell over roaring cataracts and down into the sky. No one he knew had ever seen it. He wondered who among the People had first come to this place and named the River, and if they'd seen the great waterfall. Did the Ancestors walk along its banks as he did? Lost in thought, Kaainka didn't hear the dogs until it was almost too late.

Yellow-furred bodies burst out of the undergrowth on either side of him. Kaainka froze, eyes wide, then instinct took over. He launched himself into the air. Shrieking, he heaved himself into the lowest branches of a tree that was mercifully free of thorns. One yellow dog flung itself at the tree, running up almost high enough to nip Kaainka's tail. The dog slid back and Kaainka fled higher as the pack surrounded him.

Kaainka's heart pounded. The dogs circled and growled, but couldn't reach him. He flipped his wings and tried to calm down enough to think. Something was missing. He looked down. To his horror, he saw the waterskin that Eikss had made for him in the jaws of a yellow dog. With a cry he ripped the nearest branch loose and flung it at the dog. It bounced off the creature's nose. The dog sneezed and flinched, then opened its jaws to bark, dropping the waterskin. Kaainka could see water leaking from the holes the dog's teeth had made in the leather, mixing with the dog's glistening drool. He flared his tail in rage. Then he inflated his throat and boomed at them, singing the fiercest part of the Song of the Lion. The pack paused, but only for a moment.

Kaainka turned in place on the branch, looking down at the dogs. He told himself that the dogs would lose interest. He needed to outwait them, that was all. Eventually they would grow bored, or hungry, or something, and then they would go away.

The sun fell through the sky, shadows lengthened, and the dogs settled down around the tree to wait. Frustrated, Kaainka flung more branches down at them, but elicited nothing from the dogs but growls and the occasional futile attempt to climb the tree. Kaainka paced back and forth on the branch. He considered throwing his knife, but at best he could only hit one dog. Then he would have no knife, and that would hardly improve his situation.

He knew he could not outrun the dogs on the flat, nor could he fly longer than they could run. He despaired of them ever losing interest. Kaainka looked down at the dogs, then out at the river. A plan hatched in his mind.

Kaainka shuffled sideways, and flipped his wings. A dog sat up, watching him. He shuffled the other way, clacked his beak, and shook his tail. All the dogs were watching him, now. He danced and sang, working his way lower in the tree. The pack leapt up, barking. When they were all on their feet, tongues lolling, he flung himself out of the tree, flapping hard. For one gut-twisting moment he thought he had misjudged the distance.

Then Kaainka was among the reeds. His wings banged painfully against them and his feet groped for purchase. He came to rest suspended over the water, a reed gripped in each foot and another in his beak. The dogs hit the water behind him, and the water erupted.

Kaainka dared not move his head. His eye that faced the water gave him an incomplete view of the carnage. The river's muddy froth was full of teeth as the great river-lizards tore the bloody dog-bodies to pieces. Then the splashing and the barking ceased, leaving only the hiss and snap of the great lizards' jaws.

Kaainka felt a moment of pride that faded as he considered his new situation. It was possible, he thought, that this was not an improvement. Reeds shifted around him as the river-lizards settled back into the water. He lost his grip with one foot, then another. Kaainka grabbed for the reed that he held in his beak, but it could not support his weight. Slowly, inevitably, it bent. The reed dipped him into the water with barely a splash, abandoning him to the river.

Kaainka tried to fly, but he could not push off against the sagging reed or the surface of the water. He flapped his sodden wings like paddles, trying to swim the other bank. He could almost feel the lizards' teeth closing around him. Kaainka panicked, and inhaled a noseful of water. He struggled against the river until his feathers were waterlogged and he was utterly exhausted. Then the current had him, and he was swept away.

The river carried him north, past stands of rushes and basking lizards. He tumbled through its rapids, and he had just enough strength left to keep his head above water. Then, as quickly as it had seized him, the river tossed him up against a mound of dead reeds and went on its way.

All the stars were in the sky before Kaainka found the strength to pull himself onto the shore. He huddled in the rushes, fluffing his dripping feathers away from his skin in a futile attempt to keep warm. His waterskin was lost to the dogs, and now the river had taken his knife and all of his supplies. Far from home, out of the sight of the People and alone, Kaainka shivered until sleep dragged his mind away.

The rising sun warmed Kaainka's back. Slowly, the dejected lump of black feathers on the bank of the river regained the aspect of one of the People. Kaainka stood up, and lifted his head. He could see his reflection in the muddy water: red wattles dulled by hunger, feathers that had dried into muddy spikes, and the proud casque on the top of his beak where it met his head.

He still had his life. Everything else could be replaced. He would weave a new bag, gather supplies, and finish his journey. His Ancestor's footsteps had shaken the foundations of the world before the first Long Winter. He could not fail now.

Kaainka fluffed, and began the long process of working the river-filth out of his feathers. It was, he thought, probably full of lizard dung. He looked around at the stands of cane and the river that ran through a lush, green land. He would not have to worry about going hungry, provided that he did not let himself become somebody else's meal.

And when he came home, Kaainka promised himself, he would feed Eikss entrails himself . . . And perhaps she would forgive him the loss of the waterskin.

Kaainka hunted dry cane by the edge of the river. When he found a piece he liked, he split it with a practiced blow of his beak. The sharp edges would serve as an acceptable knife until he could gather proper stones and knap a replacement for the one he'd lost. He spent the rest of the day making a fire-saw, and by sunset he was able to make a fire.

He caught leg-fish in a pool near the river, slurping the little soft-scaled bodies down whole while keeping a wary eye out for the giant lizards. He could hear the monsters lowing to one another in the distance. Out of impulse, Kaainka sang the Song of Mourning for Frog. Finally, restored by the warmth of the fire and a full belly, he slept.

Kaainka could feel the desert stalking him, though he walked through green grass. He could taste the sting of its dust when the wind blew from the west. Sometimes he could see its barren hills in the distance, beyond the trees. His new waterskin, tucked beneath his wing, comforted him a little. It wasn't as nice as the one he'd lost, but it would do.

Kaainka's last landmark rose above the horizon, and he knew it was time to return to the desert. Twin mountains stood on a plateau above the river: The nesting-mounds of the Sun and the Moon. It was time to turn west, onto an ancient road of black stone that threaded its way between the strange, square-edged mountains.

Sand blew in the wind. Kaainka squinted, walking slowly. Here, the sand covered the road; there, it was swept clear. A few paces further on, the road was eroded down to its spongy gray substrate. Rubble left by the last great war between the Ancestors and the Unspeakable lay scattered around the nesting-mounds: Shattered boulders, pitted stone, and pits half-filled with crystal.

Kaainka picked his way down the road toward the mountains. Now he could see that they were made of individual blocks of stone, too numerous to count. His heart fluttered with the knowledge that somewhere in the dim distance of history, some*one* had built mountains. His breath came quick, and he thought he could feel the ancient stones looking down at him. Kaainka began the Song of Stone, but his voice stumbled and he stopped. The stones hung silently above him, casting long shadows.

Finally Kaainka walked out into the open desert, leaving the terrible mountains behind. The road ended there, trailing off into gray rubble, but he could see his goal shimmering above the horizon. Kaainka's heart thundered behind his keelbone. As he approached, the strange house seemed to solidify out of the trembling desert air. It stood in the sand like something out of a fever-dream, white as an eggshell and sharp as splintered bone. The stories said it was a house, and indeed it had a roof, and door flanked by warding-symbols in the form of a pair enormous, beakless, two-legged beasts with serpents growing from their heads.

Kaainka flapped and hopped up the tall stone steps to the door of the huge, dead house. His feathers slicked down in wonder as he finally stepped inside. Who but the Ancestors could have built something so strange, so grand? Light filtered through the walls as if they were made of water. His claws clicked on milky stone that was strangely cool under his feet despite the heat of the sun. The floor was one smooth block of stone, and the ceiling above him curved up to a central spine like the ribcage of some titanic creature.

Kaainka stopped. His beak hung open, and he stared in wonder at the presence that dominated this house of bone. Then he remembered himself. He bowed low, spreading his wings on the sandy floor. He rattled his beak against the ground, then stood, stepped forward, and bowed again. The feathers of his wings left crescent marks where they swept the dusty floor. Kaainka danced, and bowed, and dragged his belly in the dust. Only then did he look up again.

Held in space above a dais in the center of the room, naked of flesh and gnawed by time, were the bones of the Ancestor. Though his mouth was filled with sharp teeth and he had claws in place of wings, he stood on thick legs and three-toed feet like one of the People. His tail hung in the air like a blade of grass caught in the wind. A proud row of spines rose in a wave from the bones of his back. The Ancestor stood in that strange white cave just as he had since before the War with the Unspeakable and the Long Winter.

Kaainka bowed again. Inflating his throat, he began the long, slow Song of the Ancestors. His voice thrummed with joy. The Ancestor's empty eye sockets stared into the distance, but Kaainka thought he felt the ancient one's approval. All that remained was to retrace his steps. He could already hear the drums of the People welcoming him home.

Kaainka finished his song and turned to go, head held high. He knew the Ancestors would be proud. Their children still honoured them, generation after generation. The People had kept the songs alive, through the Long Winters and the dominion of the Unspeakable. They had all survived. Now the last children of the dinosaurs stood alone, ready to re-conquer the Earth.

Originally published in On Spec Summer 2013 Vol 25 No 2 #93

Sarah Frost lives in Kansas, where she makes her living putting science on the internet. She is a member of the Science Fiction and Fantasy Writers of America. When the weather is fine, she can be found working in her garden. Online, she can be found at **www.sarah-frost.com**.

Afterword
Diane L. Walton
Managing Editor, On Spec

So there you have it. We do hope you have enjoyed this little journey through time and occasionally through space with us. So many factors influence us in the selection of an *On Spec* story, as we aim to entertain, enlighten and enthral our readers. The next twenty-five years of *On Spec* will depend on the continuing support of our granting agencies, as well as the subscription and sales revenue from our audience. If you have enjoyed this book, we encourage you to buy and read more of Tyche's offerings, and start your own *On Spec* subscription. The Canadian Science Fiction and Fantasy community is a vibrant one, and there are many amazing writers, poets and artists still waiting to be discovered in our pages. They deserve your support.

We at *On Spec* acknowledge the financial support of Canada Council for the Arts and from Alberta Culture, Alberta Multi-Media Fund, for helping to make it all possible.

onspec
the canadian magazine of the fantastic

www.onspec.ca

Expect the unexpected.